BYE BYE
BLACKBIRD

BYE BYE
BLACKBIRD

ELIZABETH CROWENS

Author Photo Credit: Kim Gottlieb-Walker

"Bye Bye Blackbird" lyrics written by Ray Henderson and Mort Dixon (1926); public domain

First edition

ISBN: 978-1-68512-840-1

Cover art by Level Best Designs

This book was professionally typeset on Reedsy.
Find out more at reedsy.com

To Lola, my lucky star

Contents

Praise for Bye Bye Blackbird

"No author can seamlessly blend Hollywood history with an engaging mystery yarn better than Elizabeth Crowens. It's a jaunty tale that could have been lifted from a Warner Bros. screenplay with all the principals from the studio's famed stock company: *The Maltese Falcon*, Bogie, Mary Astor, Greenstreet, John Huston, and Jack L. Warner. Fasten your seatbelts for a wild ride through 1940s Hollywood!"—Alan K. Rode, film historian and author, *Michael Curtiz: A Life in Film*

"Crowens does it again with *Bye Bye Blackbird*. Babs, Brandt, and Bogart make this rocking novel the stuff dreams are made of."—Reed Farrel Coleman. *New York Times* bestselling author of *Blind to Midnight*

"It's like someone shook a movie projector and out tumbled Humphrey Bogart, Mary Astor, Peter Lorre, and a duo from a struggling PI agency bringing all the lighthearted fun of a 1940's Hollywood mystery. That someone is Elizabeth Crowens."—Tom Straw, *New York Times* and *USA Today* bestselling author

"A creative twist on *The Maltese Falcon*: Dead birds show up on doorsteps. Humphrey Bogart assumes the role of a real-life Sam Spade, and two young PIs rescue every oddball animal as they investigate. Even the mogul of a major movie studio is no match for a wisecracking myna bird who sounds like a Warner Brothers cartoon. If you're a fan of Turner Classic Movies and the Golden Age of Hollywood, *Bye Bye Blackbird* will be sure to entertain."—Robert Dugoni*, New York Times* bestselling author of The Tracy Crosswhite Mystery Series

"An office full of lost pets, a strange dame drops dead in the doorway, and Bogie appears with a knock-off Egyptian hawk ... while shooting *The Maltese Falcon*. Thus begins the wild ride of Elizabeth Crowens' *Bye Bye Blackbird*. Babs and Guy, the heroes of *Hounds of the Hollywood Baskervilles*, continue in this welcome, hilarious and worthy sequel that I can only describe as *The Thin Man* meets 'hardboiled' with both tongues firmly in cheek. Famous names, Hollywood haunts, and a crime I dare you to solve, make this well worth your time. As a lover of Old Hollywood, I loved this book!"—Jon Lindstrom, *USA Today* bestselling author of *Hollywood Hustle*, 4-time Emmy© nominee, award-winning filmmaker, and veteran actor known for *True Detective, Bosch,* and *General Hospital*

"Elizabeth Crowens' *Bye Bye Blackbird* is a welcome addition to the Babs Norman Hollywood Mystery series. Set during the Golden Age of Hollywood and brimming with depictions of its personalities, Crowens succeeds in bringing Old Hollywood to life and offering readers another thoroughly entertaining installment to this series."—Annette Bochenek, Ph.D., author of the *Hometowns to Hollywood* series

"A delectable mystery set in the Golden Age of Hollywood, Elizabeth Crowens *Bye Bye Blackbird* is a fantastic addition to her Babs Norman series with a treat of a cast featuring Bogart, Mary Astor, Peter Lorre and other screen legends from the era brought to stunning life."—Lee Matthew Goldberg, award-nominated author of *The Great Gimmelmans* and *The Mentor*

Cast of Major Characters

Babs Norman, former actress, now in her late twenties and a female private investigator, head of B. Norman Investigations.

Guy Brandt, former actor, early thirties, now Babs' investigative partner.

Humphrey Bogart, lead actor in *The Maltese Falcon* who plays Sam Spade, a fictional private detective in the Dashiell Hammett book and inspired screenplay. In a stormy marriage to **Mayo Methot**, his third wife.

Mary Astor, daughter **Marilyn,** formerly married to **Dr. Franklin Thorpe**. Leading lady in *The Maltese Falcon*. A former child actress and silent screen star involved in a love triangle, causing a public scandal in her well-publicized divorce over the *Purple Diaries* and custody trial with Thorpe.

Detectives Felix Allgood and "Moe" Morris Sadowski, homicide detectives with the Los Angeles Police Department (LAPD) assigned to the Bogart case.

Abel Wiggins, Irish-born janitor at the office building where B. Norman Investigations is located. Often integral in solving the PI's cases.

Sir Henry of the Baskervilles (Irish Wolfhound mix. Known for search and rescue. Hero dog in the Asta-Rathbone case.) **Stu,** (the myna bird, formerly named Cagney), and **Bruno** (bulldog). Notable pets of the private detectives' menagerie.

The Asta-Rathbone Case – First major celebrity case for B. Norman Investigations involving the missing celebrity dogs of the actor Basil Rathbone and the canine star of *The Thin Man* movies, Asta, whose real name is Skippy and who has been featured in many other top films.

John Huston and Walter Huston – John Huston is the director and screenwriter of *The Maltese Falcon*. His famous actor-father Walter has an uncredited role as Captain Jacoby in the film.

Peter Lorre – Versatile German character actor who plays Joel Cairo in *The Maltese Falcon*.

Sidney Greenstreet – British character actor who plays Kasper Gutman in *The Maltese Falcon*.

Elisha Cook, Jr. – Prolific American character actor who plays Wilmer, in *The Maltese Falcon*.

Fred Sexton, propmaker of *The Maltese Falcon*.

Jack L. Warner, President of Production of Warner Brothers Studio and the most prominent and outspoken of the Warner Brothers. The other brothers involved with the movie studio include Harry, Sam, and Albert.

Dashiell Hammett and Lillian Hellman – Author of the original novels *The Maltese Falcon* and *The Thin Man* and his long-time playwright girlfriend.

Ida Lupino, actress who had worked with Bogart in the past on *High Sierra*.

Abdul Maljan, Jack L. Warner's Turkish bodyguard and a former boxer.

Bette Davis, actress who played the femme fatale role in the second version of *The Maltese Falcon*, titled *Satan Met a Lady*.

George Raft, popular actor and former Broadway dancer, well-known for his gangster roles, inspired by real-life acquaintances in the underworld.

Cary Grant, popular and versatile British actor, now American.

* * *

Stay tuned for the third book in the Babs Norman Golden Age of Hollywood mystery series, ***Round Up The Unusual Suspects***, featuring the stars from *Casablanca*.

Chapter One: Look at the Birdie!

Hollywood 1941

O n Friday, July 4th, only the most essential, dedicated, or insane Los Angelenos punched the clock. Established businesses that usually stayed open closed early that afternoon. For the fledgling ones, like the young private detectives at B. Norman Investigations, there would be no weenie roasts, barbeques, or national holiday celebrations. Death would soon follow. Every electric fan they owned hummed its own tune. Between the fan blades whirring and the cats purring, panting dogs, who could qualify as hotdogs, an injured pelican with its wing in a sling, and their janitor's wisecracking myna bird, the whole kit and caboodle at Hollywood Boulevard and N. Sycamore resembled a cross between the Humane Society and the Griffith Park Zoo.

Guy Brandt, more detective-partner than secretary, manned the desk upfront. On top of it: a shoebox of magazine clippings, scissors, and a stack of *The Times* and *Herald-Examiner*. He undid one more button on his clammy, sweat-stained shirt, flung his tie onto their hat rack, and took a swig of his warm Nehi orange soda, already flat. He hoped to find new clients from newspaper leads but wasn't getting anywhere. Babs Norman, who always had every pin curl in place, patted off her sticky forehead with a handkerchief. Way beyond a simple touch-up with powder and fresh lipstick, only a masterful makeup wizard, like Perc Westmore, could bring new life to this wilted flower.

1

"Wouldn't it be fine and dandy if we could afford to run an ad at least once a week saying that we're private detectives, specializing in discreet celebrity cases?" she asked.

An adventurous kitten, who strayed from the pack, latched on to Guy's sock and started to climb his leg. "Maybe we should ask if we can put a note in the downstairs lobby that we're also a pet adoption service." He unhooked its claws, returning him to his mama.

"You think that would pay off our debts?"

"Do you always have to sound like a broken record?" An Irish Wolfhound, in need of a bath, sauntered in from the doorway between the two offices. He went up to Guy and plopped his oversized, hairy head into his lap. "Dog days not agreeing with you, Sir Henry?" After rubbing the furry beast's head, he went to their icebox and plopped chunks of ice in the various water bowls scattered around both rooms. Several prostrated cats laid on their backs, trying to find coolness on the linoleum floor.

From under his pile of clippings, he fished out a copy of *Black Mask*. Babs, with a wooden clothespin clamping her nostrils shut and carrying an odiferous box of shredded newspapers, walked into his office and stopped short when she caught him reading the pulp. "You think we're going to find our next client from detective fiction? We need another high-profile case like when we rescued Asta, so MGM could go into production on their next *Thin Man* film. They paid us an unheard-of amount of money...until you lost it all."

"Stop being such a sourpuss." He refused to give her eye contact.

"Do you think I'm enjoying spending time in our stifling office? I'd rather be at the beach with the man of my dreams." Her inflection had a hint of sarcasm.

"Who's the lucky fella?"

She went over to their monstrous dog and kissed him on the nose. "Looks like it's you, Sir Henry of the Baskervilles. Instead of my frog prince, you're my *dog* prince. Ah, you're such a good boy." She stared at the bulldog in the corner. "But we really need to paper-train Bruno."

Their adopted bulldog whined. "You hurt his feelings," Guy said. "Give him a good scratch behind his ears and apologize."

She scowled. "I'll give him two more weeks, and it'll be your job to train him. Otherwise, he can go back to Wiggins, and I don't care if one of his kids breaks out in hives." She headed out the door to dump the litter.

* * *

"Our phone rang twice while you were out," Guy said. "But Wiggins' stupid bird answered before I could."

"Hello, sucker!" the myna bird cackled. "Down for the count...1...2...3. Knocked him in the kisser, didn't ya?"

"By the time I picked up the receiver, whoever it was hung up," he explained.

"It's hard to believe a bird can be so smart," Babs muttered.

"Smart-mouthed is more like it," he said. "Sounds like Jimmy Cagney, who he's named after. Maybe we should let him earn his keep. The bird can impersonate him at parties."

Babs stared at the troublemaker. "The person on the other end probably thought it was a prank." She looked around the room. "Keep it up and...I got a lot of hungry cats and canines who wouldn't mind a bowlful of myna bird stew."

Wiggins, the building janitor, propped their front door open, causing their ginger tomcat to disappear into the hallway faster than gunfire. "My wife said the same. What are the two of ya doing here on Independence Day? With the tenants gone, I heard yer bickering all the way in the basement. Sounded like a married couple in divorce court. How did ya get in?"

"We had an extra set of keys," Guy said.

Wiggins planted his hands on his hips. "More like makin' a copy of my set while my back was turned. There's no foolin' me. Come on now. Who'll be the first to confess?"

Both detectives buried their noses in their newspapers.

"All right, if none of ya willin' to come clean, why aren't you out having fun?"

"Paying our overdue office rent is my idea of fun," Babs replied.

Wiggins looked confused. Guy explained, "We're hurting. Nothing but small potatoes since retrieving our dognapped canine stars."

"We might be forced to move out, if we don't land a decent case," said Babs. "I'm not looking forward to setting up shop at my house."

Wiggins inhaled but choked. "You make sure you keep this place spic-and-span. If your neighbors start belly achin'..."

From inside his desk, Guy took out a sardine from its wax paper wrapping and tossed it to their pelican.

"*Sniff...sniff...* If you don't get rid of this stench," Wiggins continued, "my boss'll make sure he throws you out on your arse."

She plucked a bottle of cheap toilet water from her purse and spritzed the room. "Better now?"

Wiggins pointed toward the exit. "Goin' after that mouser. Left the back door open to the alley downstairs. He's liable to slip out and get lost forever."

Babs handed her partner a feather duster. "Do something." Then she returned to her lair with a stack of discarded tabloids to make fresh litter and to do her own skewed interpretation of housekeeping.

Guy reset their wall clock, which was a few hours behind the last time they had a power outage, and gave the reception area the minimal once-over by removing accumulated grime from the top of file cabinets. He was just about to straighten the frame displaying his private investigator's license, when out of the side of his eye, he noticed a shadow. A large, irregular object leaned against the pebbled glass window of their front door. At first he paid it no mind and continued his cleanup crusade.

When minutes passed and it hadn't budged, he called out just above a whisper, "Do you mind coming over? Make it quick, but be quiet."

A startled canary flew out their open transom as Babs breezed toward the front. Guy pointed to the silhouetted figure. "I tidied up, like you asked, but don't recall hearing anyone approach. This thing...it appeared out of nowhere and hasn't moved since."

Babs called out to see if it was Wiggins, but whomever it was didn't respond. She inquired again. "The door is open. Come on in. We're too hot and tired for practical jokes."

With a nod, she gave Guy the go-ahead to open the door, but when he did, a young woman they'd never seen before, wearing a hat and an oversized coat despite the heatwave, fell face-forward onto the floor.

"The casting office is on the fourth floor," Babs said, until she realized the lady hadn't moved or said a word. Horrified, she squealed and froze in place.

Guy, also shaking, reached for the phone and called Wiggins' downstairs office. His voice broke up. "Come up—pronto!"

As soon as he put down the receiver, she demanded he call the cops. Without thinking, she leapt up on a wooden chair as if she'd seen a mouse. Her legs wobbled, and she continued to holler.

Wiggins returned, heaving as if he had skipped waiting for the elevator and sprinted up the stairs. He had the missing tomcat draped over his shoulders. "Heard screams echoing down the hallway. You better keep better tabs on your tabbies. What the blarney did ya think was so important—Holy moly! Mary, Mother of God!"

Guy poked the stranger with his feather duster. Not having any luck, Wiggins, who was bigger than the two detectives combined, got a firm toehold with his work boots and rolled her onto her back. All three stared at the stiff.

"Oh, she's dead alright," Wiggins assured them. "Ever seen her before?"

Both PIs shook their heads. Guy tiptoed around the corpse and closed the front door. Wiggins fended off their curious menagerie.

"Something dark and…fea-ther-y is protruding from her coat. Like she was trying to conceal whatever she was carrying." Babs wrinkled her nose. "Smells like she or someone else doused her with…men's cologne. Not flowery enough to be one a lady would wear. Wiggins, how do you think she got in?"

"Through the back-alley door, I suppose, 'cause I locked the front. Could've snuck in and been here a while. Maybe passed out in a stairwell while my back was turned and crawled up to your floor before she expired."

Guy paced the room and checked the clock. "The cops seem to be taking

5

their time." He pulled a flask from his file cabinet and took a swig. He offered some to Babs, but she declined.

Wiggins wrested the flask out of Guy's hand and finished it to the last drop. "Sure as hell, this would have to happen on a holiday when the police are short-staffed." He took a swatter from off the wall and clobbered a pesky fly that landed on the stranger's ear. Babs trembled.

"She can feel it no more than if you were all doped up at the dentist," Wiggins said.

Babs commented that the police could examine the body. She wasn't touching it.

Guy suggested to Wiggins to wait for the cops downstairs. "They'll need you to unlock the building."

Keeping his distance, Guy asked, "Babs, how do you think she died?"

"I don't know, and I don't care." She made it clear she wasn't even interested in slipping on gloves to search for an ID.

He suggested that this could be the lead they've been looking for. She didn't see it that way. "This is no way to spend a holiday. Let the police and the medical examiner do their jobs. They've expressed they don't want us meddling in their homicide cases, anyway. I just want her out of here."

Soon, they heard footsteps and the sound of crunching paper. She took for granted the cops had arrived. "Come in. It's unlocked."

She and her partner didn't make a move until the front door creaked open.

Instead of the police, Humphrey Bogart stood there holding a parcel haphazardly wrapped in brown paper and twine. "I called twice. Assumed you had an answering service to leave a message. Dialed the right number, but someone with a peculiar voice like a Warner Brothers cartoon picked up. When I tried to explain my predicament, he mocked me and cracked a few jokes. Figured I better stop over."

"How did you get into our building?" Guy asked.

"Your janitor recognized me. When I asked to see you, he figured I was harmless. He said he was waiting for—" Babs interrupted his train of thought. Still standing on the chair, she covered her eyes with one hand and pointed to the floor without making a sound. Bogie backed up. The blood drained from his face. "Whoa! Guess he wasn't kidding when he said he was expecting the cops."

A black cat jumped on top of the victim and started making biscuits. "Oh, no, you don't." Guy bent down to throw him off.

"Wh-a-a-t happened?" Bogie's words came out choppy.

Babs regained her voice, which, at first, came out in squeaks. "Not sure. What brings you here?"

"I'm looking for a private investigator. You came highly recommended as some of the best private dicks in town."

Babs flushed. She preferred a more ladylike elucidation. With no further introductions needed, she ushered Bogart into her office, and Guy followed, grabbing a notepad off his desk. Even though she hated staring at the corpse, she kept her door open to keep an eye out for the police. She kept reminding herself to take deep breaths and not to panic.

"Do you mind clearing your desk?" Bogie held out his parcel. "I'd like to show you what I found on my doorstep this morning."

With one fell swoop of her arm, the papers went into a spare box, which Babs said she'd sort through later. Bogart put his parcel down on her desk and fanned out his jacket.

"I guess we can skip formalities when the weather beats us into submission. Mind if I take this off?" His shirt was soaked. "This has been one of those days where I've felt like an omelet slapped on the Devil's griddle."

Babs identified his mysterious object as a museum replica of an ancient Egyptian canopic jar of Horus, the Hawk, the offspring of Isis and Osiris.

"This is much smaller and lighter than the falcon prop in our movie. Ours is about forty-seven pounds of lead. If you dropped it, you could break someone's toe." Bogie lifted its lid and revealed a mummified object. Taking special care, he unwrapped its gauze, stained but far from looking ancient, to reveal a sizable dead crow.

"I have no idea what this is supposed to symbolize, but now it looks like I've got competition from what's in your front room as to which gives me the worst case of the heebie-jeebies," Bogie remarked.

Guy pulled the privacy shades down on the pebbled glass windows on the walls and door separating the front office from her inner sanctum. "One would presume to find a dead falcon, not a raven, considering you're in the middle of production for *The Maltese Falcon.*"

Chapter Two: Police Report: Not Necessarily Allies

"How did you know we're in the middle of production for *The Maltese Falcon?*" Bogie asked.

In one hand, Guy held up a copy of the *Hollywood Reporter*, in the other an issue of *Variety*. "We make it our point to read the trades."

Bogie gestured toward a collection of books on Babs' shelf. "I see you also make it a point to read Sherlock Holmes and Dashiell Hammett."

"We've had the pleasure of working with both. Well...I mean, Rathbone, Basil Rathbone, who plays him on screen," Guy said.

"It's a dead crow, not a raven," Babs muttered. She had argued with her partner all morning and was in no mood to correct him, but now, there was a stiff in the anteroom. Pretending nothing was out of the ordinary, she said, "Mr. Bogart. Tell us, what's on your mind?"

"Maybe I should ask you why there's a dead dame out front?" He tried to put on a hard-shell veneer, but it wasn't working. "Mind if I smoke?"

Noticing him shaking, Guy helped him light his cigarette. Then he lit one for himself. Babs pulled a face and repositioned her desk fan to blow the tobacco smoke out the window.

"Tragedy aside," Bogie said. "For the life of me, this isn't how I envisioned a private eye's office, but I guess this isn't a movie set."

Guy cracked a smile and leaned against the desk. "What did you expect?"

"Something a little less Sam Spade and more Chandleresque. A smoldering stogie in an ashtray. The smell of stale beer or whiskey from bottles piled

9

in the trash, fighting for space with the crumpled remains of yesterday's news… Half-eaten sandwiches, which flies continued to make a meal out of, and a radio on in the background, broadcasting a staticky speech of President Roosevelt warning us to beware of the Krauts."

Babs frowned at a Daddy Longlegs that crawled and hid behind a photo taken by MGM's photographer after they rescued Toto and Asta. "We have no shortage of insects, and this corpse has already attracted flies."

"Newspapers that have long outlived their use line our litter pans." Guy held his hand above his head. "And we've had it up to here about the nasty Germans."

Bogie almost tripped over their gargantuan-sized mutt, primarily Irish Wolfhound. Once he regained his footing, a hoard of kittens swarmed toward him. He picked up a kitten, which climbed halfway up his leg. "You running an animal shelter or something?"

"Care for a soda?" Guy took a metal slug out of his pocket and tossed it in the air. "VIPs get theirs for free."

Bogie gave a slight nod. "Nehi, if ya got it."

"We're out of grape and cherry but well stocked with orange," replied Guy, also helping himself to a cold, fizzy one.

Bogie pointed to his unwanted souvenir. "What do you think this means?"

Babs helped herself to lukewarm Chase & Sanborn and left her lipstick print on the rim of her cracked coffee cup. "Not sure, but I sense it's symbolic. Perhaps Chief Crow-Feather could shed some light."

"Chief who?" Bogie asked.

"My boss has a whole long list of so-called experts she picks up along the way," Guy explained. "Some aren't worth a wooden Indian nickel, but others—"

"Others offer more promise than the California Gold Rush," she said, finishing his sentence. "He's a local university professor and an advocate for animal preservation—"

Their conversation came to a halt. The convalescent pelican waddled in and poked his sharp bill into Guy's funny bone. "Maybe he can do something with him." He gritted his teeth, trying to suppress a loud wail.

"The chief might turn out to be an invaluable source of information," said Babs, ignoring him.

Guy winced. "Or a potential target."

"Or a suspect," Bogie said, "God knows why?"

"Stop jumping to conclusions," she snapped. "Just because he's large in stature and dresses in tribal attire, one shouldn't pigeonhole or use him as a scapegoat. Keep an open mind and give the chief a fair shake."

* * *

"Police! Open up!"

"Be my guest," Guy replied.

The older of the two plainclothesmen flashed his badge. "Detective Morris Sadowski, Homicide." He introduced his junior partner, Detective Felix Allgood, who was squattier, tubbier, and despite his youthful advantage, he looked like the "before" example of a fitness ad. Beat cops in blue piled in along with the rest of the crime scene investigation team.

Guy excused himself to guard his front desk fortress from the nosy inquisition. Babs and Bogart followed.

Allgood made mention of the business identifier on their front door. "B. Norman Investigations? The police department doesn't want the local dicks pokin' their noses where they don't belong."

Babs played tough. "It's a long while since I burst out crying because policemen didn't like me."

Raring to strike, Allgood raised his hand but stopped. "If you weren't some pretty dame, I'd slap you silly."

"Calm down," Guy explained. "The victim… She came to us."

"Who do you think you're foolin', sissy boy?" Allgood said.

Without a flinch, Guy sat up straight in his chair. "Trust me, there are things I'd rather do and places I'd rather be this afternoon."

Allgood glared at the actor. "What about you?"

"Same here," Bogie replied. "No, on second thought, I just came here for my health."

11

"Wise guy," Allgood mumbled and pointed to Babs' desk in the far room. "Whatcha got in there?" he asked. "Anything related to the unfortunate woman on the floor?"

"Hope not," Bogie replied. "Maybe it's just a coincidence."

Everyone's attention was diverted to Wiggins, who approached their front door holding a box. Whimpering sounds came from within.

"You guys are getting quite a reputation," he said to the PIs. Despite dirty looks from the police team, he circumnavigated the corpse and placed the box on Guy's desk. "Found this in the alley a few minutes ago. Barely old enough to open its eyes."

Curious, Sadowski peered inside. "A beagle puppy?"

∗ ∗ ∗

With everyone elbow-to-elbow within the cramped space, Babs collided with the busy photographer. The contents of her purse spilled all over.

"Look, lady," Allgood threatened. "Do you want me to cite you for contaminating the crime scene?"

Careful not to rip her stockings, Babs got down on her hands and knees to retrieve a tube of lipstick that rolled in between the detective's scuffed brown leather brogues.

"I want to see what's poking out from under..." She realized when she lifted her head, she was looking up at the inseam of his trousers. Not wanting the detective to read anything into it, she scooted away from the detective's crotch. "I want to know what's under her coat," she said, cleaning up the mess.

"Whatever it is, don't you dare touch it!" he warned her. "You can fill out a requisition form to see those photos and reports later."

She sneered and gave a subtle snort once his back was turned.

The medical examiner had yet to arrive. Others dusted for prints and placed markers around the room. The animals went berserk between the smell of death and chaos from all the strangers going into the crowded room. Colossal Sir Henry acted like a roadblock. Bruno served as a jumbo-sized doorstop.

"Can't you act like guard dogs once in a while?" Babs carried the abandoned pup into her office. "Don't understand why everyone thinks it's okay to drop off their unwanted pets." She took a quick glance at Wiggins. "Including a bird who thinks he's a stand-up comic."

The LAPD made it clear the civilians were in the way and warned them not to muck up their investigation. Guy and Babs escorted Bogie into her chamber and watched the scene from afar.

Bogie wanted to hire PIs and make it official. "They'll do what they need to regarding the victim. Between us, let's draw up a contract. My case needs a resolution."

Sadowski barged in while they drew up the paperwork. The myna bird flew off his perch and landed on his shoulder. "M.E. arrived. Don't want to get in his way. Best to follow Mr. Bogart over to his house and search for evidence over there."

Bogie protested, "Officer, I have no connection with the dead dame in the other room."

"That's for us to determine—*ouch!*" said the detective, who got pecked in the head by the myna bird.

"Call the cops, solve the crime. Do it on your own dime!" Cagney jabbered.

Sadowski shoved the god-awful bird aside. The myna found a new roost on Guy's shoulder. "Should I start calling you Public Enemy Number One?" The bird bit his ear—casualty number two for the day.

The detective asked if Bogie needed a ride, but he declined. "Got my own car parked outside." When the PIs insisted on following and Sadowski contested, Bogie explained, "They're on my payroll now. I just hired them to handle my own misadventure."

Guy asked Wiggins to remain behind and tend to any of the needs of the remaining crime scene team. He and Babs each took their own cars and followed the two homicide detectives to Bogie's place on Shoreham Drive, one of those adobe-style numbers built in the twenties. As soon as Bogie opened his front door, Babs tried to push past everyone to be the first one in.

13

Allgood clamped on to her elbow with such vigor that he almost dislocated it. *"Whoa!* Where do you think you're going, Miss Sherlock Holmes? Murder is for the real cops to figger out."

"More like Nancy Drew," Sadowski said, blocking the open part of entrance, glinting at Guy not to get any brave ideas. "These two dicks look like they just graduated from their diapers."

Babs gnashed her teeth and wriggled to get free, to no avail.

Bogie insisted, "I hired them. They need to know everything you know."

Sadowski asked, "Mr. Bogart, is your wife home? We'll need to question her."

"If she was, her car would be in the driveway. Maybe she's out scouting for the newest designer dress from Paris. She always finds creative ways of draining my bank account."

Babs corrected him. "Most stores would be closed for the holiday."

"She could be lunching with her girlfriends," Bogie suggested. "Whatever she's up to, her car's gone, which means she's not here."

"Has your wife seen the bird?" Sadowski asked.

Bogie shook his head. "Mayo knows nothing about it. I wanted to make sure I got it outta here before she arrived. She's prone to hysterics, and I don't need an additional headache."

"Let's keep it that way," Allgood said. "It's bad enough two civilian dicks are in on it, but we need to take a look around."

The two homicide detectives went straight upstairs. Babs wanted to follow, but Guy restrained her.

"Hey," she protested. "I'd like to examine the Egyptian artifact one more time."

"You'll get pictures, information about the victim's identity, and whatever that thing was stuffed inside her coat. You're lucky you're a lady, and they're playing nice. If I butted in, like you always do, these cops might've displaced a few of my molars."

When the police finished their inconclusive search, Sadowski gave Guy his business card. "If you call in to the station, just ask for Moe. That's how everyone knows me."

Allgood gave his to Babs. "Don't try calling me Felix the Cat. Contrary to popular belief, I don't own one of those black and white kit-cat clocks with the googly eyes and tail swishing back and forth." He gave her a wink before he made his way out.

After they left, Babs turned to her right-hand man. "Not sure if he was trying to rub in his hatred for PIs or whether he just flirted with me."

Before he could disagree, Bogie interrupted, "If you're not doing anything tomorrow night, why don't you come over for dinner? You can search my house to your heart's delight, meet my old lady, Mayo Methot. You'd wonder why we're still married, and I hadn't left her for somebody else, but that's neither here nor there. Anyways, all of us could discuss matters in private...without the cops. Sound like a swell plan?"

Chapter Three: Meet the Missus

Guy picked up Babs in his waxed-and-shined late model 1941 black Buick Roadmaster convertible. He argued she would embarrass them if she parked her three-year-old dapple-gray bargain Crosley in the Bogarts' swanky neighborhood.

"Why did you choose a car resembling a jack-in-the-box?" he asked. "At least I got something middle of the road, easy to forget, and hard to follow, not to mention more reliable."

She hated being reminded of the days when she depended upon him for rides.

"You're lucky you purchased this before you gambled away your savings," she grumbled. "Otherwise, you'd be stuck with the old jalopy that was always in the repair shop. At least I had the sense to buy something better than riding the bus or depleting my bank account on expensive taxis."

Being it was mid-summer when they arrived, it was still light out. Flocks of birds choreographed their evening flight patterns. Insects took their one last nip at floral nectars, and morning glories closed their petals until the next dawn. Traffic wound down. Neighbors walked their dogs or squeezed in a quick jaunt. One could hear an occasional splash of a pool behind high privacy hedges for a pre-sunset swim.

Guy parked around the corner in case any police cruised by on patrol. They walked the rest of the distance. By the time they reached the Bogarts' driveway, a man with a tutti-frutti-hued ice-cream truck, converted with extra windows and seats for passengers, blocked the entrance. When Guy came close enough, the jumpy, overeager man thrust a circular in his face.

"Wanna purchase tickets for you and your sweetheart for Acme Star Tours?"

"Stanford Peck?" Guy read out loud the man's nametag. "What the heck is this? How do I know you're not a phony baloney?"

"Standing in front of Humphrey Bogart's place as we speak."

"I could have told you that myself." Guy's temper kicked up a notch. "Outta my way!"

The obnoxious hawker leaned in so close that Babs could smell his raw onion breath. "For the pretty little lady, why don't I offer you a two-for-one special. That way, you can impress your date on how the better half lives."

"She's my partner, not my date, and we're here on business," Guy snapped.

Babs saw his fingers curl into a fist and pulled him back before he got within punching range. By and large, the diplomatic responsibility fell on his shoulders, but for once, she'd have to bail him out. "We're here on *police* business, and unless you want to spend the night behind bars, I'd suggest you let us enter," she said with the sweetest but firmest voice possible.

The overzealous tour guide stepped aside, took off his cap, and gave her a deep bow. "As you wish, your majesty."

Once they reached the Bogarts' front door, both detectives looked over their shoulders.

"Give me a gold star for acting," she whispered. "At least he didn't demand to see our nonexistent badges."

Guy told the ticket monger to buzz off and refused to ring the doorbell until he started his engine and rounded the corner. "Being charming once in a while can work wonders."

"You mean I'm not the epitome of congeniality all of the time?" she asked.

Before Guy could conjure more sarcasm, Bogie surprised the two by answering the door.

"Does your butler have the night off?" Guy asked.

"I'm a hands-on kinda joe. Maybe I should hire a bodyguard after finding that mummified bird on my doorstep. Why do you ask?"

"You're not worried that you might get accosted by some starstruck lunatic fan?" asked Guy. "Some jerk tried to solicit us outside. Wanted me to purchase tickets for a tour of celebrity homes. Thought I was going to have

17

to fight him off."

"Ever since my dimwitted ex-husband sent him hurtling across my office," she explained, "he's been lifting more weights at the gym. Don't know how much impact it's going to do on his slight frame, but it has brought out his more provocative side."

"Not sure if you'd be much of a match against my wife," Bogie said, dangling a cigarette from his mouth. "Welcome to Sluggy Hollow."

A Scottish terrier trotted up to greet the detectives. Babs bent down to pick him up. "Who's this handsome fella?" she asked.

"That's Sluggy, too."

"Two Sluggies?" Guy furrowed his brow. "I'm a bit confused."

Bogie laughed. "There's more than that. I nicknamed my wife Sluggy, and one of our dogs also got named Sluggy. The police came over here so many times that they named our place Sluggy Hollow, and I named our boat after my wife. Why, you ask? Haven't you ever read the gossip columns about the Battling Bogarts?"

Babs tested her memory. "That's right, I think Louella Parsons said—"

Guy shushed her and cut her off. "You've been married before, am I correct?"

"Sluggy...or Mayo is my third wife. Can't keep myself from tying the knot. I'm a sucker for a sexy dame."

Everyone heard a crash inside the house. "One word of warning, though," Bogie said. "When I say, 'Duck,' I mean *duck!*"

This time, he shouted. The three crouched low as a ceramic plate hurtled over their heads like an Olympiad's discus.

Babs brushed her hair back in place and stepped over broken shards, which littered their carpet. "Close call. What prompted that?"

"She's sharp and knows something's up," Bogie replied. "I've kept her in the dark about finding that Egyptian artifact. Mayo hates when I hide things from her. Always accuses me of this and that, including having affairs." He welcomed the detectives inside. "Come. Let's negotiate a peace treaty, but be aware. Let's hope she doesn't have any other surprises in store."

"Like what?" Babs asked.

"Once she produced a gun in front of our guests and fired at the ceiling," Bogie said.

The three went inside. Bogie kissed his wife, Mayo Methot. Being close enough in range, he forced her hand open to relinquish the last plate she had in reserve as a weapon. "Promise me you're going to be a good girl now?" he asked.

Reluctantly, she nodded as the gang headed into the den.

After everyone took seats, Bogie addressed his wife. "Brought the detectives I hired."

"Honey, why on God's earth would you need to hire private detectives?"

"All in good time. Let's say we have a drink. Ladies first." He turned to Babs. "Name your poison." She insisted on seltzer water. Needed to keep a straight head on her shoulders. Mayo said she'd concoct her own and made a beeline toward their best bottle of Scotch.

Once she got out of eavesdropping range, Bogie whispered, "Any word about that dead dame on the floor?"

"An autopsy report?" Guy laughed. "I can give it the old Boy Scouts try and call tomorrow. With the holiday? Let's just say they take their time when they're having fun."

"Then I guess you haven't heard any more about whatever you call that Egyptian jar and why we found a crow stuffed inside. That thing gave me goosebumps…and nasty dreams."

"Reminds me of the line from Hammett's book about Spade feeling like somebody had taken the lid off life and let him see the works," said Babs.

"What's next?" Bogie asked.

"I scheduled an appointment to meet with my friend, the Indian chief. There's a powwow over in Pasadena. He promised he'd slip away from his obligations long enough to speak with us. We'll solve this crime, even if it's step by step," she explained.

Their maid entered with a serving tray of canapes. She announced that dinner would be served soon.

Babs recognized the brand of Mayo's dress. "Claire McCardell, I presume?"

Mayo enjoyed the flattery. "How did you guess?"

"I follow the fashion magazines. Her designs are all the rage."

Bogie made clear he didn't want to listen to lady talk. When Guy turned down his offer of a Cuban and said he was fine with a cigarette, Bogie offered him a hand-rolled one—Sam Spade-style. The two headed outside toward the poolside patio. Their two Scottish terriers followed along with Cappy, their Newfoundland, whom the detectives rescued last year during their Asta-Rathbone caper.

Babs followed Bogie's wife to her dressing room. This could give her the opportunity to question her one-on-one and snoop around for relevant clues. Mayo enjoyed taking center stage and showed off her collection of memorabilia. By the way she carried on, it was clear to Babs she already had a few and felt compelled to brag about every little thing which came to mind.

"Bogie and I met on a film called *Marked Woman*," she said, almost spilling her drink. "Bette Davis played a bar hostess, and I played one of the ladies who roomed and worked with her. Bette testifies against her mobster boss of the clip joint where she works. He and I hit it off and got married a year later, in August of '38." She showed Babs a publicity still from the film in a silver frame. Then she took it and held it close to her heart, as if fawning over a precious child.

Mayo continued to blather about her accomplishments. "Before Hollywood, I was huge in theater. Started out in my hometown of Portland, Oregon, at the age of five, believe it or not, before moving to New York. I'm also related to one of the presidents of the United States—Zachary Taylor. Oh yes, I've always attributed my inspiration to the famous actress Sarah Bernhardt, and earned the nickname the Portland Rosebud."

Babs allowed her to brag about her career accomplishments, even if she jumbled her timelines.

"In 1930, I kissed Broadway goodbye and moved to Hollywood," she said with melodramatic intonations. "Much to my dismay, I never landed a leading role. Just got minor parts in films, most of which weren't too memorable."

Mayo explained that she gave most of it up to bolster Bogie's career.
"Had you been married before?" Babs asked.

"Twice," Mayo replied. "Bogie and I are each on our third marriage."

The ladies returned in time for the dinner bell. They rounded up the gents from the pool area, and everyone's conversation shifted over to the dining room. Dinner turned out to be an eclectic array, including a green salad with an unconventional garnish of walnuts and strawberries picked from a local farmer's market. Everything went fine until the main course of pasta, peas, and roasted duck.

Babs stared at her plate and pushed it away. "This looks like it's still alive."

Mayo said nothing. Bogie apologized. "Came from Chinatown. Must've forgotten to tell the butcher to chop their heads off, and my household staff was too squeamish to do it themselves."

Babs toyed with her side dish of linguine but couldn't bring herself to eat it. "Not that I was planning on becoming a vegetarian, but I think I lost my appetite."

While the others ignored the oversight and devoured the duck down to the bone, the small talk continued. An issue in the kitchen delayed clearing their dishes. During this lull, Guy asked his hosts, "Do you have colored pencils or crayons?"

"We should have grease pencils in several colors," Mayo replied. "We keep them in the kitchen to mark, date, and organize our food items."

"When I have an idea, I must jump on it right away," he explained. "It's kinda like a dream. When you don't write it down when the memory's fresh, you can never recall it again. Do you mind if I borrow them?"

When she returned, he took their plates and traced circles around them. Then, he connected those circles using long strands of linguine.

"What are you doing?" Mayo looked as furious as one of those cartoon characters with steam coming from its ears. "This linen tablecloth is a family heirloom!"

"Creating a diagram of who hates who in Hollywood," he explained and continued to create a map. Inside the circles drawn from the largest plates, he wrote down Humphrey's and Mayo's names, but took pause. "This is not enough. I should add your fellow cast members. Do you mind naming them? Stick to the main ones."

"Mary Astor," Bogart said, as Guy traced another circle and filled it in.

"There's Sydney Greenstreet the Fat Man, Peter Lorre..."

"Don't forget Elisha Cook," said Mayo. "I think there's a suffix after his last name—of Junior."

Able to read her partner's mind, Babs knew where this was going. They had made schematics of suspects before. Doing it on a tablecloth—this was a first.

"Figure we should toss in our director, John Huston," said Bogie.

"We can't forget him," Guy said, but this time, Babs grabbed the plate first. Using a grease pencil, she traced around it.

Guy drew another circle. Then, he held up a smaller plate with a half-eaten roll. "Next, are you aware of anyone who might want to prevent you from finishing your film? Who might be jealous or wish to seek revenge?"

Bogie knitted his brows together. "Not sure I catch your drift?"

"Let me rephrase it another way," Guy said. "Can you think of anyone who might have a beef with you?"

Mayo cut in, "George Raft and Paul Muni." She explained that both were up for the lead but turned it down.

"Is that true?" asked Babs.

Bogie nodded. "Funny, you should bring that up, but you have a point. When I accepted the role as Sam Spade, I considered this a successful coup. Prior to that, I established myself as a full-time actor, but with bad-guy roles in B-movies, stuff that padded the producer's wallets. Not that Spade was beyond bending the law to his own advantage, but with *The Falcon*, I had the chance to step into the hero's shoes."

"Muni didn't see it that way. Maybe he's too famous for his own britches. Such a perfectionist. He envisioned himself in dramatic leading roles like *The Story of Louis Pasteur* or *The Life of Emile Zola*. Not *Scarface* or *I Am a Fugitive from a Chain Gang*. He didn't want to be typecast."

"Everyone played in *Scarface*, even George Raft," Mayo said, interrupting. So did Boris Karloff. The director, Howard Hawks, even made a cameo."

"Regarding Raft… I think his agent found a loophole: no remakes," Bogie explained. "Playing a private eye in the third round at bat on a Hammett film was way beneath his caliber. Let's say he has *friends*…"

"Mob connections?" asked Guy.

Bogie pointed his index finger right at him. "A few unsavory childhood chums with influence to get him meatier parts and ways of convincing producers to comply. You might want to read up about him. Look up the name Owney Madden, a bootlegger kingpin who wound up spending time in Sing Sing prison. Raft grew up on the tough streets of Hell's Kitchen before he hit it big."

Guy stole a few eating utensils and pointed them in specific directions to indicate how people in certain circles affected others. Babs jumped in, since she knew a few things he didn't. Then he turned to Bogie. "Can you think of anyone else whose path you might've crossed?"

"There are always the minor actors, often day players with small parts." Bogie took a napkin and wiped his lips. "Huston's father Walter… I don't even think he wanted his name in the credits. He plays Jacoby, the poor sea captain who gets shot full of holes and dies delivering the bird."

"Wait a minute," Babs interrupted. "I read Hammett's novel. He was the guy who delivered the Maltese Falcon to Sam Spade in his office and dropped dead just like the Jane Doe who croaked and fell on our floor." She gave all present a look of concern and pushed her plate of uneaten duck farther away. "Don't know about you, but for me, this is getting too close to the bone."

The Bogarts' staff apologized for the delay and started to clear everyone's plates. Babs pointed to the tablecloth and panicked. Guy assured her the tracings contained all the relevant information, but Bogie stopped them before they removed it and suggested they forego throwing it in the laundry. "Fold it up for Guy to take back to the office."

When his wife complained they couldn't dine at the table with an exposed surface, Bogie suggested they eat their dessert in the den. "Perfect place for a nightcap."

* * *

The Bogarts' maid brought out their coffee and a tray of desserts. Mayo glowered at the yellowish custard lumps inside their porcelain bowls. "What happened to the chocolate soufflé?"

"Change of plans, madame. The egg whites weren't stiff enough, and it turned into soup. We improvised. Not quite *crème brûlée*, but delicious nonetheless."

Mayo sighed with a sign of defeat. "Any number of things could go wrong."

"Regardless, I'm impressed." Babs licked her lips. "Chocolate eclairs or candy bars tend to be my usual after-dinner sweets."

After everyone had settled and seemed satisfied, the PIs continued their inquiries.

Guy asked Bogie if there could be anyone else. "Maybe someone not related to your current film, but who you worked with in the past and who'd like to take you down?"

"I dunno. Maybe Ida Lupino." Bogie lit a fresh cigarette. "She hated working with me on *High Sierra*, my last film, but she's not in *The Falcon*. Not even sure if she auditioned for any of the female parts. What advantage would she have by threatening me?"

"Is there a skeleton in the closet you're hiding?" Babs asked. "Perhaps the person who delivered the artifact planned on playing that up."

Mayo looked up, confused. "What artifact?"

Bogie turned red. "Guess I'm busted. Well—"

Before he had time to explain, their doorbell rang.

Mayo turned to her husband. "That's odd. We're not expecting anyone."

"Maybe it's that idiot ticket salesman trying to sell us a tour of our own place."

She gave him a dirty look and excused herself.

While she was out of the room, Babs asked, "Any chance your wife could be behind these scares?"

"We constantly fight. No doubt about that," Bogie said, scratching his chin.

"While you gents had your smoke and she gave me a tour of your house, I got the impression she was jealous of your success."

"Many of our arguments have centered around her waning career." He was about to elaborate when Mayo returned. She explained when she opened the door no one was there.

"Maybe it was the wind blowing the chimes." Bogie came up with a quick excuse. "You know, it could've been a draft seeping from under the door."

Babs hoped to avoid another marital squabble. "That aside, is there anyone you recently encountered who seemed out of place?"

Mayo shrugged. "No one I could think of."

"What about you?" Babs asked Bogie.

"I dunno..." He stopped to smooth a stray strand of hair back in place. "Guess my mind has been so focused on memorizing my lines and hitting my camera marks that I haven't thought of much else." He smirked at his wife. "Right, Sluggy?"

Mayo poised her serving spoon like a javelin and hissed through clenched teeth. With only her eyes, Babs signaled to Guy for intervention.

"Do you remember whether anyone on the Warner Brothers lot could fit the bill?" Guy asked.

"If you're asking if I've spotted anyone abnormal, between sky-high egos and extras walking around in every sort of wardrobe-and-makeup combo possible, the whole movie industry is wacky."

"Seriously, Mr. Bogart."

Bogie swilled his ice cubes on the bottom of his whiskey glass. "Come to think of it, this guy...most of the time, I'd see him over at the commissary, but I've also seen him handle a bunch of other odd jobs."

"Hey, Babs, grab your notepad," said Guy.

"What's his name?" she asked, as she handed it to him, along with a fountain pen.

"Something so simple it escapes me. Once or twice, I've seen him come out of Lorre's dressing room," Bogie mentioned. "Come to think of it, he has this peculiar quality, which reminds me of Peter even though they don't look alike. Maybe he wants to be Peter's stand-in. Beats me."

Guy wrote down Mr. No Name—possible suspect. "Anyone else?"

"There's a quaint roadhouse joint, little farther away from Warner Brothers. Some sleazy waiter always thinks I'm rolling in the green stuff and thinks he could pimp a few little pretties, but this town is full of lowlifes like that."

The doorbell rang again. All parties eyed each other before deciding that everyone should go to the foyer together.

Bogart, with his hand on the doorknob, hesitated before opening. "Who's there?"

"Western Union," a man announced.

Guy nodded and gave the go-ahead. The moment Bogie opened the door, the uniformed messenger broke out into song:

> *Gonna pack up all my care and woe,*
> *Here I go swingin' low,*
> *Bye, bye blackbird.*
> *Where somebody waits for me,*
> *Sugar's sweet, so is she,*
> *Bye, bye blackbird...*

"What's this with a singing telegram?" Bogie tried to snatch the note away from him, but Guy stopped him.

"Let him finish. Maybe it'll clue us into something."

The man resumed his chant.

> *No one here can love or understand me,*
> *Oh what hard luck stories, they all hand me.*
> *Make my bed and light the light,*
> *I'll be home late tonight.*
> *Blackbird, bye bye.*

The deliveryman stood silent afterward. Guy whispered, "I think he expects a tip."

26

Bogie growled. He reached into his pocket. No loose change, only a fiver. "Guess it's your lucky day." He waved him off and said, "Now, beat it."

His wife poked her head over his shoulder, curious about the message. He waited until after the kid drove off on his motor scooter. When he finally opened it, he crumpled it up and threw it in the bushes.

Babs rushed over to retrieve it. "Besides the song lyrics, all it says is, 'I'm watching you.' It's signed by someone calling him or herself Birdie Wilson."

"Any idea who that can be?" asked Guy.

Bogie shook his head. "Why me?"

Mayo added, "If Birdie's threatening you, he's threatening me too. We're in this together."

"Well, at least it's not another dead—" Bogie ate his words the moment his wife gave him a dirty look.

Forced to confess, Bogie calmed her down and explained about the dead crow delivered earlier.

"Do you mind if we take your telegram as evidence?" Guy asked.

"Be my guest," Bogie replied. "No cops around to accuse you of stealing."

Babs yawned. "It's getting late. She suggested Guy grab the marked-up table covering. One of the maids placed it inside a spare wicker picnic basket.

Guy made a joke about bringing home leftovers. "This is the first time I've asked to bring home the tablecloth." Mayo wouldn't let him hear the end about ruining it.

Bogie, realizing he had too much to drink, caught himself whistling *Bye, Bye Blackbird*. "Gene Austin sang the original back in '26. Got the recording somewhere."

"I'm more familiar with Eddie Cantor's rendition." Guy waved his hands back and forth, shuffled his feet, and began doing his best vaudeville impersonation. "Should I do an encore with *Mammy?*"

Babs stared daggers at her partner. "That's Al Jolson, silly. Hand over your car keys. I'm driving."

On that note and with no pun intended, the detectives bid their goodbyes.

Chapter Four: Birds of a Feather

O n Sunday, all God's creatures stood vigil at B. Norman Investigations. Stuck with the task, sleepy-eyed Guy inserted his key in the door at a quarter till seven. The dogs needed their walks and all the zoological residents needed replenishments of food and water. Babs entered moments later carrying a bag with donuts for Guy. For her, a chocolate éclair.

"Hope you didn't blow our whole retainer on pastries," Guy joked.

"Not easy to work with a nagging stomach."

Guy yawned. "What's today's agenda? Go through the phone book and try to find a listing for Birdie Wilson?"

She licked the frosting off her fingers. "Heard on the radio Chief Crow-Feather will preside over a powwow and already arranged our visit."

While Guy turned his back to get coffee, the pelican poked his long, thin bill into the bakery bag. The moment he returned to his desk, he saw the last of his glazed donuts, bulging inside the bird's membrane pouch and not yet swallowed. While keeping a safe distance, he held out his hands and pretended to wring the bird's neck to force him to spit it out.

With her best faked Irish accent, she recited a limerick. "A wonderful bird is a pelican. His bill can hold more than his belly can."

"That bird is going to wind up in my belly like the Chinatown ducks we ate for dinner last night," he groused.

As consolation, she offered him the apple on her desk and half of her chocolate éclair. "If we can figure out how to get him into your car without becoming casualties, we'll hand him over to the chief. He's always rescuing endangered wildlife."

Guy took the Bogart's marked-up tablecloth out of the wicker picnic basket. He cradled the bird in his arms, but realized it was too large to stuff inside. He gave up, gulped down the rest of his coffee, and took a bite of apple. "Any other suggestions?"

"We got him here bundled in a beach towel. We need a similar substitute."

He tucked the Bogart's tablecloth under his arm and held it tight. "Not this; it has all my notes from last night."

Babs slurped the rest of her coffee at record speed and snagged a tatty blanket from their closet. She trapped the willful bird by throwing it over his head and gathered the excess fabric. "Hope the top is up on your convertible, 'cause I'm going to make a run for your car. Meet me there after you lock up. Hurry, if he escapes, he's liable to become the newest tourist attraction on Hollywood Boulevard."

* * *

Guy urged her to sit in the back with the bird. It was impossible for her to keep him secured beneath the blanket, but under her watch, she could curtail the damage.

"While we're stuck here for a long ride, we might as well discuss business," said Guy. "What's your first impression of the Slugger?"

"She reminds me of Ouida Rathbone from our last major case. Tough not to get reminded about Basil's irritable and jealous wife, who always set us back from solving our case."

He brushed it off. "Ah, she's not that bad."

"Who? Ouida or Mayo? I think they're both in leagues of their own."

Guy laughed so hard he almost ran a traffic light.

Babs alleged Mayo didn't stand out as a suspect. "She and Bogie have a troubled relationship, but I don't think she put the relic on their doorstep to spook her husband."

"After I get back to the office, I'm going to tack their tablecloth up on the wall. I swear it'll point out something we've overlooked."

Without a cage to contain it, the pelican walked all over his backseat and poked at him. Babs fed him stinky sardines throughout the ride to try to get him to behave. Most of the time, it didn't work.

* * *

After they reached their destination, Babs bundled Mr. Hokey Pokey, one of the pelican's new nicknames, back into his blanket. Once they got out of the car and the bird's feet touched the ground, he waddled straight toward the chief.

"His beaten-up Indian headdress looks like it was discarded in the trash from Western Costume," Guy said, whispering in Babs' ear.

She gave him a swift kick in the shin. "Give him some respect. He's taking time out of his busy schedule to help us out."

"Perhaps I'd believe his played-up credentials if it didn't look like he was wearing warpath surplus. Looks like half his beads have fallen off."

"Watch your mouth. Maybe it means he's seen real action, and you face the danger of getting scalped."

"Sounds like we got Laura and Hardy. Am I right?" asked Crow-Feather. "Care to let me in on the inside joke?"

Babs glared at her partner.

"Anyway, welcome to our celebration of the Gabrielino-Tongva nation," said Crow-Feather. The curious pelican tried to nibble the beads on his dangling leather fringe. He yanked a strand out of his mouth. "Well, who's this?"

"Call him Bill," Guy said. "I guess that name is as good as any, but beware. He steals donuts, and he likes to use his damned bill to impale me."

"Maybe you need to get protective fencing attire," Babs joked, but soon she became serious and begged the chief to take the bird. She pointed to his wing, still in a sling. "He's on the mend and can't yet fend for himself."

Guy said if he had the cash, he'd bribe him to take him off his hands.

Crow-Feather rubbed his chin and seemed skeptical. "How did you manage to acquire him?"

"We took a rare afternoon off and went to the beach," Guy explained. "She spotted him in distress—"

Babs interrupted and insisted on telling her side of the story. "We had no choice but to take him with us. If we had ignored him, he would've died."

"Despite us not knowing a darned thing about taking care of him. We had to play everything by ear."

"So now, you want to pawn him off on me?" asked the chief.

Even if they were crocodile tears, Babs put on her act. The chief called his assistant to take the bird away from curious onlookers who already started to crowd around them.

A little Indian boy ran up to Babs and handed her a necklace made of seashells.

"Wampum," explained the chief. "It's supposed to act as currency."

Guy spread on the sarcasm. "Enough to pay off our debts?"

A young Indian girl with long braids placed an ornamental headband on top of Guy's head. "Is everyone here part of your reservation?" he asked.

"There aren't enough of us left of the Tongva heritage to warrant having a reservation. Whether intentional or not, the Spanish missionaries who settled here did a good job of wiping out the population either through disease, disagreements ending in bloodshed, or by assimilating tribal members into their own religion and culture. Nowadays, we hope to pay homage to our ancestors. Little remains of the knowledge and memories that have been handed down through the generations."

Guy glanced around at the festivities. "People's costumes seem to vary."

"We've tried to reconstruct our legacy as best we could from a vanquished nation." Crow-Feather pointed to his own outfit. "Mine, for example, isn't quite authentic. I salvaged my great-grandfather's. I had to sew on extra pieces and get creative, because I'm much larger. By the way, are either of you hungry?"

"Starved. This birdbrain ate my breakfast." Guy was about to elaborate when the two young children offered him and his partner bowls of mush.

"Processed acorns, prepared to get the bitterness out, along with ground pits from the holly-leaf cherry," the chief explained. "The chunks are roasted yucca. The colorful stuff is wild berries for sweetness. Should remind you of oatmeal with different flavors and textures."

Crow-Feather excused himself to handle matters elsewhere. Babs forced a smile and raised her bowl in a toast. "*Bon appétit.*" She tasted one mouthful and puckered her lips. As soon as she was convinced their host was out of sight, she spit it out into her handkerchief.

* * *

Chief Crow-Feather returned and led the two detectives over to a less trafficked area where tribal members had erected a facsimile of a traditional thatched hut.

"Can't get more private than here," he said. "Now, show me what all the fuss is about."

Guy explained why they came empty-handed. "The best I can do is to sketch a picture. The police took Bogie's bird and artifact into evidence."

Babs lent him her notepad. "It resembles an antiquity I've seen in a museum and appears to be Egyptian."

"I hope you're aware I'm not an Egyptologist," said Crow-Feather.

"Of course," Babs replied. "With your namesake alone, I'd assume you'd know about birds and their mythological symbolism."

"I do, but you might not like what you hear," he said, examining Guy's drawing.

"Please, tell us anyway," Babs pleaded.

"Since you caught me away from my library, what you'll get is from memory of both my culture and other indigenous cultures in general." The chief went on to explain that for many tribes, a dead bird found at one's doorstep often meant misfortune or a warning of imminent danger. "A dead bird is also known as a symbol of death."

Babs shivered despite it being a warm day.

"Don't tell me you're scared and want to drop this case," Guy said.

"No. Just don't like dead things," she replied. "Not after what I went through with my father."

Suddenly, she clammed up. Guy wrapped his arm around her shoulder. While she turned her back to the chief and gave herself a moment to recompose, Guy explained, "Babs had to witness her father's murder. That's what compelled her to leave the acting profession and become a private investigator."

She patted a slight tear from her eye and forced herself to snap out of it. The chief asked if she was all right. "I'm fine...as you were saying?"

"When a bird dies, it indicates an ending, a release, and rebirth for letting go and moving on. It could also suggest something evil or wicked has occurred in one's life and a transition is necessary. Many of us view that with reverence rather than fear. A dead bird is seen as a messenger from beyond, bringing wisdom and guidance."

"What about a dead bird in one's yard?" asked Babs.

His smooth tone implied the eloquence of an educated man. "If you see a common bird like a sparrow or robin, this may signify an ending in your life, and it's time to move on. An uncustomary bird..."

Babs interrupted. "Like the peacocks my next-door neighbor owns?"

"Perhaps, but those may be seen as a message from beyond. The location of where you found this bird has a special meaning. For example, a dead bird on your porch might mean there are problems, either now or from the past, you need to resolve."

"Mr. Bogart doesn't have a front porch," Guy explained. "He found the bird on his doorstep outside his front entrance."

"A dead bird in front of your house could mean a change is pending, for better or worse. Now, if he found it in his driveway—"

Babs cut him off. "The black bird theme resurfaced when Bogie's wife received a singing telegram to the tune of *Bye, Bye Blackbird*. Guy, you still have that telegram, right?"

"In the office. For safe keeping."

"Come to think of it, I'm not even sure what that song is supposed to mean."

Guy interjected. "I've heard all sorts of interpretations from someone leaving his floozy patootie and the harsh life of the city to rush back home to his sweetheart, to leaving behind his troubles, heartbreak, and loneliness, portrayed by the black bird, for a life of hope and renewed optimism."

"How can we be sure the telegram deliveryman wasn't behind the murder?" Babs asked.

Guy added, "Nothing's conclusive, but we noticed what looked like a black bird poking from inside the dead woman's overcoat. Do you have any ideas how all this might line up?"

"First, you need to get your police report," said Crow-Feather. "Then give me the chance to go through my library to see what I can come up with. The fact that your victim was female might have a special meaning versus being male, but I wouldn't know off the top of my head."

* * *

They thanked the chief and bid him goodbye. Guy drove Babs to her house in the Hollywood Hills. Along the way, he asked, "Is Crow-Feather the real McCoy?"

"Of course. Why do you ask?"

"Are you sure he's not some actor fabricating his ancestry to access government funding?"

"I can't believe you'd think he'd stoop so low. I assumed he told us the truth. Why do you always have to undermine everything I do or say? He has multiple academic degrees and serves on the advisory board for Indian affairs for the LA County Art Museum," she argued. "Enough of your shortsighted opinions. What are your plans for the rest of the afternoon?"

"I need to swing by the office to walk Bruno and feed the hungry hoard. You took Sir Henry home with you last night, right?"

She nodded. "Having a king-sized canine around might scare off any intruders."

"Don't all Japs know special samurai fighting techniques?"

"Jap? Watch your language! Mr. Otake tends my garden, helps with my household expenses, and pays his rent on time. Maybe we should pay a visit to Dashiell Hammett. Perhaps he could enlighten us on areas we might've overlooked. After all, he penned *The Maltese Falcon* and worked as a Pinkerton's detective."

"What do you want to do with the Bogarts' telegram?"

"Show it to Hammett first. Then report it to the LAPD. If we don't, they'll cite us for withholding evidence. We'll just have to get our stories straight with the Bogarts, so we're on the same page. It's just a threat and not an actual homicide—yet."

* * *

After he dropped her off, her boarder, a Japanese gardener, Aoi Otake, rushed toward her with an urgent message. "Someone called and hung up. Several times. Maybe same person."

This could've been anyone from the murderer to her ex-husband, also a murderer. "Why didn't you answer it at first?"

"Didn't hear it ring. Summertime. Sun doesn't set until late. Was outside pulling weeds. Then...famous actress...Mary Astor called while you were gone. Your dog—"

"Sir Henry?" she asked.

"Yes, very smart. Barked and got my attention. Then picked up the receiver in his mouth. Good thing you brought the dog home last night for protection. He alerts me. Miss Astor... The lady wants you to call her right away."

Chapter Five: Purple Diaries and Purple Hearts

In a panic, Babs phoned Guy, despite it being late. "There's been another birding. Meet me at Mary Astor's. Right away!"

"I need to wash my hair and shave."

"Since when did you have to worry about a five o'clock shadow? I thought you said you couldn't grow a mustache if you tried. Come as you are. It's urgent." She explained that she'd meet him there and couldn't care less what the neighbors might think about her rinky-dink car.

He met her on Mary's front porch and looked like something the cat dragged in—tousled hair under his hat, pajamas poking out from under a light overcoat.

"You look like a bum," Babs said.

"What do you expect at this hour? You woke up my roommate. He threatened to move out and leave me alone to pay the rent if disturbances like this continued."

"Hey, finances have been tight, and I have a roommate, too. Otake was the one who took the phone message."

Guy yawned and looked at his watch. "I think our time will be better spent if we tend to our client and not our petty arguments."

* * *

After they rang the bell and waited for someone to answer, to kill time, Guy made up song lyrics but sang off-key. "My heart is blue over a scarlet woman…" He stopped, looked at Babs, and said, "I guess that doesn't make much sense—red and blue. If you mix those pigments together, you get purple, right?"

"Guy, you've gone over my head."

"First of all, you dragged me out of bed. You interrupted my wishful dream about cleaning up at the craps table, and now my thoughts are jumbled."

"What's your other excuse?"

"If you hadn't heard of the *Purple Diary* scandal, you must've been spending too much time in Poughkeepsie."

Babs raised an eyebrow. "I've never been to Poo-poo whatchamacallit."

"Just a manner of speech. If you still lived in San Francisco, I'd say you got lost in the fog. Anyways, her widely publicized divorce trial made the daily headlines."

"Maybe the heat from the long day has affected my memory."

A woman holding a drowsy young girl, whom Babs assumed was Astor's nanny, opened the door. She ushered the detectives into the living room, and explained their hostess would be with them as soon as she finished her phone call. While waiting, Babs and Guy tried to keep their opinions down to a whisper.

"I heard Mary Astor might have something going on with Bogart," Guy said.

"Funny, I suspected it was with Huston," Babs replied. "For all we know, she's having an affair with Jack Warner."

"I overheard that!" Astor entered with her hair wrapped in a silk turban with a few errant curls poking out. She wore a floor-length ice-blue satin wrap dressing gown with a flap collar trimmed in cream Chantilly lace. Her picture-perfect complexion had only a bare hint of makeup, if any. Babs turned red and apologized. In turn, Astor begged their forgiveness for calling so late and lit a cigarette. She called for her maid to bring tea and cakes and confessed, "Humphrey told me everything, from what happened twice at his house and while at your office. I'm frightened."

She disappeared into the back and returned holding a long, white cardboard box, one used by florists. Amid a bed of long-stemmed roses lay a large, dead crow.

Hesitant at first, Guy leaned in to take a whiff and commented that the bird didn't smell decayed. "Must be taxidermy or a sort of mummification like the other ones."

Unable to bear looking at the monstrosity any longer, Astor resumed her seat. "At first, I thought this was a cruel practical joke. Revenge from my ex-husband. Now, I'm not so sure. What do you make of it?"

Prompted by the smell of food, Astor's daughter ran into the living room calling, "Mommy! Mommy! Teddy is hungry." She leapt upon her mother's lap and proposed she and her teddy bear join them for tea. Astor gestured for the detectives to hide the flower box.

"Meet Marilyn, the light of my life," Astor said, slowing her breath to stave off the panic. She bounced her daughter on her knee and promised tomorrow she could have as many sweets as she liked if she'd run along now with her nanny. Given that incentive, the little girl kissed her mother good night.

Babs retrieved her trusty notepad once Marilyn and her caretaker disappeared. "In order to understand why someone delivered a similar bird, we'll need to know more about you."

Astor lit another cigarette. "What dirt do you want to know about, and we're not talking about the mulch in my garden."

If Babs couldn't remember much of the scandal that made frontpage news, Mary Astor would remind her now. "I suppose I've always been a magnet for men, but I've never known how to handle affection," she admitted. "Even when I was too young to know better during my fling with John Barrymore back in my days on stage. Old enough to be my father, but he taught me how to live—free from my overbearing parents who kept me on a short leash. He ignited the real passion from within me and mentored me in the art of acting. His influence, both paternal and as a consummate lover, helped me grow into full womanhood. With Barrymore, for once, I could breathe."

"Let me interject a moment," said Babs. "How did your mom and pop treat you?"

"Oh, God. They controlled all my earnings, squandered it by living beyond their means, and left me with a pittance of an allowance."

"Where are they now? Do they live here?" asked Guy.

"I banished them...far, far away to a farm all the way out in Lancaster. Nothing in comparison to the lush life they'd grown accustomed to with my earnings. Barrymore helped me cultivate my own strength to make my own decisions."

"Is there any possibility your parents are trying to retaliate, and they're behind these freakish incidents?" asked Babs.

Astor shook her head. "They'd have everything to lose and nothing to gain, and they'd never kill anyone or anything. Besides, why would they go after the Bogarts?"

She switched from tea to brandy and offered some to the detectives, but they declined.

Babs apologized for the interruption. "Getting back to John Barrymore, please continue."

Astor nervously twirled a stray curl around her finger. "Could you imagine how I felt when he abandoned me for one of his costars? I felt like a domesticated bird thrust out into the wild, forced to fend for myself without proper training or experience, because men still flocked toward me. So many, in fact, I felt like I had to fight them off."

Guy asked, "You had been married before, correct?"

"My first husband... So tragic."

Despite everyone being worn to a frazzle, Babs wanted to keep her on track. "You were married to Howard Hawks' brother, right?"

Astor nodded. "In 1930, my husband Kenneth, also a fine director, had his whole career ahead of him until he filmed a plane-to-plane stunt and the two airplanes collided. We hadn't been married all that long, and it wasn't the most passionate relationship, but I had expected we'd be partners for life. In a sense, I guess we were. 'Till death did we part."

She gulped down the last of her drink and refilled her glass. The detectives gave her a moment to recompose.

"Not long after he died, I approached Dr. Franklyn Thorpe in desperate need of medical treatment, and he rescued me just in time. We came from such different worlds, but, to me, I found that alluring…and comforting. Almost a respite from the madness of the screen trade. We developed a sympathetic friendship, but we both made the mistake of pursuing it further, since we were so mismatched. The American public got a front-row seat to the drama of our divorce trial. Franklyn and I each had affairs. He threatened to make public my private diaries, purple in color, thus the name *Purple Diaries*. Thorpe rubbed it in about my trysts with George S. Kaufman, the most successful playwright on Broadway, one of the highest-paid screenwriters for film, and also a married man."

Babs coughed and used her notepad to fan away the aftermath of Astor's excessive chain-smoking. "Can you give me some dates?"

Astor covered her yawn. "Hawks, my first husband, died in 1930, and I made the mistake of rushing too soon to marry Dr. Thorpe in '31. He sued me for divorce in 1935, charging me with mental cruelty and incompatibility. The court gave him custody of our three-year-old daughter, along with real estate and a sizable amount of assets. I had certain visiting rights but felt forced into giving up too many concessions.

"A year later, I hired a top-notch lawyer to overturn the ruling. I demanded full custody of Marilyn on grounds of physical abuse, a repeal of our property settlement, and a formal annulment of our marriage over the technicality of bigamy. Thorpe lied to me about a previous marriage. He had also lived in sin with a Florida woman in what was deemed as a common-law marriage. Can't be married to two at once, you know. In addition, he had several other extra-marital affairs. What a nerve he had to condemn me concerning Kaufman!

"Throughout this whole ordeal, I had to go through another trial by fire when I had to fight to keep my part in the film *Dodsworth*," Astor explained. "It starred Walter Huston and Ruth Chatterton, based on a novel written by Sinclair Lewis. The director, Billy Wilder, wanted me for the role of

Edith Cortright, the 'other' woman, who gets between them during their second honeymoon. I almost lost the part because my contract contained a 'morals clause,' something the Hays Code enforced. Hand it to Samuel Goldwyn. He came to my defense and insisted my legal battles signified my determination as a loving mother who fought for her child."

"Granted that it can't be ruled out completely," said Guy. "I find it hard to believe anyone involved in a court battle, which happened five years ago, would start seeking retribution."

"Had a secret marriage and quickie divorce since Thorpe, involving Manuel de Campo. I call him Mike. Not worried about him in the least. He left to join the Royal Canadian Air Force as a flight lieutenant. We had a son together, Tono, who is sleeping upstairs, but we've remained friends. Men seem to leave my life as quickly as they fly into it."

By midnight, everyone admitted they were too pooped to continue. Astor gestured toward the box of roses. "What should we do with the dead bird?"

"With no human cadaver involved, I guess we can keep the cops out of it," said Babs, who looked at her partner for confirmation. "Maybe we should take a chance and keep the evidence."

Guy sucked in his cheeks and blew out a low, controlled whistle. "Are you sure that's the right thing to do?" Babs nodded. "Regardless, we're going to have to get over to the studio and interview all of Mary's coworkers."

"I'll arrange for you to get studio passes and meet us at our sound stage," said Astor. "Does tomorrow afternoon work for you? It's best I inform everyone first as to what they're in for. There's no telling if Bogie had a chance to inform the rest of the cast about what happened to him and his wife, but I guarantee you he knows nothing about this."

Chapter Six: Taking Down Names

The respite from Mother Nature allowed Babs to wear her smart tan rayon gabardine suit with royal-blue trim with a demure round-necked pleated cream short-sleeved dress blouse. She pinned up her hair and topped it with a beret-like half-hat of matching royal blue adorned with a cream silk gardenia pin her mother had given her. When she arrived at the office with Sir Henry in tow, she couldn't help but notice the uncanny similarity of her partner's outfit.

Almost like a brother and sister, Guy wore a white cotton shirt, collar open with a royal blue, and a cream-colored diagonal striped silk tie with matching suspenders to hold up his high-waisted khakis. Sans jacket, he had a coordinating silk handkerchief peeping out of his trousers' back pocket. She took a lint brush to remove excess cat hair from her A-line skirt. "You're a sleuth on the case, not a hopeful for an MGM-style musical extravaganza."

He showed off his spit-shined wingtips with soft-shoe dance moves.

Guy rearranged their office decor to make space on the wall to tack up the Bogarts' tablecloth. Then he went through several boxes of clippings and a stack of entertainment magazines to locate photos of Bogie, Huston, Astor, Lorre, and Greenstreet—the major players in *The Maltese Falcon*. Taking a pair of scissors, he trimmed the edges. With rubber cement, he glued the corresponding image inside the circles already named. As he progressed, his artwork resembled a group of planets in an orbital configuration.

"How do you like my map of the stars?" he asked Babs, as their incorrigible myna bird flew over and stole a strand of linguine.

"You might have to swap out the pasta for string or yarn," said Babs. Sir

Henry got up on his hind legs and licked the linen. "Guess he smelled the spilled gravy. This could pose a problem if our four-legged friends nibble on your notes."

Their famished furry and feathery three-ring circus devoured what Guy had planned for breakfast, but he didn't seem too concerned. "We can always grab a bite on the run." They made one last check on their aviary and mammalian residents, left a note for Wiggins to walk the dogs in their absence, and hopped into his car to head over to Warner Brothers in Burbank.

* * *

Little did they know the LAPD detectives would also be there.

"Four's a crowd. I was afraid you'd show your ugly faces," Allgood snarled at Guy but gave another wink at Babs.

She spotted the veins tightening in her partner's neck as he clenched his teeth and readied himself for a faceoff. "Let the police do what they want to do while we pick up lunch," she whispered and led him toward the exit.

As they shoveled down their meal at the commissary, Guy repeatedly checked his father's old WWI trench wristwatch, now his. "We can't sit here all day. I say we head back."

The moment they stood up, their busboy cleared their coffee and crumbs. Babs stayed behind, long enough to touch up her lipstick. When she caught up, she made mention their busboy leered at her, but Guy brushed it off. "Men are always giving you looks you disapprove of. You're a knockout, a hot tomato. What do you expect?"

They made sure the wig-wag warning light was off and reentered the stage. The police tried to shoo them away, but Babs pointed out that the director was off in a corner by himself reviewing his script. Sadowski gave them the go-ahead to interview Huston while he and Allgood monopolized the actors.

"Normally, I insist on a closed set," Huston said. "In fact, I initiated a code word: Number Five, when starstruck onlookers barged in on rehearsals.

43

This cued Bogie to call Greenstreet a 'fat old fool' for upstaging him. Then I'd intervene and insist he'd calm down. Lorre also had a stunt that would have us in stitches. Whenever VIPs came to the set, Peter would come out of Mary Astor's dressing room and make it obvious he was buttoning up his fly. He loved shocking people, but policemen aren't publicists, studio executives, or gawking tourists. We had no choice but to let these guys in."

"Let the police do what they want to do, but we're going to be more thorough," Guy said. "Do you mind giving my partner and I copies of your script to compare it to Hammett's original novel?"

Huston asked his assistant to fetch two scripts. "I insisted on keeping it close to the original story. If you really want to dot every 'i' and cross every 't,' then you need to treat yourself to a screening of the two previous attempts to film his story—*The Maltese Falcon,* filmed in '31 starring Bebe Daniels and Ricardo Cortez and *Satan Met a Lady*, which didn't even have a falcon statue at all. They used the Horn of Roland, another valuable object filled with priceless jewels."

"I might've seen that film," said Guy. "Kasper Gutman's role was played by a woman."

Just like our victim was a woman, Babs thought.

"Indeed, it was." Huston chewed on his stogie out of respect for Babs, who winced and gagged the first time he lit up in her presence. "Turned out to be a comedic farce. The female lead played by Bette Davis and renamed as Valerie Purvis, still gets nailed in the end."

"About the first film with the same name," Babs asked, "any similarities to yours?"

"The Hays Commission and their censors would have the best of me if I hadn't toned down any hints of illicit sex between Spade and O'Shaughnessy. Come on; you read the book. There's a scene where Spade insists she take off all her clothes to prove she isn't hiding a thousand-dollar bill inside her brassiere. Jack Warner would've never gotten their seal of approval to distribute it to standard movie theaters unless it followed the rules to their satisfaction. Ten years ago, it was a lot easier to get away with those things. When our movie's done and on the big screen, you'll notice my choice of wardrobe. O'Shaughnessy might play the part of a seductress, but I've got her dressing like a librarian. The powers over me would've never allowed the audience to get the impression that she and Spade ever spent the night together."

"As you're already aware, Humphrey Bogart has hired us to investigate two outlandish threats he's received," said Babs. "A similar incident happened the other night to Mary Astor. The cops might know something we don't, which can compromise everyone's safety, but we're all concerned that whoever is behind them might also be responsible for the dead woman in our office, and there could be more to follow. Sir, have you or anyone else noticed any suspicious stagehands anywhere around the set?"

Huston scratched his chin. "I'd be glad to introduce you to Fred Sexton if he's around, but I can't see how he'd benefit from threatening our cast. He's our prop maker for *The Maltese Falcon*. We had two props made, a spare and the one for the film with special markings."

Babs noticed the two police detectives heading toward them.

"They're all yours," Sadowski said. "But I suspect they're all talked out."

"Take 'em while they still got a pulse," said Allgood, snickering.

"Wait!" Babs called out as they were leaving. "Did you identify the lady who wandered into our office?"

"Yeah, and what about that feathery thing poking out of her trench coat?" Guy added.

Sadowski waved them off. "Maybe someone was trying to stuff a pillow. I dunno. Call me at the precinct. Don't forget to ask for Moe, otherwise someone might try to give you the runaround."

After the homicide investigators departed, Bogart gathered his fellow cast members and made formal introductions. They pulled up their chairs and formed a semicircle with Babs and Guy in the middle.

"I hope all of you understand that we, as well as the police, have to consider each and every one of you as possible suspects or victims," Babs explained. "Let's start from the top. Our lead actor is Humphrey Bogart, who plays Sam Spade. Mary Astor plays his foil, Brigid O'Shaughnessy. Sydney Greenstreet plays Kasper Gutman, the 'Fat Man.' Elisha Cook, Jr. as Wilmer, and Peter

Lorre plays Joel Cairo. Am I leaving out anyone important?"

"My father, Walter, plays Captain Jacoby, the guy who shows up with the fake bird and has been shot full of bullets," said Huston.

Babs shuddered, considering the uncanny similarity of what occurred in their office.

"It was a bit part for one day only," said Huston. "Doubtful if he'll receive screen credit, and we don't expect him back. There are others like the actors who played Effie Perine, the police detectives Polhaus and Dundy, and Miles Archer, Spade's partner played by Jerome Cowan. However, he's already off the call sheet. We already shot and killed his character."

"All right," Babs said. "Let's go around in a circle and sound off about anything in your pasts that might set off alarms."

Mary Astor, who had been chain smoking all afternoon, lit up another. "Don't even get me started. I have an ex-husband who's refused to cut his losses."

Peter Lorre loosened his collar and smoothed back his hair, dampened from sweat. "Let's hope someone doesn't decide to hound me regarding the curse of *M*."

Babs was perplexed.

"You would've been just a schoolgirl at the time, but ten years ago, I starred in a German film called *M*, directed by Fritz Lang. It boosted my career but in a negative way. Both producers and the public typecast me as a villain. It's haunted me ever since."

Bogie laughed. "You wanna know about all our failed marriages and regrets we'll have to live with for the rest of our lives? Better sharpen your pencils, 'cause you're gonna wind up writing something longer than the Bible."

Lorre, who had been fidgeting in his seat, got up. "Excuse me, but I'll be right back."

"Are you all right?" Babs asked.

He went through the motion of checking his watch, though Babs suspected he hadn't really examined it. "Doc gave me some medication. Got busy and forgot all about it. I'm a bit overdue." He promised he'd return and sprinted toward the dressing rooms.

Babs didn't want the sudden distraction to break her train of thought. She looked Huston in the eye. "What about you?"

Guy looked at his watch and sighed. "Leave it to the coppers to waste our time." He turned to the director. "Don't you have a rehearsal in five minutes?"

Huston confirmed. Guy announced that he and Babs would have to make appointments with the individual cast members for further inquiries.

Bogie confided that, so far, he's offered to foot the bill. "If Guy and Babs are going to show up on the Warner's lot as a regular thing, they'll have to get the okay and clearance from the Big Man."

Sydney Greenstreet put down his cup of tea. "What would I have to do with it?"

"Not the Fat Man," replied Bogart. "The Big Man, our boss, Jack Warner."

Chapter Seven: Hollywood HQ

On Tuesday, the detectives discovered a crate with three abandoned mewing kittens at the front door of their office. They encountered even more mayhem once they stepped inside the reception area. Mayo's tablecloth had fallen. Two kittens played hide-and-seek within its folds. Guy scolded Sir Henry, who licked one of its corners. Bruno served as a paperweight in another and slobbered with a long strand of drool from his underbite. Since there was no linguine to be found, they assumed Cagney had eaten it.

Guy wiped Bruno's mouth and leashed him along with Sir Henry. "Gonna pick up brown wrapping paper while we're out." He further explained that he needed to transfer his drawing to something more permanent before their rescues destroyed everything.

Babs offered to take the soiled linen to Manny Esposito, her favorite dry cleaner. She also reminded him he was the same guy who could bail her out in a pinch and let her rent or buy evening dresses left behind by nonpaying customers.

She made up signs while he was out and taped them around the office, the largest on their front door: *Good Homes Needed* and *Don't Forget to Spay or Neuter*. By the time he returned, she was at her desk shooing off Cagney, pecking at their White Pages phone directory. Exasperated, she raked her fingers through her hair, realizing afterward she'd have to fix it all over again. "Tried to look up the name Birdie Wilson. Too bad, it's probably just a nickname. Can't seem to find anything. Meanwhile, someone kept calling, but as soon as they heard my voice, they hung up."

"Babs, did you try the Yellow Pages to see if Birdie owns a business?"

"Nothing under the Bs or Ws."

"Did you call Chief Crow-Feather?"

"Already thought of that. Doesn't know anyone by that name."

"What about Wiggins? He knows all sorts of vendors and handymen, people we don't necessarily run in to on a daily basis."

"Good point. Why don't I run downstairs? While the phone is free, maybe you can find out if the police know anything yet."

* * *

"Hollywood Precinct."

"Hi, this is Guy Brant from B. Norman Investigations. We're working on a case with Moe. Is he around?"

"Let me check."

Guy chewed on his pencil until the homicide detective picked up.

"Moe, here."

"Lieutenant, this is Guy Brandt—"

"Who the hell are you?"

"One of the private detectives Humphrey Bogart hired. We called you to our office—"

"Don't recall. Refresh my memory."

Guy switched from biting on his pencil to hard, nervous jabs against his desktop. "We found a stranger dead on our floor. You remember now?"

"Oh, yeah. You guys…and gals. Don't know why some dame wants to get involved with such riffraff. How can I help you?"

"I'm calling to find out if you figured out who the victim was and how she died."

"What's it to you?"

It took everything Guy had not to lash out and give this chowderhead a piece of his mind.

"Just in case someone might come back to threaten us…or our client, Mr. Bogart…"

49

"Glad you had the sense to stay clear," Sadowski replied. "We identified the deceased as Lana Pilchik, but people knew her as Pinky. Worked the concession stand at the Egyptian Theatre. Know her?"

Interesting...considering someone gifted Bogie with an Egyptian artifact... "Never heard of her. Any idea why someone might want to kill her?"

"Maybe she turned tricks on the side or worked as a burlesque performer after hours. You were wise to follow the rules and not touch the body. Besides a dead bird, under her coat, she dressed more like a cigarette girl at Ciro's."

"Maybe she peddled goods other than the obvious sweet and salty ones."

Sadowski ignored Guy's wisecrack. "Past her prime as an ingenue at thirty years old. Single. Lived alone, except maybe with rats as her roommates, off Hawthorn Avenue on the east side of La Brea in a furnished efficiency apartment. Top floor of a walk-up building with no elevator, which made my arthritis act up, and one of those with a Murphy bed."

Not far from our office. "Whatcha aiming at?"

"The only clue, which doesn't lead anywhere, is the movie theater where she worked showed a Philo Vance retrospective that week. On the day she died, we discovered *The Canary Murder Case* on the billing."

"I'm a big fan of detective movies and watched it," said Guy. "Besides the actual name of the title, the *canary* refers to a songbird, a common showbiz term, but in this case, she's a former Ziegfeld showgirl. She's not a real bird. Maybe Pinky is a chanteuse."

"Didn't know that."

Surprised that no one had made an Egyptian connection, Guy smiled and felt smarter than the cops. "My partner also mentioned she saw a black feathery object stuffed under her lightweight coat. We refused to tamper with the crime scene, but it would help us if we could find out what that was."

"We were told it was some kind of stuffed crow, but bigger. More like the size of a hawk or falcon. Beats me what that's supposed to mean. Any idea?"

Guy struck his tabletop with such force that his pencil snapped. "By any chance, you familiar with Dashiell Hammett?"

"The crime writer?"

Guy figured the detective probably read *Black Mask* magazine like he did. "Did you ever consider...when you went to Warner Brothers the other day...there might be a connection?"

"Right! They were in the middle of film production for *The Maltese Falcon.*"

"Birds...crows...canaries... Don't you sense a theme?" Guy wondered why Moe was so slow to connect the dots.

"Interesting. Need to mention that to my partner. Well, look. Gotta go—"

"Wait! Before you hang up, you didn't tell me if anyone found out how this Pinky gal died. Tell me if I'm wrong, but we didn't see any blood. I'd suspect we'd notice marks on her coat if someone had shot or stabbed her."

"You get an A-plus for being observant. From what we can tell, our victim had some kind of poison in her bloodstream, but poisoning can mean a lot of things, including a drug overdose."

"How and with what?"

"Hasn't been determined yet."

"I'm concerned for the Bogarts and—" Guy clammed up. His partner took Mary Astor's morbid leave-behind as evidence and didn't report it to the cops.

"And?" Sadowski asked. "Is there something you shamuses are withholding?"

"My mind just wandered." Guy blew out withheld breath. "All right. I'll let you fight your crimes and capture the bad guys."

After he hung up, Guy called the same veterinary office where he and Babs met Basil Rathbone and sealed the deal on their last major case involving celebrity dognapping. He begged them to take their beagle pup and at least one of their kittens, especially since new ones arrived that morning.

"I'm puzzled," he confessed. "I wonder if someone has us under surveillance and knows our weakness for rescuing animals. Every time I turn my back, I feel like there's something new at our doorstep. Anyways, this situation is getting out of hand."

Their myna bird made a smart-assed remark. "Too many kittens. Too little time. Do it on your own dime! *Squawk!*"

"Who was that?" asked the veterinary receptionist.

"A rude talking bird who thinks he's a cat." When asked what that implied, he explained, "Thinks he still has nine lives, but he's getting down to the wire."

He hung up and confronted the bird. "Instead of Cagney, maybe we should rename you. How about Stu? As in myna bird stew? You're pushing your luck."

Moments later, Babs rang from downstairs. "Hurry down here, quick! Wiggins has something to show us."

* * *

"Look what the cat dragged in!" said Wiggins, wearing work gloves. In one hand, he held a kitten by the scruff of its neck. In the other, he held a dead robin. "One of yer critters must've escaped again and found these two fellas in the alleyway."

Guy scratched his head. "Wait a minute, I just called the vet's office for them to pick up the box of critters we found upstairs."

Babs shook her head. "He's not one of ours. What's going on? It's like kittens are popping up out of nowhere."

Wiggins held out the whining stray for her to cradle in her arms. "Whatcha want me to do with it?" asked Wiggins, referring to the lifeless bird.

Babs took a few steps back and refused to touch it. Guy teased her for being skittish. He sacrificed his handkerchief, the monogrammed one his grandmother gave him last Christmas, and wrapped it up before placing it in a discarded empty Bon Ami container.

"You gonna take that down to the Medical Examiner's office?" Wiggins asked.

"Why would they be interested in dissecting dead birds rather than concentrating on human corpses?" Guy replied. "Besides, it's probably not related."

"Funny your new case involves dead birds," Wiggins said, "'Cause I have a stuffed owl in the private room behind my general work area. Always keep the door locked." He took out his collection of keys and started to open it.

"I always assumed that room was a storage closet," Guy said.

He and his partner tried to follow, but Wiggins held up his hand, preventing them from entering. "Oh no, you don't. Won't let it be on my conscience if one of you gets hurt. Too many cleaning solutions and sharp tools."

Guy remarked, in jest, "Maybe we should consider you a potential suspect."

"If that's the case," Wiggins said, "I would've gotten rid of ya a long time ago. Landlord would be keen to replace you with tenants who pay on time."

Their janitor brought out a taxidermy owl, a handsome specimen with its wings spread in an attack position. "Now, mind you, it wasn't my idea to get this. Don't know what possessed my wife to buy it in the first place. Probably figured it would remind me of the barn owls from my grandpappy's farm back in Ireland. Me thinks she found it for a cheap price at a flea market. Scared his customers away just like it did my kids.

"Wifey made me take this out of the house. Check out the wooden base it's mounted on." He pointed to a small brass plate identifying its creator. Engraved upon it: Birdie Wilson, Taxidermist to the Stars.

Chapter Eight: The Wizard of Paws

The private eyes made an appointment to meet Burt "Birdie" Wilson. Guy carried a paper bag containing the dead robin, still wrapped in his handkerchief and inside a coffin made from Wiggins' discarded Bon Ami container. Babs felt awkward delivering Mary Astor's box of fading roses with a defunct crow.

They passed the taxidermist's darkened storefront and doubled back, rechecking its address, as it gave one the impression it had gone out of business and the remaining merchandise had never been cleared out.

"I bet Birdie does this on purpose to discourage tourists and curiosity seekers," said Guy.

Once inside, both noticed a sign over the doorpost that said, "Don't be a stuffed shirt. Get your bird stuffed."

Plump and potbellied, his head was like a billiard ball wearing a Hawaiian grass skirt. Too tall to have qualified for a Munchkin role in *The Wizard of Oz*, he was still much shorter than Babs at five-foot-four. Guy, only five-foot-seven with a slender frame, towered over him.

Birdie came off as a quirky know-it-all who thought he was familiar with every private dick in town. "How come I never heard of you two?"

"We've only been in business a tad over two years," said Guy. "But those who've taken us on have trusted us more than the LAPD."

A bad choice of words, she thought, but she wondered why or how he had been involved with the cops or their competition. She shot her partner a dirty look and corrected him. "That doesn't mean we're not experienced. Most of our previous cases have involved insurance fraud or proof of cheating husbands or wives. Or they've entailed tracking down people who have disappeared, or thefts and the return of stolen property."

Guy gave her a reassuring pat on the back. "Our famous celebrity canines case, the one publicized in every paper, which started with the theft of Basil Rathbone's dog and ended with Toto and Asta from the *Thin Man* films, was the rare exception, because we had never intended to become pet detectives."

Stop rambling and get to the point. Babs spoke up. "This is the first time we've had to deal with dead bodies, whether they were human corpses or dead birds which, by the way, we brought samples for you."

The quirky taxidermist beckoned them to follow, passing through his display area of zoological wizardry.

Babs winced and whispered in Guy's ear, "This place brings back childhood memories. When I was little, my mother owned a mink fur wrap with the heads still on. Its itty-bitty glass eyes would stare at me and give me nightmares."

She almost went into shock when they passed a two-headed wolf, saddled like a horse with a monkey wearing a cowboy hat and boots riding on top, swinging a stiff lasso, frozen in mid-air.

Birdie made a grin as wide as the Panama Canal. "Don't you love it? Makes me prouder than a pride of lions. That's an excellent example of anthropomorphic taxidermy, or having the animals do human-like things."

"Makes you wonder how these poor things died," said Babs.

"If you're worried," said Birdie, "I didn't kill either animal to create this. My code of ethics: I never do. Someone found the wolf by the side of the road, hit by a motorist. Didn't know what to do with it, so they brought it to me. I decided to stitch it up with another head in need of restoration. One of my customers didn't have the heart to throw it out after it fell off the wall, and his Great Dane started chewing on it.

"Lots of the animal trainers for the movies know me and let me do my magic after their animals die. If I recall, this monkey died of old age. His owner had plenty of live ones and didn't care what I did to him. I love being creative. Like it?

"You're familiar with the circus entrepreneur, P.T. Barnum. Did you believe he had a real mermaid? He capitalized on the marvels of taxidermy."

Babs forced a smile. The sooner they got out of there, the better.

Birdie, however, continued to brag to his captive audience. He pointed to a display of tiny birds on a bush under glass. "This is a rare example of animated taxidermy."

Guy looked perplexed. "Like animated cartoons?"

"Except these are three-dimensional." Birdie inserted a key into its base, which engaged a music box. Suddenly, the birds came to life. Some flapped their wings, simulating flight. Others warbled and hopped from branch to branch. "Well-to-do Victorians were real connoisseurs for this kind of thing. Imagine impressing one's guests with such parlor tricks."

Guy took a closer look. "They resemble automatons, except these were once alive."

Horrified, Babs took a step backward and rubbed her arms, as if shivering. "This reminds me too much like creatures from Dr. Frankenstein or from Dr. Jekyll and Mr. H-i-d-e."

Birdie laughed. "In a certain sense, both of you are right."

* * *

In the rear, he had an elaborate setup of worktables. Birdie donned a protective apron over his wrinkled shirt. Then he tied a kerchief around his face like a bandit from a Western. He put on aviator goggles in lieu of safety glasses and slipped on a pair of rubber gloves.

"Harmful stuff," he said. "Wouldn't want to ingest it or breathe it in by accident. Nor would I want to absorb anything through my skin or an accidental cut. Won't affect the bird. It's already dead."

He took a few ominous jars of chemicals off a shelf. "Sorry, I don't have extra gear. I'm used to working alone." Birdie asked Guy to hand him his robin. "I'll give you a short demonstration, but you'll want to distance yourself—for safety purposes."

Birdie showed them various knives, scalpels, and scrapers and explained that taxidermy essentially entailed the tanning and preservation of the animal's skin. "Similar to making leather from scratch, but in this case, the animal retains its fur. Then it involves stretching it over a frame made of wire or plaster of Paris with lots of pinning to make sure everything stays in place."

He asked Guy to hand him the robin. "Recently deceased, right?"

"Our janitor found it yesterday." Guy explained he had kept it cold inside the refrigerator.

"Don't think of taxidermy as just a way of mounting hunting trophies or a macabre form of artistic animal sculpture. For several centuries, scientists have used taxidermy as a learning tool. Biologists used it for taxonomy or classifying how species were related to each other."

As an animal lover, Babs felt squeamish. "I'd never want to hunt and kill animals and nail them up on my walls."

"Have you ever owned a rabbit's foot for good luck?" Birdie asked.

She realized she was guilty.

Birdie made a long cut from their robin's throat to its tail. Guy flinched. "Ah, come on. It's no different from taking off a too-tight coat and socks. In this case, you're peeling the skin off a carcass. Preserving life after death started around 3,400 Before the Christian Era with the ancient Egyptians."

"With mummies," Babs piped in.

"First with humans," Birdie explained. "For religious rituals to prepare one's soul for the afterlife. With animals, they paid homage to their gods, but they also wanted to memorialize their beloved pets."

"Was it true that pharaohs often buried their wives and pets alive?" Babs asked.

Birdie ignored her query and continued. "The Egyptians used a combination of spices in their process, including cinnamon, common to most kitchens. Some masked the fragrance of death. Others, like frankincense, discouraged insects, and myrrh curtailed fungus." He continued to talk while performing his own embalming process. "Centuries later, seafaring explorers needed ways to bring back their discoveries. People came up with concoctions of whiskey, seawater, and the type of glue or tar they used to patch up holes in their ships. Maybe not too scientific, but they had to work with the materials they had on hand."

Babs tried to distinguish the labels on his motley assortment of glass bottles. Unable to decipher its writing, she started to reach for one to turn it around.

"Stop! Didn't I warn you not to touch stuff?" Birdie shouted.

Startled by his sudden outburst, she knocked over a bottle of oxalic acid onto the floor, only it didn't break. "Close call. Sorry, I guess I got too curious."

"That substance is caustic. Can burn your insides if you accidentally ingested it. It's bad enough you're dealing with a murder case," he said. "Not going to have your death on my conscience because of your refusal to listen to simple instructions."

Guy gave her the side eye and turned to their host. "What's in these solutions?"

"All sorts of nasty chemicals—naphtha, carbolic acid—don't you dare inhale the fumes from sulphuric acid. That's a corrosive. Many of these substances, if they don't kill you, will irritate your lungs, your eyes, or your skin. Breathing them can cause dizziness and vomiting.

"I'm one of the few taxidermists who does their own tanning. Most have someone else do the work. For instance, this powder you keep seeing me sprinkle on your robin like powdered sugar on a donut, that's borax. It helps dry everything out. You're probably familiar with borax as a cleaning agent." He pointed out to the Bon Ami container Guy had brought the bird in.

"Like I mentioned before, sailors used hodgepodge methods. It wasn't until the 1700s when a French biologist developed a secret formula that everyone eventually copied, but it was so poisonous for the smaller projects, they put them under glass. They housed larger ones within dioramas, like the ones you see in museums."

"Aren't you worried?" Babs asked.

"I like to use my own special ingredients, but that's not to say I shouldn't take precautions, and I won't give away my guarded secrets. People will have figured it out after I'm dead and gone. That's what makes me a cut above all my competition." Birdie explained while the robin needed to soak in his special solution, he'd examine the crow.

"As opposed to the poor robin, my guess is someone must've preserved this." Babs handed him the box. "It's never had any odor."

"I'd be willing to bet it's not my handiwork. If you still have your doubts, then feel free to examine my ledgers."

Like a surgeon, Birdie took a scalpel and peeled back the crow's feathery epidermis, revealing a wire frame. He remarked that its glass eyes didn't match. "These are too large. More fitting for a kestrel, a small raptor, also known as a sparrow hawk."

"Maybe that's why this one looks eerier than the other one."

"Lady, how many of these have you found?"

"Two—no three, even if we're only speculating about the one under the coat of the deceased. Police have it and are keeping a lot hush-hush."

Birdie shook his head as he continued to disassemble Mary Astor's specimen. "Not my doing. An admirable try, but too amateurish. Do you want this back?"

Babs grimaced. Guy asked if it was okay to leave it here for safekeeping.

After Birdie finished his demonstration and cleaned up, ditching his makeshift protective clothing, he offered to make tea. Guy admitted he felt queasy, but Birdie claimed Earl Gray and digestives should settle his stomach. "Guess you gotta have guts of steel to work this trade. You'd be surprised how many hunters come to me to make trophies who are afraid to eat the meat. I'll bag it up and make venison or buffalo jerky. 'Waste not. Want not', as the saying goes."

Guy interrupted his banter to return to more serious matters. "Do you have records of selling any stuffed crows to any of your customers?"

"For anything purchased in the last three months, I wouldn't have organized the receipts yet. You'd be surprised how busy it's been lately. Maybe it's the movies they're making. I'd have to examine my ledgers for older purchases. Been in business a while, you know."

Babs found it odd he wouldn't remember anything recent. *Did he have enough customers buying dead crows that he couldn't sort them out?*

"Do you sell any books on how to do this, you know, for hobbyists?" she asked.

"Wouldn't want to lose sales by encouraging people to try this at home. Doubt if you'd find what you needed in your public library, but I'm sure there must be mail-order catalogues. Maybe they even have correspondence schools advertised in the back pages. Everything from learning how to paint by numbers to stenography…they seem to be popping up all over the place. Probably lists schools on how to be a private eye, eh? On that note, you better start running along. Busy deadlines to make."

"Dead—lines," Guy muttered, placing his hand into his trousers pocket. He pulled out the note, which accompanied Mayo's singing telegram, and handed it to the taxidermist. "Almost forgot. Can you explain this?"

"That's a forgery." Birdie pulled out an old ledger. "Look. The handwriting doesn't match."

Considering he could've always jotted down something in front of them, which he could've faked on the fly, Babs believed what she saw. "If someone's setting you up, why?"

"You're the detective," Birdie said. "I suppose it's to shift the blame and throw off the police and sleuth hounds like you."

"While we're on the subject of ledgers," said Guy. "Do you mind if I take a peek to see if you have any records of selling stuffed crows to your customers?"

Birdie pointed to his shelves filled to the brim. "That'll take days. You'll have to make an appointment. Several, in fact, 'cause they're not leaving my office. If you have the time, be my guest, but for now, I gotta kick you out."

* * *

Babs felt uneasy. In her opinion, Birdie Wilson withheld too much information, especially regarding the exact chemicals that made up the formula he used to preserve his taxidermy specimens.

Heading back to their office, Guy mentioned, "Perhaps if I spend time on my own doing research, it'll help fill in the blanks where Birdie sold us short. Like Chief Crow-Feather, I regard him as both a source of information, but also a potential suspect. However, as an ally, he could be an asset and an advantage we have over the shortsighted homicide detectives."

Chapter Nine: Whose Bird is Cooked?

T he temptation of getting bailed out of their debts lured Babs and Guy deeper into a realm where they had dared not go, until now. After their eye-opening encounter at Wilson's taxidermy shop, Babs started having second thoughts. Her lack of enthusiasm showed as she mulled over her coffee the following morning.

She had no appetite for her favorite chocolate eclairs as she shuffled into Guy's office and offered him hers, who was willing to eat anything set before him. The moment she noticed him sipping his coffee and reading a copy of *Black Mask*, the detective pulp in which Dashiell Hammett got his start, she cleared her throat, took aim, and verbally fired. "Should I start calling you Sam Perry Marlowe, instead of Guy Brandt, the hotshot gumshoe to the stars?"

"Why? Because they serialized some of Dash's famous stories before he had them published into the works we know now? Earle Stanley Gardner, the guy who writes the Perry Mason stories, and Raymond Chandler also contributed to this pulp. Can't you give me a break? You need one yourself."

Willing to fight him just to prove she was right and he was wrong, she folded her arms tight across her waist. "As the owner of this firm, isn't it my job to make sure we don't go under?"

Sir Henry stood up on his hind legs. He licked Guy in the face with such gusto that he almost knocked him out of his chair. "Take the dogs. They're tired of being cooped up in the office. Go for a brisk walk in the hills near your house. It'll do all of you some good."

Babs surrendered. She leashed up Sir Henry. Before taking Bruno into her custody, she put in her two cents. "Wish you were better trained like Skippy, the dog who plays Asta."

"For him to bring home a paycheck and pay for his own room and board?" asked Guy.

Babs grumbled a *harrumph* before articulating, "What are you planning today?"

"Huston is messengering over a production schedule. He already gave me the heads-up that Elisha Cook doesn't have any scenes this afternoon, so I figured this would be a good time to pin him down for a one-on-one."

"Smart move. Are you sure you'll be all right without me?"

"As snug as a bug in a rug," he said, biting into her unwanted éclair. "Besides, he might feel awkward toward women and might be more open around me."

Babs knitted her brows together and gave him her inquisitive scowl. "Meaning?"

He shrugged. "Well…you know…because he has similar sentiments…"

"Which implies?"

"Since Elisha plays the gunsel. Maybe he was a gunman in the movie, but I'm convinced it also referred to the other definition of the word, which is a boy used for you-know-what purposes…by another man, and in this case, Kasper Gutman. What I'm saying is Cook might be queer in real life. Looks like it's fairly obvious in the script that Joel Cairo identifies that way with his manicured hands and his gardenia-scented business cards. I picked up on this underlying theme in the story right away."

I guess you would know. She knew he was evading a sensitive subject, one which was privy between the two of them but never spoken about in public. "If you feel he'd be more receptive to you conducting an interview, be my guest. I'm sure you'd feel the same if I needed to extract more intimate details from Mary Astor."

"The uproar about the *Purple Diaries* scandal involved some pretty *risqué* details. Anyway, Babs, are you gonna follow my advice?"

"About taking the afternoon off? You're probably right. Good luck. I hope you uncover something important so we can move along with this case."

63

* * *

"You're lucky the studio put me up in a local hotel," Elisha Cook, Jr. told Guy. "For the most part, I'm a hermit. During the summers, I like to stay in a remote cabin in the High Sierras and go fly fishing for golden trout."

Guy wrinkled his brow, perplexed at the less luxurious surroundings of where he was staying compared to most other stars with higher billing—simplistic, without a showy restaurant, more like a diner and an afterthought. Cook led him over to two wingback chairs in the lobby with a large pillar and a potted fern behind them. Before they sat down, Guy sized him up. *He'd be lucky to tip the scales at 123, and looks two inches shorter than me.*

"You make so many films. How do you manage that?" Guy asked.

Cook removed his hat and placed in on top a nearby end table. "Sure do. Been making 'em for years. Small parts. In three already this year—Joe the elevator boy in *Love Crazy*, a film starring two other actors who became famous from being in Dashiell Hammett films... You know, Myrna Loy and William Powell. How uncanny is that? A piano player in *Sergeant York* and a hotel clerk in *Man at Large*. None of them have been big ones like *The Falcon*. Can you believe I'm playing a character now who also has the last name of Cook?"

With pencil and pad in hand, Guy doodled caricatures of Cook, emphasizing his expressive, fearful blue eyes, high forehead, and wiry, brown hair. "How do the studios get a hold of you if you live way up in the mountains?"

"They send couriers to fetch me. Then, I pack my bags and head back into civilization. That's the way I like it, and it works well for me."

Guy loosened his tie. The lobby fans were going full blast, but they were more for dispelling the haze of tobacco smoke than dissipating the oven-baked heat. He took his fedora off and fanned his sweat-dampened hair for relief. "Elisha—"

"Stop right there. Call me Cookie."

"All right... Cookie, you are aware of why we're here today, I hope?"

Cook sat up straight in his chair, as if the extra inch in his spine would give him an air of authority. "Hey, just because I look like a stupid fool on screen doesn't mean I don't have any brains. No sirree. Okay, we'll start from the beginning. My full name is Elisha Vanslyck Cook, named after my pa, of course, since I'm a junior and he's a senior. *Ha, ha...* I'm on my second marriage to a woman named Mary Lou. We've been together for thirteen years, although I don't know how much longer it's gonna last."

"Do you have kids from your marriage with Mary or the one before that?" Guy asked.

"None. And I was born in San Francisco. Same town *The Maltese Falcon* takes place in."

"Interesting..." *Babs is from there, as well.*

"Acted on stage before films. My Broadway debut was a musical comedy, *Hello, Lola*, a Shubert production, but if ya really wanna know, I started in vaudeville when I was the tender young age of fourteen."

Guy put his pencil down and looked up. "You don't say!"

"Not all-natural talent. Nurtured some of it by attending St. Albans College and the Chicago Academy of Dramatic Arts to learn the craft. After a while, a friend approached and said I needed to leave New York and head out west to do motion pictures. I never expected to be famous or get the choice parts."

"Please don't tell me you're sick and tired of playing the oddball," Guy said, probing for any possibility of whether he'd consider taking revenge and *bird* people for being pigeon-holed.

"Cookie, how far are you willing to go to achieve your desires?"

"I went on a one-man strike for ten months against stage producers and refused to continue settling for small roles and wanted a shot at the leading ones. Figured I had apprenticed in the theater long enough. For me, it was all or nothing, and guess what? My stubborn insistence forced me to pump gas and work as a clerk at cigar stores to make ends meet. That's a far cry from when I started out, and I was willing to do anything. Even sell souvenir booklets in the lobby."

"You're telling me that your strike shut you out?" Guy asked.

"The theatrical world wanted nothing to do with me anymore. Now, if Hollywood wants to continue giving me such a handsome paycheck, I'll play one of the flying monkeys in a sequel of *The Wizard of Oz* if I have to," said Cook.

Guy penciled a note to himself: *Lacks motivation for any wrongdoing. Like many of his characters, seems to be an innocent bystander.* "No one's tried to threaten you yet?"

"Nope. Fortunate, I guess."

Lucky, indeed, his goose isn't cooked. "This question might sound strange, but what is your biggest fear? Everyone's got a deep, dark bugaboo they're worried about."

"Having to get a real civilian job, I guess, if my acting work ever dried up." Cook laughed. "Or maybe getting drafted if the United States goes to war, which it looks like it might. What about you?"

Guy shrugged it off. "Let's not worry about me. I need to be concerned about your well-being."

"Regarding *The Maltese Falcon*, you know, John wrote the script. Warners made it twice before that. It wasn't very good, I guess. I heard Bogie wasn't that great in pictures until John directed him. If you look at his older films...and he was under contract with Warners for quite a few years... You'll see the difference in his acting. Me? I get punched around all the time."

"You never had any leading roles?"

"No, thank you. I'll tell ya why. There was a playwright, years ago, named Owen Davis. He won the Pulitzer Prize for his play, *Icebound*. His son and I were best friends. We both wanted to come out to Hollywood. Mr. Davis told me, 'Cookie, you're gonna go to Hollywood.' Remember, this is 1937, and all supporting actors, like me, would come from the New York stage. He said, 'Just play small parts.'

"I asked, 'Why?' He said, 'I'll tell you why. You'll last a long time, and they won't be able to blame the picture on you, because you're going to make a lot of bombs. Cookie, do you know how many major studios there are on the West Coast? There must be six or seven, and don't forget, they make fifty-two pictures a year. Plus, one or two feature pictures. Can you imagine finding enough good writers for that many pictures multiplied by that many movie studios? You're going to be in bomb after bomb.' And he was right, because there just weren't that many writers and not many good scripts."

"Why do you think John Huston chose you to play Gutman's gunsel?" Guy asked, trying to pry more into Cook's personal life, especially since he mentioned earlier he was married.

"I don't know. Maybe because I have the same agent as Bogie."

"From reading the script, I get the impression Sam Spade likes to push your character around. He calls you names. Blows smoke in your face. He even traps you inside your own overcoat to wrestle away your gun. Did you ever get so steamed that you'd want to take it up with him after the director yelled, 'Cut!'?"

Cook started to develop a nervous tic and shifted in his seat. Guy sensed an uneasiness. "Spade said, 'The cheaper the crook, the gaudier the patter.' When I still tried to make a go at being an actor, I used to get all the bit parts nobody wanted—the patsy, the soda jerk, the filling station attendant who got knocked out cold by an ex-con on the lam who didn't feel like paying. When I first met Humphrey Bogart, I said that, unlike him, I could play the role, but never looked right for the tough guy part. Like most people, I didn't know what it meant to be a gunsel. I just thought it meant a gunman, not Gutman's *boy*." Cook put him on the spot. "Are you somebody's boy?"

This time, Guy assumed a defensive posture. "Of course not!"

Cook crossed his arms, as if shielding himself from further questioning and gave Guy cold eyes. "I hope this wasn't the aim of your interrogation."

Guy's Adam's apple rose and fell with a gulp, which he was certain was visible to anyone paying attention. Maybe he had been sending the wrong signals. He reached for his hat and fanned off the sweat from his long, thin neck.

From that point forward, Cook appeared to distrust Guy's intentions, and his tone switched from talkative to guarded and uncooperative. In real life, there was no Production Code censoring their conversation. Considering Cook's irrational fear and aversion toward inversion, maybe the next time Guy appeared in public, he needed to give others the impression he was Babs' husband or boyfriend. Of their clients, only Bogie knew the truth, but Guy figured him trustworthy enough to keep their little secret. Guy thanked Cook for his time. To make a cordial exit, he came up with the excuse that he had another appointment pending and had to return to his office to check his messages.

* * *

To any bystander, Babs must've appeared ludicrous, stuffing the elephantine Sir Henry and the incorrigible Bruno into her Crosley clown car, especially since most road trips involved rides in Guy's much larger Buick convertible. Once she got her vehicle started, Sir Henry rested his chin on her shoulder. With his head so large in comparison, other motorists did double-takes, thinking he was the driver.

The best plan would be to stop at her house first, feed and water the dogs, and get changed into a more casual outfit of a short-sleeved cotton sweater and high-waisted pleated trousers, Oxfords, and a floppy-brimmed sunhat, rather than a suit with pumps. She had seen Carole Lombard wear something similar in a fashion magazine. During this rare moment of leisure, she needed to dress the part.

Babs brushed Sir Henry's scraggly coat. "I'll have to do this all over again if you pick up any stray leaves, burrs, or ticks," she told him. Bruno only needed minimal grooming. A vigorous massage ending with a pat on the head and a dog biscuit made him content.

On her way back to her car, she passed her Japanese tenant, busy pulling weeds. He wore a cornflower-blue happi coat, short mid-calf trousers, and tabi socks with his sandals. To protect himself from sunburn, he wore a conical bamboo coolie hat.

"Otake-san, do you mind taking my calls while I'm out?"

"You sure? My En-ger-lish...not very good," he said in his choppy Japanese accent, combining his Ls and his Rs.

"It's good enough for me to understand. You'll be fine. Okay?"

"Okay. *So-desu,*" he said, making a customary bow.

* * *

While in theory Babs was supposed to be taking the day off. Thoughts ran through her brain like a newsreel. Birdie Wilson! Was it impossible to erase those images of dead animals glaring at her through artificial glass eyes? They reminded her of a chamber of horrors from a carnival sideshow. He claimed innocence. She and her partner still considered him a suspect. Guy was still wary of Crow-Feather.

Enjoy the scenery, she kept reminding herself, as she closed her eyes to savor the fragrant smells of cut grass, citrus, and eucalyptus, but the tempting aromas also enticed bees. Bruno kept snapping at them.

She continued up the hill, passing a group of yard workers trimming a privacy hedge. She pointed to an amaryllis, the color of a blood orange. "Do you mind?" They gave her the nod, and she plucked one and stuck it in her hatband. Each time she tried to slip another under Bruno's collar, it fell out and lost its petals.

She had thoughts of Bogie…and Mayo. *He was on the up and up. Must be a challenge to play second fiddle to one's famous husband. Would hate it if that were me. What if their marriage didn't work out? Where would that leave her? On a path for revenge? She could be the murderer. Don't rule her out.*

Mary Astor's ex-husband seemed to be a crackpot. If he was willing to ruin her reputation by exposing her private diaries to the public, Babs didn't put it past him that he was capable of anything, including freakish intimidation tactics.

Further down the road, Babs looked both ways to make sure no one was looking and plucked a pomegranate from a neighbor's tree, causing a guilty bulge in her trousers pocket.

Despite taking the afternoon off, the broad scope of their case still overwhelmed her. Who was Pinky Pilchik? What other concessions was she peddling? What about Stanford Peck, the obnoxious tour guide who badgered them in front of Bogie's mansion?

She and Guy still had plenty of interviews. He had an appointment today with Elisha Cook, Jr., a man who always got stuck in parts playing the fall guy. Wouldn't it be ironic if he was tired of being the patsy and took it out as his personal vendetta? Should she worry about Guy spending the next few hours alone with him? Was it even worth their while to track down and interview George Raft, Paul Muni, or Ida Lupino?

With her mind elsewhere, Babs hadn't paid attention to the squirrel gathering acorns. Sir Henry barked, noticing it first. The combined weight of an Irish Wolfhound and a musclebound bulldog dragged Babs into the middle of the road just as a motorist sped around the bend. She lost her grasp on the leashes and hurtled into the roadway as the terrified squirrel zigzagged to avoid screeching tires. He got spared, but the ripe pomegranate that rolled out of her pocket did not and looked like a bloodied crushed rodent on the asphalt.

The driver pulled over to the side and parked in a ditch. "Are you all right?"

Feeling woozy and weak-kneed, Babs pointed to her hat. Sir Henry retrieved it and held it in his mouth while the stranger steadied her onto her feet. "Are you sure? It's no trouble for me to get you to a hospital."

"What'll we do with my dogs?"

"Everyone can hop in my car. If you won't see a doctor, the least I could do is take you home. Agreed?"

Babs closed her eyes. For a moment, he almost reminded her of her father, whom she missed. *Darn it. Why did he have to go so soon?*

When the man came into full focus—blonde hair, a strong, commanding chin, trim and tall, an athlete in sporty tennis garb, she realized he was a handsome fellow. Could this be her lucky day?

Ready for a ride, Sir Henry took the opportunity of his open door to climb into his backseat. Bruno wriggled his piggy-like body and crawled in behind.

"Where's the squirrel?" she asked, trying to regain her bearings.

With care, he got her settled into the passenger seat. "What squirrel?"

She looked around and was dismayed she couldn't find him. "The one my dogs chased...which caused me to fall."

"Looks like he took care of himself," he said, not seeing a thing. "You need to worry about...what's your name?"

"Babs."

"You need to be more concerned about Babs, not some silly squirrel. What were you going to do with him anyway?"

Guy would've never let her hear the end of it if she brought the injured critter back to their office to join the rest of their collection.

"Tell me where you're going," the man asked. "It's no trouble to drive you. Uphill or downhill, your choice."

Still feeling disoriented, she managed to disclose her address. The driver confessed he was a dog lover and fell head over heels with Sir Henry and Bruno.

Loves dogs...a man after my own heart, Babs thought.

He pulled into her driveway, got out of the car, and went around to the other side to help everyone out.

Who is he? Am I mad to size him up?

He walked her over to her front door. Her gardener stopped what he was doing and rose to his feet.

"Can I trust you'll see her safely inside?" the stranger asked.

"Miss Norl-man, are you okay?" Mr. Otake asked. He braced Babs under her arm.

"A bit shaken, I suspect," the stranger said. "But keep an eye on her to make sure."

As the man waved goodbye, Babs spotted his wedding ring, and her heart fell.

Otake escorted her over to her kitchen table and offered her a glass of water. "Took several phone messages while you were gone," he said. "Your mother called. She sounded worried."

"Anything wrong?"

"She wants to know when you're going to get married."

Babs frowned. *When is she going to let nature take its course?*

"I guess she doesn't consider me a prospect." Otake laughed. "Funny, yeah?"

She chuckled with him, not at him, and made a long-distance call to San Francisco.

"Mom, it's Babs. What's wrong?"

"Dear Barbara, it's good to hear your voice."

"I told you to stop calling me Barbara, and I don't care if that's what it says on my birth certificate. What's going on? I've had a trying day."

"Barbara darling, when are you going to give that all up and find yourself a husband?"

She refuses to listen! "Do we have to discuss this now when I'm bone tired?"

"A woman's job is in the home. Get out while you're young and still pretty enough to snag a man and let your partner take over."

Babs rolled her eyes. Not now—not ever did she want to have this conversation.

"Without me, Guy would run the place into the ground." She faked a yawn. Maybe her mother would get the hint.

She exaggerated a kissing sound into the receiver and hung up. Afterward, she sought out her housemate. "Someone else called?"

"Detective Allgood."

"Did it sound urgent?" She didn't want to disclose too much to Mr. Otake that she and her partner were working on a murder case.

He tried to explain, "Not urgent, but still im-por-tant. You not mating this guy, I hope."

"Mating? I think you meant dating. Why?"

"Smart girl like you too good for him. Pretty girls can get millionaires."

"He can wait till tomorrow." This time, her yawn was genuine. "Right now, it's bedtime for Babsy."

Chapter Ten: Is The Grass Really Greener?

The shamuses met with Sydney Greenstreet, who had already planned on lunching at Chasen's with John Huston, providing a great opportunity to knock off two interviews in one. They had started to question the director back at Warner Brothers Studios but had to cut it short for rehearsals.

Babs found it hard not to stare at the celebrity portraits adorning Chasen's rich wood-paneled walls. She wondered if new ones had been added since she last visited. Normally beyond her budget, the last time she feasted here was when William Powell invited them to join Myrna Loy, Dashiell Hammett, and Lillian Hellman for dinner when she and Guy handled their missing celebrity pets case.

Once again, they discovered that Detectives Allgood and Sadowski had gotten there first, had worn them out, and left. Greenstreet, because of his size, positioned himself at one end of their semicircular booth. To make it easier, Huston scooted over on his side to give room.

"Those cops squeezed every last drop out of me," the director said. "Would you believe they tried to link...of all people...my father, to the dead broad at your detective agency?"

He finished his single malt and fumbled, trying to cut the tip of a fresh cigar. More than one empty whiskey glass sat on his side of the table. "Whoever is behind these absurd threats has read Hammett's book and saw the two previous films adapted from it."

He stopped struggling with his Cuban and put it away. Babs assumed he must've seen the disgusted look on her face. As a gentleman, he said he'd wait until after he departed her company. "Have you seen the other films?" Huston asked, looking at Babs first.

She reached for her compact to powder her nose, as if that might hide her slight oncoming blush. "If I have, I don't remember them."

He turned to Guy, who confessed he saw the second film with Bette Davis, but didn't think he watched the first. Babs suspected a visit to Hammett would soon be in order.

Their waiter came for the newcomers' orders. "All I want is a simple sandwich," said Guy, dumbfounded by the elaborate menu.

"Nonsense, this isn't a five-and-dime soda counter," said Huston, who said he'd pick up the tab. "Try the turtle soup or check out today's chef's specials. I hear the *Carolina Frog Legs aux Aubergines, Catalane* are excellent. Try that with a side of caviar."

Guy strained to make a straight face and chose the assorted cold cuts. Babs stood firm on drinking only water flavored with a lime and said she wasn't hungry.

Huston turned to Guy. "Any of the tough-man stuff for you?"

He gulped, hesitating before pointing to Huston's glass. "Whatever he's having."

"Good choice." Huston cracked a smile. Babs caught him winking at their server as he asked for refills. She suspected this insinuated an extra-strong drink for her partner and a possible test to see how well he could handle his liquor.

When the drinks arrived, he and Greenstreet proudly recited one of Kasper Gutman's lines in unison. "I distrust a man that says when. If he's got to be careful not to drink too much, it's because he's not to be trusted when he does." They clinked glasses afterward.

Guy made mention that Babs never glanced at her menu. "Don't tell me you're skipping lunch 'cause you're worried about your figure."

She shook her head, despite the obvious bouquet of tantalizing aromas.

Guy put her on the spot. "You wolfed down a chocolate éclair an hour ago and ruined your appetite, am I right?"

Under the tablecloth, she opened her too-tight belt a notch.

Huston caught wind of her not-so-secret action. "Do you always argue?" He pointed to one, then to the other, and laughed. "I've only known you for a short time, but you two remind me of a comedy duo...like Abbott and Costello. Are you sure you're really PIs and aren't trying to hound me for an audition?"

She took offense, assuming her partner and her patron compared her to Lou Costello, because she had only ordered seltzer and was counting her calories. "Who are you calling fat?"

Guy, who always bordered on being underweight, replied, "Who's on first?"

It took her several seconds to digest his burlesque. Abbott and Costello made their film debut in *A Night in the Tropics,* where that famous line, "Who's on first," came from.

"There's only one Fat Man at the table, and I don't see his match," said Greenstreet, using his play on words to allay the tension, even if it was comic tension.

Changing the subject and getting down to business, Guy asked Huston, "Is there anything you did, any course of action, or a film you performed in that now you regret doing?"

Huston laughed so hard that he choked on leafy remains of his cigar. "Getting so drunk that—"

Babs interrupted. "Sir, that's not what we're talking about."

He cut her off. "Just jerking your chain. People know I can be difficult. Some of us consider ourselves artists. When I was just a screenwriter, often I had to coauthor my scripts. Then they'd be turned over to someone else to tamper with. Finally, I had my agent write a provision into my contract that if the studio took up my option, I'd be allowed to direct the film. I always felt it was about time I could get control over my projects."

Guy intervened. "Let me reword our question. Can you think of anyone who'd try to prevent you from finishing your film?"

Huston confessed the police had already gotten the better of him, but he'd do his best to answer. "Mark Hellinger, an associate producer to Hal Wallis, aggrieved me to finish *High Sierra*. Had something to do with George Raft's contract. He didn't want to do the film anyway, because he was tired of playing gangsters and didn't want a project where he'd get killed in the end. So, the deal was they had to get the script to him by a certain date. If he didn't do it, they didn't have to pay. I told Hellinger to—"

He stopped, looked at Babs, and said, "I told him a few choice words, which I can't say in the presence of a lady. That didn't go over too well, especially when he shared the same sentiments with Jack Warner, who had Hellinger fired."

Guy scratched his head. "Are you saying we should consider Hellinger behind these birdings?"

"Not if he knows what's good for him."

"What about Wallis?"

"Sonny, you better quit while you're ahead. Wait till someone's birded him. On every production, there are a hell of a lot of cooks in that Hollywood kitchen. Hellinger wasn't the only person given the boot. W.R. Burnett, my cowriter on *High Sierra*, and I churned out a damned fine script. I liked to talk out a scene and dictate it. He was a wizard on a typewriter, but I think I wore him out. Warner gave Paul Muni the script after their debacle with George Raft. Muni turned it down for many of the same reasons. He didn't want a script where he'd die at the end. They'd been paying him $5,000 a week, and Warner kicked him out on his can.

"After Muni, Warner went down the list—Cagney, Edward G. Robinson, and John Garfield. With the Gangster A-List exhausted, they offered it to Bogart. I could also get into the issues we had about bringing onboard Ida Lupino, but I'm afraid I'm pretty spent from being put through the wringer by Allgood and Sadowski."

Their waiter interrupted their conversation, holding a folded slip of paper. "A phone message for Mr. Huston."

Huston raised his finger to identify himself and read the note. Then he kept his voice low so that only his immediate party could hear him.

"It's from Frank Sexton, our property master. Someone has either stolen or misplaced one of *The Maltese Falcon* statuettes. Sorry to cut this short, but I better investigate."

Not up for much talk anyway, Huston cut out early, leaving the detectives alone with Greenstreet. Guy, who hadn't had time to touch his food until now, bit into his sandwich.

"I suppose you want to know about me," said Greenstreet, who quoted from *The Falcon*, 'I'll tell you right out I'm a man who likes talking to a man who likes to talk,' but in this case, you better let the lady take over so you can finish your lunch."

All eyes were on the Fat Man as he captivated everyone's attention. "As you can tell by my British accent, I wasn't born here, and you probably already know I got my start in theater. My first opportunity to transition over to film came at the age of sixty-one, and I must say I'm enjoying every minute of it."

"Are there any roles you've played where someone might want to target you?" she asked.

"In my stage debut, I played a murderer in a 1902 production of a Sherlock Holmes story by Arthur Conan Doyle and William Gillette at the Marina Theatre at Ramsgate in Kent. However, I heard the two of you made your grand career debut in a Sherlock Holmes-like assignment."

Babs clarified, "Only if you consider working with Basil Rathbone and Nigel Bruce on a case that was widely publicized all over Hollywood. Our previous stints were more like chicken scratch."

"Talking about Rathbone, now since the talkies have replaced silent films, people love to typecast Brits like him, Claude Rains, Ronald Coleman, and yours truly as the evildoers. Anyone with a foreign accent, especially with the war going on in Europe, isn't exempt. Bela Lugosi and Peter Lorre almost always play nefarious characters.

"True heroes in real life are people like you. Nonetheless, I've played all sorts of roles over the years, including comedy. In the theatrical world, most people know me for my portrayals in Shakespeare. Somehow, my distinctive size has rarely been a deterrent in casting."

"Sir, do you prefer film to theater?"

"Don't have much to compare it to since *The Maltese Falcon* is my first film project. Warner Brothers likes our rushes and lined up several more projects under my contract. One thing I've learned so far, however, is the lens is the actor's best critic, showing his mind more clearly than on the stage. You can get wonderful cooperation out of the lens if you are true, but God help you if you are not. Pictures are much harder to do than the theater. You're at the mercy of the camera angles."

"Please refresh my memory of how John Huston discovered you."

"In New York, I played Uncle Waldemar in the play *There Shall Be No Night*. He happened to be in town and met me backstage afterward. We've been friends ever since. People in the film industry had been after me for years with no success. Warner Brother offered me a thousand dollars a week with a four-week guarantee. Since I wasn't getting any younger, they caught me at the right moment. The thought of being in one place finally appealed to me after many years on the road."

She wondered how she'd word this without embarrassing him. "Please don't take this the wrong way, but how big—"

"Five feet and eleven inches, and I weigh well over two hundred pounds."

Close to three hundred, Babs thought.

"Once I was in New York. A runaway horse and wagon knocked me down," Greenstreet said. "Thank my lucky stars, I only wound up with minor scrapes. The horse later died of its injuries. Poor animal. He died because of me. Hard to live that down."

"Oh gosh. Poor horse. Do you see any possibility that whoever is making these birding threats could've taken your commanding presence out of context?" Babs asked.

"It's not like the story of *The Maltese Falcon* was created yesterday, and some stagehand got a hold of the script and decided to go on a grotesque crime spree. Hammett wrote his original story eleven years prior. Plus, of course, the two previous attempts on screen. Perhaps, somewhere out there, is an obsessed fan who's more of a zealot—someone who's twisted the myth behind the bird to fit their own warped interpretation."

"If there's a hint of truth to your statement," said Guy, chewing and swallowing, "then any of you playing a bad guy might be considered a target."

"That would entail the entire cast," said Greenstreet. "If you add everyone who's had a bone to pick against them, you might as well check the ship manifests at Ellis Island. I don't think Hammett portrayed them as simply black or white. Even Spade could be bought for a price, or at least that's how I've interpreted it. Think of the lines at the beginning when Miss Wonderly wants to hire Spade and his partner. 'We didn't exactly believe your story.'

'Then—?'

'We believed your two hundred dollars.'

'You mean—' She seemed not to know what he meant."

"'I mean that you paid us more than if you'd been telling the truth,' he explained blandly, 'and enough more to make it all right.'"

"Let's hope I don't play this part so well that my reputation will hound me from film to film."

"Aren't you just a pocketful of quips and quotes today!" Babs remarked. "Sydney, what's your next project after *The Falcon*?"

"Warner Brothers wants to keep me busy now since I'm under contract. They want me to play Lt. General Winfield Scott in *They Died with Their Boots On*, which also stars Olivia de Havilland and Errol Flynn. Guess I'm supposed to play a grand old man of the army in a fictionalized account of the life of George Armstrong Custer."

Errol Flynn... Babs felt a heavy pang in her chest. Well aware of his reputation as a ladies' man, she had her fill of dealing with him during her Rathbone case. As her interview with Greenstreet drew to a close, she asked Guy to take over and excused herself to go to the lady's room. "Pardon me. I must've consumed at least three or four glasses of seltzer."

On the way back to her table, when she passed by the bar, a male voice called out her name. "You owe me a phone call," said Allgood. "Should I consider your motive as an obstruction to justice?"

"Have you been following me around or tapping our phone lines? How did you know my partner and I were going to be here this afternoon?" *Thanks for putting me on the spot.* "Well, if you want the truth of why I couldn't call you back, I almost got hit by a car."

"Sorry to hear that."

At least he showed sympathy. "What was so urgent?"

"It's sort of private. Let me tell ya over a gimlet. The seat next to me is empty."

Babs took a quick look at her watch before sitting down.

He sidled up to her stool, too close for comfort. "What can I get you?"

"Club Soda with a twist of lime," she told the bartender. Allgood could drink on company time. She needed a clear head.

"Got an in on a show tonight," he said. "Care to join me?"

Chapter Eleven: Conspiracy Theories

After lunch, the private detectives returned to their office. Babs made a note to follow up with Huston if he recovered the missing *Maltese Falcon* prop. The two got busy catching up when Guy grabbed his shoebox of loose magazine and newspaper clippings and noticed what looked like another shadow of a person outside their frosted glass door leading to the hallway.

"Babs, it's happening again."

Not really wanting to be bothered, Babs sauntered out with her hands on her hips.

"What now?"

He pointed to the door, his hand shaking. She muttered an "Oh no," but approached with caution. He signaled for her to help open it; the weight against their door was nowhere near as heavy as before. When they pried it open, a rolled-up carpet plopped down on the floor, sending up a cloud of dust in its wake. Bruno and Sir Henry gave it a sniff inspection. Several cats decided it was the perfect scratching post. Guy picked up the receiver and called Wiggins to remove it posthaste.

When he arrived, they noticed him holding a parcel of loosely wrapped brown paper and twine. "Found this on the streetside door this morn when I opened up yer buildin'," he said. "Figgered some bum from the boulevard tried to open it but got scared off by a street copper."

Guy motioned for him to place it on his desk.

Babs sprang to her feet like a jack-in-a-box. "Oh God. Not another dead bird."

Wiggins put on his work gloves and unwrapped the bundle as the detectives watched. He found a small briefcase. Inside were two notes, each in its own separate envelope, three overstuffed clasp envelopes, and what appeared to be a records book. Babs opened the larger of the two notes and read out loud, "Can't have either one of you working at my shop around dangerous chemicals. Here are my last three months of receipts and most recent ledger containing my transactions. These are only on loan and must be returned—Birdie Wilson."

As soon as Guy opened one of the envelopes containing loose receipts, Stu swooped down and plucked one out of his hands like an eagle making a dive after a salmon, causing him to drop the rest. His electric fan scattered the papers even further.

"Looks like you've got your work cut out for ya." Wiggins waved goodbye and said he had other matters to tend to.

While Guy tried to round up the mess, Babs shoved the second note, unread, into one of her already overcluttered desk drawers, trying to keep away inquisitive kittens.

* * *

"Saves me the trouble of having to make appointments," Guy said. "His place gives me the heebie-jeebies."

Babs helped herself to a sip of water. Afterward, she dipped her handkerchief into the glass and patted her neck. "It's one thing to have no leads at all. It's another to have too many."

"Let's examine Hammett for a moment," he said.

"We already did a thorough examination of him on *The Thin Man* when its canine star Asta was missing."

"But now we're dealing with *The Maltese Falcon*. I'm sure it was easy for him to create the character of Sam Spade from his time spent as a Pinkerton detective in San Francisco, and speaking of this famous location, who else do we know is from the Bay area?"

She got defensive. "I am, but you're not suggesting I'm part of the plot?

You're going off on a tangent."

"Let's say we give Hammett a call and see what he's doing this evening."

Babs hesitated.

"What's wrong?"

"I sort of made plans."

"What kind and with who? Remember what happened the last time you kept secrets from me?"

How could she forget that whole fiasco when Basil Rathbone's jealous wife humiliated her in front of a star-studded crowd at the Coconut Grove? The newshounds had a holiday, and the photographers captured the catfight all over the tabloids.

Guy justified his need to know more. "We lost the Rathbones as our clients, and I quit the agency. Temporarily, of course."

"Do you have to be so nosy? Someone asked me out."

"Not Huston, I hope. He's married, but that won't stop him. He'll go after anyone wearing a skirt, and I don't want you to get hurt."

Babs looked down at her feet. "Would it make you feel better if I told you this person, not Huston, by the way, might help our case?"

"That would make me more worried than ever."

She leashed Sir Henry and said he'd spend the night with her. "Forget I ever said that."

"Fine," he replied in a huff. "Just don't let me say, 'I told you so.'"

* * *

Babs finally agreed if Guy could arrange an early evening meeting, she could go from there to her date. Back at their office, Guy tried to thumb through his files while their nettlesome myna bird kept pecking his fingers.

"Shoo!" he said, taking a swift swipe at the insistent interloper. "Maybe we should rename you as Stu, as in myna bird stew, or let Birdie Wilson embalm and turn you into a statue like the Maltese Falcon. If you were encrusted with jewels, maybe someone would steal you, and you'd be off our hands for good. Go away!"

As the bird flew off, Guy felt something wet and smelly land on his shoulder. "Drop a deuce on me again, damn it, and you're chowder, I'm telling ya!"

After dealing with the obstinate bird, he became so single-focused that he almost tripped over two kittens before he found what he wanted. "Babs, it looks like we might be meeting Hammett and Hellman at the Hedonist's Haven. Guess someone got tired of paying the steep tab at the Beverly Wilshire Hotel."

"That penthouse suite must've cost a king's ransom, and I heard rumors he was indebted to everyone from his liquor store to his limo driver, but I always assumed his studio had foot the bill."

"For all we know, he rented the suite for the day just to impress us. You know how *Hollywood types* can pull a fast one."

"If he's no longer there, where is he?" she asked.

"The Garden of Allah."

They had different opinions about the infamous place owned by the former Russian silent screen vamp, Alla Nazimova. Located on two and a half acres in the west end of Hollywood, this residential hotel had twenty-five additional Spanish-style villas. Marlene Dietrich had been known to swim in the nude in their swimming pool, shaped like the Black Sea.

A gossip columnist once described the Garden of Allah as a voyeur's dream, a place for the café society to see and be seen. Every once in a while, men in white came with a van and took a resident away. Others bit the dust from bankruptcy or divorce. Some landed in jail. Many film industry aspirants came to Los Angeles only for the films they were working on, and the Garden of Allah provided a retreat from reality for those whose job it was to provide that illusion for everyone else.

Bogie had unexpected time off and called to let them know he was restless. Mayo, always the first to start a spat, threw a vase at him; it nicked him above his eye. Huston didn't want to cover it with makeup and wanted it to heal before he returned to the set. Therefore, he wanted to know if he could assist them in any way.

"We're meeting with Dashiell Hammett and Lillian Hellman," Guy said when he picked up. "Maybe they can offer us insight on this vulgar crime. Come and join us."

* * *

The three parked their cars and walked over to Hammett's residence together. The moment they entered the Garden premises, the place reminded Babs of forgotten food past its shelf life. This stale and dilapidated residential palace of former faux opulence vied to be nursed back to health.

Guy gave Babs an advance warning. "Remember to stay objective and distinguish Hammett from the characters he writes about."

Babs brushed it off and accused him of being overly cautious.

Lillian Hellman welcomed them in and wanted to know what everyone was drinking.

"You're bartending?" Dash asked. She ignored his inquiry as she busied herself over their personal collection of booze bottles, bitters, lemon peels, and mixers, as if reconjuring the days of speakeasies, Prohibition, and bathtub gin. He whispered to his guests, "I was waiting for a snide comeback along the lines of, 'Looks like we have everything in stock. Go help yourselves.'"

Everyone tried not to laugh hard enough to arouse her attention. Babs, cautious as usual, noticed they were already two sheets to the wind before they arrived. Bogie had no qualms about catching up with his hosts.

"Welcome to the Land of Marriage and Divorce," said Hellman, over her shoulder, still busy mixing her own choice of spirits. "My ex-husband, Arthur Kober, and I stayed at the Garden back in '31, where we ended our marriage."

Bogie confessed he had lots of memories, some not always so fond, tied up in this place.

"How so?" Guy asked.

"For starters, back around '36, I stayed here with my second wife, Mary Phillips, a stage actress. I played Duke Mantee for four hundred dollars a week in the film version of *The Petrified Forest*. They were letting go of a lot of actors from that film, so the Garden was the perfect temporary place to hang out. Besides, one of these bungalows always had a swell party going on.

"As the story goes, Mary got offered the chance to star in *The Postman Always Rings Twice* on the New York stage. I guess I wasn't the squeaky-clean, good little boy I should've been. While she was away, I met Mayo, who I asked to go sailing with me on weekends. Soon, she sailed into my bungalow here at the Garden.

"Well, Mary found out about my two-timing ventures and gave me the ultimatum. Had to choose between Mayo and her. I went with Mayo, which was probably the best thing for her. It's debatable that was the best option for me. Two years later, she wound up marrying Kenneth MacKenna, a story editor at MGM. If I ever feel I need to escape from my current marital situation, maybe I should consider renting another little hideaway."

Bogie asked, "Is it still true you almost never see people drinking at the bar or eating in the Garden's dining room?"

Hammett answered, "The food here is disgusting. Lillian accuses me of being undernourished and tries to force their watery soup down my throat."

"Guess nuthin's changed," Bogie replied. "A gossip columnist could hit pay dirt by mining this place."

"Don't speak so fast. You're aware Sheilah Graham spent considerable time here in the past—all because of her old lover—F. Scott Fitzgerald. She might've been an ingenue compared to Hedda Hopper or Louella Parsons, but she held her own pretty well with syndication."

"Ah, that's right. They were an item once. Poor guy. Drank himself into an early demise. Died right before Christmas last year, I think," Bogie recalled.

"Fitzgerald accused me of being a spoiled writer," Hammett said, cutting in. "Said the same about Ben Hecht, Nunnally Johnson, and Dottie Parker. Called us the 'great corruptionists,' whatever that meant."

Hellman returned with refreshments and piped in. "My time here with Kober proved to be unproductive. I did everything in the world to avoid writing, despite the generous amount of money the studios threw at me. All I did was drink, be a wife, and swim laps in the Garden's pool."

"Is it any different now?" asked Hammett, with the clear intention of taunting her. She responded by banging his drink down on the tabletop just hard enough to have it splash and make a mess.

"Anyway," said Hellman. "I left the Garden in '31 bound for New York, never to stay here full-time again."

Bogie gestured to the obvious signs of cohabitation between her and Dash. "What do you call this?"

"I never liked Hollywood and don't like the look of Los Angeles," she said. "When money talks, I come back from time to time to work on scripts, especially those of my plays."

"And to give me a hard time," Hammett added and turned to Babs. "Looks like you're getting a bit of Hollywood hearsay whether you like it or not. Comes with the territory, I guess."

While everyone else dominated the conversation, Babs observed the villa's thrift store-like décor—the threadbare rugs, cheap Oriental imitations, and bric-a-brac most likely purchased from wrapped movie sets—all pretense with little substance, accompanied with a hint of *Eau de Parfum Must*, as in musty, not musk, or must get a better job.

Lillian complained she was hungry, but all they had were *drink fixins* like salted peanuts, martini olives, and lemons, which couldn't be eaten by themselves.

Hammett continued. "I arrived in Hollywood during the perfect time, the late summer of 1930. The talkies took over the silent films, and the studios couldn't wait to nurture their new stars. Paramount took me under their wing and wanted me to write a gangster film for Gary Cooper.

"We're talking about the Depression with real crime all over the headlines. Hollywood cashed in on the action. Who needed more sappy musicals or soupy romance? Films like *Little Caesar* and *The Public Enemy* mesmerized audiences by having this gritty reality stare them in the face. I pounded on my typewriter in my room at the Hotel Knickerbocker, smoked cigarette after cigarette, and had a bottle of trusty Scotch at my side, knowing I'd receive a five-thousand-dollar bonus if I could come up with the perfect idea for Coop. I'd say that's an incentive, wouldn't you?"

No arguing that, Babs thought. By the looks of everyone else's nods, they seemed to agree. "The last time we had a meeting with you in private, as opposed to a bar or restaurant, we met with you at a penthouse suite at the Beverly Wilshire Hotel. Did the studio stop footing the bill?"

"Is that what you thought?" Hammett admitted he found that amusing.

Hellman interjected, "Between gambling away his earnings at the Santa Anita racetrack, falling behind in rent, and a mounting liquor bill with his local pharmacy, he was forced to downsize his taste for luxury. Lucky for him, he had a friend bail him out, but expected the loans to be repaid."

"Meanwhile, Lillian's career soared, while I sidestepped into the lair of Satan, of sadness, and getting sloshed." Hammett played up the melodrama. "She credits me with being her taskmaster with relentless revisions of her play *The Little Foxes*, which became a smash hit on Broadway. When she threatened to trash the project, I'd demand she return to her typewriter for another go-around.

"Meanwhile, I had this idea to write a novel called *My Brother Felix*," said Hammett. "Whatever my problem, I wasted my time with the nightclub crowd. Even got into a ridiculous match of machismo with Ernest Hemingway, who felt he could bend spoons with his biceps."

Felix...Detective Felix Allgood, Babs thought. Coincidence? Maybe. Maybe not. Since Hellman was such a fixture on Broadway, Babs asked her whether she knew George S. Kaufman.

"Everyone on Broadway knows George. Why do you ask?"

"In regard to Mary Astor. Her divorce scandal centered around a diary about their detailed escapades."

Hellman cracked a smile. "That was a juicy situation, wasn't it? Kaufman can't be behind these birdings. He's the golden boy of both coasts with way too much going on. If anything, someone might try to threaten him, but it would never be the other way around. Besides, he's moved on to another broad. I heard he ignores Mary's calls. Honestly, I don't know what she saw in him. He's not handsome and never tickled my fancy, but I guess he's known to have a way of making women feel wonderful, and that's why they fall for him."

Hammett seemed intrigued by the bizarre goings-on, which played on the theme of his novel. "I sold the film rights to *The Maltese Falcon* long ago and have no vested interest in whether the film gets completed or not. Lillian and I are more worried about being hounded by the FBI for our political leanings. They've managed to accumulate a file on us. Besides, the real falcon doesn't exist."

"Where did you come up with the idea for the story?" Bogie asked.

"My former Pinkerton partner had an uncle who lived in Calcutta. He sent him a jeweled skull of a holy man with a gut-churning legend behind it. That's probably the closest real object in existence, but to tell the truth, I made everything up."

"You must've encountered real people on whom you modeled your characters," said Guy.

"I had a secretary, Peggy O'Toole. She came to me at Pinkerton's regarding her housekeeper. I patterned Brigid O'Shaughnessy after her. Kasper Gutman came from a guy by the same name, considered to be a German spy. I have a cousin, Effie, so that's how I came up with the name for Spade's secretary."

"What about Joel Cairo?" Bogie asked.

"His character reminded me of a fellow I nabbed on a forgery charge in 1920."

"And Wilmer, the gunsel?" Bogie asked.

"Picked up a twenty-one-year-old punk kid in Stockton, California, who robbed a filling station. For the coppers, Polhaus was a former captain. I used to buy books from 'Miles Archer's wife' in Spokane, and I knew Dundee from working in the North Carolina railyards. Samuel is my first name, although I go by Dashiell. The Spade surname I stole from a boxer. I wanted to pattern his code of honor after myself in my Pinkerton days."

Babs noticed she was running out of time. She excused herself and left Guy and Bogie with the two writers.

* * *

Despite events taking a different direction, it seemed like both Babs and Detective Felix Allgood intended to mix business with pleasure. While everything was still fresh in her mind, she had hoped to see if there was any possibility of catching up on the previous film adaptations of *The Maltese Falcon* that evening. Either Allgood was talking out of the side of his mouth, or he wasn't too glib with words. He surprised her when he told her to wear "better than her Sunday best." With no advance notice or money to go shopping, Babs begged Manny, her miracle dry cleaner, to find her a last-minute solution. He bailed her out once again with a simple silk ultramarine, bias-cut off-the-shoulder gown a customer had abandoned by accident or on purpose from an inability to pay the bill.

"Don't know what I'd ever do without you," Babs said as she tried it on in front of his mirror. "With the right jewelry and a clutch purse, I'll be set."

He safety-pinned a few areas where the hem hung a bit long. "This'll keep you from tripping on it, and remember—"

"I know...bring it back exactly the way I found it," she said.

He wished her luck on her date, and she hurried home to finish her hair and makeup. She parted her longish hair, as if making a braid, but twisted and pinned it into three tight buns at the nape of her neck.

Something old, something new, something borrowed, something blue chimed in her head. Old—her mother's rhinestone bracelet. New—the dainty lady's watch for her other wrist. Borrowed and blue—the evening dress from Manny's. Sir Henry gave her a lick on the palm of her hand for good luck. Despite the silly ditty still on her mind and her mother's insistence she get remarried, Babs had no allusions about dating a cop, especially this one.

Before she pranced out her front door, her boarder, Mr. Otake said in his staccato-like accent, "You look berry purr-e-tee, Miss Norl-man. Big night ahead?" He tethered Sir Henry, who wanted to drag him across the lawn, as she waved both goodbye and Allgood's car pulled up to the curb.

* * *

90

This so-called show Allgood blathered about was more like getting admitted to a nightclub in exchange for looking the other way. He pulled up to the parking attendant, who tried to wave him off until he flashed his badge.

Ciro's...what a surprise, thought Babs. The club's exterior reminded her of a white wedding cake with a slice cut out on its second floor. Its neon sign had a giant cursive C sitting on a swooping overhang.

They pushed past the jumble of tropical plants, and Allgood displayed his police badge again at the front entrance.

Babs craned her neck to see if there was a poster announcing the headliner. "If I had known this is where you were taking me, I would've looked in the paper to see which band was playing."

"What's it to you?" asked Allgood.

"I've done my time as a nightclub singer."

"Aw, I thought you were going to say you were a drummer or played the trombone," Allgood joked.

"Something wrong with that?"

He tried to cover his tracks. "It's not too ladylike."

She put him on the spot. "Are you telling me the only opportunity for a respectable woman is to be the songbird in a sexy dress?"

"Well...that's not what I meant—"

"Oh yes, it was," she said in a huff. "Maybe I'll know some of the musicians playing tonight. Many do more than one gig an evening and hop from club to club."

While they waited for their seating manager to return, he asked her, "You've heard of Billy Wilkerson?"

"He publishes the *Hollywood Reporter*."

"He's also a former bootlegger from New York and now a West Coast transplant. After Prohibition ended, he couldn't seem to wean himself away from gambling and the underworld crowd. Opened the Trocadero in '34. Got tired of paying extortion money to the mob. Sold it after a *convenient* fire, which I could bet my pension was arson, and opened Ciro's in January, which reminded him of his favorite casino in Monte Carlo. Tonight, I need to make a little *social call*. His security goons will be less likely to harass me

91

if I came in with a swell dame on my arm. Besides, everyone who is anybody comes here."

If he was trying to impress her, he wasn't. Babs wasn't sure if she should take that as a compliment or a blatant confession that he was using her to gain entry. Too bad her borrowed evening dress wasn't bulletproof.

Emil Coleman's orchestra took the bandstand at eight. By the time they arrived at half past the hour, the band was in full swing. The first thing she noticed was that everyone who came through the front door had to walk down two steps to enter the main dining room. Klieg lights illuminated all who entered—friend or foe.

Allgood explained, "Rumor has it that Wilkerson hired Golden Gloves boxers to double as busboys and bouncers."

Ciro's interior designer had adorned the walls with rich, thick silk in apple green. She noticed its ceiling was painted a color on the opposite side of the spectrum, that of a red rose, and also the color of the benches against the walls.

Moments after their host seated them, Allgood insisted on taking a look around by himself, leaving her alone. He returned with nothing but complaints. "I expected a few regulars."

"Isn't it a bit early? I thought places like this didn't get hopping till after midnight."

Allgood asked her if she wanted to dance.

"Do you mind if we eat something first?"

He grumbled, which signaled to her that their pricey tab would come out of his city employee's paycheck. He flagged down a waiter for menus and let her order while he stuck to drinks. She figured he might've eaten first just to keep it cheap.

Babs probed Allgood with questions; he pursed his lips. "Do you really want to discuss Pinky Pilchik's toxicology report this evening?"

"As a matter of fact, yes. Do I have to remind you we're on the same side? I'd like to see justice served and a killer behind bars just as much as you."

"Waiter!" Allgood snapped his fingers. "Bring this young lady a martini. Make it a double."

"No, please. Just a club soda with ice. Waiter, I'm hungry. What do you recommend?"

"Nonsense," Allgood interrupted. "You need to loosen up."

"The *Gigot d'agneau rôti* or roast leg of lamb comes highly recommended," said their waiter.

"Anything with chicken?" she asked.

"For something different, you might want to try *Caneton à la bigarade* or duckling with bitter orange sauce."

At once reminded of the duck at the Bogarts, which hadn't yet been beheaded, she said she'd pass, but she could tell Allgood was getting impatient.

"Then I'd suggest our *Poussin à la diable*. It comes with *pommes au four* and *epinard en branche*."

Piecing together her high-school French, she said, "*Diable* means devil. I guess I feel a bit devilish tonight. Why not?"

Allgood told the waiter he wanted to show the lady a good time, and if she was a "good girl," maybe later he'd spring for a bottle of champagne.

When their waiter arrived with their food, Babs was famished. She tried not to appear unladylike, reminding herself to chew and swallow instead of scarfing it down.

"The police department is always looking for qualified civilians to cooperate and tread paths where they dared not go," Allgood said.

Babs' fork froze in midair. "You want me to work as a snitch?"

"Are you interested in a job infiltrating the mob?"

She flatly answered, "No!"

* * *

"Babs, the guys I'm looking for…I suspect they're hiding a gambling den. Most clubs like this have them." Allgood abandoned her to check out the back room. Not that it was any of her business, but she figured he might be collecting a bribe to keep the operation running—a common practice with a big city police department known for corruption.

Meanwhile, Babs observed the room. Cary Grant? She held her breath till she felt faint. His wife, date, or whoever was most likely in the powder room. Oh, how she wanted to spring to her feet, run across the room, and plotz on his lap, but she refrained.

Who else was present? Laurence Olivier and his new bride, Vivien Leigh. She wasn't going to compete with her. Who else? Jimmy Stewart! All the women went gaga over him when he almost won the Oscar for *Mr. Smith Goes to Washington. Too tall for me at six-foot-three.*

Breaking the spell of wishful thinking, she decided it best to use her time alone to befriend some of the supper club's employees. As a private investigator, she learned the value of cultivating close relationships with nightclub and restaurant staffers. Outside the club, the parking lot boys knew everyone's comings and goings. Tonight, she wasn't riding the gravy train, but she had loaded up on fifty-cent pieces.

Their waiter returned with her fancy French chicken dinner. Before she dug in, she whispered, "My date said something was happening in the back." She took out one of the half dollars and twirled it in between her fingers.

"Blackjack, craps...a few discreet card games... That's all, madam."

Babs slid the coin in his direction. He palmed it quicker than the eye could follow.

She asked him, "What's this dish called again?"

"*Poussin à la diable.* There is a line from a famous novel called *Les Liaisons Dangereuses,*" he said. "It's '*La vengeance est un plat qui se mange froid,*' or 'Revenge is a dish best served cold.'" He gave a slight bow as he transferred the coin from his hand and into his trousers pocket and bid her, "*Bon appétit,*" before backing away.

Not one to sit alone and feel sorry for herself and feeling more devilish than her chicken, she flagged down a busboy. "Both of us are coming back. Don't remove a single thing."

Needing some air, she figured she'd home in on one of the parking attendants. To make it obvious, she slipped something worthwhile into his pocket. "Expecting any action tonight?"

"Nothing more than the usual."

"What do you consider *the usual?*" Babs jumped in and explained, much to his surprise, that she was a female private investigator.

"The gangsters in the backroom are always on their best behavior. It's the jealous husbands and wives who cause all the ruckus."

Upon hearing this, she wished she had a fifty-cent piece for every word that came out of his mouth. "Really?"

"Oh yeah." He seemed proud to have such insider information. "Boss don't like bloody noses staining the furnishings. Cleanup crews are always on standby after the customers leave."

"Can't thank you enough." She tipped him two more.

Babs made it back to her table. Allgood still hadn't returned. She picked at her dinner, now lukewarm, and attempted to enjoy the music. Every so often, she looked at her watch and wondered what was taking so long.

Just before the band's set ended, everyone in the main dining room witnessed a different floor show than expected. Whistles blew, and uniformed cops stormed the club. Babs, too young to have experienced speakeasy raids firsthand, figured this couldn't have been much different.

"Everyone stays in their seats!" one cop shouted, but dancers cleared the dance floor in a flash. Some tried to rush toward the front, but another officer commanded, "Nobody's leaving!" Staffers followed orders to barricade all exits, including the doors to the kitchen.

The roar of a gunshot sounded from the back. People screamed, inciting more mayhem. Babs knew if she took deep breaths and stayed put, a trick she used to calm herself during her acting days, she'd be less likely to be swept up in the chaos. Medics arrived and carried away a bloodied victim on a stretcher. She reached for Allgood's untouched cocktail and downed it in three gulps, wincing the entire time and knowing she'd regret it later.

The scenario unfolded like a film clip. Cops rounded up the gamblers from the back room. They escorted them in handcuffs toward a paddy wagon, including Allgood, who kept insisting, "I'm a goddamned cop! If you don't believe me, check my badge."

"Babs!" he called out, pleading. "She'll vouch for me. She'll tell ya I'm the genuine article!"

Babs shrugged and said, "You think they'll listen?" There was no way he or anyone else would've heard her over the din. After they dragged him away, she enjoyed a private chuckle.

Wait till his partner catches wind of this.

The cops made another sweep of the joint. An officer grabbed her hand and yanked her out of her seat. "No one's getting away scot-free. Another paddy wagon is due in five minutes."

Chapter Twelve: You Don't Know Jack

Bogie insisted on joining the PIs to meet the ultimate big cheese, Jack Warner. Huston called the shots while on set, but the bottom line stopped with the studio mogul. Since it didn't look like this case would be wrapped in the next few days, Warner needed to be aware of the full scope of the threats.

"Besides, he knows everyone in town," Bogie said. "No sense hiding anything. He'd find out anyway."

By now, the birdings included not only Humphrey and Mayo Bogart, but Mary Astor and the private detectives. There could've been others. He hoped Warner would take over the costs of paying the private detectives and not put all his faith in the police department.

"Jack Warner is a guy you'd want to hate," warned Bogart, as the three of them headed to his office.

"Didn't he make all of his people under contract take a massive pay cut at the beginning of the Depression, but he still had a normal salary?" Babs asked.

"All the studio heads did. Common folk could no longer afford to go to the theater as much, and ticket sales were down. Penny-pinchers—all of them. One guy accused Jack of being 'the only man who had rubber pockets so he could steal soup.'"

"As much as you despised him, you couldn't live without him. Not only that, but you also had to respect him. He said he hated all actors. Secretly, the ham, in my opinion, he wanted to be one and craved the spotlight as much as we did. He certainly had faith in me by allowing me to step into leading roles. Personally, I think he liked men like me because we were short. Like him. Guess he thinks it's easier to push us around."

Head-to-head while wearing her low-heeled Mary Janes, Babs realized Warner was on the stubby side. He had a pencil-thin mustache, fashionable for the day, and a prominently receding hairline at the age of forty-nine. His bespoke suit disguised any extra weight. His grand smile would win you over in a minute, but still would keep you worrying. After a round of handshakes, he gave Babs an impish wink, and everyone took their seats. Pictures of both his blood family and his stellar family adorned his office, along with a growing collection of trophies and mementos. He almost seemed dwarfed behind his grand wooden desk covered with ink blotters.

Warner picked up a family portrait of him with all his brothers. "I might be the youngest, but I'm the only brother of any importance," he boasted, replacing that photo with another of him standing next to a German Shepherd. "Do you know who was our first movie star? A dog! Rin-Tin-Tin."

Babs sighed. "Oh, I loved watching those films. Made me beg my parents to buy me a dog."

"Don't get any wild ideas about getting another one," Guy whispered. "I'm tired of brushing fur and feathers off my clothes. Maybe I should give you my dry cleaning bills for every time Bruno slobbers all over my trousers."

She dismissed him, as if that meant, "Listen to what he has to say. We can argue about it later."

"We were also the ones who produced *The Jazz Singer*," said Warner, showing them a framed production still of Al Jolson. "This turned us into a major studio as opposed to a 'Poverty Row' studio making B-pictures."

He wanted to offer the men a round of cigars, but when he opened his cigar box, he realized he only had one left. "Need to be a gracious host and not smoke alone."

Bogie took out his cigarette case and offered everyone cigarettes in the meantime. When the three men lit up at once, Babs rose to her feet. Without even asking for permission, she rolled up Warner's blinds and opened his windows to air the place out, making her point without saying a word before resuming her seat.

While he was on the phone with his secretary, insisting she order more cigars right away, Bogie whispered to Babs, "After his brother Sam died, he took over all production. Jack loved flaunting his power. On a whim, he fired loyal and competent supporters just to prove he could. He even fired Rin-Tin-Tin and Douglas Fairbanks, Jr."

"You can credit me for greenlighting the third round at producing *The Maltese Falcon*," said Jack. "The success of this film will be my best revenge against my lack of foresight of bidding on Margaret Mitchell's *Gone With the Wind*—the biggest regret of my investment speculations."

Every time smoke wafted in her direction, Babs' nostrils flared. "Sir," she said, addressing Warner. "I'm not sure if you know the full scope of what's happening, but someone has targeted key players in your production of *The Maltese Falcon*, as if they're trying to prevent the film from being finished."

Warner settled back into his seat and nervously started rearranging bric-a-brac on top of his desk. "As Kasper Gutman would've said in your script, 'That's unfortunate.'"

"Have you heard word from any of your rival studio heads in regards to this production?" she asked.

"Nothing outside the usual squabbling. We're always at each other's throats, and they're all *gonifs*. That's Yiddish, you know, for crooks."

His intercom buzzed, and his secretary let him know that a messenger arrived with fresh cigars.

"That was quick. I wonder if they keep my favorite brand in a locked cabinet over at the commissary. Hand him a tip, send him on his way, and have Abdul bring them in."

"Sir, he's out on an errand."

"Then I guess you'll have to walk them in yourself. Show the gentleman here your shapely legs and that I have good taste in picking my secretaries."

"Why, you sly fox!" she exclaimed while everyone in the room could listen in.

"Who's Abdul?" Guy asked.

"My loyal manservant, Abdul Maljan." Warner got up and reached for one of the framed photos in his collection. He pointed to the one person who stood out and looked like he didn't belong in a family portrait. "He serves as both my chauffeur and my bodyguard. Big, brawny Turkish guy. Terrifies most. One of the reasons why I love him. No one intimidates good old Jack Warner when he's by my side."

"I'm not used to carrying around a handful of tips," Esther said. "Jack, maybe you should give me a raise."

"What? So, you can get your nails painted with gold? I pay you too much as it is."

"Let me dig in my purse." Esther placed her boss's box of replacement cigars on his desk.

Since Warner wasn't offering, Bogie reached into his pocket and handed her a fiver.

"Sweetheart, break it into smaller bills. Keep it in your top drawer for future tips. Oh yeah, and reimburse yourself. Don't want to hear any complaints that you can't pay your manicurist."

She gave him a gratuitous smile and hurried out.

Jack got out his cigar cutter, but when he lifted the lid of the cigar box, he roared and flung the box across the room. Cigars flew like launched projectiles, along with something small, feathery, and dark.

Guy leapt toward the menacing black object, which sparked the furor. Esther rushed back inside, prompted by the caterwauling.

"Call security!" Warner commanded. "Call the police!"

Sacrificing another one of his cherished monogrammed handkerchiefs, Guy picked it up and asked Jack Warner if he'd lend him one of his empty cigar boxes to put it in. Everyone else backed up and observed it from a distance.

"You've been biii-rrr-ded," Guy stammered.

Still skittish and keeping his distance, Warner replied, "So that's what birding is like. I guess everyone wanted to spare me the gore and keep me in the dark until now. *Yeeech*, I can't look at it. Reminds me once when a friend gave me his talking myna bird."

Babs shot Guy a wary glance, curious to know where this was heading.

"The bird went berserk after three days, because I could talk louder and longer than he could," said Warner. "Please, put it away."

"This one's different," Guy pointed out. "It's a tinier type of black bird. The previous ones were crows. Someone had the audacity to taxidermy this one as a private joke. They put on a doll-sized top hat on its head and a cigar stogie in its mouth. Looks like a mockery of an old-time vaudevillian."

Bogie commented that it looked more like a cartoon character.

Only Birdie Wilson or someone similar could craft something like that, Babs thought. Guess we'll need to pay him another visit.

Meanwhile, Bogie gathered the fallen cigars and placed them back in the box. Nobody was in any mood to smoke them.

"Did you have a good look at the delivery guy?" Warner asked Esther.

"Wore a cap and uniform, like one on the studio's maintenance staff. His cap seemed too large. Covered his forehead and part of his face. Nondescript. Sorry, I wasn't paying much attention."

"Make sure to repeat that to the police when they arrive, and anything else that comes to mind. Damn, I wish Abdul were here. He'd pick him up by the collar and threaten a confession out of him."

"The kid might've not been behind it," Esther said, trying to calm him down. "He just delivered it."

Babs took a deep breath to calm her nerves and glanced at her partner's wristwatch. "Off the top of your head, Mr. Warner, is there anyone you know of who might want to seek revenge?"

The studio mogul opened the cigar box a crack, took one last peek inside, and shuddered.

"It's common knowledge I have many enemies."

Babs pretended to pay no attention to the low growl coming from Bogart's direction.

"Cagney's tried to leave me—twice. Bette Davis took me to court back in '36 after she ignored her contract and ran off to London to do two pictures." He pointed at Bogart. "Even you hate me, don't you?"

Bogie nodded. "We all hate you, Jack."

"Damn it! I'll ruin you. I'll kill you if you try to abandon me." Warner realized his gaffe and doubled back. "Considering these threats...I said that in poor taste."

"Apology accepted." Bogie clicked his teeth and made one of those smirks that was hard to read, something he did all the time on screen.

With frustration mounting, Babs wanted Warner's opinion on whether he felt any of the cast members of *The Maltese Falcon* warranted revenge from someone unhinged. "In all seriousness, Mr. Warner, even if someone's anger isn't directed at you, can you think of anyone wishing anybody harm?"

Warner laughed and said his list was long. "For all we know, Dashiell Hammett might insist on more compensation, knowing on the third time at bat, his story will be a box office success. However, the only person I could think of, would be John Huston's father, Walter. When filming the scene where he staggered into Sam Spade's office holding the statue he rescued from his ship on fire, Johnny Boy, his son, made him do take after take for his cameraman. He was black and blue the next day and furious when he found out, as a practical joke, his son put Mary Astor up to pretending she was his secretary. She called Walter and said the director demanded a reshoot, and the action wasn't satisfactory.

"Then, imitating the voice of the film's producer, Hal Wallis, John Huston phoned his father the evening after the Jacobi scene had been shot and told him he was terrible in it and said he must come back to the studio in the morning to reshoot the entire sequence. Walter was furious, but agreed to the retake, having fallen for his son's practical joke. Bet you never heard that story."

Warner stopped and stared at Babs. "You remind me a bit of Bette Davis, and it's not because you're about the same size."

Babs, taken aback, asked, "How so?"

"My brothers Harry and Albert, and I like to call her the fifth Warner Brother. Would you believe that broad had the nerve to hire lawyers and rise up against us? She demanded more sophisticated roles in better scripts, or she wanted out of her contract."

The Burbank police arrived, who were quick to remind Babs and Guy to stay clear of the crime scene and leave the dirty work to them.

"I hate the cops," Guy whispered to Babs as they watched them tear up

Jack Warner's office. "They always love to make our job more difficult."

"I guess we're going to have to get used to it," Babs said, holding in most of her frustration and trying to sort the details. Several people had pointed a finger at Walter Huston, but a lot of that was in jest, and Hammett's name came up more than once. Every time she conducted another round-robin of inquiries, she felt like a steel ball in a pinball machine.

"You can continue to service Bogie and Jack Warner," said the Officer in Charge. Babs argued that the crimes were intertwined, and it would be impossible to stay out of each other's way.

As the police whisked away the crime evidence, Warner started to whistle, without thinking, the first few bars of *Bye, Bye, Blackbird*. When he spotted the appalled look on Babs' face, he got quiet. "All right. I'll stop."

He wouldn't give an outright apology, but Bogie explained, "The big boss likes to give us a song and a dance once in a while. Isn't that right? Thinks he's as talented as those he hires to do the same thing in front of the cameras. Then Bogie asked him, "I'm curious. Did your father have plans for you to be a cantor, just like in the story of *The Jazz Singer*?"

"Not in the least," Warner demurred. "We changed our Eastern European name. None of us were particularly religious. Too many people hated the movie business anyway. Called it a depraved Jewish business. Today, we can thank the people behind the Hays Code, who claim they are moral high-hat Christians, to rub that in."

Babs found all that interesting but didn't want to get Warner started while the cops were still present.

Guy asked him when he expected to wrap production and what date he planned on releasing *The Maltese Falcon* to the public.

"If we can stick to our original plans, we'll get it done by mid-July and released in the theaters by early-to-mid October of this year."

Babs still wasn't satisfied. "Whoever is doing the birding, and we still haven't concluded it's the same person as the killer and whether or not he or she is working alone, this person wants to prey on people's fears. Jack, what are you most afraid of?"

"We're just crawling out of the Depression. With *The Falcon*, I need to protect my investment. I've vowed to spare Mary Astor from any more public humiliation, and I feel confident my bodyguard would never betray me. However, war threatens Europe. I wasn't born there, but I heard plenty of grim stories from my parents. Back in '39, I got a lot of flak for producing the propaganda film *Confessions of a Nazi Spy*, which J. Edgar Hoover, the Director of the FBI, encouraged me to make. After I released the film, someone threatened to bomb my house.

"Not long ago, I attended a dinner where a British financier seemed unconcerned about granting a hefty loan to Adolph Hitler. He said he was confident the louse would pay him back. I felt otherwise and gave him a piece of my mind. I said, 'He will pay it back, sir. In bullets.'"

The cops continued to search in his office. "People have called me a jocose penny watcher, a bargain dictator, and an all-time sonofabitch. Bogie here once said I was a creep. Isn't that right?"

"*Uh huh*," Bogie confirmed.

"I'd rather you call me Sherlock Holmes Warner," he said, as he saw them to the door. "I promise to stay out of trouble, and I'll be as cooperative as possible to help you find your killer." Warner reached into his desk drawer and pulled out a checkbook. "I'm here to support you, and don't trust the police to do a thorough job. How much do you want for my portion of a retainer? It's about time we made this official. We need to stop this madman."

He took the private detectives by surprise; both were speechless. Warner took it upon himself to write out an amount he saw fit and handed the check to Babs. "Here, that should get you started."

"While you're handing things out," said Bogie, "you still owe me a Cuban."

Chapter Thirteen: Try This on For Size

After their meeting with Jack Warner, Guy returned to the office to perform animal duty while Babs went straight home. She needed to tend to Sir Henry, who had remained at her place to serve as a guard dog in case anyone tried to threaten her.

Later on, Detective Felix Allgood called. "Your partner said you were here. Mentioned an incident at the studio. Are you all right?"

"How come you weren't there?" she asked.

"Warner Brothers is located in Burbank. Their police department gets first dibs on any crimes, even if we started the investigation first in our jurisdiction."

Still a newcomer when it came to homicide, Babs wasn't about to argue. "Were you calling because you wanted me to fill you in?"

"The Burbank guys did a fair job of that already, but if there's anything you want to add, I'd be willing to listen."

"Nobody died—this time, except a bird, which is bad enough."

After a slight lull in their conversation, Allgood said, "I'm calling on non-police business. Wanted to know if you were up for going out."

"Tonight?" Not what she expected, and she still felt he used her to get into a known hangout for LA's underworld.

"Given what you just went through, you could use a break. Besides, I owe you an apology for mixing business with pleasure. It's hard not to think that way when you're a cop on a tough case."

"I was thinking more along the lines of taking a hot bubble bath, pouring a glass of wine, turning on the radio, and spending a quiet evening by myself," said Babs.

"Care for company?"

"Not in my bathtub!"

"Not what I had in mind unless the invitation was open."

Silent for a moment, she had no desire to interpret that.

"Are you still there?" he asked.

She overheard a strange medley of whistling and shouting on his end of the line. "What's going on over there?"

Allgood laughed. "A high falootin' ar-kee-tek-too-rall designer reshuffled the deck around the precinct. Not everyone's phonelines or intercom made the switch, so there's always some guy barking orders using his good old-fashioned vocal cords. Never a dull moment."

Babs visualized soothing her aching toes. Mr. Otake had already told her he would be out for the evening attending a Japanese community event. She relished the idea of having the whole house to herself and her loyal dog. Staring at Detective Allgood would conjure up thoughts of business, and she had already clocked out for the day.

"It would be a shame for me to throw out the posies I purchased for ya..."

"Roses?"

"Carnations," he blurted out. "Hate to see them wilt and die. Even worse to hear my coworkers joke that I failed to win over your heart."

To her, carnations smelled like pepper going up her nose.

"I'd like to make up for our terrible first date. Neither of us expected we'd land in jail after the raid at Ciro's. Howza 'bout another club? One the LAPD knows is clean and isn't hiding a gambling operation in a back room?"

"Please, Detective..." Her sentence was interrupted by a long, drawn-out yawn.

"None of that unless we're working the case. Call me Felix. Can't entice you with soft romantic music?"

"Another time. I'm too pooped to go anywhere. If I tried to dance, I'd trip over my own feet...and yours."

"Can I help you with anything around the house?" he asked.

That's a funny question. "No, but…"

"Whatever I do, I gotta get out of this precinct. Can't get any more work done over here if it sounds like a bunch of cowboys holding a cattle auction. Howza 'bout I come over for a nightcap? I gotta stop that way before heading home anyway."

How does he know where I live? Oh, right! He's a cop. He could always look me up, but now I'd like to know where he lives. Has he been spying on me?

"What's in your liquor cabinet?" he asked.

"Not much. In general, I don't invite many people over."

"Doesn't matter. I'm a wizard when it comes to bartending. My buddies often draft me for impromptu parties."

"Don't think about getting fresh. I have a king-sized protective bodyguard who's outperformed police K-9s and who'll do anything I want as long as I reward him with dog biscuits."

* * *

Refusing to take "no" for an answer, he convinced Babs to let him keep her company. She only agreed as long as she didn't have to get dolled up to go anywhere and could kick him out when she was too tired to act like a lady.

He might not have been thinking about official police business, but he had a personal score to settle. On his previous homicide case, he got assigned to desk duty for two agonizing months after a snide PI put egg on his face, and that wasn't the only time a low-life shamus trumped him on the job. He despised private eyes. All of them. And felt the profession should be deemed illegal and all their damned licenses be taken away. He didn't want any meddling gumshoes dicking around and mucking up his high-profile case with the Bogarts. If he was ever to get a promotion from lieutenant to captain, especially when his partner Sadowski retired, he was going to have to look like a celebrity in the eyes of his superiors.

Allgood went to the trouble and did a background check on Barbara "Babs" Norman. She had an ex-husband with a police record. Why should he trust her? Maybe she had a hidden agenda. Once he got inside her home, he could get her looped, then snoop around, and see if he could find anything to use against her. She'd never see it coming. Feeling smug, he hopped in his car and headed toward her Hollywood Hills residence.

She yawned the moment she opened her door. Sir Henry shoved his nose right into Allgood's crotch and gave him the sniff test. "You came empty-handed."

In getting so excited about coming over, he realized he forgot to buy the flowers he had lied about. "Oops! Got distracted and left them behind. Sorry, I guess you'll have to take a raincheck."

"Next time, you'll bring roses. I might be allergic to the smell of carnations."

"Why didn't you say so to begin with?"

"Didn't want to hurt your feelings."

Sir Henry showed his teeth. Babs tugged on his collar to restrain him from jumping on top of Allgood and knocking him down.

He asked, "Are you gonna let me in, or is this pooch gonna consider me as his midnight snack?"

* * *

Babs dragged Sir Henry inside, hooked a leash to his collar, and looped it over a doorknob inside her kitchen. "Stay! Don't you get any funny ideas." She commanded him to lie down, still concerned since this wasn't the most secure restraint. With her house's open layout, at least she could keep an eye on him from the other room.

"Hope you're still up for a nightcap." Allgood surveyed the room, picking up small desktop framed photographs and sentimental knick-knacks.

She caught him in the midst of his probe. "Excuse me, can I help you with something?"

"Oh, just looking for your liquor cabinet. Guess I got distracted. Always curious about people's personal memorabilia collections."

"My husband used to be a little too fond of his cocktails. I almost never touch the hard stuff," she said, leading him over to the proper hutch. "I wouldn't even have this clunky piece of furniture if we hadn't received it as a wedding gift."

"You're not still married, I take it. Don't see no ring on your finger," he said.

"I should've specified. He's my ex-husband. We didn't stay hitched for very long."

"Mind if I ask what happened?"

"Actually, I do. Let's not talk about him. That would be one way to ruin my evening...or should I say, our evening."

"Then let's see whatcha got." Allgood felt like a Boy Scout on a scavenger hunt. "What's this?" he asked, pulling out a bottle filled with dark-brown liquid. Someone had removed its original label and replaced it with homemade gift wrap.

"It's chocolate liqueur. One of my clients gave it to me last year for Christmas."

He took a whiff to see if he could identify this drink by its odor. "If you got cream in the house, I could whip up something that will taste like a chocolate éclair."

They both headed back to the kitchen. Sir Henry got anxious and circled in place as she retrieved a small bottle from her fridge.

Allgood requested a few other ingredients. "How 'bout glasses? You don't expect us to drink from this pitcher."

Babs seemed to be at a loss. She opened several cabinets and complained that drinking had been her husband's pastime and not hers. Ignoring her sink full of dirty dishes, she rummaged through her cabinets and discovered her wine glasses, given to her for wedding presents, were chipped. As a substitute, Babs selected two silly sentimental Mr. and Mrs. Santa Claus mugs. "These'll have to do."

He poured his concoction. "Let's take these back to the living room. Your couch looks a lot more comfortable than your kitchen chairs."

She sank into her seat, and commented her drink was strong. He couldn't wait for her to get tight enough that he could make out with her.

A rustling from the bushes broke their concentration as they both looked at each other in alarm and spotted shadows flitting back and forth.

"There might be a prowler out there," said Babs.

Allgood patted his jacket, signaling to her that, if need be, he was armed.

Sir Henry howled, followed by incessant barking. He must've broken free from his tether, because he gamboled into the living room, put his paw on Babs' leg, and drooled in Allgood's lap.

He pushed the giant beast away and grimaced at the slobber near his inseam. "Maybe I should check this out. Got any enemies I should be aware of?"

"As many as you do, I'm sure."

He suggested he should go outside. She insisted on accompanying him.

"No, you're staying put. You're safer here."

"Then let my dog accompany you. He's gentle as a lamb but a force to be reckoned with if prompted."

* * *

Allgood made several rounds of the front and backyard. When he couldn't seem to uncover anything, he figured it was just a raccoon. He and Sir Henry went back inside to discover Babs had passed out on the couch.

Assuming this was his only chance, he peeked into her desk drawers. He couldn't believe she could run a business if she was this disorganized.

He continued to open everything from closets to kitchen cabinets until Sir Henry caught him in the act. Confronted with a snarling dog ready to feast on him, Allgood covered Babs with a blanket and left her a note saying, "Sweet dreams." He backed away slowly from Sir Henry, shut the front door, and bolted for his car.

Chapter Fourteen: Killing Two Birds

Refusing to back down after last night's thwarted efforts, Allgood asked Babs out again. Shouldn't she be keeping him at a distance? They were still embroiled in a case and not necessarily allies. "I'd rather stay clear from the clubs," she said. "How about a detective film?"

"Don't we see enough action from our profession?"

This time, she'd use him to kill two birds with one stone, even if she had to fudge the truth. "Believe it or not, I don't think I've ever seen a film at the Egyptian Theatre."

Her instincts told her the medical examiner's office and the police department were withholding information about the first victim, Pinky Pilchik. Babs also couldn't dismiss the "Egyptian" connection between the canopic jar Bogart found, timed with the poor gal's demise.

Allgood said he'd scrounge for a newspaper to get the movie times and get back to her. Meanwhile, she took a hot bath and jumped into loungewear.

He called back within the hour.

"Anything look worthwhile?" she asked.

"Tonight's lineup features films with Peter Lorre."

Babs figured it wouldn't hurt to catch up on his other films, since he'd made so many. If only she could familiarize herself with all the films from the cast members of *The Falcon*, but that list was too long to be practical.

"We can catch a six o'clock show of *M*, if you don't mind contending with German subtitles. If we go for that one, we'd have to plan for a later dinner," he said.

"Dinner's not important. What else is playing?"

"At eight, there's *The Man Who Knew Too Much*."

"Isn't that a Hitchcock film? I think it's also the first one Peter did in English, which he learned phonetically in the process of filming."

"According to the blurb in the paper, the film's about a London couple on holiday in Switzerland who suddenly find themselves entangled in a case of international intrigue after their daughter is kidnapped by spies plotting a political assassination."

This would be a longer night than expected. "Intriguing, but by the time it ends, it'll be past my bedtime. There's a good chance I'll fall asleep. You wouldn't want that, would you?"

"Well, no, but—"

She didn't want him to get any fresh ideas. "Let's go for the earliest show. It's doubtful I'll last through another."

"What about dinner?"

When she suggested they could always pick up something at the concession stand, alarms went off in her head. Pinky Pilchik had worked there.

"Why don't I pick you up at five to get a lead on the traffic? If we get there too early, we can always walk around and stretch our legs."

* * *

Allgood put a placard on his windshield to identify himself as a plainclothes cop. "Don't want any meter maids giving me a ticket," he said. "You won't find me feeding coins to any greedy person or machine. Not when being a cop has its privileges."

They started toward the theater, and her stomach started to rumble so loud that Allgood heard it over the sound of the traffic. "Didn't I hear you say earlier that dinner didn't matter?"

"Well, I wanted to catch the six o'clock and didn't want you to go to any trouble."

"If your tummy is going to talk that loud, it's gonna spoil the movie. Back in the nickelodeon days, people had to smuggle in food from the outside. I don't go to the movies too often, but if you're willing to settle for popcorn and hotdogs, stuff you'd find at the circus or a carnival, the concession stand should have them."

"As long as we don't encounter a shooting gallery," Babs muttered. "You're the only cop I need to deal with for the rest of the evening."

"What's that supposed to mean?" he asked, taken aback.

"You'd better get used to my sense of humor. It comes out whether you like it or not."

Babs wanted to spend a few moments outside in the courtyard before buying their tickets and marveled at the Egyptian's architecture. "I remember reading about the design of this theater patterned after the temple at Thebes with sphinxes and tall, vertical columns. Inside, on stage in front of the curtain, is the image of Khepri, the scarab god who represents the rising sun.

She couldn't restrain her enthusiasm. "They used honest-to-goodness hieroglyphics on the walls copied from the real ones. I hear there are seats inside for more than seventeen hundred people, and it's owned by Sid Grauman, the same guy who built the Chinese Theatre down the street a few years later. On the day of its opening, it was a spectacular affair—way before my time in 1922. Played the silent version of *Robin Hood* with Douglas Fairbanks, Jr., accompanied by a Wurlitzer organ. Have you ever been to Egypt?"

"Haven't traveled much except to local crime scenes."

"Ever had an interest in foreign cultures?"

"Not beyond our Port of Los Angeles."

"Too bad. Some would say in relocating from San Francisco to Hollywood I made a bold move, but one of these days I hope to explore the world—Paris, London, the Orient..."

"After the war situation is settled."

She felt like he had stuck a pin in her pipe dream balloon. "Let's hope it soon all blows away. Hate those damned Nazis."

"Their threats are not just from overseas. They've got supporters crawling around like cockroaches invading Los Angeles. Wouldn't trust the Japs, either."

113

She worried about Mr. Otake. Considering Japanese aggression in the Far East, everyone was quick to put the blame on anyone from that part of the world.

"Know anything about canopic jars?" she asked, changing the subject.

"What are those?"

Babs suspected he didn't care or wasn't too well educated.

"For a weeknight, the place has drawn an unexpected crowd," he said. While he went to see what kind of snacks he could rustle, Babs spared no time asking employees if they had known Pinky.

She spotted the manager by his nametag. "Did you know much about her? Any unusual behavior?" she asked. "Did you ever see her have any suspicious conversations with questionable customers?"

He snickered. "Anything can happen in the dark, I guess."

Thrown off-kilter, Babs asked, "Have you caught your workers doing anything that—"

The manager laughed. "No, I haven't come across any hanky panky in the projection room."

Her eyes grew wide. That wasn't the answer she would've expected, but nonetheless, he vowed he ran a clean ship. She had hoped to speak to a few others, but Allgood returned with hotdogs in hand, two bags of popcorn in the crook of one arm, and Pepsi bottles poking out of his overcoat pocket. He told her to grab the soda. "The vendor popped the bottle caps already. If we aren't careful, it'll bubble out, and I'll get soaked."

They found seats toward the middle. She wished they had picked ones closer to the aisle for a quick exit, if necessary. Allgood tried to get amorous. She came up with the excuse that every time he tried to touch her, it made her itch.

"I'm not a mosquito," he said in frustration. "I'm not trying to give you malaria."

At one point she let him give her a little peck on the neck, but she timed her rebuff by overstuffing her mouth full of popcorn, which spilled into her lap. Another time, she could feel him scoot closer. She loaded her mouth with sticky candy, making it impossible for him to kiss her.

However, they encountered a distraction that neither one counted on. A woman sitting two rows behind kept screaming. If she wasn't reacting to what was on screen, she argued with her friend. Angry patrons continually shushed her.

Another woman made her opinion known. "If she screams one more time, I'm going to give it to her in the kisser."

Allgood chuckled. "Dames are too sissy to act out like that."

The annoying woman hollered again. Babs turned around, ready to start a fight and prove Allgood wrong, but he grabbed the sleeve of her jacket. The other woman surprised both by throwing her popcorn into the offender's face, beating her to the punch.

"This is an outrage! I'm going to call the cops," the screamer shouted.

"Calm down. Calm down," Allgood said. "I am a cop."

"Then you better have better control over your wife...your date...or whoever she is," referring to Babs, as she brushed the popcorn off her lap. She pointed at the one who had emptied her popcorn for revenge. "And arrest this one while you're at it." Then she left in a huff.

Babs giggled, whispering to Allgood that the disgruntled old bat still had popcorn stuck in her hair. At least she only had to put up with his amorous advances for a little over an hour and couldn't wait to leave the theater. As they headed toward the exit, the manager called out to her attention.

"Hey, lady...one more thing I forgot to mention."

She sprinted ahead of Allgood, who puffed to catch up with her.

"That Pilchik gal...I spoke to a few of her coworkers..."

"What did you find out?" she asked.

"Apparently, she was a bit of a hustler. Always wondered why her car looked a little too swanky considering her paycheck."

"Many people juggle more than one job, especially if they're trying to get established in the acting or musical profession." What came to mind were people like that repugnant tour guide or the Western Union messenger she encountered at the Bogarts' mansion. "Any idea what line of work?"

The manager shook his head. "Sorry, I figured anything could help."

"I appreciate your honesty. One last thing. Did anyone ever notice any repetitive theatergoers who seemed to come here all the time? Especially ones who might've purchased tickets for the same showing and watched it repeatedly."

"Paying cash for a ticket doesn't write your name on a register."

"Maybe your ushers noticed a familiar face."

"I could ask around, but their priority is more about making sure no perverts bother any unaccompanied ladies or no fights break out and, of course, cleaning up spilled popcorn when the lights come back on. Otherwise, none of my employees mentioned anything other than the usual. If you're dropping a hint that someone might've been obsessed with Miss Pilchik, that would've been easy. She was a hot number."

Babs thanked him for his time, but Allgood blocked her path on the way to the theater's exit.

"Were you conducting an investigation behind my back?"

She could tell from the rims of his ears turning red that he was getting steamed. "Do I have to answer that question? I have a headache."

"That's what all the dames say when they don't want a confrontation. Cough it up."

"All right. I'll come clean. Yes. It's in my blood, I guess. When I see an opportunity, I can't pass it up."

* * *

Wanting to avoid a continued argument at all costs, Babs asked him, "What did you think of the film?"

He mumbled, staring at the ground. "Didn't think it won any Oscars."

Like he really knows who won the gold statuettes last year or any year for that matter. "I always struggle following films with subtitles," she replied. "From what I gathered, the ending seemed to preach a moralistic message."

He grabbed her arm. When she tried to resist, he explained in as few words as possible that it was for her safety. "Purse snatchers and pickpockets always look to target couples who tend to be distracted. They love to prey on crowds coming from movie theaters."

"Thank you for treating me to the movie." *Showing courtesy might soften his mood.*

"*Uh...*you're welcome."

Unconvinced he only said it to be polite, she kept their conversation going. "What are your favorite sort of films?"

He did his best Cagney impression, but it was clear he wasn't a professional actor.

"Action... I like lots of shoot 'em ups...rat-a-tat-tats." Allgood used his arms and fingers and pretended to shoot a Tommy gun. "Cagney is one of my favorites. Like *The Roaring Twenties* and *The Public Enemy.*"

Babs laughed. He took offense. "Are you mocking me?"

"I was going to ask you if that's what inspired you to join the police department."

When they took a different route down Hollywood Boulevard, they stumbled upon a roped-off crime scene in front of Birdie Wilson's taxidermy shop. Several black and whites, doubled parked. A uniformed officer stood in the street redirecting traffic. Another warded off curiosity seekers on foot.

Moe Sadowski recognized his partner and vented his furor. "Since you weren't in the office, I called you at home, and nobody answered. Where were you?"

"Takin' this lady to the movies. What's happening?"

"Looks like someone wanted to play a sick joke but went too far."

Allgood pushed past the crime scene barricades. When she followed, Sadowski held her back. "Found dead blackbirds on the dead man. Like the gal in the morgue."

Babs struggled to push past him. "Then I'm involved too. Humphrey Bogart's been birded and—"

"Who else?" he asked.

Babs held her tongue, realizing she and her partner had kept quiet about Mary Astor. "Bogart is my client. It's my right to know."

"As a civilian, it's our right to keep this among ourselves to ensure your safety," Sadowski explained.

Babs had expected to mull over the plot of the film to see if she could draw any meaningful parallels to her case. Instead, she had to return to Birdie's wretched place to assess how a murder unfolded. Sadowski insisted she wait outside. Allgood vouched for her good behavior. "Besides, she's better off sticking with me than waiting outside on the street by herself. Especially in this neighborhood at this hour."

Reluctant, Sadowski complied.

Upon first glance, someone had ransacked the shop since the last time she saw it.

"Stay back!" said one of the crime scene examiners, who looked around at spilled chemical bottles.

Wilson looked almost unrecognizable: skin ashen, back hunched over his workbench, and his fingers like claws curled into a frozen position like an unfurled fern. Babs remembered how he warned her about the dangerous compounds he worked with, but then again, for as long as he had been in business, she assumed he knew how to take his own precautions. Regardless, she couldn't disclose anything to the police about their previous meeting.

"Maybe it's best I take a taxi home," she said to Allgood after taking in all she could handle. "Looks like you might be here a while."

He seemed upset they didn't get to spend more time together, and their evening wound up as another homicide investigation. Before he had the chance to speak, however, Detective Sadowski opened his wallet and handed her the fare for the ride home.

"I reckon this should be enough for the ride and a tip."

Without hesitation, she snapped up the bills. "More than enough," she said, heading toward the front of Birdie's store.

"Call you tomorrow?" Allgood said.

I'm getting the feeling he might be bad luck.

Chapter Fifteen: Close Encounters

The next day, upon hearing strange noises in the office hallway, Babs opened the front door to greet her partner and almost had the fresh pot of coffee knocked out of her hand. Guy stumbled inside, lugging Bruno on a leash while juggling a thermos, the morning edition, and a box of donuts. As soon as he could kick their front door closed, he dropped the leash and plopped their breakfast on top of his desk.

"Since when are you man's best friend?" he asked the obstinate bulldog. "Glad you slid so easily on the tile floors when I had to drag you out of the elevator."

Sir Henry, overeager for affection, knocked over Guy's thermos. He picked it up off the floor. By its rattling, he confirmed its glass lining had broken.

"What prompted you to bring it?" Babs asked. "We always have coffee."

"I thought we were out." Guy placed his ruined thermos in the trash. "Besides, I like the diner's brand better. Maybe I should make you—doggy—yes, you...replace it." Sir Henry licked his hand, as if that was his canine way of apologizing.

Babs poured him a fresh cup from her pot and took her éclair out of the bakery box. Without thinking, she popped it in her mouth and started asking questions. Guy couldn't understand a word she said as her cheeks puffed out like a squirrel.

"For crying out loud, Babs, don't talk with your mouth full."

She reached for her coffee to wash it down. When she regained her voice, she said, "Guy, I'm having second thoughts."

"About what?"

"Bogart's case has led us nowhere." She was about to say two people had already died, but realized she'd been too traumatized last night to call after she stumbled upon the crime scene with Detective Allgood. She also didn't want him to get any cockeyed ideas as to why they were together. "I'm worried one of *The Falcon* stars will be next."

"Finish your breakfast. Business can wait." Guy exaggerated the act of chewing and swallowing, using his donut as an example. "When I drove down Hollywood Boulevard, I saw barricades in front of Wilson's taxidermy shop. Figured I should skip the trades and pick up a normal person's newspaper to figure out what the hoopla was about."

He swished Stu, now the myna bird's official name, away from his crumbs. "The wind blew the first newspaper out of my hand. Mr. Blockhead, here," he said, pointing to Bruno, "thought I was paper-training him and piddled right on it. The furious vendor made me pay for it, so I had to buy another."

"At least he's learning what he's supposed to do." After inspecting it, she commented, "I thought you picked up a copy of the *Herald Examiner*. This looks like some kind of police blotter."

"Bruno soiled the last *Examiner*," said Guy. "I had to settle for this." It took him a while to find what he was looking for, but on page six, in the bottom righthand column, he read out loud:

Birdie Wilson,
Famous Taxidermist to the Stars, has Gone to the Birds
At 8:30 p.m., police discovered the body of Burton "Birdie" Wilson, male, age 62, purveyor of props for movie productions and known for his macabre shop of curiosities on Hollywood Boulevard.

Authorities found the proprietor unresponsive, speculating he might've been poisoned, but nothing confirmed.

The only notable, but inconclusive, evidence found at the crime scene were three large taxidermy raven specimens on top the body.

She played dumb. "Birdie had not only been birded," she said in between mouthfuls, "Birdie had been murdered!"

Guy scratched his head and tried to think hard. "After Jack Warner received a bird in his cigar box, my immediate hunch told me that Wilson warranted another visit. I would've bet my money he was behind the hijinks and the murder of Pinky Pilchik."

"You're not allowed to bet money on anything!" said Babs, indignant.

"Oh, stop acting like my mother...or my father. I'm your partner, dammit."

Stu kept flying from one detective's shoulder to another, taking sides as the tension escalated. Sir Henry barked, provoking a curious cat, who hissed back at him. Wiggins, their janitor, who must've overheard the commotion from the hallway, burst into their office. He yelled, "Stop!" and stood between the sparring partners with outstretched arms like a referee. "Are ya going to duke it out as to who is better than who, or are ya going to solve this case?"

Babs looked at him, bemused. "What I meant is we'll never get another chance to access his shop again for more evidence—whether he did it or not. Birdie admitted he was behind with his accounting. He hadn't had time to tabulate any recent receipts."

"Aren't you forgetting we still have his registers?" asked Guy.

Babs slowed the blather to take a deep breath. "You have a point, but we can get cited for withholding evidence."

"We still need to make photocopies and never found time to do that. Maybe we need to hire an assistant."

"That was your job, and you're my assistant," snapped Babs.

Wiggins intervened. "Took less than a minute for you to act like bratty bairns again. If I can get you kids to stop spattin', I'll be your bloody first mate. Just don't ask me to type. Now, what sort of squabble did I walk in on?"

"No argument at all." Babs grabbed Guy's handkerchief and patted off her neck, dampened with perspiration. "We're discussing business...as usual."

"Ya know what I think?" Wiggins said. "The two of you need a separation."

"Like a divorce?" Babs asked. "I already fired him once during our last huge case."

"Clearing your heads with time apart will do both of you a helluva lot of good."

Guy reworded it with more class. "Like cleansing one's palate during a multi-course meal."

She took one last look at Guy's article. Relieved no one mentioned her name or took photos of her at the crime scene, she still refrained from disclosing the off-duty occasions she spent with the homicide detective.

A loose curl grazed her shoulder. Just by feel, she knew her hair was in disarray. Pinning it up would only serve as a temporary fix. "Man the fort in my absence," she told Guy, and called her hair salon, booking an emergency appointment. "The least I can do is look presentable while trying to solve crime."

* * *

Too perturbed to tie a turban, Babs grabbed a silk scarf and hid her messy hair babushka-style like a Russian peasant. Donning her sunglasses to appear even more anonymous, she revved up her Crosley and thought, a vacation? The Fourth of July was over, and she already considered that a working holiday.

The signs were evident that Babs needed a break. At a four-way stop, she had a near-miss at the intersection. When she tried to use her rickety rear-view mirror to touch up her lipstick, the car behind her almost rear-ended her when the light turned green.

If the adage was true, bad luck came in sets of three. After emptying her change purse to feed the parking meter and hoping her hairdresser would be quick and take her right away, Babs spotted her two arch enemies seated side-by-side under hair dryers and having their nails done. Inside the salon, she detected Mayo Methot, her present-day foe, as if the mere mention of her name earlier conjured up the Devil incarnate and her previous nemesis, Ouida Rathbone. The two vixens chatted away like old chums.

Why did a simple cut, wash, and curl have to be so complicated? Babs' brain sorted out every possibility this close encounter could go wrong: Mayo drank—too much. This meant secrets were no longer sacred, and loose lips could sink ships. What if Mayo leaked to Ouida that her husband hired private investigators? Once she found out who, what if Ouida planted false notions in Mayo's head that Bogie might be having an affair with her? For God's sake, none of that was true!

Exit Stage Right: she pushed her dark sunglasses up higher on her nose and pinned her scarf tighter so it wouldn't fall off. There was no way she could show her face around those two; it would be the Fourth of July all over again.

Babs made a beeline for the nearest phone booth to cancel her appointment. Her excuse? Not the obvious truth. Even worse, she felt the need to tuck into a bar and drink herself silly. That, or stuff her face full of chocolate éclairs.

Chapter Sixteen: The Not So Obvious Suspects

Meanwhile, Guy felt a sense of wanderlust. After Babs departed for the beauty shop, he couldn't picture himself spending the day trapped in the "monkey cage," one of the many new nicknames he called their jam-packed office-turned-zoo. The last thing he wanted to do was to plow through dusty ledgers while breaking up catfights and listening to Stu's recitations of dirty limericks. Besides, the weather was too perfect to remain inside.

Taking the chance that what the police didn't know about Birdie's registries wouldn't hurt him or his partner, he set his sights on going after some of the not-so-obvious suspects: Ida Lupino, Bette Davis, and Fred Sexton, *The Maltese Falcon* propmaker, who never seemed to be available at an opportune moment. There were others, like Abdul Maljan, known around the Warner's lot as Abdul the Turk, Jack Warner's massive bodyguard, and George Raft, or Paul Muni, who had turned down the role of Sam Spade, but nabbing three interviews in one day would be considered a good score.

Ladies first, he thought. With them, he decided on a direct approach. After digging around to obtain numbers, he called Ida Lupino at home. Her housekeeper picked up, and said she was out of town.

"How long has she been away?" he asked.

The woman mumbled in a heavy Spanish accent. It sounded like she was in-between productions. Then she mentioned, *"Ido a Mexico..."* Guy strained to get past their language barrier. Unable to determine when she was due to return, he thanked her for her time but didn't leave a message. From what he had already gathered from Bogie, Lupino sparked a lot of jealousy from Mayo when she played his leading lady in *High Sierra*. Guy got the impression nothing happened. Any hints of a romance between them were strictly on screen. Otherwise, they didn't care much for each other. If anything, the relationship that developed off-screen was between Bogie and John Huston, hired as one of the film's screenwriters. They became drinking buddies and realized they had much in common, which carried over into the present.

He put a question mark by Lupino's name for now and dialed a few numbers to get tabs on Bette Davis. After getting the runaround, a publicist at Warner's, satisfied that Guy wasn't a gossip columnist, said she was in between films and gave him the number at the Los Angeles Tennis Club. He also gave Guy a heads-up. "She's a fool for romance and a pushover for dogs. If you woo her like Errol Flynn but promise to be faithful or bring along a four-legged friend, she'll melt in your hand."

Guy thanked him for the tip. He leashed up Sir Henry, a far more personable conversation starter than the bulldog, and hopped in his car, hoping to catch her before she left.

* * *

"Your new name, just for today, is Flynn," said Guy to Sir Henry. He snapped his fingers and called him "Flynn" several times to see if he'd respond, hoping he'd keep it up. Sir Henry licked his face to assure him everything would be fine.

Flynn, being so grandiose, so gray, and hairy, drew immediate attention the moment they got out of the car. They checked into the clubhouse, where one of the staff members paged Miss Davis.

The moment he saw Bette Davis approaching, he wondered if she remembered them from the MGM celebration after he and his partner rescued all those dogs in their previous high-profile case. As president of the Tail Waggers Society, she knew the countess, who had been one of his main suspects. Would she remember Sir Henry's name wasn't Flynn?

"What was so urgent that you had to interrupt my game?" Davis waved a cigarette in one hand and her tennis racket in the other. Her smokescreen shattered the second "Flynn" nuzzled his nose into her chest and licked her bosoms, which she didn't seem to mind.

"Well, who is this handsome gentleman?" She stamped out her cigarette and placed her tennis racket aside. Beaming with delight, she petted his scruffy head.

"Errol Flynn," Guy replied. "For short, I call him Flynn."

"You know I worked with Flynn."

"Did you?" Not having time to read up beforehand, Guy knew he'd have to wing it.

"A few years ago, in *The Private Lives of Elizabeth and Essex*. He could be a perfectly delightful person, but he was no actor and would admit as much. Always forgot his lines, and would laugh it off afterwards.

"Meanwhile, I'd get lost in a daydream, wishing instead he was Laurence Olivier, my dream hero, especially during our kissing scenes. After a night of drinking and whoring, Flynn disgusted me when he'd stick his tongue in my mouth. You know, one of the producers I worked with, Hal Wallis, said this of Flynn, 'He wasn't an admirable character, but he was a magnificent male animal, and his sex appeal was obvious. It seemed not to matter whether he could act. He leaped from the screen into the projection room with the impact of a bullet.'"

Sir Henry woofed every time he heard her mention "Flynn." She rubbed her nose against his like an Eskimo kiss. "Sweetheart, did you think I was talking about you?"

"He probably did," said Guy. *Seems like she didn't recall Sir Henry's real name.* "Do you mind if we sit down?"

Miss Davis led them over to a lounging area and summoned tea and extra biscuits for "Flynn." "A shot of bourbon in my tea," she added and looked at Guy. "What about you?"

"I'll just take mine straight."

"Straight bourbon for him," she told the server.

"Oh, God. No." He blushed. "Straight tea, without lemon or sugar. Thank you."

At least she loves the Wolfhound, Guy thought. He helped her light her cigarette before filling her in on the birding incidents.

"If you were in my shoes, Miss Davis, would you consider Ida Lupino a viable suspect?"

"How should I know? I don't keep tabs on her. She travels in other circles than I do."

That backfired. He hoped he hadn't offended her.

"All right, you starred in *Satan Met a Lady*..."

"Don't you dare remind me of that abomination! That was the all-time worst film, well...maybe the second worst film I ever acted in. Heard it bombed. Serves Warner's right. Hope they sent those idiotic screenwriters packing for Iowa. The only reason why I did it was because I was under contract—a complete farce!"

Guy felt tongue-tied. "Did you audition for the part of Miss Wonderly or Brigid O'Shaughnessy in John Huston's version of *The Maltese Falcon?*"

"In *Satan*, they renamed my character to Valerie Purvis. Maybe after the box office failure of the first *Maltese Falcon* film...maybe not. If you saw the rotten thing, you'd also know the Fat Man became a Fat Woman. All of this was probably done to protect Hammett's intellectual property, but I guarantee you, there was nothing intellectual about this comedy, and that's what it was—a comedy."

"Were you jealous Mary Astor got the current part?"

"Why should I be? I kept telling Jack Warner I needed better scripts. Why would I want to be on a picture that failed twice already?" She waved her cigarette at him like it was a conductor's baton. "Your name again is?"

"Guy Brandt, from B. Norman Investigations. Humphrey Bogart hired us and—"

"I don't care if Rudy Valentino hired you."

"Valentino's dead."

"That's the point. I still don't give a damn. Look, you interrupted my game while I was on a winning streak. Now, I'm in the mood for a bourbon.

A straight one and I think you and I are done."

"Flynn" approached Bette Davis. He placed his heavy head in her lap and gave her the sad eyes. "If your master made himself scarce, you could hang around with me a little while longer."

"Sorry, but we're a team. Come on, Flynn," he said, and reattached his leash. "Thank you for your time, Miss Davis."

Once he and Sir Henry returned to his car, Guy jotted down in his steno pad that Bette Davis had been an uncooperative subject.

* * *

After those two thwarted attempts, it was getting too late in the day to pester Raft or Muni, and Sexton slipped his mind. He still needed to tail Jack Warner's bodyguard. Without making it obvious, he needed to question others, the ones around the studio whom no one gave a second look, the invisible folk who might've been aware of Abdul's normal routines and activities. They could lead him to the secondary sources: an off-site barber, a gas station or parking lot attendant, the maître 'd of Warner's favorite restaurant, a bartender—all invaluable cogs in the wheel, which kept the dream machine revolving around the studio mogul.

"Warner refers to him as his shadow," said Earl, the gateman, as Guy drove up to the studio entrance. "Seems to be a jack-of-all-trades. Pushing sixty, but you'd never know it. He keeps in shape."

"How did Jack come to employ him?" Guy asked.

"Former boxer. Came to Los Angeles because he had relatives. At first, he worked for Mack Sennett as a trainer, masseur, and bodyguard. When Warner put a steam room in at the studio, he hired Abdul for a daily massage. Now, I hear our boss pays him $200 a week. More than I make in two months."

"Where does he park?" Guy asked.

"Today's your lucky day." The guard wrote something on a slip of paper. "Someone's chauffeur picked up the big boss to go to some off-the-lot meeting. Abdul took his own car today, and this is where he's got it."

Guy's generous tip caused a whistle reaction, one which sounded lyrical enough that one could suppose the guard had a background in music. "Hope you won't suffer the fate of the Happy Gate Man," Guy said.

"No, sirree, not me." The guard laughed. "Personnel Office already warned me. After dark, Jack Warner used to like to make his rounds. I hear he still does, although I only work the dayshift. Every penny counted, and he wanted to make sure all unnecessary lights were turned off. One night, he overheard one of the guards singing his heart out. Opera, I think. Big mistake to tell his boss that he took voice lessons when off duty. Warner fired him."

Without appearing too obvious, Guy figured he'd wait close by. Eventually, he'd follow Abdul and keep an eye on him.

While biding his time and knowing the people who worked the front gate and over at the secretarial pool and the commissary were in positions to possess all sorts of behind-the-scenes gems of information, Guy called out to a young bicycle messenger, who appeared to be transporting dailies to the film editors. "Hey, ever have contact with Jack Warner?"

"Here and there," the timid man replied. "Why?" He had tucked his necktie into his shirt to keep it from flapping in the breeze and had bound the legs of his trousers to keep them from getting caught in the bicycle chain. On his head, he wore a newsboy cap and clip-on sunglasses.

Finding it hard to tell his age, Guy asked, "Where's your studio ID?"

With a nervousness that appeared to be faked, the man reached into his shirt for his lanyard, but it wasn't there. "Must've fallen off. Where's yours?"

"I have a guest pass." Guy flashed a dollar bill, and the man's eyes grew wide. "Tell me something about that big guy who follows him around."

"The Terrible Turk?"

Guy nodded and handed him the dough.

The messenger's fidgety manner and shifty delivery seemed to hide more than he was letting on. He started stuttering. Guy couldn't determine whether it was a speech impediment or an awkward effort to hide a foreign accent. "He's a former boxer. Could've been a champ. Fought against Jack O'Brien for a world champ-ion-ship. Sometimes, he spars with the old man.

Likes to keep him in shape. Has been with him for years. Wheeling and dealing might ex-er-cise the brain, but it makes the body flab-b-b-by. I've overheard him say that." He appeared proud to know that tidbit.

Guy, making a quick look over his shoulders to make sure no one was looking, waved more cash in front of his face. "I heard Warner has a steam room on the studio lot. Know any way I could get into it?"

"If you're looking for a job as a masseur, the Turk takes care of that." The young man gave him a curious look. Guy tried to read into it but couldn't. "I suss-s-s-pect it's private. For executives only," he stammered. "My guess is if you look like you belong—like a maintenance worker—maybe you could sneak in...if you're lucky."

Well, I used to be an actor. Might have to put those skills to work yet. Rats! I'm not a mechanic. What I need is a passkey. This keeps getting more complicated.

He was about to hand the kid his final payout when he noticed the distinctive ring on his finger—a black onyx signet engraved with the German double-eagle.

"Where'd ya get the unusual gem?" Guy asked, trying to act assertive but not too intrusive.

"Aw, you know...picked it up in a secondhand shop. American soldiers, who returned from the Great War, snatched them as souvenirs. Everyone wanted 'a piece of Fritz' to take back home."

"You sure?"

Eager to please, the kid bobbed his head up and down like a wind-up toy that would never stop.

Guy wasn't buying it. To him, it sounded like he tried to cover up an embarrassing German accent. It was hard to discern his age. He could've served in the war, but on the other side. "You're not worried someone might think you have pro-German sentiments when people are worried about what's going on in Europe?"

The man shook his head so hard that his harsh denial made him even more suspicious. Guy handed him the promised payout and let him go but wished he had held him a bit longer for further questioning.

Minutes later, Guy spotted a groundskeeper. Another possible informant.

"Do you know anything about this steam room of Jack Warner's?" Guy realized he'd have to make this up on the fly. "I sell fixtures and upgrades and can do a free inspection."

He gulped and hoped it hadn't been too obvious. What the heck did he know about steam room renovations?

"That area is off-limits," the man said in an obvious Eastern European inflection, which he made no effort to hide. "No one but Warner and his friends go in there."

He did, however, manage to query three others; the first, a grease monkey named Ernie, who, when he wasn't tinkering with the nuts and bolts, went around buffing scratches and giving celebrities' cars a spiffy wax and shine.

Then there was "Ready" Eddie Plunket, whom Guy recognized as one of the lot projectionists, and he even ran into Errol Flynn, another Warner's contract player, whose name had surfaced in his recent conversation with Bette Davis. Flynn confessed that the Turk had made him a laughingstock in one of his man-to-man challenges. "Don't ever think you can win," he warned him. "I might've started a lot of foolhardy fistfights in my time, but I was no match against his brute strength and quick wit."

Given sound-alike names like Arnold, Ernie, Edward, and Errol Flynn, keeping all those facts and figures straight in his head could prove to be an issue. At last, Guy recognized Abdul from photos he'd seen in Warner's office. He began his tail, following Abdul to a gym off the Warner's lot. Once again, he'd have to think on his feet and come up with something convincing enough to let him into a private establishment where he wasn't a member.

"Any way you can give me a free pass for the day, in case I want to join?" Guy asked the front desk clerk.

"Let me ask the boss."

While the man stepped away, Guy craned his neck to see if he could determine Abdul's whereabouts, but he seemed to have disappeared. The clerk returned with a temporary pass.

"The big man...who came in ahead of me. Any idea where he went?"

"He likes to sweat it out in the steam room. Then he tries to rustle up a contender."

Guy played dumb. "Is he some sort of boxer?"

"Used to be, but he likes to stay in shape. Always looks for a victim to pick on. Men around here fear him. He's already sent a few poor saps to the hospital."

"Victim? For what?" Guy asked, getting nervous and wondering if this would turn into a setup.

"As his sparring partner. In reality, more like his punching bag."

Egads...what did I get myself into? "Got some workout clothes in the car, but I didn't really come prepared. Do you have—"

"We got towel service, if that's what you're asking."

* * *

Guy retrieved a duffle with workout attire and a padlock to secure his street clothes inside a locker. He figured he'd try the steam room first. If anything, maybe that would help him relax before the brute beat him to a pulp. After he ditched his clothes, he wrapped a towel around his waist and inspected his reflection in a nearby mirror. True, he had toned and put on some bulk since Troy Ulsterman, Babs' ex-husband, gave him the one-two punch, but he was imagining things if he thought he could match up with the Terrible Turk.

Guy ambled into the steam room, and there was Abdul, lost in thought amid a cloud of haze. *Come on...relax. Enjoy your free pass and the afternoon off. Leave the big lug alone.* Guy's rational mind kept telling him that, but he knew he couldn't.

Abdul cracked open one eye to give his intruder a once-over.

Not used to inhaling a lungful of steam, Guy choked and tried to catch his breath. Abdul took a ladle, dipped it in a bucket, and poured it over Guy's head. "Feels better, yeah?"

"Uh-huh." *Make him talk. Don't get cornered into talking about yourself.*

"Married?" Abdul asked.

Did Abdul notice I'm not wearing a ring? "Too busy. Work comes first."

"Same here." He grinned. "I take sports car and drive to Hollywood and

Vine. I see good girl, put her in car and drive to Hollywood Hills. Many times, they bring their friends. Come join me tonight."

"Keep them for yourself," Guy said, wheezing.

"First-timer?"

Guy felt even more self-conscious of their size differential. Abdul outweighed him at least two to one. "Considering joining. Need to work out more. Bullies like to pick on the smaller guys...like me."

Abdul placed his dampened towel against the wall as a cushion. He took a second look at Guy. "Your muscles—how do I say? Itty bitty? Well, if you can give me a run for my money, you can best the rest of them."

Guy sat up straight. "Pardon me?"

"Always looking for a seasoned slugger. The regulars around here are afraid of me."

Slugger? Guy knew he couldn't have been referring to Bogie's pugilistic wife. Not wanting to appear chicken, he tolerated about three more minutes in the steam room without coughing his head off. While Abdul had his eyes closed in his meditative repose, he tried to sneak out, but a beefy hand reached for his towel and yanked it off.

Shocked, Guy covered his private parts with one hand while grappling for his towel with the other. Did Earl the gateman alert the big man that he was being followed? Someone must've reported him for loitering. Despite being a greenhorn detective, were his shadowing skills that obvious? He felt betrayed.

"Sit down, pal. Not so fast."

"Give me back my towel!" he yelled, furious the Turk had called his bluff. "I made no deal."

"Yes, you did...the moment you stepped in here alone with me. That's the unwritten rule. Those who dare to sit with me in the steam room get to trade punches with me."

Guy begged for mercy. "Was thinking of joining this gym, I mean...but I think you made that decision for me. Let me out!"

Abdul clamped an unyielding grip on Guy's shoulder. He shoved him out of the steam room and into a cold shower. Guy yelped as the ogre lathered him up and rinsed him off.

"Change into boxing shorts so no one has to look at your shriveled nuts. Three rounds, and I'll let you go home."

Guy had been bullied before but never like this. He'd try to talk his way out of it. "Look, honestly. I don't know the game. You'd knock me out before the match ever started."

"Nonsense. I'll give you a handicap…like in golf."

"I don't know the rules of golf, either."

The Turk kept his towel wrapped sarong-style. He kept a watchful eye as Guy got suitably dressed and pushed him over to a small boxing ring.

"Lace me up," he said, nodding to the attendant to act as their referee. Then he chose an oversized pair of leather gloves with his name already inscribed.

"Wanna see how long this punk can last?" the man asked.

"Seriously, I don't fight. I don't box. I don't know a thing about the game. Only from what I've seen in the movies, and you know that's all choreographed. You have all the advantages. This is unfair, and you know it," Guy pleaded. He looked around to see if he could make a run for it. Prospects looked grim with only one exit. Between the attendant and Abdul, he'd never get past them.

The champ sat on a stool and waited for the ref to lace up Guy's gloves.

"Hey, wait! Aren't you supposed to state the rules?" Guy asked.

"No rules," the ref replied and rang a bell.

Guy moved the wrong way, leaving himself wide open. Abdul grazed him along the cheek. For sure, tomorrow, he'd have a black eye to show for that blunder. The giant struck again. Guy missed avoiding a punch to the gut, but as soon as he doubled over, Abdul gave him a hard uppercut. Losing his footing, Guy saw stars and landed hard on the floor. He wasn't sure if he heard a bell or if he imagined it.

"Put up your mitts and get ready for Round Two," the attendant said.

Stay there. Don't get up, Guy said to himself. *It'll be over as soon as it started.* Then he realized he couldn't get up. His muscles and reflexes refused to respond. Despite any exaggeration, the pain was real. *This is where my acting skills will save my life...I hope.*

Thoughts became foggy. Maybe he did, in fact, suffer a concussion. Ice...bruises...there would be a helluva lot of explaining to do the following morn...if he remembered anything.

Chapter Seventeen: Crisis on the Homefront

Babs knew Guy would see right through her disguise of wearing a snood to hide her unkempt hair, but at this point, she couldn't have cared less. He, on the other hand, couldn't conceal yesterday's misadventures. She found him sitting behind his desk, fighting off the dogs, while holding a sirloin steak against his face.

"What did you do? Fall and trip over Birdie's ledgers?" she asked.

Making his swollen eye and fat lip disappear wasn't so simple. "Don't ask," he said. "I had a bad day."

"You wanna compare notes?" She reacted to his shiner, now in full view. "Please don't tell me someone harassed you because—"

He shook his head. "No one called me a sissy. A suspect caught my bluff. Taught me a lesson, but good."

"Maybe you should learn how to box."

Guy cringed at that thought.

"In our line of work, learning hand-to-hand combat techniques couldn't hurt. All the soldiers who came back from the First World War learned a few handy tricks. I should probably learn jujutsu so as not to feel at such a disadvantage, especially as a woman."

"If you're picking a fight, you've got me at an unfair advantage," he replied. "Isn't it obvious I've already lost the first round?" He tested his teeth to make sure none were loose. "*Ouch*, it hurts just to speak. Say, if you promise not to talk about it, I won't ask why you never made it to the beauty shop. Deal?"

Saved by the bell, Guy picked up the phone. When he said it was her mom, Babs took the call in her office and made sure she closed her door. She adjusted one of the bobby pins on her hair net. Did she look that awful?

"Ma, is everything all right?"

"Your ex-husband… He's sent me threatening letters demanding to see you. At night, I keep feeling like there's a prowler outside. I'll keep my curtains closed, but I see shadows and hear noises like someone's tiptoeing around and rummaging through the trash."

More than once, Babs and her partner sifted through a suspect's rubbish to uncover a piece of damning evidence, one of the less glamorous aspects of being a private eye. "You sure it wasn't a raccoon or a stray cat?"

"If I turn off the lights, I've spotted flashlights. A car drives away afterward."

"Have you called the police?"

"They'll accuse me of imagining things and won't bother coming out unless there's a real crime. Creampuff, I'm scared."

Creampuff. No one had called her that for a long time. "Mom, are you sure it's Troy?"

"Has to be. Those letters are a giveaway."

"Did you show those to the cops?"

"I offered, but they—"

"Won't do anything until he takes action on one of those threats," said Babs, finishing her sentence. "Hate those procedural guidelines. It makes no sense to become a victim, before they'll get involved. You keep your windows and doors locked, I hope."

"Can't turn my house into a hot, airless prison in the middle of summer. If I can't feel safe in my own home, what's the point?"

"What do you expect me to do?" Babs asked.

"Come up here and tell him off. Maybe convince the local police this is serious."

"Troy doesn't respond to reason." *He refuses to accept I annulled our marriage. The idiot wants to reunite and control my life.*

"Then what does he respond to?" her mom asked.

"Jail time, and I'm in the middle of a huge case. I can't come up to San Francisco every time you panic."

Babs heard her mom's muffled sobs through the receiver. She also heard a knock on her door and assumed it was Guy. "Let me call you back."

"Be your wife...control my life," uttered the myna bird, as if he could read her mind.

"Come in!" she outyelled the noisome bird and threw a wadded-up paper ball, which bounced off his metal cage. Guy drifted in with both dogs at his heels. He tossed the steak into the anteroom, where Sir Henry and Bruno played tug-of-war over the spoils.

She summarized the gist of her mom's call and asked for advice.

"Suppose you make a visit and befriend the local police," he replied. "It couldn't hurt."

"What about our case? I can't leave you on your own, especially in that condition. What if someone's after you as well?"

He tried to scratch the back of his head but winced. "If I can't fend for myself, what good am I to you?"

"Now, you're sounding like Mom. She always feels I need a man around to protect me. That's the point of owning a gun."

"Don't brandish it about to prove you're tough. How long has it been since you've traveled home to see her?"

Babs had gone out of her way to bury the past. Not only would her mom pressure her about getting remarried, but the Bay Area was Troy's turf. Despite his arrest in Los Angeles during the Rathbone-Asta case, from her mother's description, he was no longer behind bars. He almost killed her once. He might try to kill her again.

"Well...okay, but you'll get all the credit and solve this case without me."

"We're a team. Since when was there competition between us? Babs, how many times in the past few days did I tell you to take time off? Between me and your Japanese gardener, we'll care for the animals and man the battering rams. Go see your mom and put this to rest once and for all. While you're gone, I promise to make headway with Birdie's material."

* * *

If she was going to follow his suggestion, she'd have to tie up a few loose ends. Detective Allgood called later that afternoon and wanted to ask her out again. Not that she was superstitious, but disastrous things happened every time he was around, like a jinx, and wasn't it a conflict of interest for them to be seen together in social situations? Furthering their involvement could backfire in so many ways.

Babs didn't want to assume cops and private detectives were always at odds, but so far, she felt like the two of them did little more than take advantage of each other. Maybe this sudden trip to San Francisco would be the impetus she needed to break it off. She just needed to come up with the best excuse. It backfired.

"I don't want you traveling up there alone." Allgood stood firm on accompanying her. "I pulled Troy Ulsterman's police records for the incidents he caused in Los Angeles. Found a complaint filed by the concierge at the La Dolce Vita residential hotel on threats of physical abuse and loitering. Also found a disturbance at your office where he picked up your partner and slammed him against your desk. Care to explain why you had to fire a warning shot?"

"Didn't scare him in the least. Thank heavens, between Sir Henry's teeth clamping on to his leg and a few neat tricks my janitor learned as a seaman, they pinned him down until the police arrived."

"To be honest, I can't exercise my jurisdiction out of town, but since I am a cop and can bring copies of his arrest records, I'm more likely to get cooperation from the local law enforcement. Otherwise, unless Troy seriously hurts someone, commits an obvious crime such as vandalism to your mom's house, or murders someone, the local police will brush it off as a minor nuisance complaint, still putting her at risk."

Babs sighed. Nothing she already didn't know, but while doing his homework about Troy, did he also discover her arrest record? She spent the night in jail for trespassing on Countess von Rache's property with possession of illegal German spy equipment during the Rathbone-Asta affair. Would he eventually find a way to hold that against her? She made up an excuse to get off the phone and told him she'd get back to him later.

"What's wrong now?" Guy asked.

Unable to mask the worry plastered all over her face, she withheld confessing her extra-curricular social activities to her partner. "Detective Allgood wants to accompany me. He uncovered Troy's arrest records and doesn't trust I can handle him alone."

"Maybe that's a good thing," said Guy. "I'd rather have him on your side than working against you."

* * *

With much to do and little time, Babs called Chief Crow-Feather to update him about Birdie Wilson and the second unsolved murder. Minutes after she hung up, Dashiell Hammett phoned and asked the detectives how they were progressing. Curious as to what he had to say, Guy picked up his receiver and joined the call on the other line.

"Maybe it will be beneficial to make a short trip to San Francisco, especially since this is the second time you've had to solve a crime involving one of my stories," Hammett suggested. "For all we know, you might come upon a clue on Sam Spade's home turf."

"Funny, the thought never came to mind," Babs admitted.

"If you could walk the walk of Spade or my Continental Op, perhaps a brilliant solution might fall right into your lap. You never know."

"Yeah, you never know!" chirped Stu, perched on Guy's shoulder, and who must've overheard. "*Awk!* You never know."

* * *

Bushed from all the preparations necessary to make a spur-of-the-moment trek, that evening, Babs told Detective Allgood she needed to be by herself. She treated herself to a glass of warm milk with a shot of rum and fished out her dog-eared copy of Hammett's *The Maltese Falcon* to skim through it one more time.

"Bogie's no blonde Satan," she said to herself, laughing at Hammett's visual description of Sam Spade. "And they were right about toning down Mary Astor's con artist character to appease the boys enforcing the Hays Code. Brigid O'Shaughnessy, in the original novel, made her role in the third film adaptation more like a prim schoolmarm."

Her Japanese housemate peeped through her open door and offered her saké.

"Thanks, but I'm well covered," she said, raising her mug, laced with her own rum concoction, and wished him sweet dreams.

He raised his tiny porcelain saké cup, toasted with a *kampai*, and in return said, "There's an ancient saying in Japan that life is like walking from one side of infinite darkness to another, on a bridge of dreams. They say we're all crossing the bridge of dreams together."

Chapter Eighteen: Falcon in the Fog

So much for dreams. Babs drifted into a restless night of tossing and turning and kicking off her bedclothes onto the floor at least twice. Her overactive mind flitted like the overtalkative myna that she and her partner vowed to get rid of. She also wasn't sure if traveling back to her home turf with Allgood was a wise move. Dot Norman, her worrisome mother, proved to be way too eager to marry her off to any levelheaded male on solid ground. Even worse, Stu's incessant chirping replayed in her semiconscious state. *"Awk!* You never know... You never know."

* * *

Guy and Wiggins swore to ensure everything concerning their menagerie would be under control in her absence. Her Japanese tenant promised to keep a watch on her house.

She and Detective Allgood each purchased tickets for the Lark, an overnight Pullman that left Los Angeles at 9:00 pm and promised to arrive at its final destination in San Francisco twelve hours later at 9:00 in the morning. Babs looked forward to a good night's rest, even if it took a nightcap before getting relaxed enough to sleep through the jostling and percussion of the rails.

Allgood felt terrible he couldn't treat her to a fine dinner first. "You know how impossible it is to make a last-minute reservation unless you're somebody famous."

"Being a cop isn't influential enough?" she said with a smile, part tongue-in-cheek.

"Unless he's the chief of police, one of the Sunset Strip gangsters is liable to wield more influence, but I do need to make it up to you after the lousy dates we've had so far. Too bad I can't take you for a steak at Musso & Frank, but let's see what our dining car's chef can whip up."

Ready to brush him off and turn in early, Babs' stomach answered in the guise of a gastric growl.

"Sure, have a talkative stomach, don't you? When we went to the Egyptian Theatre, I worried you'd disturb the audience."

"I got busy for this trip and doubt if I ate a bite since breakfast."

After they settled their belongings inside their separate sleeper cabins, Allgood put his arm around her waist in a butter-fingered attempt to show affection and escorted her to the dining car.

Musing over the Lark's menu, she wished she was riding in luxury on the Orient Express to Istanbul on an exotic holiday, not to her old hometown to rescue her desperate mom.

Allgood leaned in across their table. "A penny for your thoughts?"

A blush broke out across her cheeks.

"Okay, I get the hint when to back off." He hid behind his menu to spare her eye contact.

Their waiter took their orders and placed a plate of dinner rolls with butter on their table to tide them over.

"Just curious," he said. "What made you decide to become a private eye? You're the first dame I met in the profession. Didn't you say you gave up a career as an actress?"

Did he discover that as well while unearthing her own police records? After all, she got arrested and grilled by the police and the FBI during her last significant case. Babs didn't remember telling him. She took her time and bit into a roll. If it had still been daylight, she would've stalled by glancing at the scenery. Babs had always wiggled her way out of answering that question with any number of tall tales except for Guy, the only one who knew the truth up till now. Knowing she'd better not hide anything from a cop, she came clean.

"When I was a young girl, I solved a crime."

"Give me the scoop."

"Perhaps I should fill you in on some backstory." Babs took a sip of her water and gave a quick look over her shoulder to see if their waiter was coming. "When I made the decision to change my name and move to Los Angeles, I expected, through thick and thin, to be everything that was the opposite of my mother."

"Refresh my memory. What are your folks' names?"

"Mom's full name is Dorothy Norman, but she goes by Dot. My dad's name was Clifford. Everyone called him Cliff, but I thought I told you that already."

"You said your dad's name *was* Cliff. Did he change his name like you did yours?"

"Daddy's dead." She waited a beat. "As I was saying, I didn't want to be like my mother, who depended on my father. In her mind, he brought home the bacon; she ruled the roost, but she faltered trying to assume both roles when he suddenly died.

"Even when I got married to that idiot Troy, I didn't expect him to bail me out as my caretaker. Turned out that was a smart attitude to take. Mom's mind has been stuck in the last century. She believed a woman couldn't succeed on her own and needed to be married for survival. Sometimes, she'll get on her high horse and say I'd be better off returning to my abusive ex-husband than living alone and running a risky business. Don't get me wrong. I don't have a problem with getting hitched, but I intend to prove her wrong."

Babs didn't hesitate to dig in when their waiter arrived with their orders. "What convinced you to be a cop?"

"The old silent serial Westerns had some influence," he said bashfully. "Always liked the gun action and the shoot- 'em-ups."

"Wanted to be the tough-talking sheriff in town?"

"Yeah…kinda like that."

Babs wasn't sure if she bought his story, but then again, why should he believe hers?

"You know, my partner Moe. He's getting up there in years. Soon, he hopes to retire."

"Got your eyes on his spot?"

"Moving up the ranks wouldn't be so bad."

"Are you willing to assume the extra responsibility?"

Allgood brushed the shoulder of his jacket as if sweeping away invisible dandruff. "Nothing I couldn't handle."

Babs buttered him up as she buttered another roll. Something didn't quite add up, but she couldn't pinpoint it. When they first met, he had nothing but distaste toward private eyes. Acting lovey-dovey didn't make sense.

She and her partner needed to prove they were legit PIs who could be trusted to cooperate with the police. Most of their peers didn't and were generally despised by law enforcement. Many in the department already considered Babs and Guy as young, inexperienced fools, especially after the stunts they pulled onboard the Queen Mary regarding the thefts of the celebrity dogs in their Rathbone-Asta caper.

"One wonders if people's given names reflect their personality," said Babs.

With his mouth half-open, Allgood looked up from his roasted chicken, proving the question went over his head.

"Felix Allgood...are you *all that good?*"

Their waiter returned and handed them dessert menus. Babs got the hankering for a chocolate éclair and a cup of coffee.

"Join me for a glass of sweet dessert sherry instead," he said.

Drinks and socializing—Babs knew they went hand in hand but often were her Achilles heel. She wrinkled her nose and made an excuse. "What if I don't like it?"

"You've never tried it?"

She shrugged and smiled sheepishly.

"One for me and the little lady," he told the waiter. He excused himself to use the men's facilities, and she was glad he didn't notice her suppressing her angry grunt in reaction to one of the nicknames she hated—*little lady*.

Upon return, Allgood spotted the two glasses on the table. Babs had already taken a few sips from hers. "See, it's not so bad. Didn't poison you after all."

Going through her sweet-tooth phase, she gave him a wink, finished the rest of hers in one gulp, and ordered another.

"You still didn't tell me how you solved your father's crime and what compelled you to leave acting and become a private investigator?" he asked.

Did she really have to disclose everything about her father's murder—a surefire way to put her in a wretched mood? "Guess I got sidetracked." The alcohol also started hitting her all at once. She braced herself by holding onto the edge of the table until the wooziness stopped.

"For years, I had a ready-made story about how Daddy died, and I was only around nine or ten when it happened. No one wanted to listen to the truth and few would believe it. Dot...Mom...her explanation shifted from whatever she wanted to believe at the moment."

A sudden screech of metal grinding against metal jolted Babs' silverware, which flew off the table. The remaining contents of Felix's sherry stained their tablecloth.

"Debris on the track! We'll be moving along shortly!" bellowed a porter who took long strides through their dining car and into the next.

Babs wiped up the spills to prevent them from spoiling their clothes. Allgood offered to escort her to her room.

* * *

"Sure, you don't want me to come in for a nightcap?" he asked.

Pushy as usual. "After our dessert sherry?"

"I was only halfway through my second glass."

She unpinned her hair and started laying out her nightclothes, but soon realized she had signaled the wrong impression. He continued to block her doorway. She faked a vociferous yawn.

Finally conceding, he said, "The train pulls in early. Get your sleep. We'll catch breakfast near the depot before hailing a cab to your mom's."

* * *

Drinking wine did little to turn off her thoughts. Maybe Allgood's presence was a godsend, but could she trust her mom? She couldn't help but recall when her mom, after being pressured by her ex and so desperate to see her married, gave Troy the address of her LA office. Those words still rang clear, like a memorized script. "What's so bad about him, Barb? You really need a husband."

She argued back, "Have you forgotten Troy Ulsterman nearly killed me on the first night of our honeymoon? He forced me to have sex when I was too tired from drinking and dancing. When I wouldn't comply, he slapped me around and finally dangled me over our hotel room balcony—by my hair! I screamed until someone called the police.

"After I had our marriage annulled, he stalked me. That's when I ran off to LA and used a different first name, and for my last, I went by my maiden name instead—respect for our family and common enough he'd never find me—unless you spilled the beans, without thinking."

"I just want to see you happy...and married."

"Mom—be strong. Fight him off. Hit him with a broom and a dustpan. Crack an empty milk bottle over his head. If you care about my best interests, don't betray me."

I don't want him or any of his friends to find me—ever again.

A memorized script. For once, she understood what it was like to be typecast. Humphrey Bogart and Peter Lorre lamented its curse. Mrs. Norman refused to see her daughter in any other role besides being a dutiful wife and mother.

Halfway through the night, Babs woke from loud pounding on her door. "Who? What?" she mumbled as she groped to turn on a light.

"Miss Norman?" asked a baritone male voice, so deep and low it frightened her.

"Who is this?" she asked.

"Jasper Bottoms, your porter. We received an urgent radio telegram from a Japanese guy who claims he's your roommate."

147

"Mr. Otake? What's wrong?"

"Say's it's confidential, but urgent."

Babs sighed, trying to find her dressing gown. "Slip it under my door."

"Very well, then. Sorry to have disturbed you," the porter said and left.

Under the dim light, it said, "TROY CAME TO HOUSE. STOP. SMASHED WINDOW. STOP. COME HOME NOW. STOP."

She slipped into her shoes without her stockings, which always gave her blisters, and tore a hole in the hem of her long, satin dressing gown. Throwing on her raincoat for extra modesty, Babs scrambled over to Allgood's cabin.

Knocking on his door, in a voice hopefully loud enough to rouse him but not the other passengers, she called out, "All abort!"

"Don't you mean All aboard?" he responded, semiconscious. "We're already aboard. Is this some kind of joke?"

She opened his door, which he'd left unlocked. "No, rise and shine."

While Allgood was at a loss for words, she turned on his lights. "Quick! Pack your bags. We need to get off at the next stop and turn back."

He rubbed his eyes and stared at her impromptu outfit. "We'll never catch another train until tomorrow. What's the rush? What time is it?"

"Just received an urgent telegram. Troy isn't in San Francisco. He's made his way to Los Angeles and vandalized my house."

Her sparse words prompted him into action. Babs stuffed everything she had unpacked into her carry-on luggage, which she was glad she took with her instead of checking them into the baggage compartment.

At an ungodly hour between midnight and dawn, the two somnambulants disembarked at the San Luis Obispo rail depot.

Babs dropped her luggage on the vacant and dark platform and looked around, confused.

"I've never been here before. Have you?"

Allgood shook his head. "I think there's a National Guard camp in this town. What else? I have no idea."

She went to see if anyone was running the ticket office, but the lights were off, and everything was locked. "All I know is we're not far from where William Randolph Hearst lives—the millionaire who owns all the newspapers. What do we do now?"

"Does the old man owe you any favors from a previous case? Maybe he has a spare guestroom."

She gave him a mean stare with her hands placed firmly on her hips.

"Okay. Just thought I'd ask. Guess we'll have to hoof it and find a hotel." When he noticed she looked lost as to what to do with her suitcases, he asked, "Need help?"

She carried what she could. He struggled with her load in addition to his, having to put it down every few feet to rub his back and catch his breath.

They hobbled over to what looked like the nearest main street and into a hotel. Allgood rang a bell to summon the desk clerk, who looked like he wasn't expecting visitors.

"How may I help you?" he croaked, shoving his shirttail into the waist of his pants and adjusting his suspenders.

"We had to get off our train in a hurry," said Allgood. "Gotta take the next one heading back home."

"Where ya from?" the clerk asked.

"Los Angeles, and we're sleepy. Got any rooms?"

"Only one vacancy," the man replied.

"One?" Babs couldn't understand how this one-horse town could have only one spare room. "Sir, we're not... He's...he's my uncle." Afterward she realized she probably should've said cousin. Felix wasn't old enough to be her uncle unless they came from one of those backwoods families where people married each other in their early teens.

"If you're family, then you won't mind sharing." He pointed to his register and told them to sign in.

"How much?" asked Allgood, taking out his wallet. The clerk pointed to a sign. "Three dollars! For a fleabag like this in the middle of no man's land? I should ask how much your competition charges."

"Did ya take a look around? Ain't got none. We keep a clean ship here, sir. No fleas or bedbugs to report. We got some pretty little Mexican girls who come daily and make sure our domicile is spic-and-span."

Not thrilled with the lack of prospects, Babs plucked Allgood's wallet out of his hand and handed the clerk three bills.

"There's a small bed, but there's also a comfy couch someone can curl up on," said the clerk, putting the cash into his register. He took the last lone key from a hook on the wall and handed it to her, not him. "I'll let you draw straws as to who gets what. Come, follow me."

He helped with her extra luggage, which burdened Allgood earlier, and took them upstairs.

"When can we catch the next train back to Los Angeles?" she asked.

"Didn't you check the timetables before leaving the station?" the clerk asked.

Allgood had a ready excuse. "Too dark. Even if we found the schedule, there weren't any lights to read it."

"Not until late night…or the wee hours of the morning. Depends on how you look at it." The clerk wished them a restful sleep and said his wife would set up a breakfast buffet in the dining room downstairs, which would remain until ten.

"This isn't what I planned for," Babs muttered. She kicked one of her bags with her foot as it slid across the room's wooden floor.

"It might've been smarter if we'd stayed onboard to go up to Frisco…stayed at your ma's, and then gone back. Didn't you say she had a guest room for me?"

Babs could barely utter the words, "I'm taking the bed. You're taking the couch."

"But—" Allgood was about to suggest an alternative. She wasn't going to let him have the last word.

"No buts. I need my sleep," she said, and knew he'd try to convince her to share the bed with him, but that wasn't going to happen.

Chapter Nineteen: Hold the Mayo!

T he Bogarts received an invitation to attend a party in Mandeville Canyon. Those who remembered what this posh Brentwood neighborhood was like in the early part of the century reminisced on its hiking and riding trails through the canyons and into the mountains. Equestrian events for the 1932 Olympics had been held there, and it was also well-known for polo. After the Great Depression curtailed economic expansion and devastating floods in '38 destroyed the lower-lying areas, people rebuilt during the early forties. Rustic homes cropped up, and the well-fixed revived their love of horseback riding.

Friends of friends put Bogie and Mayo on the guest list. They didn't know their host, a local amateur polo enthusiast with the forgettable surname of Roberts, and they knew little of any plans he had in store except it would be a charity event. The couple had been at each other's throats all afternoon. He hoped getting out of their house would be the best panacea, despite not being in the most social state of mind.

She resumed their feud on the way to the host's front door. "Who did you say invited us again?"

"I reckon one of Hal Wallis' lackeys at the Warner Brother's production office told me about it."

"Wallis? Who's he?"

"Sluggy, you know the answer. He's Jack Warner's production czar. Can't remember the details now, except I marked it on my calendar for some kind of pro-democracy fundraiser against the war in Europe." He patted his jacket pocket. "Was told to bring my checkbook."

"Will Warner be there?"

"Beats me. I suppose so. Why?"

"You're going to be a big star after *The Maltese Falcon* comes out. Maybe he should take out his checkbook and raise your pitiful salary."

"Only if we can finish it without any more dramatic interruptions," he grumbled. "It still needs to be edited."

"Well, this better not be a costume party," Mayo carped. "Because you gave me no time to go shopping."

"I wouldn't have allowed you to waste my money even if it was." Bogie lit a cigarette. "Looks like you showed up in one anyway…wearing a flashy fur stole in the middle of summer."

She got on the defense. "What's wrong with my Russian sable?"

"What'll be wrong is when a hoity-toity whistleblower accuses you of being a card-carrying Commie 'cause you're sympathetic to the Bolsheviks, or when the dry cleaner says you'll need to replace it, because your sweat stains won't come out. Forget perfume. You'll smell so feral coyotes will follow you home and threaten our puppies."

On that remark, Mayo whacked him in the kisser with her black-velvet clutch purse.

"*Ouch!* What's in there? A brick?"

"It would serve you right if I did. How dare you insult me!"

He rubbed his smarting jaw and shook his head to snap to his senses. Enough liquor would be just the cure to loosen up both of them.

* * *

Mayo handed her sable wrap over to an attendant who sniffed it and gagged, as if to drop a not-so-subtle hint. The couple passed through the foyer, arm in arm. Bogie gave a quick nod to acknowledge those he recognized. Other than those he knew by reputation, most of the actors he spotted had contracts with rival studios. None of his fellow cast members from *The Maltese Falcon* were present.

"Maybe there's someone who'd like to cast me in their next picture," Mayo cooed, looking hopeful. Every time she inspected an attractive woman in a gorgeous gown, her envy erupted, as if she could name its designer by sight alone.

Bogie condemned her behavior and made clear he should've left her home. He continued to flash obligatory smiles and said through closed teeth, "I'm not even sure what our host looks like."

Mayo viewed the host's stock of liquor like being let loose at a giveaway in a Beverly Hills jewelry store. He dropped her off to flirt with the bartender and split to canvas the floor.

Harry Warner, Jack's older brother, circulated among the guests. Bogie had never met him but recognized him from photographs. Feeling he needed more than one opinion, he asked several guests, "Besides his wife, who's the young man who keeps following him?"

Partygoers claimed he was a political activist, a lawyer, and his name was Leon Lewis. "I've heard he runs a network of spies," one person whispered.

Bogie accompanied a group of men who congregated in the host's private screening room for a discussion led by Harry. Several hired hands set up the film projector and lowered the projection screen. The film *Confessions of a Nazi Spy* became a loaded and controversial topic.

"J. Edgar Hoover stipulated we make it as an exposé to the American public, most of which was blind to such atrocities," Warner explained. "Despite being a lifelong conservative Republican, I knew backing F.D.R. was the way to go. Prior to the conflicts overseas, my brothers and I produced a series of film shorts, which glorified America's fight against Germany during the First World War. By the autumn of 1938, we prevented the distribution of our films in Nazi Germany and its ally Italy. We also spent an enormous amount of money getting our relatives and employees out of these countries."

He elaborated on several other projects he had produced in the past few years: *The Life of Emile Zola*, a historical drama about the wrongly convicted Alfred Dreyfus, a victim of antisemitism; *The Sea Hawk*, an attack on King Phillip II of Spain, a despot with parallel qualities to Hitler; and *Black Legion*, a story inspired from the headlines about vigilante hate groups.

"We made no bones to disguise anti-Nazi propaganda and cast accomplished actors of Jewish heritage, such as Edward G. Robinson and Paul Muni, for many of the hero's roles. In a sense, we moved from producing films like *Little Caesar*, *The Roaring Twenties*, and *The Public Enemy* to pointing the finger at the men who proved to be far worse than gangsters. Our enemies are any people or groups who tout intolerance."

While Harry orated from his soapbox, he withheld introducing the man whom Bogie was told was Leon Lewis. Bogie assumed if this guy was sending spies to infiltrate the local German American Bund and other pro-Nazi hate groups, then anonymity was key to his organization's success and survival.

Bogie turned to one guest and asked for a light. "If Harry's here, I'm surprised Jack isn't. I always pictured him running their offices out of New York," he said to make conversation. Roberts' party seemed to have so many people he didn't know, including people not even affiliated with the film colony.

"Not surprising at all," the stranger replied. "Harry now lives with his wife and kids on his ranch near Calabasas. After the death of their father, Jack and Harry have barely spoken to each other. I guess he wants to be closer to the action to keep tabs on his brother's spending habits."

Makes sense, Bogie thought, suppressing a chuckle and relieved he didn't have to make nice to his boss this evening. Harry announced that he'd rally all the studio heads together to finance Lewis' operation. Even if the Warner brothers had done their darnedest to assimilate, their forebears came to America because of prejudice or political persecution.

Bogie got bored and lost his tolerance for hearing any more banter about politics. Even though there seemed to be no reported account of Harry getting threatened, he wondered if this birding vendetta had to do with someone acting out against the brothers and the threats against cast members of *The Maltese Falcon* circled back to the studio moguls.

Editors had put together clips from the longer feature films and spliced them into a presentation with one of Warner's anti-war shorts. Bogie felt particularly on the spot when part of their presentation included scenes from *Black Legion*, which he starred in back in '37.

Bogie slunk into his seat, withdrawing into himself, almost hoping he wouldn't get recognized, but all eyes turned to him. He felt singled out. "Didn't you pay attention to the note after the film's credits? It said the characters, the story—all the incidents and institutions in the film were fictitious. Don't look at me. I just do what I'm paid to do. Don't confuse me with the man you saw on screen."

"You knew what you were doing," one person shouted. "Why didn't you speak up and say something?"

"The whole point is the writers wanted to rouse your sensitivity against injustice. I'm just a contract player who was expected to make a certain number of B films per year in a supporting role. Not like Bette Davis, who hired a lawyer to get her better scripts."

At last, Harry, looking for an equivalent to an alms basket, dumped out the wax fruit from inside a cornucopia and passed it around for donations. Several guests complained they didn't realize this would turn into a fundraiser and apologized for not having more cash. Bogie took out his checkbook, put his John Hancock on a contribution of one hundred dollars, and tossed it onto his seat. "Here. If you don't believe me, then don't cash it. I'm going to monitor my wife to make sure she doesn't drink herself under the table."

Excusing himself, he headed over to the bar. Mayo had never left her stool the entire time.

"Where were you?" she asked, slurring her words.

He ordered a bourbon and savored the moment. "I expected to get free booze and to get drunk at this party. Not to listen all night to political proselytizing."

Ida Lupino, whom Bogie hadn't noticed earlier, took a seat at the bar. Since they worked together before, he tried to make cordial conversation but Mayo, already plastered, burst into a fit. Ever since Lupino costarred with her husband on *High Sierra,* she resented her.

Unable to cope with competition, Mayo hurled a glass ashtray and hit her tipsy husband so hard that she knocked him off his stool and onto the floor. She seized his car keys and stormed out, leaving him stranded. Bogie struggled back onto his seat, asked the bartender for another round, and got drunker. His host, after hearing his guests complain about his tasteless marital spat, booted him out.

Unsure what to do, he got the crazy notion to walk home. The problem: he was too soused to know which way was home. Heading in the wrong direction, he wandered too close to a stranger's yard and alerted their two Dobermans.

He climbed the closest fence to avoid having the dogs tear chunks out of his trousers, but their yowling and relentless barking caused nearby lights to turn on. Their owner almost called the police, but refrained when she recognized him from her favorite films. She tied up the dogs, who continued to howl, waking the neighbor who lived on the other side of the fence.

Peter Lorre, with his hair disheveled and wearing rumpled pajamas, stumbled outside with a Scotch in one hand.

When he asked what Bogie was doing, Bogie replied, "Your neighbor's attack dogs nearly mauled me." He also explained how his wife left him high and dry. "Maybe she's been my personal nemesis all along if she's always been jealous of my success."

Lorre interjected, "Aren't you forgetting, she's got nothing against the other actors, the director, or the producer of our film? If anything, she'd profit by cozying up to John Huston or Jack Warner to further her career. However, that wife of yours…"

"What about Mayo?"

"She'll make you turn gray and lose your hair before your time. A good toupee could work wonders, but I don't trust wigmakers," said Lorre. "Those never look natural beyond the stage or movie sets."

"Wouldn't make any difference if I turned gray or if I lost it all, would it?" Bogie sniggered.

Lorre helped his friend climb down from the fence. "Wig or no wig, it's time for bed, my friend. You're lucky we have an empty guest room."

Chapter Twenty: Sing a Song of Sam Spade

L orre allowed Bogie to sleep off the sauce. When the clock's hands crept close to noon, he roused him from his slumber.

"What's the deal?" Bogie tried to fend him off before rolling over and mumbling about ruining his dream about being deserted on a desert isle with Hedy Lamarr. Once he was able to focus his eyes, he stared at his host. "Hey, why am I here?"

Lorre was taken aback. "You don't remember a thing from last night?"

"'Fraid not."

"Nothing about me rescuing you from two vicious Dobermans while you roamed drunk into my neighbor's yard? God knows what trouble you stirred up before that."

"My memory's a blank."

"Since it's Sunday and we have the day off," Lorre explained, "I promised the Fat Man to meet for an early afternoon brunch. There's a new French and Creole restaurant near the beach in Santa Monica he's been dying to try. They don't have bistros like this back in England. Not many places like that here either."

"As long as we don't all die eating there," Bogie muttered. "Heard the Cajuns serve up some spicy numbers—the Devil's cuisine or voodoo victuals, some say."

"Nobody's going to die today on my watch. Besides, our pantry is bare. Don't think you want to dine on fistfuls of flour."

Lorre handed Bogie bath towels. "I'd lend you one of my fresh suits to replace the...*schmutzig*... How do I say in English? *Uh*...the un-hy-gienic ones you came in, but they'd never fit. You're much taller."

Bogie sat up in bed, realizing someone had stripped him down to his T-shirt and his Jockey-style briefs.

"While you shower," Lorre said, "I'll have one of my housekeepers press out the wrinkles. Glad you only wore a stylish dress suit last night. You'd be overdressed for brunch had you worn a tux."

* * *

"Sorry. I got hungry and couldn't wait." Sydney Greenstreet, seated against the wall, had already made headway on his *Shrimp Étouffée* when they arrived.

"We're the ones who should be begging your pardon. I ran late because of unexpected company." In an unsubtle manner, Lorre cocked his head to indicate Bogart. "Do you mind?"

"Not at all." Greenstreet gestured toward an empty chair. "I always request an extra-large table, usually reserved for more customers, only because I'm a rather king-sized customer."

Lorre snickered, "I'd say more along the lines of an emperor like Caesar or Napoleon."

Greenstreet went on to explain he had no idea what he was eating. "I took one look at the menu and told the waiter, 'That's most unfortunate. I can't translate the French.' Instead, I persuaded him to describe a few appetizers and took one of his suggestions."

"If you need help, I can translate," said Peter. "After I escaped Germany, I lived in Paris. I had no choice but to speak French before Hitchcock sponsored me for a film over in England. Took a rather roundabout route before coming to America."

"Let me take a look," said Bogie, picking up the menu. "Had to learn French in prep school and practiced it in the navy during the last war."

"I would've never guessed you to be the prep school type," said Lorre.

158

"You'd never know by the roughhewn characters I play, but I grew up in Manhattan. My father was a prominent surgeon and my mother a successful commercial illustrator. Often, she made more than he did. Would you believe when I was a baby, she used a drawing she made of me for a baby food advertising campaign?"

Their server returned and gave the newcomers menus. Greenstreet ordered Oysters Rockefeller, pointing out to his friends that their chef defected from Antoine's in New Orleans. When President Roosevelt visited the famous restaurant, the oyster dish was his favorite.

"Are you sure that's enough?" Lorre asked. "I think this is just another side dish."

Greenstreet patted his belly. "Fine with me. I want to save room for dessert."

"What about you? What strikes your fancy?" Lorre asked Bogart.

"While we're harping on influential leaders, why don't I go with their *Boef or Beef Robespierre?*"

"As long as you don't lose your head," chuckled Lorre, who decided to order pheasant under glass.

Greenstreet pointed out a historical tidbit written on the menu. During Prohibition, Antoine's served hooch in coffee cups. They were carried through the ladies' powder room and into one of their secret dining nooks.

"I see they also serve *Café Brûlot*, another signature item they stole from Antoine's," Bogie added. "They describe it here as a drink blended from coffee, orange liqueur, cloves, and garnished with lemon peels and a cinnamon stick. When served for dessert, the coffee is set on fire, like a flambé."

"After last night," Lorre whispered to Bogart, "maybe you should abstain from indulging in anything alcoholic. At least for a few days."

"Nonsense. As long as I'm paying for my own meal, I'll eat or drink anything I want."

* * *

When the waiter returned with their orders, he placed a silver tray in front of Peter with an opaque metal lid.

"I'm confused. Isn't the whole point of calling this dish pheasant under glass that it's served under glass?"

"Not sure," their server said. "We think the restaurant ordered the correct glass lids, but they arrived broken, and we had to make a quick substitute."

When it came time to lift the lid off Lorre's meal, everyone encountered another eye-opener: with all its feathers intact lay another dead crow drowned in a grave of gravy.

Lorre shrieked; the shock sent him vaulting backward, where he almost fell out of his chair. The waiter promptly slammed down the lid, splashing gravy onto their tablecloth. He whisked it away and scuttled it back to the kitchen.

Greenstreet, who had been facing outward with a view of all the alarmed diners, shooed away curious onlookers. "Nothing important. Just the wrong dish. A poor practical joke with bad timing."

Lorre slowed his heavy breathing. He still had a feverish sweat and continued shaking.

"Peter, are you all right?" Bogie noticed his friend looked ill. "You didn't eat any of it, I hope?"

Lorre's eyes looked vacant; he stared off into the distance. "I think I'd rather starve."

Bogie asked if Peter wanted to call a doctor, but he declined.

Greenstreet attempted to buoy his spirits. Nonsense," he said, indulging in another oyster. "Order something else, but I think we should call the cops."

"I'd like to keep them out of it," Peter replied.

"Why? Do you have something to hide?" Greenstreet asked.

Lorre shook his head and stared at the floor. "I don't like cops or authority figures, for that matter. Reminds me of what I escaped from in Germany and Austria. No place was safe on the continent. Not from those stormtroopers. I want to consider America as my refuge and the one place where I'll never have to worry about persecution for who I am or where I came from."

Bogie scratched his scalp and couldn't recall how he got the bump on his head, but fragments of Harry Warner's lecture speech last night resurfaced. "You're here, and they're there. If you keep your nose clean, you'll be all right."

"Nose clean?" Lorre asked. "What's that mean? Stay away from cocaine?"

"Hope you're not on the stuff..." Bogie gave him the death stare. "Anyhow, it's just American slang for staying out of trouble. I'm sure our waiter or his supervisor already phoned the police, but I wish one of those private dicks I hired were present."

Lorre looked at Greenstreet with disgust every time he swallowed another oyster. "Can't believe you're still hungry."

Bogie tried to put levity into their morbid situation. "Guess that puts a new meaning into the old saying of eating crow but pardon me. I'm going to make that call to my investigation team."

* * *

Upon return, Bogie announced, "Before the whole Los Angeles police department interferes, let's put our heads together."

"Are you now stepping into the shoes of Sam Spade?" Lorre asked.

"So to speak. Figure this...Cookie and Huston are the only ones of *The Maltese Falcon* inner circle who haven't yet been birded."

"Wrong on that account," Greenstreet interrupted. "Whoever's behind it has spared me, so far."

"Then I take that back. Oh, and when the police do arrive...don't breathe a word about Mary Astor getting the bird. I think our guys are keeping that under wraps since no deaths were involved."

Meanwhile, Humphrey Bogart retraced his steps. "My retentiveness from last night is still a bit hazy. We watched a film compiled of segments from other films. What I can tell you, besides Harry Warner's feathers getting ruffled about a group of people who gave Jews a hard time, was the feeling I got upon discovering one of those clips featured me in a despicable role. When the film ended and all eyes glared at me like a lynch mob, I had to

161

explain I was nothing like the swine on screen." Getting that off his chest, he reached for a glass of water and drank it down in one prolonged gulp.

When he finally put his empty glass down and heaved a sigh, Lorre said, "Sounds similar to my curse."

Greenstreet bellowed like Old Saint Nick. "Since when did you have a curse on your head? Given this is a Creole establishment, maybe you should ask if someone can lend you an extra voodoo doll to reverse the spell."

"Maybe I should." Lorre resembled a shrinking violet. "In my case, it pertains to the curse of *M*."

Bogie raised his brow. "The German film you starred in that Fritz Lang directed, and his wife wrote the script, correct?"

Lorre tried to light his cigarette; his hands were shaking. "An acclaimed hit in Germany and all over Europe, but I had no idea of the extent it would come back to haunt me. I had played villains before, but nothing with such impact. Everyone needed their scapegoat, and I seemed to fit all their excuses."

* * *

Sooner than a wink, Guy Brandt joined their party. "Came as fast as I could. What's so urgent?"

"Where's your little lady partner?" Greenstreet asked.

"She had to rush out of town. Her mom had an emergency."

Bogie needled him about his black eye. "What's with the shiner? From the rainbow colors it's turning—patches of mustard yellow blending into blues and purples—looks like you've been nursing that whopper for a few days."

Guy, who was ready to blame his black-and-blues on tripping over the dogs in his overcrowded office instead of getting K.O.'d by Jack Warner's bodyguard, told him they needed to concentrate on what was more important.

Bogie filled him in on Lorre's unpleasant pheasant incident. "Can't figure why the cops are taking so long. Guy, who else do you still need to question?"

"Neither my partner nor I have made any headway with George Raft or

Paul Muni."

"*Hmmm*, the guys who turned down my role. They might as well kiss their careers goodbye if they prompted these birdings."

"Sexton never seems to be around. Then again, Huston informed me they found the missing spare falcon prop." Guy squinted, testing his memory. "Come to think of it, we never got to interview you at length, Mr. Lorre."

"Then I guess it's high time you did," chimed in Greenstreet, who remained chipper and unfazed. "Mr. Brandt, I bet all these tantalizing aromas are making you hungry. Why don't you join us for dessert?"

He hailed their waiter, glanced at their dessert menu, and said, "Their boysenberry pie sounds superb," and ordered a whole pie for their table. "Tea for me. I suspect coffee for everyone except Mr. Bogart, who wants to try the *Café Brûlot* with the flaming spirits. Oh yes... Bring some bicarbonate of soda for Peter. I'm sure that cruel prank still is giving him a case of Dicky Tummy."

Bogie laughed so hard, his cigarette fell from his mouth. "You'll have to translate that into American English."

"It's a British expression referring to dyspepsia. In my opinion, to quote the King James Bible, 'it had nothing to do with godless myths and old wives' tales,' but I heard it got even more popular after a silent film actor named Richard Stomach became afflicted with the trots on the set."

"Sydney, you're a riot," Bogie roared and pounded his fist on the table.

Lorre stirred bicarbonate of soda into his water glass and gulped it down, following it with a belch.

"Feel any better?" Bogie asked.

"Maybe, but I hate the word boy-sen-berry," he mumbled. "Sounds like poison berry, don't you think?"

Bogie gave him a friendly punch on the shoulder. "Now you're being silly. I'm sure it'll be delicious. Otherwise, our savvy detective wouldn't have accepted our offer."

"In your absence," Greenstreet said, addressing Guy, "Humphrey here has assumed the guise of Sam Spade. He refuses to understand it's our day off and when we have permission to revert back to normalcy."

"Since I'm shy of my partner, I could use the extra assistance," said Guy.

Their waiter wheeled over a trolley with cups, saucers, and large pots of coffee and hot water for Sydney's tea. He asked Peter if he was feeling better and apologized that their pie would be a few minutes longer.

Guy sipped his coffee to make sure it was sweet enough. "Two lumps of sugar..." he chirped. "Can't say that without thinking of someone like The Three Stooges or an old vaudeville act."

"Their hijinks originated from the stage," Bogie said.

Greenstreet peered at his pocket watch. "Can't figure what's taking the police so long. They should've been here by now."

Lorre's whispering was barely audible. "They can take their own sweet time."

Guy asked if the gentlemen would retrace the events that transpired in the past twenty-four hours. Bogie apologized for his lapse of memory. Greenstreet said he hadn't done anything outside his normal routine. He also had an alibi. For the most part, Lorre said he'd been preoccupied with sobering Bogart and rescuing him from his neighbor's attack dogs.

Everyone had already started on their second cup when their waiter arrived with a gigantic pie, fresh out of the oven with steam rising from the slits in its crust.

Bogie licked his lips and readied his napkin. "Boy, oh boy! Does that smell scrumptious."

"What does a boy have to do with it?" Lorre asked. "Because it's boys-en-berry."

"Naw, just another Americanism," Bogie explained. "The longer you're out here, the more you'll pick up on our linguistic nuances. It would be the same with me if I were to live for any extended time in a foreign country like the one you came from."

Greenstreet took a deep whiff. He had the same anxious look in his eyes like he did when he, as Kasper Gutman, unwrapped the long-lost Maltese Falcon.

Steam escaped as the waiter cut into the pie's puffy crust. Taking special care with the first slice, he cut a long, vertical incision across the diameter of the pie as if performing surgery. The knife tumbled out of his hand.

Guy rose to his feet to lean in closer. He grabbed his fork to separate its contents. He looked at Greenstreet, who had been so eager to dine on the fruity confection. "You've been b-i-r-d-ed, sir."

With difficulty, Greenstreet heaved himself off his wall-side bench and stood to take a closer look. "By Jove! I think you're right."

"Let me take it away," the server said, putting it back on his trolley.

"Leave it," Guy said. "The police will need it as evidence."

The waiter offered to get him another one of those opaque lids to hide it from others, too curious for their own good. Lorre cowered in his seat and mixed a second helping of stomach medicine.

Surprisingly, Greenstreet took the whole incident in stride. He took his fork and continued dissecting their tainted dessert. Unable to make headway with whistling, he began humming.

"How can you think of music at a time like this?" asked Lorre, still green around the gills.

"Isn't that the nursery rhyme?" Bogie asked.

"*Sing a Song of Sixpence*," Greenstreet replied.

"Correct," said Guy, poking into their dessert using his eating utensil.

Peter clasped on to his wrist and pulled his hand away. "Please don't make this any worse than it already is. Let the police department do their duty."

Guy turned to Greenstreet. "Being English by birth, you're probably more of an expert regarding the song's meaning."

"My grandmother always told me this was a coded message used by Blackbeard, the pirate, to recruit shipmates. He'd pay a weekly wage of sixpence and a pint of whiskey. The 'pie' referred to his galleon, and the 'blackbirds' were Blackbeard's subordinates."

Not being much of a vocalist, Bogie recited the poem. "Sing a song of sixpence, a pocketful of rye, four and twenty blackbirds baked in a pie. When the pie was opened, the birds began to sing. Now wasn't that a dainty dish to set before a king?"

Guy took over where Bogie left off. "The king was in his counting house counting out his money; the queen was in the parlor eating bread and honey.

The maid was in the garden hanging out the clothes when along came a blackbird and it nipped off her nose."

"My nanna told me a different story," said Bogie.

"Pray tell," Greenstreet replied.

"She always said most nursery rhymes we know today originated in the time of Henry VIII. The sixteenth century was a time of great strife between the Tudors and the Stuarts, and good ole Henry had an 'off with her head' thing going on with his wives he no longer liked."

"What's that got to do with it?" Guy asked.

"If you'd allow me to finish, I'd spell it out. The part of the song or rhyme that says 'The king was in his counting house counting out his money; the queen was in the parlor eating bread and honey,' the monarch, of course, is none other than Henry VIII. The queen refers to Catherine of Aragon, one of his wives. 'The maid was in the garden hanging out the clothes,' points to Ann Boleyn, his mistress at the time, but whom he married against the dire warnings of the established church and who he later executed. 'When along came a blackbird, and it nipped off her nose.' I think the blackbirds referred to church officials, and the snipping off her nose meant Boleyn's execution, but don't quote me on that."

Bogie finished his coffee. The moment he lit his cigarette, Detective Moe Sadowski arrived with his crime squad.

"Where's your partner?" Guy asked.

Sadowski, who had a toothpick hanging from his lower lip like a stogie, gave him a jaundiced look. "You, of all people, should know. He accompanied *your partner* up to Frisco."

Guy was speechless and embarrassed that so much had transpired he had forgotten.

"Man, if you can't get your facts straight, maybe you need to take a refresher course in *How to be a Successful Gumshoe*."

The detective kept taunting Guy to the point where Bogie had to intervene. "Officer, do you mind having your boys take this evidence away, so we don't have to stare at it any longer."

His team not only took the pie, but requested the kitchen staff retrieve

Lorre's tampered-with pheasant under glass. Greenstreet, who seemed capable of distancing himself from the melee, complained he still wanted dessert. Despite groans and protests, he ordered more pie to be brought to the table.

"Make that with vanilla ice cream," he said.

Detective Sadowski demanded to speak with the top dog in charge of restaurant operations. "I want a detailed list of everyone who works here." He bellowed so loud it broadcasted throughout the dining room. "Including part-timers and temporary hires."

"What's this with Babs and Detective Allgood?" Bogie asked. Guy waved him off. "Why don't I pretend to be your partner since the little lady is out of town? Before you joined us, Peter mentioned the curse of *M*." He homed in on Lorre. "Care to elaborate?"

If it were physically possible, Lorre's bulging eyes seemed to retreat in their sockets. "I've played mostly madmen—killers—but the audience loves me. You know, I can get away with murder, but if you remember the film, I played a disturbed man—Hans Beckert, a fictional character. Many said he was based on a real murderer named Peter Kürten, whom the press called the Vampire of Düsseldorf. He went on a sickening killing spree back in the twenties.

"After the film was released, people would torment me in public. They accused me of things I never did or would ever dream of doing and sent me hate mail."

"Of course, you would never commit such heinous acts!" Greenstreet contended.

"For the type of parts I play, I should be booed. But it's odd, fans just adore me. I can't explain it. Convincing the general public is another story. People have confused my film character with the actual serial killer. Somewhat similar to what our friend Bogie experienced last night, but on a constant, prolonged basis. Many times, I've feared for my life."

Chapter Twenty-One: Going to the Birds

Despite all the recent excitement, Guy kept his promise and made a dent in Birdie's bookkeeping, but two particular customers stood out by nature of their metaphoric connotations: Chickie Crane and Swifty Herren, both nicknames.

Chickie, whose real name was Charles, had an address only three doors from his. Early in the mornings and around dusk, Guy recalled seeing swarms of birds making figure-eight formations. Growing up in the Midwest, he used to observe bird migrations and flight patterns, but never thought much of it. Funny, he thought, how most of the time when one lives one's life in a big city, they almost never look up, but a resident on his block must've had a pigeon coop on top of their roof.

"Are you aware of anyone else nearby who does this or has a similar fascination with birds?" Guy asked.

His neighbor turned out to be an elderly balding man who wore beat-up overalls with one of its straps undone, underneath, a work shirt. "I belong to a pet pigeon appreciation society. Our members meet once a month."

Assuming this must be a private group of only a handful, Guy doubted they'd have an official clubhouse or be listed in the phone book. "Does your organization include any well-known people?"

"Just us common folk."

How do I ask this guy if he knows any social deviants capable of killing others? "Any chance I can get a hold of your membership list?"

"Let me see." Chickie began counting on his fingers. "There's Peter Leffer…"

"Peter Lorre?" Guy asked.

"Oh no, he spells it L-e-f-f-e-r. I can testify to that because he always owes us back dues, and I handle the bookkeeping." He resumed counting. "There's Harvey Bialystock. He owns a Jewish bakery over in the Fairfax district. Then there's Mousie Gainsboro…"

"Sounds like a gangster's name," Guy chuckled.

"Far from it. Mousie and his wife are church-going folk. Insists on tithing his ten percent."

"Where did he get his name from?"

"Quiet and shy as a church mouse, I suppose. Gee, my memory's shot. Maybe I should try to compile some kind of list."

Guy worried the deeper he probed, the more he'd scare the man into keeping mum. Therefore, he switched his queries to what it entailed to raise pigeons. "Is there a particular kind of cage you need?"

"We call those coops," Chickie corrected him. "Others call them lofts. They should allow at least ten feet of space per bird. After all, they need to fly around. It's not like penning a dog or a cat."

"I guess you're right." Guy mused over the idea of asking Chickie if he'd take Wiggins' myna bird.

"Their housing should have at least three separate sections: one for old birds, one for the youngsters, and one for breeders. You also want to build their coop high enough, so you don't always have to bend over. It'll kill your back."

Thinking about his everyday challenge at the office, Guy asked the delicate question of how do you keep it clean?

"Ya want to scrape their droppings from their perches and boxes and the floor. Otherwise, you'll track shit all over."

"Besides a love of birds, what else would attract enthusiasts to such a hobby?"

"For some, this is a profession. People race the birds, you know."

"I wasn't aware of that. For big bucks?"

"Oh, yeah, and there's more. You would've been too young to serve, but during the First World War, the military trained pigeons. They delivered messages for the troops when it was too dangerous for a real person to relay news on foot. They also had the risk of being shot. Someone even experimented with mounting a spy camera on birds. They scrapped the idea; it didn't work out too well."

"Can't see how it could've." He handed Chickie his card and said he'd stay in touch. His next challenge: circumnavigating the pigeon poop to the stairwell so as not to ruin his spectator shoes.

Regarding Swifty Herren, Guy had a hard time linking the birdings to his profession as a pediatrician. Dr. Herren, whose full name was Dr. John Wilford Herren, Jr., had a reputation for stitching busted knees from overzealous kids. He did not, however, indulge in the habit of slicing open dead animals and turning them into trophies. When queried, he made it clear he abhorred the idea of hunting for sport. The only reason why he had done business with Wilson was to purchase several Victorian-style animated shadow boxes. He showed Guy a similar one to the sample with hummingbirds he'd seen in the taxidermist's shop. Its tune lifted the spirits of sick children scared of visiting the doctor.

Otherwise, he had plaques adorning his walls with testimonials praising him for his exemplary community service. His photos indicated he had a wife and three sons who were all Boy Scouts, and he volunteered as their troop leader. Discounting his incriminating-sounding name, Dr. Herren didn't appear to be much of a murder suspect.

* * *

After the upset at the Cajun restaurant, Guy couldn't determine whether Detective Moe bucked his calls or had been too busy to return them. By now, the police should've given him the full scoop on Pilchik, but so far, he'd received little more than the press. Even if he had to go through the files in person, he still wanted to find out if Chickie Crane or Swifty Herren had prior police records.

Unable to wait any longer, Guy drove over to their precinct, realizing since he'd started this case, neither he nor Babs had visited the detectives on their home turf. He showed his identification and put in his requisition at the front. Then he asked for Moe, figuring by the time they pulled his material, he'd be done with the detective.

Moe couldn't understand why it was so urgent to come in person. "Like coffee?" he asked.

"Would love some," said Guy, imagining its savory aroma.

"Too bad, 'cause mine's awful. Allgood's the culinary crack shot around here. The crap I brew, you wish you died and went to hell for, but I'm surprised you have any appetite after yesterday's luncheon."

Guy grunted. He hoped that ended his goading.

Sadowski's makeshift office only had a single desk and two chairs in a corner, and looked like it had been converted from a storage closet. With no windows to the outside world, it appeared like someone punched a hole in the wall to add one facing the bullpen.

"Assuming you don't share a desk, where's your partner set up?" Guy asked.

"We had a few departmental transfers and switcheroos. From the looks of things, crime around here has grown so fast we've had to pack 'em in by adding more personnel. Allgood's in his own cubicle on the opposite side of the room."

More crime, more work for me. I wonder if more Feds are surveilling the streets since the possibility of war is looming. "Isn't that a bit inconvenient?"

"Kinda, but I can phone him on an interoffice extension. Then I don't have to stare at his ugly face when up to my neck in paperwork. He's also a bit of a slob, and I insist on everything being tidy. Tell me, what's buggin' ya now?"

That should be obvious. "Did your team find out anything more about the pie or the pheasant under glass?"

"Too soon to tell."

"Did you have time to do background checks on the restaurant's personnel?" Guy asked.

"Been shorthanded without my regular partner. The temp they assigned me…he's not quite up to speed. What I know, so far, is the restaurant has had a lot of turnovers. They've also dealt with short-termers to fill in the stopgap."

"Any leads on who might've been behind the birding at Warner Brothers?"

"Our precinct was at the mercy of the Burbank Police Department. Investigations always slow down when people got to pass the baton."

Guy made note of it in his steno pad: could be anyone from a disgraced workhorse denied a promotion to a nameless entity from the rank-and-file, someone who would use any means to one-up Jack Warner. *Good luck trying to figure out who and how many he's fired.*

"You should've come up with a conclusion about Birdie Wilson by now."

Frustrated, Moe rummaged through some of his files to no avail. "Left the papers in Allgood's pigsty. Follow me."

They stopped at a cubbyhole with a desk buried under unopened mail and memoranda. Sadowski wrinkled his nose and groaned. He plucked the remains of a leftover lunch, now decomposed, and tossed it in the trash.

"I feel kinda sorry for you," he said while rummaging through the mess. "As long as the two of you are involved in this case, my partner's always going to have a bad taste in his mouth."

"How come?"

"You shouldn't accuse him of being a bad cop, but before he worked with me, he'd been screwed by some shady PI. Can't remember exactly what the shithead did, but he stole evidence. The damned dick got all the credit when Felix felt he deserved the praise. Even worse, it turned out this jerk had been his best friend from grade school, who got drafted in the Great War, and they had lost track of each other all these years. Not that it justifies rude behavior, but you know what I mean."

Sadowski disposed of a few solicitations and old racing forms, which had accumulated since Felix's leave in Frisco, and finally lucked into the initial report on Birdie Wilson. He took it out of its interoffice envelope, skimmed through it, slipped it back in, and refastened its folder. Then he looked at Guy and said, "Also poisoned."

"What kind?"

"What's it to you?"

"Depending upon what it is, it might offer some insight. Do you mind if I take a look?" Guy asked.

"Yes, I do. It's privileged information. Classified as an open homicide case and why it's still in our department. Don't waste your time trying to do a background check. What I can tell you is his last name wasn't Wilson."

"It's not?"

"We dug up his birth records. He seems to come from one of those many Jewish immigrant families who've changed their name to fit in and assimilate to avoid religious prejudice. His family's name was Wasser. I'll let you chew on that. Otherwise, that's all you need to know."

Guy protested. "Come on, throw me a bone. That's not enough information for me to go on, and you know it."

Sadowski stood firm. He blocked Guy from reaching around him and shook his head. "No can do. Don't want any outsiders making hash out of it."

"With Birdie... What if it was an accident?"

"What makes you say that?"

"I've met the man before."

"How?"

"From a previous assignment." A white lie, but nothing he could get in trouble for.

"Anything you care to tell me?"

"Client confidentiality privilege," Guy uttered. "Wouldn't do you any good anyway. Not related whatsoever."

"What if I requisition your records?"

Can he do that? "All I can say is this: when I met Birdie Wilson or Wasser or whatever you want to call him, he gave me a brief demonstration of how he prepares a dead animal for taxidermy. He warned my partner and I to stay clear and watch from a safe distance. Both he and Pinky, whom you still haven't given me much to chew on, were poisoned. In Pinky's case, she didn't seem to have good cause to be around such substances. Wilson, however, used toxic chemicals on a regular basis. There's always a possibility the poisoning was because of slow and prolonged accumulation, like what happened to the Mad Hatter in *Alice in Wonderland.*"

"Sounds like you've been reading too many books, smarty-pants."

"The public library is my second home on my days off, but that's beside the point." Guy didn't want to admit he was new to the sleuthing biz and there was a lot to learn, but weren't cops supposed to learn stuff like this during their basic training? Maybe not.

Detective Moe continued to fish through Allgood's stockpile. He discovered what looked like a sweepstakes ticket and thrust it into his pocket, but in the process, he knocked two four-by-six-inch picture frames onto the floor. While Moe braced against the stacks of papers to prevent an avalanche, Guy bent down to pick them up. "What's this?" he asked, examining what looked like typical family photographs.

"Felix Allgood with his wife and kids. He's got three of them brats. Glad mine are grown."

Guy got to thinking. Allgood had accompanied Babs to Frisco to help her mom, but he hoped their association hadn't gone any further. What if it did? Her ex-husband hurt her so bad already, and she was the kind of lady who would never start a relationship with a wedded man. *How do I tell her?* The police were notorious for baiting PIs at any given chance. Sadowski just admitted it. Was Allgood playing on her emotions only to take her down?

Moe gathered Allgood's mementos and placed them on the seat of his chair. "That's all, folks!" he said and accompanied Guy back to the front reception area.

Once Sadowski was out of range, Guy leaned over toward the front desk manager. He put his finger to his lips and whispered, "*Shush!* Don't announce it to the entire precinct. Have you pulled my requisition yet?"

The man handed him a pass. "Follow this hallway to your left. Turn right at the end. In Room 29. Stuff's waitin'."

He perched his hat lower on his crown. Not much of a disguise, but he hoped he wouldn't get recognized if he ran into Moe again.

"We're not used to receiving visitors, especially in the middle of office renovations," said a clerk behind a wire cage who handed him a stack of files. "Guess you can avail yourself of one of the interrogation rooms. Just make sure you find something to use as a doorstop to prop it open, 'cause the door locks behind you, and I don't carry the correct keys to let you out."

Great! Just what I need—to be treated like a prisoner. Guy found a vacant room. Despite his fear of someone's revenge, he tried to make himself comfortable. Tackling Birdie's file first, much of it was a work-in-progress. The medical examiner and his staff hadn't signed off yet on a final report. They, however, had plenty of time to analyze Lana "Pinky" Pilchik. Except for getting beyond the medical and scientific notations, Pinky had been poisoned. Guy searched his memory. He could remember some of the chemical compounds Birdie had mentioned, but not all. Other than that, Pinky had one minor arrest for the possession of marijuana with no additional notes she might've attempted to sell it.

Didn't Babs mention that Pinky's coworkers said she was always juggling some sort of side business? Guy shoved his hat even lower on his forehead. Between the light fixture's overhead glare and his mounting frustration, it must've affected his memory. He constantly glanced toward the door he propped open with the wastepaper basket to make sure no one pulled a practical joke.

At the bottom of his stack: files on Dr. John "Swifty" Herren, Jr. and Charles "Chickie" Crane. The doctor had filed a report on a patient who refused to make good on past-due bills. Otherwise, he seemed to be in the clear. Chickie, on the other hand, had once been arrested for loitering. He claimed he was chasing after one of his birds, which escaped. They dismissed the charge.

Chapter Twenty-Two: Sleepless in San Luis Obispo

The two weary travelers overslept and missed breakfast.

"Where else can we go?" Babs asked the desk clerk's wife as she cleared her dishes.

"There's a diner on a side street near the train station. Prices are reasonable. The food...I guess it's edible."

"What time is checkout?" asked Allgood.

"You missed that window, too, but we won't charge you."

Allgood felt a bit of relief. "Do you mind if we leave our luggage while getting something to eat and figuring out when the next train leaves?"

"Sure thing." The woman nodded with a warning. "Take heed to read the timetables. Not all trains that pass through go from Los Angeles or San Francisco. Some branch off and head into the desert."

"Thanks, we'll make note of it." He turned to Babs. "Hungry?"

"Then, as soon as we're done, we need to call my mom. She's expecting our arrival and will worry herself into the grave if she doesn't hear from us," said Babs.

* * *

With only a daily chalkboard instead of menus, Babs and Felix ordered the "Breakfast Rush" of bacon, eggs, toast, and coffee, except it didn't appear like anyone could be in a hurry in such a sluggish city.

"Even after several arrests, I can't believe your ex-husband still won't give up," said Allgood, in between sips of coffee. "Didn't you change your name, on purpose, so he couldn't find you?"

"Didn't disguise it well enough, I guess, by keeping Norman as my last name," said Babs. "Mom couldn't take his threats anymore and gave him our office number the first time he tracked me down in LA."

"Don't blame everything on her. Your ex could've checked her outgoing mail and found your address. All it would take would be a call to an operator to get your phone number."

"Guess I never thought the private investigation business would get dangerous enough to require unlisted numbers."

Allgood shouted to the diner's proprietor, "Hey, buddy, ya got any train schedules over here? I'll take a postcard while you're at it." He snickered after the last statement and whispered across the table to Babs, "Heh, heh... Don't think this place gets many tourists. You think?"

Their chef-plus-everything-else didn't quite get the postcard joke, but he said they'd have to pick up their schedules at the depot like everyone else. "Hard as heck to interpret," he warned them. "Takes me three times to figger dem out. Hate fine print." He placed their plates on the counter, and they remained there until Allgood realized there wasn't a waitress and decided it was their job to take them to their table.

"All this worry had me work up an appetite," he said, digging into his eggs. When he noticed she just sat there staring at them, he asked, "What's wrong? They won't cluck back at ya."

"Almost too tired to eat," she said, reaching for her fork. She looked at her wristwatch and noticed it had wound down. "What time do you have?"

"Almost one, why?"

She reset hers and commented, "Might as well consider this lunch."

Three-quarters through their meal, Allgood asked, "Hey, I'm still waitin' to hear the story of why you became a gumshoe. You've sure done a good job of skirting around the answer."

"I got fed up with being an actress." Babs added an extra dollop of strawberry jam onto her toast. "Callbacks turned into auditioning for dates and how well I'd rehearse in the bedroom. If you're too pretty, that's how producers and directors viewed you…or how they perceived me."

"There are actresses like Marie Dressler who became successful in their careers."

"Correct, but if you're not beautiful enough, they expected you to do comedy—"

"Babs, you're pretty funny."

"Thanks a lot!" She patted her lips with a napkin, leaving a crimson lipstick print. "You mean you've never taken me seriously?"

"Sweetheart, I didn't mean it that way. Please continue."

"In most cases, humor will get you so far." She started to sniffle, and her eyes began to glaze over with tears. "My interest in being a private detective…started with Daddy's murder. Like most during the Depression, he took whatever odd job he could find. Guess I was about nine or ten. Maybe eight. I try my best to forget. Mom had to clean houses and do laundry. He sold used cars. No one had any money, but cars still broke down, and it was more likely for most to purchase a used rather than a new one. Do we really have to talk about this now?"

"Give it to me straight, miss," he said. He flashed his badge, if only in jest.

"If you insist. On a Saturday when I wasn't in school, Daddy took me to work, since he couldn't afford a sitter and didn't feel it was safe to leave me alone. He asked me to bring my favorite doll so I could occupy myself and stay out of trouble. You know how bored kids can get.

"Well, anyway, he showed one of his cars to a customer. I sat in the driver's seat of another nearby with the door ajar. When Daddy finished his sales pitch, his customer pulled out a gun, grabbed the car keys out of his hand, and shot him. He intended to steal the car, but I swung my door all the way open and knocked him down. His head hit hard on the concrete. While stunned, I kicked him in the face. I swatted his hand so hard with my dolly that he lost his grip on his gun, and it slid too far away for him to get it without effort. I picked up his loaded gun and ran screaming into the dealership's office. The manager called for the cops and an ambulance. By the time they arrived, the man had already gotten up and run off the lot, and it was too late to save Daddy."

"I'm so sorry." Allgood reached out and clasped Babs' hand. His sympathy appeared genuine. "Your instincts told you what to do, but you were so young, and—"

"It shouldn't have happened. I described the crook the best I could to the police, but it still wasn't fair. Daddy was dead, and this jerk got away scot-free."

"How did your mother take it?"

"Not well, as could be expected. She had to support me all by herself."

"No help from relatives nearby?"

"Who had extra money to spare? Mom expected me to chip in, which meant making useful household items like potholders and throw rugs from rag pickings and setting up a roadside lemonade stand using the lemons that grew on our backyard trees. Anything that didn't cost much to procure but could turn a profit."

"Did you have to quit school?"

"No, I managed to finish my education, but it irked me how I stuck my neck out and told the police everything I knew, and I still couldn't save my father. Even worse, they refused to believe my testimony, only because I was so young, and because I was a girl!"

"But you didn't decide to become a private investigator right away. You went into showbiz, right?"

Babs nodded. "Troy Ulsterman and his partner, Douggie Bendel, did radio shows back in San Francisco, my first foray into entertainment. They ran a classified ad in the local paper saying they needed a female to complete their singing trio, and I nailed the audition."

"You're a songbird?"

"Used to be, but now I'll be lucky not to wind up as a dead bird like the ones we've been finding."

"Bet your mom pressured you to get married when she noticed he took a liking toward you, right?"

"She knew what it was like struggling on her own and wanted to see better for her daughter. He was cute...and a great dancer. I just had no idea he

179

was downright demented. Anyways, I had a short-lived singing career in the Bay area. As I was saying before, once I relocated to Los Angeles, all everyone wanted to do was to get under my skirt. Wondered half the time if any of my auditions were legit. Then I met Guy Brandt, one of the few men who didn't harass me at an audition, and who was having his own issues making headway with his acting."

"'Cause he's a queer, right?"

"I wish you wouldn't call him that. Like most others who got ostracized, he did his best to keep it under wraps, but attitudes like that didn't help. We did what was necessary, and eventually got our private investigator's licenses."

"Quicker and easier than becoming legitimate cops?"

Babs drew her eyebrows together. "We liked our independence and never wanted to become cops."

* * *

After breakfast, they tried calling Mrs. Norman from a public payphone, but no one answered.

"Can't understand why she didn't pick up. Wasn't she expecting us?" he asked.

"Knowing her," Babs said. "She panicked and went to the police station."

"Let me call your local precinct."

"Might just complicate things. If she went there to file a report, I'm sure she's already left. Better to get those train schedules and try again later."

On the way to the station, both detectives saw one of the locals trot down the street on horseback. Out of ignorance, Allgood blurted out, "Looks like that animal has got some kind of disease with all those brown and white splotches."

"It's an American Paint," Babs said, correcting him. She rushed up to it as its rider slowed to a stop. When asked, the old homesteader gave her permission to pet her.

"Her name is Scheckey. My wife named her after the German word *schecke*

180

for a dappled or piebald horse. Got an apple in my saddlebag if ya want to feed it to her."

Babs clapped her hands with zeal. The horse made a loose, lazy swish with her tail, lowered her jaw, and softly curled her lips, mirroring Babs' enthusiasm.

"Do you ride, missy?" the man asked. "You made her happy. Guess she wants to return the favor."

"It's been years. When my father was still alive, throughout the summer, we'd go camping on weekends. He sure loved to go fishing. Sometimes, we'd go on hayrides. When I got older, he'd let me ride the trails. Always wanted to own a horse but couldn't back home in the city."

"Where was that?" the farmer asked.

"San Francisco."

"Maybe in the old mining days you could…in the heyday of the Gold Rush, but you don't look old enough to be born way back then. Wanna ride her?"

Allgood cut in. "Looks like people gave up riding their nags around here a while ago. Don't see any horse troughs or hitching posts like you see in those Wild Western films. Aren't you worried about dodging the cars?"

"We just finished our local *La Fiesta de la Flores* Parade. Had one every year since 1925 to celebrate the founding of the Old Mission Parish, which caused the town of San Luis Obispo to flourish. With a possible war on the horizon, we're not sure how long we'll be able to continue.

"People dress in all sorts of costumes from Mexican cowboys to ancient Mayans and ones where they dress as animals or let's pretend ones, which make the wearer look like they are riding a horse or a bull. Farmers show off their farm equipment, often pulled by a team of horses. Skilled equestrians perform trick riding stunts. Others ride because they don't feel like walking on foot, and the brave cowboys ride bulls. We also got marching bands, majorettes, and ornate floats, which seem to get fancier every year.

"Scheckey's trailer is hitched to my pickup. I just took her out for a little exercise. If you wanna go riding, you'll have to hop in my truck. We'll drive over to my ranch."

"She's a lot larger than what I'm used to." Babs stopped, examined her skirt and her flats, and realized she was wearing all the wrong attire. "Don't think I'll pass too well for a cowgirl."

"Nonsense. How 'bout I give you a boost, and you can ride sidesaddle?"

"I wouldn't know what to do if I couldn't wear boots and put them into the stirrups."

"What if you sit behind me? Scheckey can handle it. Won't be running any races with that getup. I'll just strap on an extra blanket."

"What about your stockings?" Felix asked.

"For this? I'll replace them."

"It's not like there aren't opportunities near Los Angeles, Babs. There's gotta be some place to rent a horse near Griffith Park."

Babs gave Allgood the puppy-eyes. She wasn't going to leave town without taking advantage of this offer.

"You sure have a soft spot for your four-legged friends," Felix muttered.

"What's wrong with lovin' God's critters?" the farmhand asked. "They just might come to your rescue one day when you least expect it."

"Make it snappy," said Allgood. "After all, we're not on vacation."

*** * ***

The two hopped into the farmer's truck. This gave her an opportunity to take in some of the local scenery. Their horseback ride took much longer than anticipated. At one point, Babs didn't hold on tight enough. She lost her grip and slid off.

"Are you hurt?" the farmer asked.

Still smiling, she dusted herself off. "Will definitely need a bath once I get settled."

By the time they returned, Felix was pacing back and forth.

"He took me to an old Spanish mission. There was an amazing church, which must've been at least two hundred years old, built by monks and settlers. Love that kind of architecture. Scheckey got hungry. We had to feed and water her, and—"

"We have a train to catch, or were you having such a good time you forgot?"

The man helped her down. Babs kissed Scheckey on the nose, gave her one last stroke, and thanked her tour guide for his generosity.

Felix clamped on to her hand to make sure she wouldn't get distracted by anything else and dragged her over to the depot.

"You need to purchase any late-night train tickets ahead of time," the station sales clerk warned them. "The ticket window closes after 8 p.m."

Despite each other's counsel, both read the weekday rather than the weekend schedule and didn't realize that the train they purchased tickets for would leave them in Barstow. They finally got a hold of her mother and explained they'd gotten detained and had to seek out expedient lodging.

* * *

After all the unforeseen and embarrassing delays, they finally made it back to Union Station in Los Angeles. Allgood drove her back to Hollywood. Not to rouse suspicion, he parked his car a few doors down from her house and killed the engine.

"Leave your bags. You're coming with me, and we're using the back entrance." Once he knew she was safe, he'd go back to fetch them. He also instructed her to take off her shoes and stockings so as not to leave telltale footprints. "Did your boarder call the police?"

"You know how most people think of the Japanese these days. Everyone's afraid they're going to drag us into a war."

"Them…along with the Krauts. Is he legal? Does he have all his immigration papers in order?"

Now was time to summon up her acting chops and put on a mask of fear. "I don't know."

"Honey, you could be aiding and abetting a spy at your house and not even knowing it. Have you ever noticed any radio transmitters he's hidden among his effects? Ever get a surprise visit from the FBI?"

Babs felt her bile churn. *Did he look at my arrest files or not? Then again, maybe the FBI didn't always reciprocate their information with the local police.* "Not regarding Mr. Otake. The only strange stuff I see of his are some of his exotic gardening tools he brought from Japan. He's got these steel instruments. They look like hammers and sickles—" She put her hand to her mouth and realized she'd used the wrong choice of words.

"Then he is a Commie."

"No. That came out wrong. The only red book I've seen of his has Buddhist prayers in it."

"How do you know it wasn't a Japanese translation of Karl Marx's *Communist Manifesto*, or a code book to intercept U.S. Naval signals? Can you read Japanese?"

"Don't be ridiculous. Otake-san is the sort of guy who'd find a spider indoors and deposit it outside in the garden before I got scared and stomped on it."

"Next, you're gonna tell me that giant Wolfhound can sniff out a Commie and gave you the clear signal on Mr. Sukiyaki," he scoffed.

"It's Otake...and no!" Babs felt her blood rise to her face. "*Ooooh!* You can be such a boor when you want to!"

They approached the house, cutting through several neighbors' backyards, causing a dog to bark. As they got closer, Babs pointed out her kitchen light was on and suspected either Mr. Otake was home, or he left it on to mislead Troy.

On the windless night, a sudden rustling cut them short. Allgood crouched low and put his finger to his lips. Then he cupped his hand to his ear. He gestured for her to stay close. "We better quit yakking. If that's our man, he's liable to hear us—"

They heard sounds of movement a second time.

"What should I say if it is Troy, and he confronts me?"

"Tell your ex you've got a boyfriend already, and he's a cop!"

Unable to put her entire trust in somebody else, when Felix drew his concealed pistol, Babs fished her firearm out of her purse.

His eyebrows arched. "It had better be legal."

"Of course, it's registered, but I don't walk around with the paperwork." Another light turned on inside the house. "He woke up my tenant."

Allgood insisted they change their plans. Blending in with the trees and shrubbery, they circled around toward the front. Someone, probably Troy, had smashed and broken her porchlight. Taking care not to step in the shattered glass, he also seemed to be picking the lock of her front door using a makeshift toolkit.

"Put that gun away and approach as if you know nothing," Allgood instructed.

"You're making me a decoy?"

He took a flashlight and a pair of handcuffs out of his glove compartment. "I've got you covered."

She put her shoes back on and readied her keys in her shaky hand, swearing she'd pretend everything was normal. To avoid making too much of a racket, she approached on the grass until the very end when her shoes made impact on a stepping stone to rouse his attention.

"Hey!" she confronted Troy and raised her purse to strike, if necessary.

He grabbed her so fast that her purse flew from her grasp. When it hit the ground, its clasp opened, and her pistol tumbled out. Troy nosedived straight for it. Then he sprang to his feet and pulled her by the fabric of her jacket, holding her at gunpoint. Babs gave him a swift kick in the shins, which hardly fazed him. She tried to fight him off. Her aim was to get inside, lock the door, and let Allgood handle the rest.

Troy grabbed her by her hair and dragged her away from the house and toward his car. Not wanting to reveal their covert plans, she cried out for Otake-san instead of Allgood. When he failed to show, she finally yelled, "Help! Police!"

On that cue, Allgood blinded Troy by shining a flashlight in his face. "Okay, you big lout. Hands up. Your fists aren't going to get you out of this mess this time."

Chapter Twenty-Three: On Familiar Turf

When she finally made it back to the office, Babs continued to needle Guy about the black eye he had before she left town. She wanted to know if he had been beaten and bullied because of his sexuality. He blamed it on the dogs. To avoid further questions, he skirted the topic and briefed her on the events at the Cajun restaurant and how Sadowski still held back important facts from the autopsy reports. Although he hadn't yet found any conclusive evidence, at least he relieved her of some of the worry; he hadn't ignored Birdie's account records.

Babs wanted to get on with business as if nothing unusual had happened regarding Troy, her mother, or Allgood, keeping any answers to his questions short and to the point. What was the status between her and the homicide detective? Guy knew her too well. If he had led her on, she'd be outraged. Did she know he was married? He wasn't sure how to break the news.

Bogie dropped by unannounced. Had someone else gotten birded? Calm as a clam, he lit his cigarette and said all he wanted to do was to welcome her home.

"You missed the din of our din-din," he said with a half-smile, waiting a beat for her reaction. "Fate paired me with two of my fellow actors after Jack's brother was the guest of honor at a party hosted by a polo player, but I was so drunk I can't recall much of it. Peter had to spoon-feed me information he had gleaned from other sources and only because he made a few calls and asked around. Harry Warner seemed to be concerned about war sentiments, both pro and con. Tell me if I'm wrong, but I get the impression you should question Lorre a bit more. Maybe Harry Warner, too, and the young guy he dragged along who kept quiet the whole time."

Guy stepped in and explained that although he hadn't been present when they first discovered the pheasant under glass, he witnessed the second birding *du jour* at dessert.

Piecemeal information came to Babs from all directions and often out of order. "Hold on, gentlemen," she said, holding up her hand. "One thing at a time. Bogie, you mentioned something about a young man you didn't know who stuck close to Harry Warner, correct?"

Bogie nodded. "I think he had a connection with an organization that needed funding. For what? I can't tell you."

"No formal introductions?"

"If they did, I was too blotto to care."

"Would your wife have any idea?"

"No, I'm the one who received the invitation. She accompanied me but snatched the car after we got into a spat. That's how I wound up sleeping it off at Lorre's."

She looked at Guy. "Your assignment today is to call and find out who the polo player was who hosted that party, and what organization he backed. Got it?"

"Any ideas?" Bogie asked.

She gave it a moment. "The head of that *charity* could've been Leon Lewis. He runs an underground network of spies and whistleblowers on the types of hoodlums we busted during our Asta-Rathbone case. For safety's sake, he keeps a low profile. Howard Strickling, the chief publicist over at MGM, quietly introduced us when he made a brief appearance at the party in honor of us returning all the missing celebrity dogs."

"That's where I first met you because you found my Newfie, Cappy, and Pard, the scruffy terrier who costarred with me in *High Sierra*," said Bogie. "Outside of the catering staff, I'm surprised I didn't notice anyone from outside the business."

"Confidentiality is vital to the success of his operation. Lewis didn't want any fanfare and shied away from public introductions. The studio moguls support him one hundred percent. Nearly every one of them comes from a Jewish background. With the war threatening those in Europe, many people who support American isolationism have been quick to hop on the bandwagon to blame our people over here for any ridiculous thorn they have in their sides. He's wanted to ferret out these rabble-rousers and set the record straight while protecting the innocent. If that was him, Guy and I should try to pay him a visit, contingent on if we can locate him."

Babs reached for her memo pad. "How come you're not at the studio?" she asked.

Quick to comment, Bogie explained, "We wrapped production on the evening of July 18th. Considering what we've gone through in the past few weeks, I felt the urge to let loose at the party, even if I did go overboard."

"Then I guess you didn't experience any more delays or threats."

"Not sure if you want to count what happened at the restaurant."

Babs rubbed her chin. "Tends to make me think the killer had some other motivation and didn't care whether your film got finished or not."

"That doesn't mean the danger has gone away," said Bogart. "Several people have died, and no one's been caught."

"Correct," said Guy. "Let's hope that'll help narrow down the possibilities."

Bogie noticed the time on Guy's Felix the Cat wall clock and said he had to go. Stu had other designs. He flew across the room and perched on his shoulder.

"You sure we can't convince you to take the bird?" Guy asked.

Bogie shook his head and demanded that Guy put him back in his cage so the bird wouldn't follow him out the door.

* * *

"How do we track down Lewis if, by nature of his mission, he doesn't want to be found?" asked Guy.

"Since we haven't established a relationship with Harry Warner, why don't you phone his brother?"

Guy got hopping on his new assignment and spoke with Jack's executive assistant, Bill Schaeffer, to find out when was the best time to pin down his boss. "Given the recent course of events, do you recall Jack or any of his brothers being involved with any particular anti-war organizations?"

"Around three years ago, Harry had a gathering in his Santa Monica home with Warner Brothers production executive Hal Wallis. He brought in people from MGM like Al Lichtman, Harry Rapf, and Jerry Wald. He invited heavies like David O. Selznick, a distribution guy, Sam Katz, director Mervyn LeRoy, and actor Paul Muni—"

"Why Muni?"

"He's Jewish. Wallis, too. His birth name was Aaron Blum Wolowicz. Like many others, including the Warner Brothers, Muni came from the Ukraine, anglicized his name, and got his start in Yiddish theater. As I was saying, Sam gathered his industry colleagues but not for a fundraiser. Just a discourse about a book written by a World War I veteran, Morris S. Lazaron, titled *Common Ground: A Plea for Intelligent Americanism*. In his opinion, prejudice was, 'not just a Jewish problem. Jews, Catholics, and Protestants were all Americans.' If we brought over notions of intolerance from Europe, then we are 'lifting a banner other than the stars and stripes.'

"A few months later, Harry Warner addressed Daniel Doherty, the National Commander of the American Legion with a hundred or more members, and Frank Merriam, Governor of California. Jack served as the toastmaster. Leon Lewis was also present. This was all before *Kristallnacht* caused such tragic devastation to the lives of Jews and their businesses in Germany. Lewis provided intelligence to the studio heads who financed his operation. At the same time, Harry had his studio produce a series of short patriotic films. To spread the word, he encouraged journalists and teachers to be aware of them."

"That's a lot to digest," Guy said. He explained that if he and Babs could get access to Lewis, it might shed light on their case. "Someone has already birded Jack Warner, and two people are dead. Please share Lewis' contact information, if you have it."

* * *

This was not a time to come off as a fashion hound. Babs advised they both go home and change into more nondescript attire so as not to draw attention. For her, she'd find a cotton housedress, something she'd use for yard work and would've never worn to the office. For Guy, she suggested work clothes he'd wear to wash his car.

Guy noted the address and proposed they drive Babs' Crosley instead of his jazzy automobile. "Don't want anyone getting any bright ideas about stealing my tires...or my car, for that matter."

Lewis, himself, was a tall, handsome man over six feet in height. Babs whispered to Guy, "He has a certain look in his eyes and elongated face that reminds me of a younger George Gershwin, the famous composer, or he could've easily been mistaken for a film studio executive."

"You'd never suspect people have called me 'the most dangerous Jew in Los Angeles,'" Lewis said. "By trade, I have a legal practice that has suffered a significant decline since I've spent so much of my time and energy fighting societal injustice."

He apologized for having them meet in the slums and ordered them coffee. "Couldn't risk one of my enemies following you to my office. Despite appearances, the food is decent at this diner."

"How long have you been on your..." Babs didn't want to use the word "quest." That sounded too much like he was Robin Hood. He was no swashbuckler, robbing the rich and giving alms to the poor, and not in the same league as Errol Flynn. Instead, she chose her words with care and used "crusade."

"Nazi sympathizers tend to be two different types," said Lewis. "The first kind are the ones who believe there is strength in numbers. They identify and align with a particular organization, become dues-paying members, swear oaths of secrecy, and aren't afraid of wearing uniforms in public. Long before the United States had issues with those Hitler acolytes, there were hate-mongering confederacies such as the Klan."

Guy shuddered. "Are they the most dangerous?"

"Not always. The others are the independent ones, the lone wolves. They might not own the extensive arsenal, or have the advantage of financial

190

backing from a large group, but they can be loose cannons. Sometimes, these renegades have become threats to the larger organizations, even though they share similar ideologies. They even could've been former members and had gotten thrown out for being either too extreme, or they could've become involved in political in-fighting, such as being bitter because someone passed them over for a promotion. You never know."

"How long have you kept tabs on these dissident groups?" Babs asked.

"Since '33, when Hindenburg appointed Hitler as Chancellor of Germany, and I'll refuse to stop until these firebrands are eliminated, unless they get to me first."

"Let's hope that doesn't happen," said Guy.

"Have either of you been to Europe?" Lewis asked.

The detectives shook their heads.

"It's rapidly changing and not for the better, like someone is turning back the clock of progress to the ruthless times of Genghis Khan. Maybe that's an exaggeration, but you get my point, and don't be so sure the same nightmare can't happen here. The entire world felt the impact of the Great Depression. In the United States, like their fascist counterparts in Germany and Italy, Nazis blamed their economic plight on the Jews. Even the world-famous aviator Charles Lindbergh or "Lucky Lindy," whom many have considered an American hero, has supported The America First Committee, which has voiced controversial opinions against Britain, The FDR Administration, and has blamed the media and motion picture studios 'who are run by Jews.' They and similar fascist supporters have pressured President Roosevelt against his 'Jew Deal' and petitioned him to remove all Jews from public office.

"In my opinion, I think your perpetrator falls into the latter category, the one who acts alone," Lewis explained. "He or she moves undetected. People like this often work undercover within a large organization. Don't discount the notion that it could be an establishment, which isn't obvious, because it might have nothing to do with politics. In other words, they can remain anonymous and use that to their advantage."

"Do you think it's an organization you're aware of?" asked Babs.

"I do, and it's been right under your noses the entire time."

"Leon, you've got us holding our breath. Who or what?"

"Warner Brothers."

"Not Jack or Harry."

"That's doubtful, especially since Jack has already been targeted. My assessment? I think it's someone on staff who is frequently on the studio lot, privy to conversations but low enough in the rank and file whom you'd never suspect."

Babs tested her memory. "I get the impression both Jack's receptionist and executive assistant seemed trustworthy. Then again, it could be his barber...a tennis partner. Surely, there are a whole bunch of disgruntled writers in his circle. Who else?"

"I didn't get too far tailing Jack's bodyguard," Guy said. "He beat the living daylights out of me in a boxing match."

Babs put him on the spot. "So that explains the bruises you blamed on Bruno and Sir Henry. Shame on you!"

Lewis addressed both. "Put on your thinking hats to see who else might fit that description. I hope that helps, but for now, I have deadlines and will have to see you out."

Chapter Twenty-Four: The Man Who Turned It Down

With *The Maltese Falcon* in the can, it was now in the editors' hands who were trying to ready it for an early October release. After Leon Lewis disclosed his theory that their culprit had to be someone hiding in plain sight, most likely on the Warner Brothers lot, the private detectives needed another excuse to pay a visit. Mr. Moneybags, Jack Warner, had withdrawn his fiscal contribution toward the detectives' fees, but at least he didn't rescind their parking privileges. Bogie pressed the actors and director to pull together their resources to keep his PIs on the investigation.

Meanwhile, everyone looked forward to their next projects. Even before *The Falcon* wrapped in mid-July, Sydney Greenstreet had started work on an Errol Flynn war flick about the Alamo called *They Died with Their Boots On*. Elisha Cook, Jr. bounced between two pictures for two different studios: *I Wake Up Screaming* for Twentieth Century Fox and *Hellzapoppin'* with Mayfair Productions for Universal Studios. He had yet to get birded, but the detectives wanted to assume he'd be too preoccupied to mastermind a birding crime.

Still under contract with Warner Brothers, Bogie barely had time for a good night's sleep before he jumped into *All Through the Night*, directed by Vincent Sherman, who cast him as Broadway gambler "Gloves" Donahue. Peter Lorre also had a small part in the film and admitted he had nonstop work lined up afterward. The only people who seemed to get a breather were

193

Mary Astor and John Huston. She would be on a loan-out to Paramount in late fall for *The Palm Beach Story*, and Warner's had slated Huston to direct *In This Our Life*, a drama starring Bette Davis, in October.

* * *

Guy's next mission was to track down Paul Muni and George Raft, the others who had turned down the part of Sam Spade.

After making calls to both the studios and the news desks, they discovered Paul Muni's last film for Warner's *We Are Not Alone*, a tale set in WWII, had been released in '39. Twentieth Century Fox had produced *Hudson's Bay*. Released in January '41, it provided evidence that he had already jumped ship and with little chance he'd be wandering around Warner Brothers.

George Raft seemed a stronger prospect. Released in July last year, he costarred with Ida Lupino and Humphrey Bogart in the acclaimed film *They Drive By Night*, thus sharing a bit of history with their main client and one lukewarm suspect, whom they never had the chance to query at length. This year, from March through May, he filmed *Manpower*, which came out in theaters on August 9th.

"Wasn't this another one of those films where art imitated life with both men after the same dame? I think I remember reading that in *Variety*." Guy lifted his foot, which Bruno had used as a pillow. With care, he swiveled his leg to reposition the sleepy bulldog. Once free of the canine sandbag, he went over to one of his file cabinets near his desk, which was one of those off-limits areas where Babs always had to ask permission, before taking a look.

"I read somewhere they fought over acting styles and creative differences," she said. "Robinson had trained in method acting. Raft was a streetwise kid with good looks who caught the eye of producers. When it came to acting, often he improvised and played himself."

After she touted her know-how, Guy pulled out a folder, retrieved a few clippings, and read, "*Manpower* is a story about two blue-collar workers fighting over one woman. In real life, Edward G. Robinson, who played the role of Hank 'Gimpy' McHenry, and Raft, cast as Johnny Marshall, feuded over Marlene Dietrich's affections. She played Fay Duval, a former prostitute who marries McHenry. Raoul Walsh directed the film."

Stu also seemed to have an interest in Guy's clipping files. He made a nosedive for an open manila folder. Using his beak, he stole a short article on Raft and returned it to his cage to add to his collection. It happened so fast, neither detective could've outrun him.

"I wish you didn't leave his cage door open," griped Guy.

Babs tried to stick her hand inside his cage, but every time she tried to retrieve it, Stu would stab her with his pointy beak. "*Ouch!* If I close it, he'll jibber-jabber nonstop and drive me nuts."

"Sounds like he tries to mimic you and how you drive me mad. You know, they learn to talk by listening to the people they're around the most."

"This bird knew how to curse and swear longer than he knew me. Didn't Wiggins say he won him in a bet at an Irish bar, and the loser had already run out of cash? *Ow!* Stop poking holes in me, you stupid bag of feathers!"

"Leave him be. Two paragraphs? It was a tiny scrap of paper. At least we don't have to deal with Bill or Pokey the Pelican now since Chief Crow-Feather took him off our hands."

Babs extracted her hand from Stu's cage, inspected the mark he made, and rubbed it, hoping the prickling would go away. "Maybe this would be more along the lines of the gossip columns, but I wonder if you also have an article about when the gangster, Bugsy Siegel, visited his friend George on the set. There's a scene when he leaves a gin joint. Raft hands Virginia Hill, playing a hat-check girl, the remains of a chair he destroyed during a bar fight. Afterward, George introduced Hill to Siegel. It didn't take long for the two of them to become lovebirds."

Guy scratched his head. "Seems like old Georgie boy gets into scuffles with everyone, including Warner."

* * *

A few calls later, a publicist on staff at Warner's suggested they could find Raft cleaning out his bungalow. He heard rumors that Raft would be moving over to Universal Pictures, but his agent could confirm whether it was true.

Bill Schaeffer, Jack's executive assistant, gave the PIs their own permanent parking passes. They hopped into Guy's car, to see if the publicist's tip checked out. While she distracted the gate security guard, Guy noticed Raft had signed in on his register. He found a parking spot, loosened his collar, and said, "Babs, I can really use a cup of coffee. Do you mind if we stop at the commissary first?" Her mouth watered for a plump, creamy éclair.

Always ones to look around to see if they spotted anyone famous, they noticed Peter Lorre, sitting by himself and wearing an overcoat a bit too heavy for the seasonal climate. He appeared lost in thought over a half-empty glass of milk and looked like he had a case of the blues.

"Mind if we join you?" Guy asked.

Babs put her hand on his shoulder. "Looks like you could use a little cheering up." She noticed he looked wan, perhaps suffering from overwork and poor health.

With three shaking fingers, Lorre signaled for a lunchroom server to bring coffee and extra cups and saucers for his friends. "What brings you here today on this gloomy, overcast afternoon?" he asked.

"Darn tootin'. It sure ain't sunny," Guy said in an overblown Midwestern country accent, trying to brighten Lorre's sullen mood.

Peter took a napkin to wipe his bulbous, watery eyes. Babs wondered if he hadn't been crying; maybe he was coming down with a bug. When their server returned with coffee, she asked if they had her favorite pastry.

"You're in luck. Today, we had a fresh delivery."

She rubbed her hands together like a child with eager anticipation. Guy gave the man a second glance and asked, "You look familiar. Aren't you the bicycle messenger I ran into the other day who gave me the skinny about Abdul Maljan?"

"You're mistaking me for someone else," he replied in a clipped monotone, then turned to Babs. "Miss, let me get your éclair." She noticed a peculiar stare between him and Peter.

"I swear that's him," Guy moaned. "Just that he's wearing one of those envelope-style kitchen worker's hats. His hair is combed forward, and he's not wearing sunglasses."

Babs noticed the veins tightening on Guy's neck as he curled his hand into a fist. "Are you talking to yourself again?"

"If he is the same person, I'd like to give him a piece of my mind for setting me up as Abdul's punching bag."

Lorre intercepted. "You're getting all worked up about nothing, and he's a nobody. I'm sure you came over here today for something far more important."

Babs mentioned they were trying to pin down George Raft.

"Who turned down the part of Sam Spade in *The Maltese Falcon*," Lorre replied. "Am I correct?"

"Have the two of you ever worked together?" asked Guy.

"The person you need to ask is Bogart. I only know of him by reputation or through mutual acquaintances."

"Yeah, we know. They were in *They Drive by Night* together."

Lorre added, "Also did *Invisible Stripes*, a picture where the two of them had their fateful first meeting in prison."

A different server returned with Babs' pastry.

Guy gave him a mean stare and was ready to kick himself. "Can't believe I failed to notice if our first server was wearing a German signet ring. It would've been his giveaway that he was the same guy, and he lied."

Peter changed the subject. "You're aware I have experience being a detective."

That came out of the clear blue, Babs thought. "How so?"

"Kentaro Moto, International Police, from my Mr. Moto films." He dampened his handkerchief by dipping it in an unused glass of water, slicked back his already pomaded hair, and fished a pair of phony spectacles out of his pocket, the lenses of which made his buggy eyes look even bigger.

He thrust his jaw forward to accentuate an overbite of his teeth, which already had gaps in front. "Can't really fake the wispy goatee unless I want to get my face dirty, but they call him the Oriental Sherlock," he said with a sly smile.

"Do you always walk around with a pair of prop glasses in your pocket?" Guy asked.

"Only when I think fans might stop me for autographs. I'd rather they recognize me as the master detective than one of the many villains I tend to play. Wouldn't you do the same?"

In his character's clipped dialogue, Peter explained that Mr. Moto always drank milk, never alcohol, but today he ordered it 'cause he had an upset stomach. "Please don't expect me to show you athletic moves in judo or jujutsu. For those scenes, I have a stunt double, despite being taught a trick or two. Otherwise, may I offer you my humble assistance? I'm easy to imitate. All you need are the soft-boiled-egg eyes and a bedroom voice."

To Babs, still in disbelief, the only "Hollywood Sherlock" was Basil Rathbone, her former celebrity client.

"If you'd give Mr. Moto a chance, maybe he could enlighten your case," Peter said.

Babs was skeptical. "How do you propose to do that?"

"Are you aware Raft and Muni did a picture together?" Peter exaggerated Moto's accent and overbite, keeping in character.

Guy scratched his head. "Did we overlook something?"

"I thought you two gumshoes went to the movies all the time. What about *Scarface*, back in the early thirties?"

"That came out during the thick of the Depression. Before my time in Hollywood, when I would've been sweeping my pop's floors in his general store. Back then, I would've saved my precious pennies to sneak off to matinees whenever possible, but I couldn't afford to see everything."

"All I'm saying is your two suspects had a bit of history together. Now...I can't vouch for how they felt about each other, because I wasn't there, but I read in the trades that Raft got to meet face-to-face with Big Al."

"Capone?" Guy asked.

Lorre nodded. "In *Scarface*, he played a fictionalized version of his bodyguard. The real mobster wanted final input even though Howard Hughes financed the film."

Guy looked genuinely surprised while Babs chewed her lip and gave their tag-along detective a scowl.

Lorre noticed and put her on the spot. "What's with the sour face?"

"On principle, I despise the idea of using white actors cast in roles made for Orientals. Same with Mexicans and American Indians. I thought it was criminal to make up Edward G. Robinson as a Chinese hitman in *Hatchet Man*, and don't even get me started about how I feel about blackface performers. Of course, it started in vaudeville long before silent pictures. Even May West performed in blackface when she started out, but I hate it.

"Not that my boarder wants to break into pictures, but if I were in charge of casting, I'd give a Japanese guy like him a paycheck—someone who really needs it." She apologized to Peter for ranting. "Nothing against you, sir. You were under contract and doing what you're told."

Guy gave her one of those "here she goes again" stares. "If you keep yapping your opinions, we'll never finish our agenda."

She elbowed him in the ribs.

Losing his patience, Peter stood and took her by the arm. He escorted her out of the commissary a few paces ahead of her partner. "Who do you think you are? Nick and Nora Charles?"

"You're not the first to accuse us of being like the *Thin Man* sleuths."

"If my memory's correct, there was a scene from their first film when Nora insists on joining her husband, but he's worried his meddlesome wife will be put in danger. So he tricks her and locks her in their closet. Maybe your smarter partner needs to devise a similar tactic."

"Are you insisting I keep my trap shut, or do I sense you want to join us?"

"If it's all right, I would like to accompany you," said Lorre. "George might feel less pressured if another actor were present rather than being badgered by two nosy private eyes who won't stop bickering. Regarding your opinions, to each his own."

Guy couldn't see why not. Bogie had assumed the role of Sam Spade in their real-life investigation; why not let Mr. Moto take over? Therefore, the three picked up their pace and headed over to what would soon be Raft's former bungalow.

* * *

Guy knocked. He put his ear to the door. "Sounds too quiet."

"Knock harder," Lorre suggested.

Guy tried the door handle and discovered it was open.

"Guess we arrived too late," said Babs, noticing the office had already been emptied.

"What next, boss?" Guy asked.

Peter offered his advice. "Call his publicist back. See where he likes to hang out. His favorite nightclub. He's still a handsome man about town. Betcha if he's not busy in films, he wants to see a little action or go to the track."

"Isn't he married?" she asked.

Guy thought she came off naïve and laughed. "Since when did that stop anyone?"

She glared at her partner. "We're staying far away from racetracks after—"

He cut her off. "You don't have to announce to the world how we lost our savings."

Babs plucked a single black feather stuck in her scalp. She looked at it in disgust before tossing it aside. "Can't believe I walked around with this in my hair all afternoon, and none of you said anything to me. Peter, how about adopting a myna bird? Free for the taking."

Guy rubbed in the sarcasm. "Oh, I thought you were trying a new fashion fad."

Peter intervened. "Stop right there. Mr. Moto says, 'Those who argue can keep their differences behind closed doors.' Maybe Confucius said that, but then again, he was Chinese. How about I propose this? You two go home. Settle your differences.

"Give me the number of his press agent. If I can pin him down, it's going to be a long night. You might as well rest up. Babs, you can wash your hair if you think your pet bird deposited more leave-behinds. At least you didn't get birded with a dead one. Deal?"

Babs thought it odd that Peter had been wearing his coat the whole time and seemed to be shivering when she and her partner were becoming uncomfortably warm. He also looked pale, and his pupils were dilated. "Are you all right?"

He scratched his arms and shifted his gaze to avoid eye contact. "We all need to prepare for the evening ahead. While you get ready, I'm going to call my doctor for some new medication. Been feeling out of sorts, and whatever he's given me doesn't seem to be working."

Chapter Twenty-Five: Ciro's

Peter got a lead to expect Raft at Ciro's after ten. Babs prayed their evening would wind up on a different note than when her supposed "date" with Detective Allgood landed them behind bars. She called her miracle worker dry cleaner to see if he had a new gown she could borrow. While she had him on the line, she asked about the Bogarts' tablecloth that Guy marked up with grease pencil. That's where his magic fell short. None of his secret solutions could do the trick. They'd have to throw it out, and Mayo would be foaming at the mouth.

The bouncer recognized Peter and, without hesitation, allowed the trio to enter. This being Guy's first time at the club, he remarked about its furnishings, and was curious who designed the place.

"George Vernon Russell," said Babs, knowing her design-conscious partner would be impressed she had a ready answer. "He installed phone jacks at every table for customers to receive urgent calls without leaving. Imagine such luxury and fine service at your fingertips."

"If he's going the extra mile, you better keep your lips sealed in the powder room. It might be bugged with hidden microphones. Talking about hidden, I heard rumors the famous gangster, Johnny Roselli, hid a gambling parlor somewhere in this joint," he said.

Babs didn't want to spend another night in the pokey, but luck seemed to be in their favor. The band went on break just as they spotted Raft, sitting alone, with his back against the wall at a table at the far end of the club. Even more so, they didn't expect him to welcome them. Perhaps it was from regarding Lorre as a fellow member of the Hollywood film elite, and he desired company. Raft ordered everyone drinks, perhaps to kick off his own celebration where there hadn't been one.

"Are you sure we're not intruding?" Babs asked.

"My friends are late, which is no surprise. You might as well warm their seats. Come, let's get this party started."

*I guess it's true about his cunning, subtle smile...and shiny hair resembling black patent leather shoes...*Babs had only seen pictures of Raft and articles in the trades and couldn't recall much if she had seen any of his films, but all of that was one step removed from being right smack in front of him. First off, Peter explained that his companions were private eyes and not to get alarmed. Raft grimaced, swallowed his olive, and ordered another martini.

Undaunted by any notions of discomfort from their host, Guy was eager to start prying. He asked George upfront, "Did you leave Warner Brothers?"

"Just my place on the lot." He paused to take a sip of his fresh cocktail and gave Babs a flirtatious wink. "I've begged Emperor Jack to get out of my contract but never get too far. In a few words: I was sick and tired of being typecast.

"My first picture at Warner's was *Invisible Stripes*," said Raft. "The director complained I was upsetting Humphrey Bogart, William Holden, and the other cast members by changing my lines. I didn't want to come off like such a thug. I even heard a rumor...behind my back...he wished he could just fade me out of the film."

"How did they resolve it?" Lorre asked.

"Good old Jack said, 'Change the script and kill off my character early on by having a prison guard throw me down the stairs.' Afterward, I put my foot down. I wanted no more scripts where I'd have to play a crook. Also, I'm superstitious about being in films where I die at the end.

"The studio wanted to pair me up with Bogart one more time in *Manpower*. I refused to work with him again. Instead, they reassigned Eddie Robinson as a substitute. We didn't get along too well, either. Especially since we both had the hots for Dietrich."

Guy flashed an "I told you so" at Babs. When Raft expounded on their differences in acting styles, she flashed a glance back.

"Our director had enough of my cursing and swearing. At one point, after it turned physical, and I have to admit I pushed the little twerp around more often than not, Raoul Walsh shut the production down for a few hours to let me blow off steam. Sometimes, I wanted to pick Eddie up by the collar and kill him. Well, not really, but you get my drift."

"Is it true Universal gave you a better offer?" asked Lorre.

Raft nodded. "A chance to star with Rosalind Russell with a salary of a hundred and fifty grand. Couldn't pass that up. I needed to finalize a divorce from my estranged wife. At decision time, I flew all the way to New York to plead my case to Warner, who was staying at the Waldorf Astoria. Then we shook hands on it.

"We didn't have anything in writing, but who needed it once I had Jack Warner's word? Can't believe I was that stupid. He did an about-face and said I had to finish five more films before I could get out of my contract. Still need to complete a few more, but I was so angry that I no longer wanted to keep my office as a reminder of being a slave of the studio system."

Bogie...Lorre...even Basil Rathbone complained of being pigeonholed into Sherlock Holmes in our last case. Now Raft. She bit her lip and hoped he wasn't under the impression Jack Warner had sent them as spies.

Raft insisted on dinner. His treat. He appeared open and cooperative and showed no remorse about turning down any of the parts that fell into Bogie's lap, despite tensions between them from working on previous films. His hatred toward Warner—understandable; however, he had no reason to deliver dead birds to Greenstreet or Astor and seemed completely at ease around Lorre. Regardless of Raft's history of befriending mobsters, it gave the detectives the impression he had nothing to do with any threats or birdings against Bogie or anyone else for that matter.

"About this typecasting issue," Babs said. "Everyone thinks you play a gangster so well. Isn't that where you've pulled your inspiration?"

"Gangsters ain't so bad," George demurred. "I always thought fellows like Benny Siegel, Frank Costello, Joey Adonis, Lucky Luciano, and Owney Madden were the greatest guys in the world. They all had Duesenbergs and 16-cylinder Cadillacs. One of them said, 'When there was money around, you might as well step on some of it.' Police captains and politicians bowed to Benny, so why shouldn't I be like them? But regarding my role models…"

"*Uh, oh,*" said Guy, putting down his fork as the rumbling and the razzmatazz in the restaurant dropped a few decibels. "I think the answer is walking right toward us."

"What? Where?" Babs asked.

Guy took her chin in his hand and forced it in another direction hard enough that she felt her neck crack. "For God's sake, don't stare."

"*Ouch!* Who do you not want me to look at?"

"If you don't know who he is," Guy said, "you're reading the wrong newspapers."

All eyes fixated on the legendary mobster, Benjamin "Bugsy" Siegel, who entered with his gal, Virginia Hill, on his arm and flanked by bodyguards.

Barely able to get the words past his lips, Guy whispered, "I thought he was in jail."

"So did I," Lorre said. "I read that his girlfriend had chefs from Ciro's cater him gourmet meals while awaiting charges in the "Big Greenie" Greenberg murder trial. Heard he had 'conjugal' visits with Hill, if you could even call them conjugal since his real wife and kids lived back in Scarsdale, New York."

Guy checked his tie to make sure it was straight. "I heard tailors altered his prison uniforms to look like bespoke couture. He maintained being well-dressed, even behind bars."

"He better not try to hit me up for another loan," Raft mumbled. "I can't lay my hands on that kind of cash right now. My wife just cleaned me out."

Peter asked, "Doesn't he have enough money of his own?"

Raft kept watch on Siegel, who flashed a wad of greenbacks at a cigarette girl. While his mobster friends rummaged through her inventory for their favorite brands and stopped every other second to chat with friends, George broke out into a sweat. "He should, but as soon as he makes it, he loses it on the ponies."

"Aren't you supposed to be on his good side?" asked Guy.

"Ben, Benny, or Benjamin…by the way, that's how you need to address him, and he'd just as soon put a hole in your head than let you get away with calling him the *other name* he despises. He considers me his closest friend, but never listens to my advice."

"Then how did he get the *other name?*" Babs asked.

"Back in the old days in New York, folk called him Bugs 'cause he was hotheaded. Even when he and Meyer Lansky formed their alliance, the cops and the press called them the Bugs and Meyer mob. He graduated from doing the rum runner's dirty work on the East Coast to establishing a wire service monopoly to compete with Capone's bookies in Chicago.

"Once he established a foothold in California, he started a racket of extorting the movie studios by taking over the local unions like the Screen Extras Guild and the Teamsters. He'd organize a strike, forcing the studios to pay him off, so everyone could get back to work. With too much moolah at his fingertips and the bookies in his back pocket, he gained a reputation for borrowing money but never paying anyone back. Who, in their right mind, would dare demand restitution?"

Bugsy flashed another glance toward George, who raised his chin to note he was still aware he was heading their way.

"Smile and acknowledge him," George said to Babs. "He savors the grins of pretty dames."

Concerned, she looked at her partner and back to their host. "How do you expect me to do that when the sight of him terrifies me?"

"You're supposed to be an actress. Use your talent," Lorre warned her.

"Do yourself a favor," said Raft. "Make up something on the fly, but whatever you do, don't tell him you're a couple of PIs. Get it?"

George gave Babs one more wink and flipped a coin like he did in *Scarface*. This signaled to Siegel it was safe to approach with his entourage. The nearest waiter brought more chairs. Upon seeing Lorre and the two detectives, whom he didn't recognize, Siegel was ready to explode, but Raft seemed to know the magic words to douse those flames.

"They're not here for you, Baby Blue-Eyes. They're here for me. Besides, since when did you start monopolizing our friendship?"

Baby Blue-Eyes, Babs thought. Within seconds, Siegel seemed much calmer.

"Since when does my Hell's Kitchen compadre get center stage?" Siegel asked. "You could've given them your autograph already and sent them on their merry little way. Hey?"

Raft, who stood and pulled out a chair for Virginia, laughed and lied his way out of an impending confrontation. "They're casting for a producer who's had his eye on me."

Babs gulped. She'd have to come up with a convincing cover.

"Maybe they'll consider giving me a part, but what's the deal with Mr. Moto?" He stared at Lorre. "Why is he tagging along?"

"Just friends. Beats me. I didn't bother asking."

"Hey, pop-eyes, scram!" Siegel commanded.

Raft intervened. "He's harmless. Leave him alone and order a drink. On second thought, take mine. Service is a bit slow tonight."

Siegel slapped him under the chin. "Not for me, it ain't."

"Looks like you need this martini more than I do," said Raft, rubbing his stinging face.

* * *

This, being no *Three Stooges* stunt, was Babs' cue to turn her attention elsewhere. In trying to break the ice, she complimented Virginia on her lilac orchid corsage. The woman ignored her. Babs' next challenge was how to continue to interrogate Raft when the narcissistic Siegel wanted their discussion to be all about him.

"You think this mug has a chance?" Bugsy flashed a smile at Babs, leaning in so uncomfortably close she could smell his spicy aftershave.

Virginia seemed more preoccupied with seeing who mingled in the crowd and had become numb to Bugsy's fooling around. Babs wouldn't have been surprised if she indulged in her own fair share of infidelity.

Turning her attention back to Siegel, Babs asked, "Have you arranged for a screen test? It's surprising how many people look great in person but discover they're unphotogenic."

"Hey, I thought I looked pretty damned good in my mugshots. Isn't that a sort of preliminary screen test? Trained hair and makeup artists should be able to take care of the rest."

"It's one thing to feel at ease among friends. Another when a director and crew are putting you on the spot," said Guy. "Nothing's worse than feeling confronted and forgetting one's lines. I can vouch from personal experience."

"You're tellin' me that being handsome ain't enuf?"

"'Fraid so. Most people must develop their talent. There are plenty of acting schools and voice coaches in town. If you want, I can get you a few numbers."

With an eye out for the who's who of the club's clientele, Virginia Hill rose and excused herself. Bugsy took her leave of absence as an opportunity to scoot closer to Babs.

Maybe he sensed her distress, but Raft picked up the ball and diverted away from the detectives, getting his friend an acting gig back to the old times they spent in Gotham.

"Before my big break with the Broadway crowd, I was a terrible pickpocket, but a good shoplifter. Often hung out in pool rooms and slept in the subway."

"Yeah, before your Irish hoodlum friend bankrolled your exit to Hollywood," said Bugsy. "Didn't you also work as a stand-in shooter at floating crap games?"

"What's that?" Guy asked.

"When the players were tipped off about an impending raid, Georgie and other out-of-work bums would take over the dice from the big timers...like 'The Brain'...Arnold Rothstein. The coppers would arrest them in their place. They'd pay a small fine and get a fiver for their services. Kinda like a stand-in for the real actors in the movies. Shortly thereafter, the game would resume," Bugsy explained.

"I always felt there was no difference between a detective and a gangster. Their jobs use many of the same methods. They just try to outsmart each other," said Raft.

Bugsy checked his brand-new Rolex luminous dial wristwatch. "It's about time Virginia planted her ass back here." He abruptly stood, the tipsiness causing him to bump into Guy, and without so much as an apology, he held out his hand to Raft and asked, "Whatcha got?"

Raft shook his head. "No dice. Got my friends to cover, and I'm staying clear of the tables tonight."

"But I'm not. Run a tab and pay it later. Billy and his boys know you're good for it."

Babs assumed he referred to Billy Wilkerson, the owner of Ciro's and of the *Hollywood Reporter*.

"Ben, I'm not a bank on two legs," said Raft. When Bugsy gave Lorre one of his give-it-to-me glares, as if he must've had enough in his wallet to satisfy his demands, Raft placed his hand on Bugsy's shoulder as if to break the spell. "Don't put the squeeze on my pals. This is between you and me. Didn't I just see you impress a cigarette girl with your wad?"

Fondling the pistol under his jacket, Bugsy wasn't going to back down. "Well, then?"

Raft growled. He reached for his wallet and handed Siegel nine one-hundred-dollar bills, which Siegel counted.

"You're not going to round that out?"

"Leaves me with only five Andrew Jacksons for tips and taxis. Can't put those on a tab," replied Raft.

When their waiter came over to clear empty glasses, Siegel grabbed the unsuspecting victim's shoulder and hurled him into the diners at the next table. Shocked and furious, one of the patrons, with no clue as to who they were confronting, yelled for management. Tensions escalated. Weapons caught eyes. Someone called the police.

This time, the gangster wouldn't outwit the men with the badges. Raft complained that he'd just given his "bribe money" away to Benny. Normally paid off to ignore the club's illegal gambling, the police had good cause for a raid.

Babs wondered if the cops had a secret quota they had to fill, and this time, Siegel had rolled a hand of snake eyes. The fuzz crashed their party like angry waves pommeling the shoreline. They threw anyone who didn't escape the melee into paddy wagons, including Lorre, Guy, and Babs. When the cops separated the men from the women, Babs struggled to break free, but to no avail. "Don't I get a phone call?"

Perhaps because she didn't look like one of their rabble-rousing regulars, one of the arresting officers escorted her over to a payphone. She gambled on calling Detective Allgood to bail her out.

"What time is it?" he asked, yawning.

"After midnight, I guess. Cops confiscated my wristwatch."

"Gotta change out of my pajamas," he complained. "I'll get there when I get there."

* * *

Allgood arrived wearing a wrinkled shirt buttoned wrong. Under his hat, his hair looked uncombed. He chewed on a toothpick while staring at Babs behind bars—not exactly presentable to a woman whom you've been affectionate toward. "Ciro's? Did you forget what happened when I took you there? This had better be good."

"Yeah, but—"

"You should've known better. A gambling joint like Ciro's could get busted." Allgood enjoyed taunting her.

Lorre called his wife, who bailed out all three. "She's the bookkeeper in the family and knows whether there's money for emergencies like this."

Babs reunited with Guy and told her side of the story while waiting for a taxi outside the precinct. "What good is dating a cop if he can't spring you from jail?"

Up till now, she was under the impression her partner knew he accompanied her on business to San Francisco. Only after she blurted this out did she realize she'd ruined the secret of their closer association.

"Babs, are you aware he's married?"

This was the one time she wished someone could've locked her inside a closet. The crushing blow was so intense, she couldn't hide her tears.

How long did Guy know, and how did he find out? Why didn't he tell her right away?

She had too many questions, not enough answers, and her tongue was tied, because their agency was still in the thick of this murder investigation. Unless she wanted to drop Bogie as their client and go back to scrounging, she'd have to buck up and take it in stride.

Chapter Twenty-Six: Satan Met a Lady

While the two PIs discussed business in her rear office, their front door swung open, and a male voice bellowed, "Fly me to the East Coast! I'll hang out with Meyer if I have to. Lansky can find another stool pigeon to take over my dirty work. This town's for the birds!"

Having had little sleep after spending a night behind bars, the sudden jolt from Bugsy Siegel's arrival was more effective than the strongest of coffee. Their door crashed into the wall with such force that its pebbled glass window shattered. Bruno started to howl which incited Sir Henry to barrel out of Babs' inner office toward the commotion.

Guy alerted Babs by pointing his index finger and balled up the rest in the shape of a gun.

"Left it at home," she whispered.

"Shoot the beast!" Siegel shouted.

"No, wait!" Babs screamed, and Guy followed. "He's harmless, as long as you don't hurt us!"

The goon on Siegel's right had his pistol readied. The bruiser on his left clutched a brown paper bag with his quarry. Stu leapt and, for a few startled seconds, hovered in midair, with a cry that sounded like he was being strangled.

Babs crossed her arms, determined to stay in control. As if that would stop bullets, she thought. Fat chance! He was tough, but she would be even tougher. "What's so important?"

Siegel cleared the loose papers off Guy's desk. A few caught enough of the breeze from his electric fan to scatter like tumbleweeds into the hallway. The hefty muscleman placed the bewildering parcel in the vacant spot.

"Open it!" Bugsy demanded. "I'm not touching it."

Guy backed away. She stood her ground. Taking extra care, his lackey pulled out a large, stiff, white feathery object. Babs gagged. This repugnant specimen reeked of recent death. Taking another step backward, Guy slammed into the wall and knocked off their wall calendar, alarming the animals. Babs inched forward.

"Have you ever seen such an outrage?" Bugsy yammered.

"Looks like our killer is experimenting with seagulls," she said, remaining calm.

"No *schmuck* is going to have designs on me! I'll personally see to it he croaks first."

Guy reached into his top desk drawer for a pair of protective gloves. He turned the bird over, then back to its original position.

"You've seen something like that before?" Siegel asked.

"Several times," said Guy. "Why don't you take off your coats and close the front door."

* * *

Dreading the outcome of his visit, Babs offered to make coffee. Guy took his vending machine slugs out of the desk drawer and asked if anyone wanted a soda.

Bugsy addressed the PIs in a manner that sounded like a condemnation. "Guess your little secret came out last night when we were all arrested."

"We weren't going to lie to the police," Guy said.

"Seemed like you already had an inside track with the cops," he said to Babs.

Siegel now knew she had a connection, although tenuous, with Homicide Detective Allgood. "Our goal was to speak with your friend George," she said. "We had no idea you'd show up, and, in fact, everything would've been better off if you hadn't come to our table."

"You mean you weren't there to take me down or bribe me into doing something against my will?"

"We had nothing to do with the raid," said Guy. "You mucked up our plans as much as we did yours."

Bugsy gave them the Bronx cheer. Babs figured it was curtains. One of Bugsy's men shrugged. The other nodded and said, "Hear them out."

"Anyways, you're the experts," Siegel said with hesitation. "What's with some jerk giving me the bird?"

"Mr. Seagull... Pardon me, Mr. Siegel." *That could've been a deadly slip of the tongue.* In her thoughts—a private joke: *Birdsy Seagull. Better not laugh.* She might only have seconds to live.

Babs assumed he accepted her apology and started to pace the room. "Our case began with a threat against Humphrey Bogart. Then the threats extended to other cast members of *The Maltese Falcon* along with Jack Warner, who needs no introduction.

"We wouldn't be doing our jobs if we didn't question everyone who might've been upset about finishing the film. This would include anyone, actors or a director, who either turned a part down or got passed over. That's why we were interested in George Raft. He rejected several roles, which Jack Warner had Bogie take over. Peter Lorre, who we ran into at the Warner Brothers commissary, gave us a few leads where to locate George, which led us to Cairo's."

Siegel interrupted, "You mean Ciro's."

Babs made a nervous laugh. "You're right. Ciro's. Not Cairo's. I must've been thinking about Joel Cairo, Mr. Lorre's character from *The Maltese Falcon*. Well, it was pure chance that both of us were there, when police had already planned a surprise raid. A matter of bad timing. Nothing more."

Bugsy's eyes went to the dead gull, still on Guy's desk. "What do you make of this?"

"Not sure," Guy said. His nose wrinkled as he tried to breathe through his mouth to avoid the offensive odor. The others, including Babs, had pressed their handkerchiefs to their faces. "In most of the *birdings*, as we call them, someone preserved the birds, using taxidermy. This one...looks more like roadkill, or it had died by some other means and hadn't been maintained. George didn't mention a word about getting targeted, which makes me wonder what it is about you that would be of particular interest to our killer."

"You mean the person who's been leaving these dead birds has killed people?"

"Sometimes yes and sometimes no," said Guy.

Sir Henry seemed curious about the trio and approached to sniff them out. Mr. Trigger Happy pulled his pistol.

"Stay, Sir Henry! Sit!" Babs cried, offering to take him into the other room and put him on a leash. "He might be a giant, but he's as harmless as an overgrown toddler, as long as you don't pull a fast one."

Bugsy ordered his *bag man* to place the decaying bird out in the hallway and to close the door, despite its glass being shattered.

"Betcha it's one of Capone's guys getting back at me for setting up a rival wire service on the West Coast," Bugsy said, addressing his buddies. "He hates me 'cause I'm not Italian, nor subject to his commands. He accuses all Jews of being Commies, because he supports free enterprise—black-market or legit. What the hell is with that? I'm no card-carrying communist. I worship the God of Money...just like him."

Siegel took out his wallet. "See? The fruits of capitalism." He flipped through his cash like a dealer shuffling a deck of cards. Probably the same dough he bummed from Raft the night before. "All I can say is, nobody had dared threaten me. How much do you need to make sure I don't get *birded* again?"

Babs took special care in choosing her words. "Mr. Siegel, at the moment, we're overwhelmed with our current caseload, and I'm sure you'd want your matter to take top priority."

"Of course. Name your price."

"Sir, it's not a matter of..." *Think fast!* "We're working in conjunction with the police."

"Too bad. That kinda puts a dent in it."

Babs nodded. "Way too many complications. Besides, I think the birding might've been a warning."

"Nobody tells me to back off!"

Guy jumped in. "I can't believe you're in danger. It's doubtful you have anything in common with the previous victims."

"Don't play me for a birdbrain. Why me? After all, no one's bothered Georgie?"

"Not yet," Guy said. "If you're concerned, I'd play it by the book and file a police report."

Bugsy spouted venom about not wanting to step foot near any police station when the detectives' janitor, who'd been making his rounds, entered.

"I saw a package outside your door surrounded by broken glass. Figgered I'd better sweep it up before anyone steps in it, but..." Witnessing their weapons and seeing that his friends were being held hostage, Wiggins uttered, "Me broom's downstairs anyways. *Uhhh*...I think I'll come back later."

With a look of do or die, Mr. Trigger Happy waved his gun toward one of the office chairs and ordered Wiggins to stay put.

Not thrilled they dragged Wiggins into the mess, Babs figured at least they'd have another witness, unless Siegel's thugs decided to do them all in.

Bugsy continued to put the screws on them. Babs suggested, "Sir, if you tell us how and where you found the gull, maybe we can be of help."

Siegel's bag man answered, "His driver found the dead bird tucked under his windshield wiper in the parking lot at Ciro's. Broke the damned thing. Wouldn't work afterward."

"Before or after the raid?"

"Before."

"He knew his boss was inside. Why didn't he say something?"

Bugsy answered for him. "I ordered him to stay with my car...under the threat of death if he did otherwise."

So much for intimidation tactics, Babs thought. They could backfire.

"When did you find out?" Guy asked.

"After the cops released me on bail. By then, the bird had started to rot."

"I bet." Wiggins chuckled to himself. "I've cleaned enuf trash to know."

Bugsy overheard his remark and slapped him on his cheek so hard that his chair teetered before coming to a stop. "Who told you to speak? Yeah, right. A janitor will wind up solving this case. Ha! That'll be a first."

Stu bawled, and the gunman punched him away with his fist.

Wiggins seemed to have no concern for his own neck. "What does *Bigsy* have to do with *The Maltese Falcon* unless it's his affiliation with Raft?"

Siegel aimed his gun. "Hey, stop callin' me names!"

Guy held up his hands. "*Whoa!* Hold on. You've never met our friend Wiggins until now, and you're liable never to encounter him again. Leave him out of it. Be rational. Think about what you could have in common with some of the others who've received the same threats?"

Babs picked up the slack. "Both Jack Warner and Peter Lorre got birded."

Bugsy volunteered a clue. "Could it be because we're all Jewish?"

Babs scrunched her eyebrows.

"Peter Lorre's real name is Laszlo Lowenstein," Guy said. "He'd still have a thriving career in Germany if it hadn't been for the Nazis. Remember how Bogie told us of that fundraiser by Harry Warner? His studio has been on the warpath against such fifth columnists for several years now."

"What's that got to do with me?" asked Siegel. "I've wanted Warners to put me under contract, but they seem to want nothing to do with me, despite Georgie Boy's influence."

Everyone batted around ideas while the three hoodlums continued to hold the three hostages at gunpoint. Wiggins had left his trusty mop and pail downstairs. Babs had left her firearm at home. Sir Henry was smart enough to know to remain in place. Bruno slept and snored the entire time. Stu stayed put rather than pecking at anyone's heads, and the cats were no match against these human time bombs.

The phone rang. Then it rang again. On the third annoying ring, Guy spoke up. "Do you mind? It could be the police."

"We'll gun them down if they show their faces!" Siegel shouted, but Mr. Trigger Happy reprimanded him.

Bugsy nodded and gave the go-ahead to Guy, who leapt into action. "B. Norman Investigations," he answered, paused, and looked at Bugsy, who gave him approval to continue.

"Who is it?" Bugsy asked.

"A confidential client," Guy told him. In Babs' ear, he whispered, "It's Mary Astor."

Babs gestured to switch seats. She whispered, "Call later."

Mary wanted nothing of it. "The diaries...I swore I destroyed every last one of them," she ranted. "By now, it's been a while. Newspaper headlines called it the *Great American Sex Scandal of 1936*."

"That was five years ago," Babs murmured.

"What if the judge decided to reverse his ruling? I'd lose custody of my daughter."

"I think there are laws as to how many times one can try and appeal a case." Babs needed to get rid of her.

"I've been through this once before and will die if I have to go through this again."

"No one will die over this. Thorpe's record isn't squeaky clean by a long shot." Dreadful ex-husbands, Babs thought. *I can relate.*

"Don't be keeping no secrets," Bugsy boomed.

No acting talent could hide Babs' nerves. She patted her dampened neck with her handkerchief and turned to her captors. "Do you mind if I take the call in the other room?"

Sir Henry agreed with a resonant woof, which must've sparked sense into the gangster's head. Fed up, he ordered his men to holster their weapons. He muttered to the detectives, "You're useless," gathered his guys, and left.

Chapter Twenty-Seven: Dead End Detectives

Babs sipped on cold coffee and, without thinking, she disconnected Miss Astor by accident. She had dragged herself to the office today out of habit and necessity. Even worse, she had Bugsy Siegel to contend with. What she failed to do was to give herself the time to lick her wounds after finding out Allgood was married. Not that she had fallen in love, but now it would make it even harder for her to open her heart to any man.

Wiggins had returned and was finishing sweeping up the broken glass. Birdie Wilson's ledgers lay open on Guy's desk. He got up and grabbed his hat and jacket. "We broke the law by not reporting Bugsy and his gang. At this point, if we turn them over to the police, being honest would only get us in more trouble...I've had it, Babs."

"Please don't tell me you're giving up on this case, or even worse, quitting altogether?"

"Raft slipped me his number down at the police station," he explained. "I'm going to put any suspicions about him to rest once and for all."

"Guy, we've tried to narrow this down, but the list of suspects seems to get wider. *The Falcon* already premiered in New York. Soon, it'll open here in Los Angeles. Who haven't we spoken with in a while who hasn't gotten birded?"

"Wilmer...Elisha Cooke, Jr. Neither has Huston. Maybe we should ask the police to keep a special eye out."

Turning his back, he waved goodbye and headed out, leaving Babs on her own.

* * *

Thoughts stopped her in her tracks. *Sexton...sex scandals... Arrrgh! Raft... Kaufman...two guys named George!* The chatter in her brain became so overwhelming she was about ready to give up for good, and another part of her wanted to take revenge against that two-timing Allgood. She mused that a facial and a soothing steam room would do the trick, and the Roosevelt Hotel spa was right down the street.

"Isn't that right, Sir Henry?" She addressed the dog as if he could interpret her thoughts and knew what had been on her mind.

She took over her partner's chair and tried to make herself comfortable at his desk. When a kitten tried to snag her stockings, she picked him up and stroked him in her lap.

With a fresh pair of eyes, maybe she could find something Guy overlooked. She paged through Birdie Wilson's account books, taking care not to disturb the loose pieces of paper he had inserted while making personal notes. Figuring he combed through these ledgers with half his attention, when she took her crack at it, one repetitive entry stood out with a name that sounded so common and nondescript. Until now, it never came up—E. Knoll.

The note! Birdie had stuffed a memo inside one of the binders. To keep it safe, she secreted it away inside one of the drawers of her desk...but which one?

As opposed to Guy, who was always neat, precise, and persnickety in his obsession for orderliness, the contents of her drawers looked like the aftermath of the San Francisco Earthquake—a joke her partner would always drive home. Between Sir Henry the wolfhound and Stu the myna bird, both of whom had the capability of opening her drawers, she got into the habit of locking them. Fine and dandy, but she always misplaced the key. Babs rummaged through her clutter until she found the desk key under a cushion on her couch.

"Stupid Stu," she murmured, "I bet he stole the key and stashed it there." She unlocked every single drawer until she got her hands on Birdie's note. He scribbled the message: The mailroom.

That's all? She cross-referenced addresses and found three customers who had their orders delivered to the Warner Brothers mailroom. *How could my partner have been so jaded or distracted that he overlooked this?* One placed more orders than the others. Next to those ledger entries, the name: E. Knoll.

The phone rang again. Since she didn't want any nosy animals poking through open drawers in her absence, she answered it at her desk.

"B. Norman Investigations."

"Babs, this is Leon Lewis—"

"Yes, I remember. The lawyer. Is everything all right?"

He hesitated, then replied, "Someone tried to threaten me with one of those dead birds."

"Where? How?"

"For obvious reasons, I keep a low profile. Your friend, Chief Crow-Feather, however, he's rather fearless when it comes to appearing and speaking in public. He addressed a rally of protestors in Boyle Heights about redlining."

"Isn't that where huffy conservatives try to prevent what they consider undesirable ethnicities from settling in their exclusive communities?"

"In layman's terms, you could say that. The Boyle Heights vicinity has become a major melting pot in the Los Angeles area. While we were still in the Depression, political leaders went so far as to repatriate Mexicans, many of which had been born here and had never stepped foot South of the Border.

"Desperate people looked for any excuse to blame others as to why they were out of work. When times were tough, even those with education were needy enough to take the most menial jobs. They felt the newcomers needed to be sent back to their ancestral countries, even if they'd been born and raised in the States and had never even been to those other places."

"Guess it was before my time in Los Angeles, but that's awful," said Babs,

"People got away with it?"

"Since Boyle Heights has a large working-class Jewish community, I wanted to be present, but without being recognized to observe any reactions and, if need be, report any disturbances from outside agitators."

"Was anyone threatened?"

"Just the usual name calling and, 'I'll speak to my city councilman.' Otherwise, nothing we hadn't already anticipated."

"Except what happened to you."

"I discovered it after the event ended and the crowd dispersed, but I wanted to speak with you first. It's always hit or miss as to who might be sympathetic in the police department. Many, I've found, support a few of the homegrown fascist movements that my office has tried to take down. Considering this rally took place in a neighborhood with a significant Jewish population, an insider might've tipped someone off that I might be present."

"Did anyone pose a threat to the chief?"

"Not that I'm aware of. The police managed to keep everything under relative control."

"Exactly how did you get birded?" asked Babs.

"Found a starling tucked under my car's windshield wiper."

"Just like Bugsy Siegel," Babs muttered.

"Did you just say Bugsy Siegel...the gangster?"

"*Uh, oh...*" Babs realized she shouldn't have blurted that out. "You're not supposed to know that."

"Well, I do now. How can we be connected?"

Wiggins popped his head through the door. "Sorry to barge in. An operator called me on my downstairs phone. Mary Astor has been desperately trying to get through to you, but your line's been busy. She was worried you were in danger, or your phone had been knocked off the hook."

Oh, gosh...I never called her back. "Leon, I don't know what to say. File a police report. They are already aware of similar situations. This is urgent. I must call my client."

Babs thanked Wiggins for the reminder. Feeling bad that now Leon might be at risk, she hung up Guy's extension and returned Mary's call.

Babs put her empty coffee cup down on her saucer. "Your custody case is closed."

According to Mary, it wasn't. "That amoral, unprincipled New York reporter, Florabel Muir, covered our trial. Can you believe back in the 20s, to get a scoop, she'd bribe law clerks, kidnap witnesses, and break into peoples' desks? All for a sordid story! She's relentless and must've gotten her grubby hands on my diary and either copied or took photos of it. Whatever trick she used, she had no qualms exposing its contents and printing them in the *Daily News*."

Babs sank into her chair, kicked off her shoes, and rubbed her temples. She forced herself to remain calm, almost to the point of sounding apathetic, but she felt like she was trying to talk sense into a tempest.

"Kaufman claimed he was my friend, like many others in Hollywood," Mary raged. "He refused to stand up for me and screwed me in more ways than one."

"I'm convinced Dr. Thorpe is not our birder, nor our murderer, not even for a copycat crime," Babs said. "Neither is Kaufman." She found a tin of aspirin in her partner's desk drawer and choked down two of the tablets dry.

"Rest assured," she gagged on her answer. "The police will have so much security at the *Falcon*'s LA premiere, you'd think they were stopping Hitler's army."

Chapter Twenty-Eight: Showtime!

O n Friday, October 3, 1941, *The Maltese Falcon* premiered in New York. The critics plastered their accolades all over the trades, saying, "Three Times a Charm!" after the two prior attempts to adapt Dashiell Hammett's bestselling novel to screen got panned. Sadowski and Allgood assured the young PIs that the LAPD coordinated with the New York Police Department to make them aware of what had transpired and to be on the lookout for shenanigans. In lieu of being able to witness the event in person, Babs tuned in to every radio station. She also made calls to the news desks at the *LA Times* and all the trades to see if they had received any word from back east. Everything turned out fine.

Warner's planned their Los Angeles premiere for Saturday, October 18th. Humphrey Bogart pulled the proper strings to get Babs and Guy onto the red carpet. At first, they figured they could be each other's date. On second thought, they felt it a wiser strategy to split up. Allgood accompanied Babs, despite her bitter feelings. He made it clear not only was he still on the job, but so was she. Convinced there would be no threats from her litigious ex-husband, Guy would chaperone Mary Astor, who could've had any number of suitors trying to woo her favor but happened to be in between marriages.

The two private detectives convened at their office before parting for their respective engagements. While putting together the finishing touches, Guy had a standoff with Stu, who refused to relinquish his perch on his shoulder.

"Get rid of him," griped Babs. "Throw a handful of birdseed across the room. It works like kibble with dogs."

Guy swatted the myna with the lint brush he had used to remove cat hair from his tux. Every time he took a swipe, Stu dug his claws in deeper and pecked at his face. "Babs, help me, for heaven's sake. Get this insipid bird back into his cage before he ruins my suit!"

"He's already poked holes in it, but at least it's on black fabric. It'll be dark outside. No one will notice them." When Babs rushed to his aid, Stu freed his feet and plucked a strand of hair from her up-do, which he deposited down Guy's collar. "Now, I'll need to restyle my hair."

"Tomorrow, I'm letting you loose in Griffith Park," said Guy. "See what it's like to fend against the predators. Wait till you wind up as a falcon's dinner."

Stu, still fastened to his jacket, mocked Guy with a clicking and whirring that sounded like a windup toy. He put down his convertible top and drove to Mary Astor's, hoping the wind would blow the stubborn fowl away.

* * *

Upon their arrival, Mary Astor gave the photographers complimentary smiles as if nothing was out of sorts. The garish flashbulbs almost prevented Babs from keeping an eye on the crowd, but the steadfast myna grabbed the spotlight. "That idiotic creature," she said, mumbling to herself.

Bogie made light of the situation and told one reporter, "Don't think we're sneaking a double feature on you all by showing a secret version of *Treasure Island*. All this kid needs are a peg leg and an eye patch, and you could pass him off as Long John Silver. Right, bro?"

The newshound addressed Stu. "Let's see how smart you are. Say something."

Guy bit his lip as the pesky bird cawed insults to the pressman, "Ah, matey. Yer just as smart as paint! *Accck!*"

Word for word, the man wrote it down and walked away laughing. "Too bad we couldn't have recorded that quote for a radio show."

"Wallace Beery, I am not," said Guy, referring to the film Beery did about the legendary pirates.

Despite threats, Stu nearly pecked a security guard's eye out when he tried to bash him with his baton. Guy justified Stu's behavior by giving the guard his business card and said he was helping him solve a case.

Hesitant at first, the guard admitted Guy and his feathery sentry but insisted they find alternate seating in the back row. Astor, who didn't want to leave Guy, assured Bogie they'd reconvene later.

"You need to remain here," Bogie suggested. "I expect we'll be called up on stage to introduce the film."

Huston agreed. "Most likely, the press will want us to return for questions and answers." He proposed that Guy take a seat by himself. Mary needed to remain with the rest of her cast in their designated section.

Reluctant to separate from his clients, Guy did his darnedest to hide his disfavor but agreed to a seat in the rear.

* * *

When the film ended, as expected, reporters asked Huston and his stars to come on stage for questions.

Afterward, Allgood assigned uniformed cops to escort the *Falcon* gang outside. "Make sure they're safe from anyone who tries to push past the barricades."

Left on her own, as the moviegoers started to exit and despite the din of the crowd, Babs swore she heard someone perform a combination of singing and whistling, "Nobody seems to love or understand me...black bird, bye-bye."

Unable to determine its source, she spotted Guy heading her way with Stu still latched onto his tux. "Did you or the bird just sing a tune?"

Guy shook his head. "No. Why?"

Stu had to put in his two cents. "Myna birds don't sing—*whoo hoo! Awk! Mynas* dance." He started rocking back and forth in place but did not relinquish his perch.

Fed up with his antics, Guy took a swipe at the bird, to no avail. Babs glanced at the crowd and shuddered as she spotted Basil and his wife, Ouida

Rathbone, exiting with the VIPs.

* * *

Bogie approached the couple. "Kinda unusual you'd show given you're working for one of Warner's competitors. Aren't you under contract with Universal?"

"James Cagney gave me his invitation," Rathbone replied. "My wife didn't want to pass up a chance for publicity. After all, I don't expect to be typecast as Sherlock Holmes for the rest of my acting career."

"Ha! Most likely, Cagney was teed off 'cause he hadn't been offered the role, and I stepped out of his shadow. Reviewers are giving it the thumbs-up."

Taller than most, Rathbone peered over peoples' heads and examined the crowd. "How come there seems to be more of a police presence than usual?"

"Why do you care?" Bogie asked with a guarded tone. "Is Sherlock Holmes on the clock tonight?"

"I had hoped he'd get the night off, and Spade would be on the case," said Basil, reacting to his *bon mot*.

Bogie played into their repartee. "Who says the two detectives can't solve a case together?"

Basil loosened his tie. "Are you expecting criminals to spoil our evening?"

"Thugs and thieves like to have a good time, too." Bogie exuded a cool casualness that everything was under control.

Basil sighed. "Holmes' creator, Conan Doyle, seemed to have him at his prime back in 1895. Then again, I've heard our producers have asked our scenarists to update him to modern times. Saving England against the Nazis...or something like that."

Bogie offered Basil one of his cigarettes and lit both. "You don't say?"

"If one did the math, that would age him far beyond a normal retirement, but I guess the producers figured their loyal fans would overlook that."

"According to Jack Warner, they were the first studio to crank out anti-war films."

Basil blew out a puff of smoke. "Then it's not inconceivable Spade and

Holmes could partner on a case, but I'm not sure how Doctor Watson would like it."

"I'm not so sure how Spade would take it either. He's used to working solo or with his partner Miles Archer," Bogie replied. "Lucky for me, I guess, that Georgie Boy turned it down."

"Who ya callin' Georgie Boy, you punk!" Raft, emphasizing a streetwise New York accent, had poked his nose into their conversation.

"Your ears must've been burnin'." Bogie scanned the crowd to see if anyone had tagged along with him besides his female escort. "Hope you left your doppelganger at home."

Raft glanced over both his shoulders to make sure no personal enemies were eavesdropping. "Benny Siegel? He's back behind bars. Lawyers still want to pin him with a guilty charge on the 'Big Greenie' murder case. He claims he's innocent."

Bogie snickered. "Don't they all?"

A photographer barged in, holding his press camera and looking to corral the celebs for a picture. "Look at the birdie!" he shouted, referring to the small dead stuffed sparrow mounted on his camera. Blinding everyone with his flash, he vanished into the night.

Mary became faint and lost her footing. Bogie caught her in his arms as she started to collapse.

His wife Mayo had fire in her eyes, but he justified his gallant act.

"Look, she'd been drinking all afternoon and called me earlier, all paranoid. She feared her ex-husband was going to take her back to court over the *Purple Diaries* scandal. To be honest, she just saw spots in front of her eyes."

Allgood left to fetch medical help.

Bogie warned his possessive wife, "Don't you dare accuse us of having an affair. Any gentleman worth his salt would rescue a fainting broad. Just happens that I'm quicker on my feet than the other screen hero bystanders." With a nod of his head, he acknowledged Basil's presence with slight sarcasm since he was well-known on screen for his derring-do and athleticism.

Stu surprised everyone by flying off his perch and onto Basil's shoulder. He stabbed his neck with his sharp beak and cried, "Look at the birdie! Look at the birdie!"

Basil tried to swat him away without success. "*Ouch!* Would someone remove this pest?"

"Maybe he's trying to tell you something," Bogie chuckled. Basil was nonplussed.

"Killer in the crowd. Dead man will follow. *Accck!*" Stu jabbed Rathbone in between rounds of squawking.

Basil complained, "I'm going to need medical attention if someone doesn't stop this bird from spearing me for no reason."

Allgood returned with an ambulance attendant. Both recommended they take Mary Astor to a hospital for observation. Basil stressed that he accompany them to have his wounds examined. He grabbed his wife's arm, but as they stepped into the ambulance, Stu unlatched himself from Basil's shoulder and resumed his perch on Guy's. Allgood told Babs she was on her own for the rest of the evening.

* * *

Babs' concerns about Ouida Rathbone or Mayo Methot got thrown into the shade when the police could no longer control the crowd. Guy clutched on to Babs with as much vigor as the myna bird did to his jacket. They broke into a sprint as fast as she possibly could muster while wearing high heels and an evening gown.

"Guy, wait!" Babs said, stopping for a second to catch her breath. "Did you get a good look at that photographer?"

Stu sounded like a broken record. He cut her off with his repeated warning, "Killer in the crowd. Dead man will follow. *Accck!*"

Pushing and shoving from all directions. "How's Mary going to get home?" she asked.

"Worry about that later. Come, we're wasting time arguing unless you want to get trampled."

Babs wanted nothing of it. She needed to know what the ruckus was about and dragged him back toward the mayhem. One panicking pedestrian plowed into Babs and knocked her onto the pavement. Detective Sadowski, who happened to be nearby, helped her back to her feet. While he worried she might've gotten hurt, she took that as an opportunity to break through the police barricade. Guy scrambled after her. Everyone huddled around a dead body.

"Isn't that...?" She was at a loss for words.

"The annoying tour guide we encountered in front of Bogie's mansion," Guy finished her sentence.

Sadowski ordered two of his uniforms to restrain them. "You can identify this man?"

"Stanford...Peck. Works for...Acme Star Tours," Babs replied.

"Put that in past tense, lady," replied one of the uniforms. "He *worked* for Acme, but not anymore."

"Mind if I have a closer look?" Guy asked.

The cop gave Guy a bewildered look. "What's with that bird?" he asked.

Guy ignored him and showed him his private investigator's license.

"He's here on official business," Sadowski replied, but signaled he was needed elsewhere. The uniformed officer would supervise the private detectives from here on. He looked at Stu in disbelief but finally nodded and gave Guy the go-ahead.

Guy bent down to examine the corpse. "Just like the dead woman we found in our office. There's another stuffed bird under his coat, but what's the point? The film is in theaters now. Why would anyone continue these shenanigans?"

Babs showed her ID, as well. "Look at the bruises on Peck's neck!" She pointed out other signs that indicated he might've been strangled rather than poisoned, which was the cause of death the Medical Examiner's Office always gave them.

"Hey, check this out." Guy pointed to contusions and indications of blunt force trauma on the man's head. "I think he might've been knocked out first, then strangled to finish him off."

"All right...all right." The presiding officer helped Babs up. "You've seen enough. Go join your friends."

Chapter Twenty-Nine: The Calm Before the Storm

The private detectives had to contend with another working Sunday. Babs arrived first to tend to the animals. An hour later, Guy tramped in, holding a squirming bundle.

"Not another birding," she cried out.

"I wish this one were stuffed." Guy explained he had no choice but to take Stu back to his shared apartment in West Hollywood after he acted up at the premiere. He made an unsuccessful attempt to shove Stu into his cage but gave up and let him loose.

Babs laughed. "What's the point? He's going to do what he wants anyway." She drew his attention to a cardboard box on his desk. "Help yourself to donuts. They're fresh. The coffee should still be hot."

Guy reached for the only uneaten éclair. Babs tried to grab it away, but he bit into it first.

When it came time to recap last night's events, Guy complained he couldn't see anything after the photographer's flash bulb blinded everyone.

"Didn't you find the small, stuffed bird mounted to his camera a bit out of the ordinary?" she asked.

"Not at all. That's where the old expression comes from. The phrase 'look at the birdie' or 'watch the birdie' originated in the last century. When a portrait photographer needed to capture his subject's attention, especially with children, while he was hiding behind a large camera, often with a black drape over his head, he operated a mechanical brass bird so his client would look in the right direction. Some of them made chirping noises. The man who approached us—"

"More like assaulted us," Babs said.

"He looked like he had a homemade version of one of those bygone-era gimmicks."

"Except it looked like one of the taxidermy specimens we saw at Birdie Wilson's."

"Well, that too."

Babs repositioned one of her hair combs. She had rushed to get ready and already felt like everything was coming apart. "Maybe we should check on the members of the *Falcon* troupe and see how they're doing, especially Mary Astor. Poor woman..." Bruno, the bulldog, waddled over and chewed a buckle on her shoe. "Seems like drama always nips at her heels," she said, using her foot to shove him aside.

"I'm sure it's nothing serious," said Guy. "She just got overexcited."

Babs gestured to his desk phone to make her point.

* * *

A sudden knock on the door startled the detectives, who hadn't expected any visitors. The one advantage they had after Bugsy Siegel had shattered their pebbled glass window was they could see who approached. Since Wiggins had replaced it, it obscured everyone's features just like before. All they could determine was their guest's shadow showed signs of movement. Welcome or not, it appeared to be a slender male (clearly not Wiggins), and over six feet tall and alive. Whoever he was, he took advantage of their front door being unlocked. Babs held her breath. The doorknob slowly rotated, and as the door creaked open, she finally exhaled with relief to identify their interloper as Basil Rathbone, their former client.

He observed the menagerie that had taken over Guy's front office. "A few changes since the last time, won't you agree?"

Like the infamous WWI flying ace, Baron von Richthofen, Stu dive-bombed toward Basil's felt Trilby hat. With a response more expedient than if Zorro were his opponent, Basil used his well-known skills in swordsmanship to swat his aggressor in midair, using a nearby umbrella. The bird let out an ear-piercing chirp.

"Foul ball!" Guy rushed to the waste can where Stu crash-landed.

Basil groused about the wounds all over his neck, stained with orange Mercurochrome antiseptic, after last night's onslaught. "Good heavens! He attacked me first."

Guy locked Stu in his cage. Babs couldn't stop giggling. "What brings you here on Sunday? Shouldn't you be out playing cricket?"

"My appointment to meet Doctor Watson, or should I say, Nigel Bruce, isn't for another two hours. I had time to spare and figured I could get in your hair, but it seems like I had to give your feathery fiend a stop hit."

"What is that?" Babs asked.

"A fencing term, which I guess I can't expect you to understand since you don't engage in the sport. In other words, beating him to the punch or stopping a hit before it could be launched. I haven't caused any permanent damage to your companion, I hope."

"He's no friend of mine," Guy muttered. "But please don't tell me you've lost one of your dogs again. We're not in the business of being dogcatchers, and we're in the middle of a far more serious case."

"None of the sorts," Basil replied. "But—"

"This time, it involves murder," said Babs.

"In fact, several murders have gone unresolved," Basil replied.

"How come you know?" Guy asked.

"Sherlock Holmes has his methods."

Babs felt an unsettling sense of déjà vu. Between suspects and victims, there were already too many people involved, including the unpredicted twist of George Raft's association with a notorious gangster. She had no control over what the police leaked to the press. Neither she nor Guy had time to stay on top of every gossip columnist. What next?

"Your presence, although always welcome, threw me, and I'm sure my partner would agree. Basil, how can we help you?"

He reached into his pocket and retrieved his wallet. "Actually, I came to help you. When I spotted you last night, and it was hard not to with that pesty bunch of feathers on Guy's shoulder, I had hoped to have a word with you, but my jaundiced wife's reaction to Mary's fainting episode and my animal attack precluded any opportunity for a normal conversation."

From his wallet, he took out several bills of a high denomination and placed them on top of Guy's desk.

"What's that?" Guy asked. "A retainer to hire us on another case?"

Basil shook his head. "On the contrary, this is the balance due for the reward for rescuing my dog from those fiends who almost shipped him to Japan. As I told you at the celebration party at MGM, my wife handed the reward to the police, and you were the ones who should've gotten it. Therefore, I scraped up whatever available cash I could find around the house on short notice and gave it to Babs, but it wasn't much and nowhere near the amount I promised in our original contract."

The detectives gawked at the startling amount of cash. One of their many kittens used Basil's trousers to climb up his leg. Taking care not to hurt the little fellow, he plucked off the kit and addressed the taciturn detectives. "Cat got your tongues?"

"Guess…it did." Guy stumbled over his words to get that much of a reply.

Babs wanted to slap her face as if she'd been dreaming. "There's leftover coffee, but I don't mind boiling water. Tea, perhaps?"

Basil made himself at home on one of their chairs, as if he had planned on staying.

"I'm afraid you'll have to make do with a tea bag," said Babs. "We don't keep loose tea leaves and a strainer in the office."

Meanwhile, Stu resented being caged and became talkative. "Elementary! You know my methods, Watson!" he blurted out.

Guy was flabbergasted. "How can this bird know quotes from Sherlock Holmes?"

"Well, I did just say, 'Sherlock Holmes has his methods.' If he's that smart, he probably just repeated what he had picked up elsewhere," Basil said and got up to examine him.

"Free to a good home," Guy chirped. "You must love birds, because I know you have canaries."

"I tolerate them, and they amuse our cats. They're my wife's doing, but after last night, if this bird wants to curry my favor, he owes me some sort of concession."

Sir Henry the wolfhound got up to sniff Basil's hand and wanted him to scratch his head. Bruno planted himself on top of one of Basil's feet.

Babs gestured at their accumulated fauna collection. "As you can see, we have way more than we can handle." She didn't want to be rude and kick out their guest, especially after he handed them a large sum of money, but unless he was biding his time until he had to meet with Nigel Bruce, she still wanted to know why he continued to linger when they needed to get back to work.

"I'm curious. How did you get invited to last night's premiere since the two of you no longer work in the acting profession?" Basil asked.

Babs swiped the last bite of the éclair Guy had stolen. When he gave her a dirty look, she replied, "If I hadn't eaten it, Sir Henry would've."

The detectives concocted a quick summary of the birdings, the mysterious murders, and all those who became the target of threats. Despite the film getting made and finally in theaters, whoever was behind these outrageous acts hadn't been caught.

"Every time we make progress, we run into another snag," Guy explained. "The latest involves George Raft, who was up for the part of Sam Spade in *The Maltese Falcon* but turned it down."

"Isn't he best friends with that gangster...Bugsy Siegel?" Basil asked. "If so, you need to drop this case and leave it to the police. You don't want to be associating with the likes of any of his companions. They're liable to put you out of business...permanently."

Basil took his cigarette case out of his pocket. He offered one to Guy, who took one and, in turn, offered Basil a light. "Hope I'm not being rude," he said to Babs, but if I recall, you don't smoke."

She promptly opened her office windows, turned on a fan, and propped open their front door. "Are you volunteering your services? We can't afford to pay you as a consulting detective."

"I'm not so sure how Humphrey Bogart would feel about it," Guy said. "Imagine if another notable sleuth impinged on Sam Spade's territory."

Basil made a long, deep exhaled breath, blowing his cigarette smoke away from Babs. "I think you're wasting your time with Siegel and Raft."

"What makes you think that?" Guy asked.

"Let's go over the facts. The film is done and out in theaters."

"After the sensational death at the film premiere, reporters were everywhere, but police are probably trying to suppress the news as much as possible," said Guy.

Babs crossed her arms and stiffened. "That's not going to stop the presses."

"Do you know the identity of the person who died and whether he had a connection with the film?" Basil asked.

"We met him once when the Bogarts invited us over for dinner. He worked for Acme Star Tours. Bogie said he always hung around his place, ringing the doorbell to get him to show his face for his customers. I think he also told us that once he threatened the jerk with a shotgun to get off his lawn."

"He never badgered Humphrey Bogart for a job?" Basil asked.

"As what?"

"For a part in one of his movies."

"Not that we know of," Guy added. "That's why we can't figure out why he became the next target. It just doesn't make any sense, and opposed to being poisoned or possibly drugged, when we got a closer look, he showed clear signs of getting bashed on the head and choked to death."

Basil steepled his fingers, touching them against his lips. While the remains of his cigarette smoldered in a nearby ashtray, at last, he replied, "Maybe that's exactly what the killer wanted."

Guy showed Basil his brown paper map, which had remained tacked to the wall. Then, he pointed out the analogies he made to certain suspects. Babs explained that he originally had stolen the Bogarts' tablecloth before transferring his notes to paper, and how it conjured the Goddess of War when Mayo wouldn't let them hear the end of it.

"Thinking along the deductive lines of Sherlock Holmes rather than the flawed rationalization of Rathbone, your criminal could've preplanned this chap's demise, but intentionally switched his techniques of rendering death in order to throw the police off his scent," said Basil.

He lit a fresh cigarette and mused, "There's nothing more deceptive than obvious fact. Crime is common. Logic is rare. Therefore, it is upon reason rather than upon the crime that you should dwell. When you have eliminated the impossible, whatever remains, however improbable, must be the truth."

Babs wondered if their Holmesian thespian would turn out to be their eleventh-hour patron saint.

"Have you followed up on all of your actors since *The Falcon* wrapped?" Basil asked.

"We know of their schedules and have been in the process of making in-person appearances," said Guy. "We already encountered a false alarm with Mary Astor regarding her ex-husband. He claimed he had located the *Purple Diaries* and threatened once again to expose them to the public."

"That would incite quite a scandal," Basil said. "I remember the stirring headlines the first time."

"Tomorrow, we're supposed to meet with Peter Lorre," said Guy. "He's rehearsing with Cary Grant on a film adaptation of the stage play *Arsenic and Old Lace*. Are you dropping a hint that you'd like to join us?"

"None of the sorts. Although the Great Bard wrote, 'All the world's a stage and all the men and women are merely players,' I don't think it's my place to perform on those sound stages. Especially when they're at Warner Brothers, and now my contract is with Universal. You're on your own, I'm afraid."

Basil looked at his watch, thanked them for the tea, and said he mustn't forget his engagement with Nigel Bruce, his on-screen sidekick. In turn, the detectives thanked him for acknowledging their efforts toward retrieving Leo, his Cocker Spaniel, and bid him adieu.

Babs took one last sip of her tea, now cold. "I guess a penny's worth of Holmesian advice is better than none at all."

Guy had other thoughts. He, who always preferred sugary orange Nehi soda for a pick-me-up rather than the more bitter beverages of coffee and tea, tossed a slug into their vending machine. After taking a long, satisfying slurp, he scooped the reward money into one of his drawers for temporary safekeeping, be it from a random breeze or an inquiring hound. Then he turned to Babs. "There's been a third murder."

She gave him an incredulous stare. "What else is new?"

"Now, since Basil dumped all these dollars in our laps, maybe we should pull out of this case. We really should leave homicide matters to the police. That's Sadowski's and Allgood's specialty. Not ours. We've never dealt with anything like this before."

She opened Guy's desk drawer to recount the money. Earlier she had only gotten a visual glance and wanted to know how much Basil had given them. "This might seem like a lot of cash, but what will we do when it runs out?"

"So, you're telling me you want to drive this nail to the board?"

She gave one firm, confident nod. "I wouldn't consider otherwise."

Guy shrugged and started to head for the exit. In an almost imperceptible tone, he babbled, "What's the point? She's going to do what she wants anyway."

"I heard that!" she called out.

"You're acting just like Stu, except I have the option of putting him away in his cage and covering it with a towel to make him calm down and go to sleep."

She hesitated a moment to digest his insult. "Are you walking out on me again…like you did on Basil's case?"

"No. Just heading outside for a smoke." He took his cigarette case and lighter out of his pocket. "Being courteous since you hate when I do it in your presence."

Bruno agreed with a growly woof that only a bulldog could muster, and Babs waved him off to get back to her paperwork.

Chapter Thirty: Arsenic and Old Spite

Not long after *The Falcon* premiered in LA, rehearsals commenced on *Arsenic and Old Lace*. Cast and crew played musical chairs between three Warner Brothers sound stages where the painters and carpenters were putting on their finishing touches. Peter Lorre invited the private detectives to meet him on the set of the Brewster aunts' boarding house, where he and Cary Grant planned on going over their lines.

Who wouldn't want an excuse to orchestrate a closer encounter with Cary Grant, one of the world's most debonair leading men? Babs' ego needed a boost after getting jilted by Felix Allgood, but first, she wanted to take a detour and swing by the mailroom. Her partner had plenty of time when she was away in San Francisco to scour Birdie's records. He could've connected the entries of a repeat customer with deliveries to Warner's, but either couldn't or didn't.

"I think we're getting close. The name E. Knoll showed up with a frequency worth noting," Babs explained. "He, however, only gave the address of the studio's mailroom, or he picked them up in person."

"Birdie never mentioned anyone suspicious when we met him," said Guy.

"We'll never know, which makes me more concerned that he might've covered up for him."

They arrived close to lunchtime. Most of the mailroom employees were on break or out on errands. One of the few who remained said E. Knoll stood for Eric Knoll.

"Do you have any idea why he had his deliveries sent here rather than home?" she asked.

"Heard from my coworkers that Knoll complained about thieves stealing packages. Sometimes, he leaves memos giving permission for others to pick up his mail."

"You wouldn't happen to have any of those memos lying around?" Babs explained they could compare those to the handwriting on Mary Astor's note which was signed, "Birdie," which Wilson swore wasn't his handwriting. Unfortunately, they discarded all of them.

"Have you ever met Knoll?" Guy asked.

The mail clerk took a quick bite out of his sandwich. "Naw, I'm a new hire. Haven't met many of my coworkers."

"Any of your colleagues mention if he looked or wore anything out of the ordinary?" asked Guy.

"Can't help you on that one. We have a lot of employees here. Many part-timers."

"You wouldn't happen to have any pictures of Knoll?" asked Babs. "Perhaps headshots?"

"On the offshoot chance a casting director wanders over here, and he'd get discovered?" the employee said, laughing.

Unable to retain her poise, Babs snorted. "That's not what I meant."

The man apologized. "Personnel should have a copy of his ID in his file."

"They'd also have his home address." Guy took out his wallet, making it clear he had a little extra cash to fork over if this man was willing to talk. "Can you tell us anything about Knoll...like how long he's been here?"

"Like most of us, I think he works here on and off...a few hours a week and does other odd jobs on the side. Other than that, beats me."

Guy handed the man a fiver and thanked him for what he was able to provide.

The detectives made a quick pit stop at personnel. Knoll only provided a P.O. box. No photos. Taking for granted he used the standard spelling, on one form his name was spelled E-r-i-k. Another person wrote it as Erich, and someone had it misspelled as Erica. Since people had goofed with hers, spelling it Barbra instead of Barbara, her real name, the one which she didn't want anyone to know, she didn't think much of it.

* * *

They located a production chalkboard indicating which stages were used for their current productions. The problem was it was being filmed on Stages 6, 9, and 19.

"Either Peter didn't tell us which stage or—" said Babs.

"You failed to write it down."

Feeling her recent headache making an encore, she pinched her eyebrows together.

"I've had a lot on my mind."

"The choice is yours," said Guy.

She picked the closest. They tiptoed through a cemetery with fake gravestones while stagehands tested out their wind machines. Guy had to chase after his hat, which flew across the set. Both ended up picking dried leaves out of their hair.

They got lucky on their second try and found Peter rehearsing lines with Cary Grant on the set of the interior of the Brewster spinsters' house.

Babs noticed Grant had his arm in a sling. "Did you get injured, or is that part of your costume?"

"Oh, no. Hurts like the dickens. I fell face-first over a chair during a scene where I chased a prospective boarder out of the house. I was trying to prevent him from being poisoned. Not in real life...in the script, of course. The director expected me to give him a healthy dose of my famous physical comedy, but I guess I went overboard."

"None were too happy when they thought it might hold up production," said Lorre. "The production staff had to juggle our schedule accordingly to accommodate time for our star to recover. Now, he must constantly remind himself not to get carried...*ha-ha-ha*...*Cary-ed* away."

"You might find that amusing," Grant retorted. "But you're not the one who wakes up in the middle of the night with a sore shoulder."

Lorre took a flask out of his jacket pocket and guzzled it down. "It's a mere scratch. Nothing a swig of this stuff couldn't make disappear."

Grant shook his head when offered. "That moonshine will make me lose my wits for good."

"It's lemonade," Lorre said with a smirk.

"Yeah, right, and Napoleon Bonaparte retired at a beach resort in Bermuda and took Jack Warner's private masseur with him!" His statement caused a few raised eyebrows. "Well, anyway, the show must go on. Peter warned me two young detectives would drop by, and I assume that's you. What brings you here?"

Babs deferred back to Cary's injury. "Will that hold up production?"

He raised his brows and screwed up his face in a comedic fashion. "Who knows when this film will come out? I've heard there have been contractual delays, because *Arsenic and Old Lace* is still playing on Broadway. Might be related to having to wait until the run of the show is over."

"Hey, as long as our checks clear at the bank," Peter said, "I don't care when it winds up in the theaters."

"Fill me in 'cause I didn't have time to do my homework," Babs admitted. "What's this story about?"

Cary had trouble lighting his cigarette with his arm in bandages. Lorre asked if he could have one and lit them for both.

"A Brooklyn writer, Mortimer Brewster...that's me...known for his books on the futility of marriage, ties the knot with his childhood sweetheart. Things get even more complicated on his wedding day when he discovers his maiden aunts and delusional uncle have murdered a dozen or more tenants and have buried their corpses in their basement."

"Are you the delusional uncle?" Babs winked at Lorre with a slight snicker.

"I don't want to brag, but I can make people laugh and then be terrified. To answer your question, Mortimer has a homicidal brother named Jonathan who's escaped from an asylum for the criminally insane. He's enlisted the assistance of Dr. Einstein, that's me. He's an alcoholic plastic surgeon, who keeps operating on him so he can hide from the police. Einstein's last botched job made Jonathan look way too much like Boris Karloff, and he gets furious if anyone brings it to his attention."

"What's even funnier," Cary added, "the real Karloff is playing Jonathan's role in the Broadway production."

"Who's playing him in the film?" asked Guy.

"Raymond Massey," replied Lorre. "He's a fine performer with a wide range. He can appear quite scary when he wants to."

"Not sure about my acting," said Grant. "In my opinion, it's way over the top and one of my worst performances ever, but our director seems to like it. Looks like I'm just going to have to write this film off as one of my silly obligations under contract and nothing more. I doubt audiences will like it—"

"But the checks have cleared at the bank." The words rolled off Peter's tongue as he gave him the side-eye.

"All right. You've given us a rundown as to what *Arsenic and Old Lace* is about," Guy said. "Let's take that theme and compare it to *The Maltese Falcon*."

Grant was nonplussed. "What does your last film have to do with this one? I can't think of any similarities."

"Maybe not," said Guy. "But Peter is in both of them, and we want to make sure he doesn't get threatened again."

Cary held up his hand. "Hold on! No one informed me at all about threats. Care to put me in the loop?"

"We'll address that in a minute, but first, hear us out," said Babs. "In *The Maltese Falcon*, San Francisco private detective Sam Spade takes on a case which inadvertently causes his partner to get killed. Next thing he knows, he's in up to his neck with a seductive femme fatale who's a consummate con artist and three unpredictable, unorthodox criminals, always looking after their own necks and at odds with each other. It's winner takes all when it comes to finding a priceless and legendary, but elusive, artifact in the shape of a bird."

"You should be awarded an honorary PhD for that discourse," said Grant, tongue-in-cheek.

Babs blushed. "You're next, Peter. We need your input."

"I'm still not convinced this doesn't have to do with the curse of *M*."

Grant looked back and forth between Peter and the detectives so fast that he thought he gave himself whiplash. "Curses and dead birds! Does anyone care to fill me in?"

"Fritz Lang directed *M*. Typical of his reputation of being cruel to his actors. Lang had me thrown downstairs and into a cellar over a dozen times. His wife wrote the script based on a newspaper article," Lorre said, lighting another cigarette.

"Isn't Thea von Harbou, Lang's wife, a Nazi sympathizer?" asked Babs.

"What does that have to do with a dead bird?" Lorre asked.

"We're aware there are underground groups of fascist supporters living in Los Angeles. Right now."

Lorre's lip started to tremble. His first words came out as a stutter. "Y-o-u mean they fol-lo-wed me here all the way from Ger-ma-ny? I thought I was safe here in America. Don't tell me Hitler is trying to deport me."

"That's doubtful," Guy said with assurance. "But we can never fully rule it out."

"Did you know his ministry made a propaganda film called *The Eternal Jew*? In it, they used a clip from *M*. Are you aware that I'm Jewish?"

There was a brief silence as the bemused detectives looked at each other and frowned. In her head, Babs tried to sort the facts: Jack Warner, Bugsy Siegel, and Leon Lewis were also Jewish, and they had all been birded.

"Goebbels has commissioned many films to denigrate the Jews and anyone else he doesn't like. Let's hope this isn't a case of relentless persecution," Lorre said, grinding his cigarette into an already overfilled ashtray. Ashes spilled out onto the top of an end table.

"Tell me about these," Guy said.

Lorre vigorously rubbed his arms as if the room's temperature had dropped thirty degrees. His teeth chattered. "De-spi-cable in-doc-tri-nation. They portray Jews as uncivilized, par-a-si-tic, abnormal, and depraved. Fritz Hippler directed *The Eternal Jew* on orders from Goebbels, Nazi Germany's Minister of Propaganda. It included documentary footage taken shortly after the Nazi occupation of Poland. These vicious attacks resulted in the 1938 pogrom of *Kristallnacht,* which translates to the Night of Broken Glass. I'm sure you heard about that."

Babs also felt an icy chill and donned her jacket, as if his mere words caused her to live through the terror.

Peter continued. "Aside from the footage shot in Poland, the rest of the film consisted of photographs and footage from feature films like *M* and *The House of Rothschild* about the family of European bankers, which was made in Hollywood. Mind you, they altered many details in the Rothschild film, making much of it fictional. I'm sure the Nazis took these film clips without permission. By the way, they put it together...edited, you know, they meant it to look like documentary footage. De-cep-tive, right? Just like most of the things they do."

"There has to be a common thread among these films," said Guy.

"Maybe I should get the reward, if there is one, for solving this case," said Grant, quick to answer. "It doesn't take a genius private detective to figure it out. Our friend Peter's in all of them."

Before they had a chance to discuss it further, a messenger dropped off boxed lunches for only the actors. There was an extra brown paper bag with a note for Peter saying it was from his doctor.

"My new prescriptions." He held the bag close like guarded treasure. "Excuse me. It's a special preparation, and I'd like to take it in private."

While Peter disappeared, Cary asked, "It would be rude of me not to ask, but are you hungry?"

Babs' growling stomach spoke for her. Meanwhile, one of the properties assistants left a bottle of wine on the table between them.

"Looks like you're doing lunch in style," Babs commented. Her guts gurgled again.

"It's for an upcoming scene," said the kid, who took a rag and wiped off the dust on the tabletop. "Please leave it alone. I think it's supposed to be in a decanter on a shelf, but that's for my boss to decide."

Cary offered him a tip. "I know it's not in your job description, but do you mind getting two more boxed lunches for my guests?"

"Sure thing, Mr. Grant," he said and sped off.

* * *

Lorre returned from his dressing room wearing a light coat over the jacket he'd worn earlier. His face looked ashen, and he didn't seem too steady on his feet. Babs paid particular attention to his sniffling where, on occasion, he rubbed his nose.

Always a gentleman when it came to manners, Cary insisted on waiting to open their boxed lunches until the stagehand returned with extras for Guy and Babs. Realizing her momentary chill was due to an attack of nerves, Babs removed her jacket.

She couldn't understand why Peter kept his on since his face and hair showed signs of sweat. "Peter, please take off your coat. Just looking at you is making me feel overheated."

"Me, too," Grant said, loosening his collar. "You've been acting kind of peculiar lately. Are you sure you're all right?"

Hesitant, he undressed, but as he swung it around onto the back of his chair, Cary sprang to his feet. "Look!" he cried, pointing to a chalk mark on his topcoat.

"Someone branded you with an M!" Guy exclaimed. "Just like your film."

Seeing it for himself, Peter jerked like he'd been pinpricked. He shouted in German, "Oh my, God!" and threw his coat onto the floor, scared to get closer.

Guy tried to stay calm amid the panic. "Who gets access to your dressing room?"

"The lock doesn't work. I keep all sorts of personal items in there, which are nobody's business, but there isn't any way to keep anybody out."

Cary looked at the gang for a volunteer. "Call security, right away!"

Peter held up his hand, still shaking. "No, wait. I'm sure it's someone's idea of a practical joke. Perhaps Horton, who plays the Happydale Sanitarium director, or John Alexander, the actor who believes he's Teddy Roosevelt. They don't know me well enough or realize, to me, it's not amusing."

The four debated the best way to handle it until the properties assistant returned with the extra lunches. Peter decided he'd take the marked coat to the production office, but after they finished dining.

"Well, I don't know about you, fellas…and ladies…or lady, since there's only one of you," Cary said to Babs, "I'm famished and suggest we eat. Does everyone agree?"

Guy glared at four identical white cardboard boxes. Cary switched them around like a shell game. "I'm sure whatever's inside is all the same. If not, we'll get pleasantly surprised. Now, let's eat."

Babs, whose innards were never subtle, plunged in first.

"Whatcha got?" Guy asked.

She scrutinized its components, dipping her finger and tasting it first before giving it the A-okay. "Slices of turkey, gravy, stuffing, and cranberries. What about you?"

Guy opened his. "The chef might've made up a pre-holiday smorgasbord. I've got candied sweet potatoes, green beans, and baked ham."

Peter opened his next. "Might be Beef Wellington," he said, picking at it with a fork.

Cary tucked his napkin into his collar. "Can't get gravy on anything."

"That's not your film wardrobe," said Peter.

"Doesn't matter. Who has time to worry about dry cleaning?"

"Isn't that what your wife or your valet is for?" Peter asked.

"My valet has other things to worry about, and right now, I'm in between wives."

Imagine landing the world's most handsome bachelor! Move aside, Errol Flynn. Babs felt a sudden tingle, hoping no one noticed.

Cary Grant cracked open his container. The urbane comedian, always full of quips and comebacks, suddenly became inarticulate. Guy peeked into the box, grabbed an ashtray, and placed it on top to keep the box from reopening.

At last, he regained his speech. "What was that?"

Raising his brows, Guy looked at Babs. "Not a crow. Another kind of bird...covered in gravy and no Thanksgiving turkey, for sure." Guy took one more peek. "Don't think it's my imagination, but this one isn't dead. I swore I saw it move...just a little. Then again, maybe I shook the box. It looked drugged and was beginning to wake up."

"I think that was meant for me, except you mixed them up and moved them around, which messed up somebody's plans." Peter inched closer. "Mind if I look?"

Babs choked down her food. "Yes, I do. Guy, call security. We need to turn this over to Allgood and Sadowski."

"Are you certain? This is Warner Brothers, and we're in Burbank. The Burbank police will tamper with it before it gets over to the Hollywood Precinct."

She patted her lips with her napkin and applied fresh lipstick. "Do this by the book. We have no business holding on to it."

Everyone stared at the box, which appeared to make a slight rattle.

Still confused, Grant asked, "Does anyone care to explain this? Seems like I only know part of the story."

Lorre cut in. "I could see if this were an April Fool's joke, but it's October, and we're nearing Halloween."

"This seems to be more of a trick than a treat," said Grant. "Wait a minute! Are you telling me this has happened before?"

Peter dropped his shoulders and nodded.

Guy excused himself in search of a phone. "I'm calling Bogie. He needs to be here when the police arrive."

"Humphrey Bogart?" Grant asked, "Why him?"

"He's our paying client and the first to get birded like this," said Babs in haste. She turned to Peter. "We need to examine all angles as to why somebody wanted to single you out above the rest of your cast members and be willing to follow you to your next project."

Chapter Thirty-One: Trapped

Flanked by studio security guards, Jack Warner announced he had already put a call in to the police. Lorre worried the next time, he'd be a dead man. "Someone has birded me twice. As the saying goes, three strikes and you're out, right?"

Warner took command. "We'll require sign-in sheets at all entrances for the three sound stages we're using for *Arsenic and Old Lace*. Security will monitor everyone until we catch this killer."

"How do we know the killer is also the birder?" asked Grant. "He might have an accomplice."

"Soon, we should find out. It's clear it's someone who's gotten onto the studio lot," Warner said.

"Not necessarily," said Babs. "It could be someone who's instructed another to do their dirty work."

The studio mogul gave her a stare like he resented anyone, giving the impression they were smarter. "Anyway, we'll keep an eye out for packages going in and out of our mailroom." Then he leaned over to Grant and whispered, "I'm going to let you in on a little secret. This is a personal matter. Someone has birded me, too."

The stage door opened, and everyone expected it to be the Burbank Police. Humphrey Bogart bounded in, with his bowtie askew and hair out of place, looking like he had just gotten out of bed or into a fight.

Guy kept his voice low. "What time did you roll in last night?"

He took a comb out of his back pocket and did a once over. "Had a little trouble at home. Sometimes I wonder which is more of a threat, my wife or this maniac leaving dead birds as calling cards."

"Can I trust Sam Spade to resolve this case before anyone else?" asked Warner.

"Don't you go running around confusing me with my character," Bogie said, cracking a smile, but soon shifting to a serious frame of mind.

Big Boss Warner ordered the actors to resume their rehearsal and ignore any onlookers. Babs, in trying to sort everything out, muttered out loud to herself. He snatched a megaphone and yelled, "Quiet on the set!" reprimanding her for not being silent. She nearly jumped out of her skin.

Peter reached for the spiked bottle of wine. Grant yelled, "Stop! Remember the script? Mortimer Brewster's crazy aunts concocted a murder cocktail of arsenic, cyanide, strychnine, and elderberry wine. It might be poisoned—for real."

Lorre withdrew, clutching his chest and breathing heavily. Warner ordered one of his guards to seize it as evidence. Meanwhile, Babs' brain brimmed with deductions. She couldn't get it out of her mind that the person they were looking for had birded and killed others outside of the film's immediate cast, making the murderer's motivation even more complicated.

"You know, all movies have a properties department. Don't you think we should make a few inquiries?" asked Grant.

"Speaking about props and property masters," Guy whispered to Babs. "We never pinned down Frank Sexton, the sculptor of the *Maltese Falcon.*"

Warner looked at his watch and complained the cops were taking way too long. The actors resumed their rehearsal until someone started hammering. Cary could no longer tolerate the distraction. "For heaven's sake, don't they know we're trying to work?"

"I think they'd have the same argument with you," Peter commented. "Maybe we should head over to the commissary. Lunch should be over by now. We ran our lines there earlier until it got too noisy and crowded."

Warner started fuming. "For crying out loud, ignore it. Didn't I mention that I like to keep our projects secret from others? Who knows what sorts of spies from rival studios might be lurking around our lot?"

"Boss, all it takes is a look at the chalkboards to know who is filming what and where," Cary explained.

Warner wanted the last word. "It's a lot easier to lock down a set than it is to prevent someone from eavesdropping in the lunchroom."

With their argument going nowhere, the performers continued their scene until Lorre, who looked peaked to begin with, slumped over in his chair.

Guy splashed water in Lorre's face to revive him. "He mentioned his doctor had given him new medication. If we can get him to talk, he'll know how to contact him."

"No...not that one." Hardly intelligible, Peter beckoned the detectives to come closer. "I've had this problem with pain in my back...and in my stomach. Troubled me on and off for years."

Guy got wise. "You took drugs that you shouldn't have, didn't you?"

"Can't seem to shake my dependency." He groaned, doubled over, and nearly fell out of his chair. "Earlier, I told you that the lock on my dressing room door is broken."

Guy cornered Peter. "You think someone tampered with them?"

From the far end of the stage, someone started singing. "It's that darned song, again," said Babs. "Someone is obsessed with *Bye, Bye Blackbird.* Why?"

From behind the constructed walls of the set, they heard movement.

"I thought no one could come in or out," Cary said.

"This is a massive stage. What if they were already on the set before security locked it down?" Bogie asked. "There are those who work behind the scenes, the ones we rarely pay attention to who know of all sorts of catwalks and cubbyholes we'd never encounter. In theater, I've worked with trap doors and revolving walls. Stage magicians use these tricks all the time."

Everyone grabbed the nearest object that could double as a weapon. Peter found a broom. Bogie went for the wine bottle. Guy struggled to pick up a bundle of cables meant to power the movie lights. One of the juicers from the electrical crew confronted him.

"Hey, don't recognize you as one of my union boys. Better keep your hands where they belong."

Guy jumped and dropped the heavy cables on the man's foot, who was ready to raise his fist. Babs intervened and used her charms to calm the irate stagehand. He gave Guy a warning about safety on set and left cursing.

Once he was out of earshot, Babs asked, "Guy, what were you planning to do?"

"Guess it's a bit clumsy to swing it like a whip, but I had no idea it would be this heavy. What should we do now? There's bound to be more stagehands like him milling about."

Beyond their immediate setting, most of the vast stage hid in darkness. Every snap or pop made someone shudder. Moments passed. Everyone got restless. Then the door leading to the Brewster's basement rattled. Warner signaled everyone to stay put.

Cary spotted a large stage light already plugged in. "I don't care if that big brute tries to bully me and cites union regulations or not." Everyone heard a powerful whoomph, a hiss, and a crackle of power surging through the cable as he switched it on and pointed it in the direction of the basement door. "Learned this from cop movies," he said. "The police would shine a searchlight into the criminal's eyes and blind them, halting them from going further."

This time, when the door vibrated, it appeared that someone was trying to open it but couldn't. Finally, a man dressed in street clothing but wearing a crude falcon mask of unknown folklore covered with black feathers kicked it open. He pranced forth and broke into a tribal-like dance, whooping and hollering a chant which sounded like German. Peter shuddered, as if he knew its meaning.

"Crow-Feather?" Guy whispered.

She shook her head. "Too short...and slim."

When finished, the Bird Man pulled out a gun and pointed it at Peter.

"Drink the wine!" he demanded with a high-pitched voice that cracked.

"Don't you dare!" shouted Grant, who whisked the possibly tainted bottle away.

"Halt!" cried one of Warner's guards, who tried to shoot the intruder, but missed.

Seeing beyond his disguise, Guy pointed at the Bird Man and shouted,

"He's got the ring! The German signet ring. He's the same guy...the bicycle messenger. You set me up to get clobbered by Abdul!"

Taking no chances, Babs took her gun out of her purse and fired, grazing his leg to hinder but not to kill. The man screamed and dropped to the floor.

"Did you forget I had a gun?" she said to Guy, but everyone looked shocked when the Bird Man clutched his leg to stop the bleeding and broke down crying, in part from pain, but as if wracked with remorse. In a strange twist of logic, the bizarre Bird Man ranted about wanting to take revenge against the Germans, but he was German, therefore he must be condemned.

"The Nazis have turned my country against me. Germany is no longer the land I knew, but there is a monster screaming inside of me. Such agony. I wanna run...run away, but I can't. I can't escape from myself. I want to kill all the Germans."

By the time the police and two ambulances arrived, the Bird Man had lost consciousness. Babs accompanied Peter in his ambulance. Guy and the police kept watch over the crazed Bird Man in the other.

* * *

While doctors and nurses attended to each patient, the hospital staff ordered the PIs to remain in the waiting room.

Babs blew her nose and complained she hated the antiseptic odors typical of hospitals.

"What's this big ado about a ring?" she asked.

"After I noticed him wearing it the first time, I was curious and looked it up," Guy explained. "*Ringvereine* signet rings, identified a member of a ring club, or criminal gangs operating in the German Weimar Republic. Around 1933, the Nazis outlawed them. Like the Mafia, these underground networks of former convicts had a code of conduct. Since these groups practiced witness intimidation and members provided alibis for one another, it was difficult to prove their involvement in crimes. Our Bird Man, who I suspect is this Eric Knoll we've been looking for, insisted he got his ring from a pawnbroker. He thought it signified nobility or an honor for military service, but I believe he lied."

"How would that relate to Peter?" asked Babs.

"Perhaps he feels the need to act as some sort of vigilante, but I'm convinced Knoll is consumed with the film *M*. He must've put the chalk mark on Peter's overcoat. In *M*, Berlin's police director, in pursuit of the murderer, makes it tough for the established criminal gangs to continue their operations. One of the crime bosses steps forth and summons the other heads of Berlin's *Ringvereine* to take matters into their own hands and organize the street people to help capture the killer.

"Babs, when Hans Beckert encounters another young girl, the blind balloon peddler recognizes his whistling of Grieg's *Hall of the Mountain King* and tells his friend. At the earliest opportunity, the man chalks a large "M" for *Mörder*, or murderer in German, on the palm of his hand. He pretends to stumble and bumps into Beckert, on purpose, marking the back of his coat so others can identify and track him. When Beckert realizes he is being watched, he makes a break for it, sparing the girl, but I wonder if our Bird Man was actually part of a real ring club in Germany. Perhaps Peter knows."

"Can't understand why, but in this case, he obsesses over the song *Bye, Bye Blackbird,* and actual black birds," said Babs. "However, this seems like a case of mistaken identity. This masked man is confusing Peter Lorre for his character. Just like people tend to assume George Raft is a real gangster or Bogie as Sam Spade."

A man with a resonating voice approached from behind. "Are you still getting hung up about black birds?" The detectives turned around, surprised to encounter Chief Crow-Feather in "civilian" attire. Instead of his native dress, he wore an open-collared khaki gabardine work shirt with flap pockets tucked into belted khaki high-waisted pants and with his long hair slicked back and tucked under a Panama hat.

"What brought you here?" asked Guy.

"Can't make a living performing drum ceremonies. Besides teaching our native culture to local college students, LA County brings me in to make behavioral assessments on suspects and prisoners who don't fit the norm.

Among my multiple college degrees, I have a background in psychology," the Chief explained.

Babs would've never guessed. "Is that something new with police investigations?"

"Many in the police department consider getting a psychologist involved as a bunch of hoodoo, especially by a person with my tribal background. I'm hoping these groundbreaking criminology methods will become more common rather than the exception."

Guy tried to fill him in. "The long list of celebrity birdings had been kept discreetly out of the press, until recently, when the body of Stanley Peck, the pushy and obnoxious Acme Star Tours guide, shocked everyone at the Los Angeles *Falcon* premiere. I had my concerns this would spawn the emergence of amateur sleuths with every friend and neighbor vying for a piece of the action, making our jobs even more difficult."

Babs gave him a friendly poke. "Maybe you should share your theory about the shooter's fascination with Peter's movie."

The conversation never went that far. Somebody shouted, "He's escaped!" Heads turned in the waiting room. A group of cops blew their whistles. With guns drawn, they stormed past them, accompanied by hospital personnel. Babs grabbed her partner by his shirt. "Rules or no rules. Let's follow."

* * *

Knoll's hospital bed was empty, and an orderly lay stunned on the floor. Two cops stood in his wake, and a nurse hovered over her associate with smelling salts.

"What happened?" asked Babs.

One cop gave her a funny look as to why a woman led the questioning. "Sadowski handed him a pen and a pad and tried to get a confession out of him. He scrawled something down, but nobody had a clue what it said. When he got called away on an emergency with the other patient, Allgood took over and coerced him to rewrite it, but legibly.

"Who in their right mind would dress up as a falcon and pull a gun? He wanted to know what made this guy tick. Not sure if you know how in-your-face Allgood could be, but he must've gotten under the prisoner's skin. Heard he stabbed the detective in the face with the fountain pen, bashed his head against the metal guardrails, and knocked him out long enough to pull a Houdini. Did the same with the hospital attendant. Wasn't there, but that's all I can tell ya."

"Where's he now?" asked the chief.

"Beats me." The officer shrugged. "He flew the coop."

Babs feared the worst. "Peter could be in danger!"

The police on hand rushed to Peter's room. The PIs and Crow-Feather tagged behind, out of breath. They found him unharmed and conscious, but delirious.

"He forced me to make a confession...but I didn't do it." Still under the influence of tainted drugs, Peter kept talking to himself, unaware others watched and listened. "'I couldn't help myself. I had to kill them!' Those were lines said by Hans Beckert, my character in *M*, but the killer wanted me to recite them...to believe in them."

One cop asked Crow-Feather if he understood what he was saying.

"Sounds like he's trying to make him feel guilty and atone for Beckert's sins."

With no nurse in sight, Babs couldn't believe they'd left Peter unattended. She took her handkerchief and wiped the sweat off Peter's forehead. The officer in charge ordered round-the-clock security. Knoll was still at large, and his whereabouts unknown.

Chapter Thirty-Two: Round Robin

The PIs returned to their cars after security booted them out of the hospital.

Guy wasn't willing to give up. "Once Peter's well enough, we should get the Bogarts to host a party. I'd bet that would lure the Bird Man back."

"Mayo will turn the place into a free-for-all if she starts one of her flare-ups." Babs' weariness turned to cynicism. "Why don't we invite everyone in the Hollywood phonebook? Throw in a parking valet from Musso & Frank's while we're at it, or Bette Davis. She always conjures up controversy."

"If we try hard enough," said Guy, "everyone in town will have a slight connection to who's been committing these crimes."

Babs one-upped him and took the cake. "The heck with it! Invite Errol Flynn and Basil Rathbone and see if they'll wind up in another sword fight like the last time we put them together in the same room," she said, referring to their last big celebrity case and their showdown on the *RMS Queen Mary*.

* * *

Despite the obvious danger from Knoll, the Bogarts wanted to share their appreciation for everyone's combined efforts. On Saturday evening, instead of an elaborate sit-down affair, they arranged an informal, last-minute get-together with a buffet.

Babs and Guy took advantage of the balmy night air. He kicked off his shoes and socks. She ditched her stockings, and both sipped drinks while cooling their toes in the pool. This gave them the opportunity to still observe the other guests through the French doors, which led to the Bogarts' den and game room.

"I thought you shied away from alcohol," Guy observed.

Babs plucked off its stem and swallowed her maraschino cherry. "Sipping on a Shirley Temple."

Guy reached for a souvenir menu sitting on top of one of their wrought-iron tables. Using it as a fan, he swatted a few infernal gnats in another direction. Afterward, he examined it.

"From Chasen's, which Jimmy Durante happened to have signed. Can't believe they had this lying around where it could've been picked up by a breeze and landed in the pool. You know how much I could get from an autograph hound for one of these suckers?"

Babs ignored his remark and kept watch on the guests. Couples danced the foxtrot to Tommy Dorsey's *Blue Champagne*. When the song ended, Cary Grant, who showed up dateless, returned the record to its jacket and tuned into a radio station playing Bing Crosby's, *It Makes No Difference Now*.

"That's the attitude you need to take," said Guy.

She took offense. "It *does* make a difference. Don't know how everyone can relax and stay civil with Knoll on the lam."

"Why don't you make a play for the world's most eligible bachelor now that he's single and available?" Guy suggested. "Might help you get your mind off Allgood, for good."

Babs growled. She didn't want to be reminded of how he deceived her about being married. She also resented having similar misfortunes when it came to other men. Guy took her by the hands and forced her to her feet. "Come, now. You wouldn't hesitate to jump into action if Cary Grant considered hiring you."

Hesitant to admit he was right, she grabbed her sissy Shirley Temple and headed toward the action. Detective Sadowski intervened before she could corner Grant alone. Being a corpulent man, he stepped into her path and scrutinized her cocktail.

"Drinking on the job?" he asked.

"Sugar water and non-alcoholic." She examined his. "What about you?"

"Coca-Cola when I'm a guest-on-call. So far, the party's been quiet."

She took a deep breath and tried to see past him to determine what Grant was up to, but the oversized detective blocked her eyeline. "Where's your partner?"

Babs said that to hide her intent of homing in on Mr. Savoir Faire. She would've been content if she never ran into Allgood again.

"He's trying to blend in and hopes no one notices him."

"By going undercover?" Babs asked.

"Trying to hide all the nasty lumps and bruises."

Babs belted out a laugh but needed to compose herself.

"Besides getting attacked in the hospital, his wife smacked him with a cast iron frying pan after discovering he had a secret girlfriend."

Maybe he deserved it. After all, she had a moral code and would've never dated Allgood had she been aware he was married. Now that his wife had taken her revenge, she felt somewhat vindicated.

Sadowski picked the worst time to disclose his discoveries about the illusive Bird Man during his brief stay in the hospital. The more he chatted, the more he decreased her chances of getting time alone with Grant.

"We did a background check and found out Eric Knoll was German, not American," Sadowski said. "Maybe Mr. Lorre can enlighten us more on those matters, but don't worry about him. My men are working the catering crew tonight."

Ignoring what he had just said, Babs was more concerned that Sadowski obstructed her view from keeping watch on the handsomest man on the planet. He failed, however, to shield her from spotting his partner stuffing his face with hors d'oeuvres. She also acknowledged Leon Lewis mingling among the guests.

The unexpected arrival of Jack Warner and his wife crashing the party caught everyone's surprise. "How did you manage to wrangle an invitation?" Bogie asked.

"A slip of the tongue from my personal assistant," Jack replied. "Couldn't keep it a secret, I guess."

For Babs, it proved to be a challenge to keep tabs on everyone and every little detail. Meanwhile, Bogie's wife slipped in and grabbed Grant by the crook of his arm. Mayo ushered him away from musical duties and toward the steps leading upstairs, bungling Babs' chance to attract his attention.

The bartender freshened her drink and turned it into a Dirty Shirley instead of a Virgin Shirley by adding vodka. Babs returned to the pool to rejoin her partner, where she caught him slicking back his hair to perfection.

"That was quick." Guy straightened his tie and flashed her a smile. "Did you fail to nab the most eligible bachelor at the ball? Except me, of course."

"As a...well, you know. A man who..." She took a deep, calming breath of the evening's jasmine while she groped for words.

"Prefers other men?"

"Yeah, that. You don't count."

"I guess not. Anyway, while you were gone, I put my singing talents to good use. Listen."

Guy swallowed juice from his cocktail lemon to clear his throat and started to whistle. It didn't take long to summon a symphony of tweets, trills, clucks, and warbles from the Bogarts' backyard birds.

A songbird sang, "Cheep, cheep." Two more landed next to him and formed a boisterous trio. Guy chirruped, "*Cheap! Cheap!* Meet the Warbler Brothers. The one on the left is Jack Warbler, short for jackdaw." He doubled over, hee-hawing like a jackass.

Babs burst out laughing. "You're mocking the Warner Brothers."

Using only his voice, Guy mimicked the birds. They responded like a chorus of flutes and piccolos. Then he cooed, cawed, screeched, and bowed the Chasen's menu to simulate the flapping sound of wings. Joining in, her gargling trills made her throat sore, so she switched to drumming her fingers on top of a wooden card table to replicate a woodpecker.

Several birds flew in closer. The first to respond were three Black-capped Chickadees. The detectives debated whether their calls sounded more like *chicka-dee-dee-dee-dee* or *cheeseburger-cheeseburger*. They called on the nearby crows. They compiled a melodic choir but soon became silent.

Babs and Guy looked at each other. "*Shush,*" he said. "I hear footsteps."

"*J-j-j-j jeer. J-j-j-j jeer,*" a blue jay cried.

"I think he's trying to tell us something," said Babs.

Evocative Mourning doves moaned *who-who* and another *who* that went up a few notes and then back down with a final *who*.

"We already know who," whispered Babs. "It's Eric Knoll."

Guy pointed beyond the far side of the pool. "Sounds like it's coming from that direction. Quick, grab your shoes and follow me. Since they can fly and we can't, and maybe with the advantage of a bird's-eye view, silly as it sounds, they might lead us to him."

She had her doubts, but figured they might not want to wind up as stuffed and preserved like their taxidermized colleagues.

As they snuck out the back way, she asked, "Even in times like this, why didn't the Bogarts hire security?"

"Tonight, they left the front gate open for their guests. I guess they felt having cops inside was good enough."

The detectives followed the birdsong, trying their best to interpret its meaning while listening for human footsteps. One bird, whom Guy couldn't identify, screeched three times. Guy swore he said, "*You're it, you're it, you're it.*" Babs accused him of being overimaginative.

Then another bird cooed, "*Here, here.*"

"Babs, they're trying to warn us that the birding killer is stalking the Bogart estate and is ready to strike again."

She was about to accuse him of being as insane as the Bird Man, but the moment they spotted him, Babs took a whistle out of her purse. She hoped she could blow it loud enough to alert everyone inside.

Detective Sadowski darted forth, gun in hand. Allgood and the cops dressed as servers followed. "Put your hands up and step out into the light where we can see you," Sadowski shouted.

Knoll pulled out a knife, but dropped it as other officers closed in.

"What's with his bird costume? He looks like someone tarred and feathered him," Allgood remarked.

Sadowski shouted one more warning. As the cops tried to corner him, the Bird Man tried to flee. Allgood pulled his gun and fired. The Bird Man went down. The backyard birds chattered as if they were cheering while the crowd gathered. While the victim lay bleeding, Bogie's wife ran inside to call an ambulance.

While he was still alive, the homicide detectives tried to force a confession. "What was the big deal 'bout Pinky Pilchik?" asked Sadowski. "The gal only sold popcorn at the Egyptian Theatre. Damned poor excuse to have to kill her."

The Bird Man moaned in pain on the ground.

"Not sure if that's the only thing she sold." As Babs explained that she interviewed Pinky's manager, who was convinced she picked up other work on the side, she noticed Peter trying to fade into the background.

"Not so fast." Allgood grabbed hold of Peter, who looked like he was making a quick exit. "No one goes home till I get a few answers. Was it you who killed the tour guide during *The Falcon* premiere?"

Peter gulped and started shaking. "That's absurd. Why would you assume that?"

Allgood showed him his fist and turned back to the killer. "Cough it up. Tell us why you murdered that Birdie guy."

Knoll groaned, unable to articulate.

"I think I can answer," said Peter, cowering.

Everyone got quiet. Allgood raised his brows. "If you've withheld vital information, you can be cited for obstruction of justice."

Lorre hesitated, but finally got his long-held secret off his chest. "A long time ago, I started taking painkillers for serious medical issues. Doctors have tried to get me off them for years. When they threatened to stop prescribing them, I had to find outside sources. Eric Knoll was my supplier. My addiction to these narcotics could've killed me long before Knoll did. That's why I fainted on set and wound up in the hospital, except this time, I suspect he spiked my supply with chemicals used in the taxidermy or tanning processes, which got me sicker than usual.

"Birdie knew all about it because Knoll was a hobbyist and a frequent customer. I met Birdie once or twice, but if you think his shop was wild, you should see Knoll's apartment, but I suspect Knoll didn't trust me. He always told me to shut up, because I asked too many questions. You've heard this before, but everyone needs their scapegoat. I seem to fit all their excuses."

Sadowski asked, "You think Birdie supplied his dead animals?"

Babs jumped to his defense. "Birdie swore he never killed an animal. He explained to my partner and I that they had already died before they came to him. Knoll, on the other hand, gave me the impression that he was the kind of kid who'd pluck the wings off butterflies or pull the legs off a cicada to watch its head decapitate—"

"I thought it was only a rumor," Guy said.

Allgood shook his head. "Nope. I tried it. Those suckers pop right off. Some people fry them and claim they taste like popcorn."

Feeling skittish that she ever trusted the lout, she turned to Sadowski. "Wait a minute. Your report said Pilchik was poisoned…with what? That part you never told us."

"I suspected drugs all along," Guy said. Then, he pointed out that Knoll's hair looked different. "If you can see beyond his outlandish disguise, for some reason, now he reminds me of the man in the commissary who always served us coffee."

Babs got confused. "I thought you said he was the bicycle messenger who set you up with Warner's bodyguard."

Guy scratched his head. "I did, but remember what the man in the mailroom told us. Many employees are part-timers, and they juggle a few jobs to get by. I think he's both. He just changed his looks when he changed positions."

"That's exactly what Pinky's manager said about her at the movie theater. Her coworkers suspected she had a gig or two on the side. Maybe she peddled drugs for the Bird Man."

"Or used them," said Guy.

"Or both," mumbled Sadowski.

"With all these facades and others in cahoots with his schemes, maybe that's how it was easy for him to mercurially slip in and out of situations and bird people without them noticing," said Babs.

The ailing Bird Man grunted and drew his last breath.

Frustrated, Allgood kicked over a wooden patio chair and tossed his Bloody Mary into the pool. "That bastard! Guess we'll never know."

Bogie gave him the evil eye as he watched Allgood's discarded cocktail dissipate into the water. "If you feel like listening to my two cents, Peck knew the location of stars' homes. He also had the unfortunate provenance of his surname—Peck, something associated with a possible attack from a bird. For all we know, Peck might've gone to Knoll for hop. Maybe even stronger stuff. I swore I smelled a skunky aroma when I first warned him to get off my property, but I still can't figure out why or how a tour guide would've been enough of a threat to our killer to get bumped off."

"Being an Acme Star Tours guide, he knew where everyone lived, and some of them might've also been customers of Knoll's illicit merchandise," said Guy. "You never know who'll bend under pressure and rat him out."

"Seemed like it was a close call for me, but why would he want to kill Peter?" asked Grant.

Bogart mentioned, "Maybe it's a little late to dig up any military records, but he could've served in the last war and is pretty upset it's happening all over again now. There are plenty of men who served and witnessed such horrible atrocities that they still can't shake it off, and this is his way of acting out."

Guy recalled Knoll often sounding inarticulate, but, in fact, he must've tried to cover up his accent. "That ring! The signet ring he wore identified members of criminal gangs, although I'm not sure if I trust anything he told us about its origin. Considering he birded Leon Lewis, who had nothing to do with *The Maltese Falcon*, I wonder if Knoll's threats had anything to do with acting out against Jews."

Babs stopped scribbling in her casebook and looked up from her notes. "By no means should we downplay its severity, but I suspect there are a lot of factors that went into this stew. Reminds me of one of those Depression-era dinners where you scrounge through your leftovers, throw everything in one pot, and turn on the heat."

She wished the Bogarts would've invited Chief Crow-Feather to their party. He could've added his insights, using his expertise, instead of everyone taking police opinions at face value. In comparison, for her, it was like being asked to perform Grand Opera when all she had was experience singing popular tunes on the radio and in an occasional nightclub with no formal voice coaching.

Medics arrived and removed the body. Just as the situation settled down, George Raft, who had kept a low profile and stood among the onlookers, stepped forward.

"You were so quiet, I didn't even realize you were here," said Allgood.

"To be honest, I worried you'd point a finger at me. Since I know big shot gangsters like Owney Madden and Benny Siegel, you'd assume I must've been connected to the killings. Am I right? 'Cause of my pals, people accuse me of all sorts of things all of the time."

"Just to set the record straight," said Guy. "On the night of the LA premiere, I can guarantee you, he didn't kill Peck. George had an ironclad alibi."

"Spit it out," demanded Allgood.

"He endured Stu's antics, even got thrashed with his wings several times, but George sat next to me throughout the entire screening."

"That just goes to show," said Raft, who winked at Bogie and Lorre for confirmation. "Typecasting can be treacherous."

Chapter Thirty-Three: The Dawn Before the Doom

Back at B. Norman Investigations, it was already the first week of December and almost Christmas. Babs brought boxes of holiday decorations to make their office festive. While tidying up, Guy found a stray feather of Stu's and stuck it in his hatband.

"For a job well done, I deserve a feather in my cap," he said with a smirk.

She debated whether she should try once again to visit her mom in San Francisco.

"Your hare-brained ex-husband is in prison," Guy said. "Dip into the funds you earned from bringing *The Falcon* case to a close. Spoil her with something extravagant. Something she always wanted but never could afford, because she wound up as a struggling widow...like a luxury cruise to the south of France."

"Not now, unless you want her to get torpedoed by U-boats."

Guy turned red. "I take that back, but you know what I mean."

Prior to this case, they scraped by picking up small and insignificant assignments and finders fees here and there, some almost embarrassing for professional detectives. Set for now, Babs finally forgave her partner for losing their nest egg from their last high-profile case with the celebrity dogs.

"Next time you borrow money, maybe I should consider having you sign an I.O.U." She enjoyed putting him on the spot.

Using some of his earnings, Guy updated his wardrobe, which included a new pair of wingtip shoes. That meant he'd have one more shoebox to create a new clippings file for *The Maltese Falcon*. It swooped into theaters back in October. Reviews continued to trickle in long past Thanksgiving. Its success elevated Humphrey Bogart from playing a two-bit hoodlum to a respectable leading man. It did nothing, however, to appease his wife's histrionics, which erupted over the most trivial issues.

The Falcon had marked a turning point in Sydney Greenstreet's career. Formerly a Lunt-Fontanne player in the theatrical world, he decided to remain in Hollywood and had a whole lineup of offers. Peter Lorre promised everyone he'd dry out from the morphine and painkillers, which had kept their stranglehold for way too long, and Mary Astor focused on spending more time with her daughter rather than worrying about future revenge plots from her former husband. Critics proclaimed John Huston's directorial debut was Oscar-worthy, and he had a bright future ahead of him.

"Listen to this," said Guy as he found another review. "*The Maltese Falcon* turned the Critics Circle into a bunch of *raven* maniacs. This dashing Dashiell Hammett yarn, adapted and directed by John Huston, was endorsed by the press and backed up by the public as a Warner-Wallis winner of major proportions. Bosley Crowther said, 'The best mystery thriller of the year, and young Mr. Huston gives promise for becoming one of the smartest directors in the field...'

"Film critic Howard Barnes said, 'A tremendously effective screen melo-drama. It has been filmed before, but never with the smashing impact and tough overtones.' Bill Boehnel commented, 'It's going to be tough to top this one... It is told with conspicuous skill and brilliant economy. It races with nervous excitement, and it zooms to a terrific climax... He (Huston) brings vigor, freshness, and originality to his direction.' Kate Cameron gave it three and a half stars: 'Young Huston's direction is comparable to Alfred Hitchcock's at his best.'"

Feeling like she might draw the winning raffle ticket, Babs reached into his clippings box and pulled out another article. "This critic makes a reference to Hammett," she said. "'Author Hammett, 47, onetime Pinkerton detective, white-haired and very thin, has not written a book since his memorable *The*

Thin Man (1934). Since then, the once-undisputed champion of U.S. crime-story writers, has been scripting his thrillers for Hollywood. For a long, long time, he had his sixth book—now titled *There Was a Young Man*—underway. He swears it is almost finished...' That doesn't put Hammett in the best light."

"There was talk of a sequel, but he wanted $5,000 to write it. In advance as a guarantee. Warners wouldn't give it to him," said Guy. He seemed to be content organizing his collection while Babs skimmed through the trades, scouting for their next assignment.

Chief Crow-Feather stopped by a while later to find permanent homes for their fostered kittens, who were now more than old enough for adoption.

Babs wanted his opinion on why Knoll acted the way he did.

"It's too bad we never met," said the chief. "Therefore, I had to draw my conclusions about Knoll's psychological profile after the fact from police reports.

"Knoll was difficult to pinpoint, because he worked on-call at a variety of menial jobs, including his side venture in the drug trade. For the most part, he performed various duties at Warner Brothers where he was positioned to overhear many private conversations, but one of the most interesting insights surfaced from his confessions."

"The ones they coerced him to write before he escaped from his hospital bed?" asked Guy. "I thought they turned out to be gibberish."

"They were scribbled in old-school German, which I happen to read. Lorre probably could've translated it, but he was lucky to be conscious."

"How many languages do you understand?" Babs asked.

He started counting on his fingers but stopped. "More than you care to know, including Tongva and several other native dialects. Well, anyway, after Knoll was already dead and it was too late to make significant headway, they let me take a crack at it. When he lived in Germany, he was part of a ring gang, as Guy suspected. Mind you, I had to dig through back issues of German newspapers in the public library to uncover this, but he accidentally killed a young girl named Elsie while on a *Ringvereine*-sanctioned assignment."

"Elsie was the name of the first murder victim in *M*," Guy blurted out. "I wondered why he broke down crying when he confronted Peter on stage."

Babs shushed him and insisted he let the chief continue.

"Trust me, it was a challenge unearthing records on Knoll. It wasn't like I could just send a telegram over to Germany and get cooperation when they're at war with half the world. After Knoll killed the girl, I suspect something snapped. In *M*, Beckert becomes taken over by evil compulsions and can't control his actions. Maybe Knoll felt the need to mirror the life of Beckert, but to also identify with his gang, who banished him afterward for that act of misjudgment. No longer under their protection, he went rogue, but grappled with feelings of revenge aimed toward them versus guilt and remorse for the girl.

"Compound that with the probability that he already had a mental abnormality to begin with, and he might've used the drugs he dealt. Stuck like a scratch on a record that causes it to play the same section of the song over and over again, Knoll got obsessed and couldn't let it go. He might've been cognizant of this, but it was doubtful that he realized the real villain came from within. The only way he knew how to end it was to stop its outside source. If threats didn't work, he'd kill his subject."

"How do you explain his unusual behavior toward birds, particularly black birds?"

Her query cued Stu to chase after Bruno. In turn, he tipped over the box of kittens reserved for the chief. Sir Henry turned the box upright with his snout and rescued each one by picking them up by the scruffs of their necks.

"That's one smart dog," said the chief.

"He's not for the taking," said Guy, scooping up spilled litter that Sir Henry left behind. "You're welcome to take the myna bird if you like."

Crow-Feather shook his head. "I'm still nursing your pelican back to health. He's not ready to be released into the wild."

Stu flew past the chief so close that he almost gave him a mouthful of feathers. Crow-Feather spit into his handkerchief and grimaced. "Babs, getting back to your question about Knoll's preoccupation with black birds, besides the obvious symbolic connection to *The Maltese Falcon*, he might've had a traumatic experience getting attacked by a crow. Who knows what goes on inside the criminal mind when he's beyond logical reasoning?"

She wanted to know what he thought the victims had in common with *The Maltese Falcon*.

"Maybe Knoll thought by preventing the completion of the film that was his way of getting to Lorre, who concealed how he was connected with the three people who died," the chief suggested. "Pilchik and Peck used and distributed Knoll's drugs, making extra income. Peter didn't need the money. His acting career was more than sufficient. He had to contend with his addiction and will probably always have to deal with the stigma of *M* and people's reactions to other nefarious characters he's played.

"Peter kept us in the dark the entire time that he knew Eric Knoll and about his eccentricities with taxidermy and protected his interests because of his drug dependency. Despite what Peter knew, he couldn't visualize this man as the killer, much less someone who might want to kill him. However, when Peter lived in Germany, he might've been aware of Knoll's accidental murder and his *Ringvereine* affiliation."

"Why would Knoll kill the taxidermist?" asked Guy.

"Delusional people like Knoll might need someone they could confide in to justify their motives. It's my guess he realized he disclosed too much, just like he had with Peter. If he could no longer trust him, he had to eliminate him."

"Do you think antisemitism played into it?" asked Guy.

"That could've been another scratch in the record, so to say, which caused Knoll to get stuck. His fixation on Lorre could've rubbed off and transferred to target people like Jack Warner and Leon Lewis, the latter having nothing to do with *The Maltese Falcon* film. What he was after was the shock value of repeated birdings."

"Legally, won't Peter get in trouble for failing to disclose those secrets?" she asked.

"If I were him, I'd be more concerned about the exposure of his illicit drug use. Since he helped solve the crime, most likely, he'll be able to talk his way out of the other charges. Although we'll never know the entire story, since enough has already surfaced, I'm relieved law enforcement officials have put their personal prejudices aside, and they no longer consider me a suspect," Crow-Feather said in confidence.

Babs scratched her head. "Wait a minute. Since when did they think you were responsible for the birdings?"

"Perhaps you weren't aware, but Sadowski and Allgood had their own agenda. They never trusted you and had one of their undercover men follow when you visited me at our Tongva gathering. I noticed right away when they began to tail me. Mind you, when they found out I freelanced as a consultant in a different division of their department, I'm sure they received a severe tongue-lashing. However, they didn't exonerate me until it became obvious Knoll committed those murders."

Babs cuddled a kitten in her arms and shook her head.

"In movies, people like us—the Indians, though none of us ever came from India, we always play the bad guys. Even worse, when others call us Injuns and refer to the phrase, 'honest Injun,' as if that insinuates our kind hedges the truth. Police and officials, who should know better, jump to conclusions. It's unfortunate that widespread ignorance casts us in such contemptible roles."

"I'd like to see someone from your community play the hero for a change." Babs handed the kitten back to the chief. She got out her checkbook and donated a portion of her reward money to his animal rescue efforts.

The chief was ready to head out with the box of kittens in hand.

"So would I."

* * *

Already missing the kittens, Guy turned on the radio and said that would keep them company. Goals achieved; conflicts overcome...for now, but it didn't take long before breaking news interrupted their musical broadcast:

Tragedy at the American naval base in Pearl Harbor in the Territory of Hawaii. At 7:48 a.m. Hawaiian Standard Time, Imperial Japanese aircraft attacked and destroyed roughly 21 American ships, 350 aircraft, and killed more than 2,400 civilians and military personnel. Among those sunk were the battleships the USS Arizona and the USS Oklahoma. In a conversation between President Roosevelt and Britain's Prime Minister Winston Churchill, Churchill said, "We're all in the same boat now."

The startling announcement of the impending global crisis rendered the detectives speechless. Several calls came in. They couldn't motivate themselves to answer them, which, in turn, prompted Stu to become their new receptionist. The smart-alecky myna bird knew how to take the phone off the cradle and speak into the receiver.

Later that afternoon, Bogie dropped by unannounced. "Tried calling earlier. Couldn't get through."

"Did you hear the news?" Babs asked.

"Yeah...installed one of those fancy...and expensive radios in my car. The station repeated the announcement. Missed it when it was happening 'cause my wife wasn't in the mood to listen."

"Don't know what's going to happen now," said Babs.

"They'll probably ramp up the draft, and we'll have to start conducting blackouts and rationing like they do over in Britain," Bogie replied. "Getting back to why I showed up on your doorstep, since when did you hire Mel Blanc to answer your phones? Felt like I was being pranked by one of those Looney Tunes."

"Eh, what's up, Doc?" Stu mimicked.

Babs' jaw dropped. "How could he have managed to watch one of those cartoons? No one's brought a film projector over here."

"Maybe a former projectionist owned him, and that's who Wiggins inherited him from," Bogie suggested.

"One of these days...I'm gonna..." Guy was ready to blow a fuse. "What's the lifespan of one of these varmints? Hey, if you like him, he's yours."

"That's all folks!" Stu squawked.

Gesturing with his hands, Guy pretended to wring Stu's neck. Not taking any chances, Stu flapped his wings in Guy's face before flying off and landing on Bogie's shoulder. Guy tried to put him back into his cage, but the bird clamped his talons onto Bogie's jacket.

"Looks like you're stuck with him unless you want him to ruin your suit," said Guy, giving up his struggle to outwit the bird.

"So, you're giving me the bird," Bogie said as he twisted his neck to look the myna in the eye. Stu rubbed his feathery head against his ear and mimicked the purr of a kitten.

"Hate to say this, but, Guy…"

"What, Mr. Bogart?"

"I think this is the beginning of a beautiful friendship."

Historical Notes and Disclaimers

This novel is a work of fiction. Although the author attempted to depict historical references as best as possible, she altered some details in 1941 for artistic license.

Acknowledgements

My agent Elizabeth K. Kracht, who rescues cormorants, seagulls, bees, and an occasional pelican, Verena Rose, Shawn Reilly Simmons, and Deb Well from Level Best Books, Grace Bradley, Kathy Bennett, Teel James Glenn, David Kaye, Laura Frankos Turtledove, Linda and Wolf Hein, Beth Barnard, Jerry Kegley, Dr. Katherine Ramsland, Dr. Robert Stek, Christopher Zordan, Elena Gaillard, Thomas Kessler and Brittany Webb from the History Center of San Luis Obispo County, the staff at the Special Collections at the Lincoln Center Library of the Performing Arts, the Margaret Herrick Library, Bree Russell at the USC Warner Brothers Archive, and the Los Angeles Public Library Special Collections Department, my Sisters in Crime – LA crit team: Sonya Steele and Susan and Gary Baughman, and Dashiell Hammett.

Book Club Questions for Bye Bye Blackbird

1. What was your favorite part of the book?
2. What was your least favorite?
3. Which scene stuck with you the most?
4. Did you feel the book was educational? Did you learn something new from the book that you hadn't expected?
5. What surprised you the most about the book?
6. Does this book remind you of any other books or films?
7. Would you ever consider re-reading the book? Why or why not?
8. If this book were adapted to film, who would you like to see in the cast?
9. What characters did you like the best? Which did you like the least?
10. How did the setting impact the story? Would you want to read more books set in 1940s Hollywood?
11. Which twist surprised you the most?
12. Did you guess the ending? If so, at what point?
13. Would you definitely recommend this author and read other books that will come up in this series?
14. Are you curious about the other books this author has written, even if they are in a different genre?

About the Author

Elizabeth Crowens is bi-coastal between Los Angeles and New York. For over thirty years, she has worn many hats in the entertainment industry, contributed stories to *Black Belt, Black Gate, Sherlock Holmes Mystery Magazines, Hell's Heart,* and the Bram Stoker-nominated *A New York State of Fright*, and has a popular Caption Contest on Facebook.

Awards include: Leo B. Burstein Scholarship from the MWA-NY Chapter, New York Foundation of the Arts grant to publish the anthology *New York: Give Me Your Best or Your Worst*, Eric Hoffer Award, Glimmer Train Awards Honorable Mention, Killer Nashville Claymore Award Finalist, two Grand prize, six First prize, and multiple Finalist Chanticleer Awards. Crowens writes multi-genre alternate history and historical Hollywood mysteries.

AUTHOR WEBSITE:
www.elizbethcrowens.com

SOCIAL MEDIA HANDLES:
Facebook.com/thereel.elizabeth.crowens
X.com/ECrowens

Instagram.com/ElizabethCrowens

LinkedIn https://www.linkedin.com/in/elizabeth-crowens-5227804/

Goodreads https://www.goodreads.com/author/show/15173793.Elizabeth_Crowens

BlueSky: elizabethcrowens.bsky.social

Also by Elizabeth Crowens

Hounds of the Hollywood Baskervilles, Book One in the Babs Norman Golden Age of Hollywood Mystery series. First Prize winner of the Chanticleer Review Mystery & Mayhem (M&M) and Mark Twain Awards, Finalist in Killer Nashville's Claymore Awards

New York: Give Me Your Best or Your Worst (photo-illustrated anthology), Grand Prize winner of the Chanticleer Review Shorts/Anthologies Award

Three novels in the Time Traveler Professor series (alternate history):
Silent Meridian, First Prize winner of the Chanticleer Review Goethe Award
A Pocketful of Lodestones, First Prize winner of the Chanticleer Review Paranormal Award
A War in Too Many Worlds, Grand Prize winner of the Chanticleer Review Cygnus Award

www.ingramcontent.com/pod-product-compliance
Lightning Source LLC
Chambersburg PA
CBHW020603110726
47899CB00002B/352